THE MAGIC OF CHRISTMAS

Emma Craig
"Jack of Hearts"

Emma Craig "knows how to wrap her characters around your heart."

—*Romantic Times*

Annie Kimberlin
"The Shepherds and Mr. Weisman"

Stray Hearts "is a masterpiece of storytelling, real people, and all kinds of love."

—*Under the Covers*

Kathleen Nance
"The Magic of Christmas"

"*Wishes Come True* is a delightful story that takes the Aladdin/Arabian Nights theme and adds a uniquely modern twist. Ms. Nance has a winner!"

—*Romantic Times*

Stobie Piel
"Twelfth Knight"

"Ms. Piel keeps us on the knife-edge of curiosity as she tantalizes us with her imaginative plot."

—*Romantic Times* for *The Midnight Moon*

Other *Leisure* and *Love Spell* holiday anthologies:
CHRISTMAS SPIRIT
SANTA PAWS
A TIME-TRAVEL CHRISTMAS
HOLIDAY INN
A WILDERNESS CHRISTMAS
THE NIGHT BEFORE CHRISTMAS
THEIR FIRST NOEL

THE MAGIC OF
Christmas

Emma Craig
Annie Kimberlin
Kathleen Nance
Stobie Piel

LOVE SPELL BOOKS ◆ NEW YORK CITY

LOVE SPELL®

November 1998

Published by

Dorchester Publishing Co., Inc.
276 Fifth Avenue
New York, NY 10001

ISBN 0-505-52283-7

JACK
OF HEARTS

EMMA CRAIG

For my evil twin, Sue Cass,
who likes hunky angels.

Chapter One

September 12, 1851
Dear Mama and Papa,

Uncle George and I have arrived in San Francisco in fair health, although very weary. The city is booming, and appears to be bursting at its very seams with men come here to seek their fortunes in gold. There are very few women, but I shan't repine, as Uncle George has promised to take good care of me.

It grieves me very much to tell you in this letter that Jonathan succumbed to the rigors of the ocean voyage. As we rounded Cape Horn, he contracted the fever so prevalent in those parts. He was buried at sea, with many prayerful wishes from all who had come to know and love him on the arduous voyage. My heart aches as I write this, for I loved my brother very much, and we had such grand plans for our sojourn in California. I miss him awfully, although I know he is now with

7

God and, therefore, immune to all earthly suffering forevermore.

I shall keep the Bible Jonathan carried, and will send his other belongings home to you as soon as may be.

Your loving daughter,
Merry

November 30, 1851
Dear Mama and Papa,

Uncle George and I have traversed as far as Red Bluff, where Uncle George believes he will be able to stake a claim with some fellows with whom he has become acquainted.

The landscape hereabouts is beautiful, although I greatly fear the accounts in some of the newspaper articles we read back home in Maryland were grossly exaggerated. I have not yet met one man who has discovered gold lying on the ground, and no one merely scoops it up out of the river, but must work very hard to find any gold at all—"hitting color" the miners call it. They use many quaint expressions in California, many of which I have yet to comprehend.

The fellows who seem to prosper here are those who supply goods to the gold-miners.

As for me, in an effort to keep myself occupied (as I am a female and thus, according to Uncle George, unfit to help him with his claim), I believe I shall set up as a laundress. I must tell you that cleanliness, while next to godliness, appears to be next to impossible in California. Some of the miners actually send their clothes to be laundered in China! Have you ever heard of such a thing?

Uncle George is calling for me now. Please relay all my love to my sisters and brothers, to my grandparents, and to all my aunts, uncles, and cousins. I do miss you all!

Your loving daughter,
Merry

Chapter Two

Christmas Gap, California, December 1851

Smoke curled up from the remains of a fire still smoldering in the fire pit miners had dug out of the earth and lined with rocks a couple of years before. In the fading winter afternoon light, Levi Harte watched the smoke snake its way into the tall firs and pines edging the gold camp. He smelled it, too, for it had permeated his shirt and hair. He felt grit from the fire in teeth that had lately chewed the remains of a chicken. His last chicken.

He'd have to shoot a squirrel tomorrow unless he could trade food for something—he didn't know what—with one of the other miners. He probably could. Most of the men in Christmas Gap had been in Levi's fix at one time or another, and were sympathetic.

Or he could ask at Gus's place, and see if Gus could use himself a grocery clerk. Shoot. Levi used to think that farming was the lowest life a man could sink to. Shortly after he'd made his way to California, his heart full of hope and his head filled with golden fantasies, he'd learned that farming wasn't anywhere near the bottom.

At least when Levi was a farmer, he'd had food to eat and a roof over his head. He hadn't eaten a decent meal for so long that his clothes now hung on him like rags on a skeleton, and his roof was a canvas tent that leaked and let in the cold like nobody's business. He'd relocate to Marysville for the winter, except that he didn't know how he could support himself in Marysville any more than he knew how he could support himself in Christmas Gap.

Levi inhaled deeply of the piney, smoky scent of the gold camp, and then expelled his breath on a sigh. What a life.

The woods were almost quiet now, the evening silence punctuated every now and then with a muffled laugh or a curse. And, of course, there was always the river.

That river taunted him. It rushed gaily down the mountainside, laughing at him, hiding its gold from him, teasing him for being such a fool as to think he could steal its treasure.

Levi couldn't see the river from where he sat, but he heard it well enough. It flowed through his mind's eye like a running joke. It was all he'd seen for the last eighteen months, just about. From where he sat on his rock by the fire, he heard the *chunk-chunk-chunk* of Ben Budlow's sluice box as water diverted from the river flowed through the sluice and out the other side.

Ben swore he'd hit color one of these days, what with him working days and his sluice-box working nights. After all this time, Levi doubted it, especially since the snows would come pretty soon, and all the miners in Christmas Gap would be out of work entirely. He didn't know how Ben kept his spirits up. Whiskey, Levi supposed, like most of the other men—except Levi. Low he might be, but he refused to sink *that* low. Cripes, life was hard enough sober.

As for Levi, he stared into the ruins of that once-roaring

11

campfire and contemplated the ruins of his once-happy life. He fingered the pencil in his right hand and knew he had to set it to the piece of thick foolscap in his left hand pretty soon. He'd paid five cents for that one sheet of paper. He wasn't about to waste it.

It was hard maintaining his lie to the folks back home, though. He hated lying—but he'd die before he told them the truth.

"Writin' a letter to your ma?" Kanaka Lou looked up from the stick he'd been whittling and nodded to Levi from a rock on the other side of the fire hole. It was interesting, Levi thought, the different things the men here did to keep from losing their minds. Kanaka whittled. Ben Budlow drank. Levi brooded. He had a feeling Kanaka and Ben's methods worked better than his.

"Yeah."

"You can tell her that you're all growed up now."

"I'll do that." Levi smiled at Kanaka. He was used to being ribbed by the other miners about his relative youth. At twenty-one, he was the youngster there; all the men joshed him about his age and inexperience.

Not that many of the other men living in Christmas Gap were old. Or had much experience. Nobody but a young idiot would brave the rigors of a California gold camp. It took youth to survive one. Even with youth on your side, survival was moot. Levi's partner, who'd been barely older than Levi, had died of the ague in August. Now Levi worked on alone, for all the good it did him.

Levi had loved the chanciness of this life once. Tonight he felt old and tired, his stomach felt much too empty, and he wished he could go home again. If there was a way to do it without proving the folks at home right, he'd head back to Ohio in a second.

If he left Christmas Gap, he'd be branded a quitter, however, and he wouldn't do it. Not in this lifetime. After he was dead—which shouldn't take too much longer, the way things were going—he didn't guess he'd care if his friends shipped his carcass home in a pine box. At least he would have died without having given up, even if he hadn't achieved his goal.

He'd come to California to see the elephant, dad-blast it, and he wasn't going to let his family know the beast had trampled him flat. He could envision the triumph in his father's face, almost hear the lectures sure to follow, and tasted the gall of them both two thousand miles away. No way in flinders would Levi let his old man say *I told you so.*

Levi looked up from the glowing coals, diverted from his melancholy by a buzz of approaching excitement. The rumble began in the woods and rushed toward him on a tidal wave of speculation.

Someone was riding into camp. The stimulation inherent in such an event was palpable, and it raced through the evening air like wildfire. Grateful for an excuse to put off writing lies home for another little while, Levi carefully folded the piece of paper, jammed it into his shirt pocket, then stared at the stand of trees some thirty yards removed from the fire pit.

If he'd been asked, he wouldn't have been able to tell how he knew the visitor would emerge from just that spot, but he did. With a bitter, twisted grin, he acknowledged to himself that at least he'd learned *something* in the two years since he'd made his way to California to seek his fortune.

When he saw Gentleman Jack Oakes emerge from the twilit trees on his big black horse, Pete, Levi's spirits lifted in spite of his glum mood. Although he'd never actually met him, Levi'd seen Jack before. Levi knew Jack Oakes was a square fellow. He was all right. All right? Shoot, Gentleman Jack was a legend in the California gold camps.

Gentleman Jack Oakes didn't allow life or people to get him down. He was dapper. He was a slick operator. He was a smooth talker with a silver tongue. He was a gambling man. What's more, Jack seemed to be winning here in this devilish place while all the rest of them were losing faster than they could breathe.

Levi had heard that Gentleman Jack was a whiz at card tricks, too, and could make a card—invariably the jack of hearts—materialize right out of thin air. Everyone knew it was a trick, but no one knew how he did it. Jack never told, either.

Now there was audacity for you, in Levi's way of thinking. Self-confidence. Savoir faire. A gambling man performing card tricks. It didn't matter to Jack that folks might interpret his skill at tricks to condemn him as a cheater. No siree. Jack's honor at the table had never once been challenged.

Levi admired Gentleman Jack's spotless reputation as true blue and rakish at the same time. Although Levi regretted it because it pointed out his own callowness and feeble character, he secretly idolized Gentleman Jack Oakes. He'd like to be like him in another life. He knew he'd never make it in this one.

He gawked like the country boy he was when he realized that Jack had a woman with him. A young thing, she sat like a queen before him, looking neither to her right nor to her left, but scowling straight ahead as if daring anyone to question her unusual mode of transportation. Levi knew how she felt and honored her determination to defy the world's opinion.

A gaggle of miners trailed after Jack and the woman. Females were scarcer than cleanliness in Christmas Gap. If a fellow needed a woman—and some of these men claimed they did from time to time—they had to ride all the way to Oroville or Quincy to scratch their itch.

Levi wouldn't know about that. Oh, he had urges enough for any man. He'd never had one of them satisfied, though, in the conventional way. He guessed he was better off not knowing what he was missing, even if it did seem slightly pathetic that a twenty-one-year-old man hadn't lain with a

14

woman yet. At least it seemed pathetic here in California, where there were no laws or parents to prevent him from doing whatever he blasted well pleased.

Like a showman, Jack rode slowly into the camp and drew his horse to a halt. Levi'd heard that Jack always wore black, and he was pleased to have the rumors confirmed. This evening Jack had on a black frock coat, black trousers, black vest, black hat, and a black tie. Tidy fellow that he was reputed to be, he probably had on a clean collar and cuffs, too, although it had gone too dark for Levi to tell. Even Jack's hair was black. Levi envied the fellow his cachet, his élan. Levi wished he had cachet. Shoot, at this point, he wished he had anything at all.

Gentleman Jack slid the woman down from his horse, then he himself dismounted. He was quite a bit taller than she was, although he wasn't an especially tall man.

She was dressed in a smudged dress that looked as though it had been blue once. The fabric had turned gray now and was torn in spots, but she wore it like a duchess. Levi marveled at her dignity, given the circumstances. The idea that she and Jack suited each other entered his head, disappointing him for some reason. She wore no hat, which surprised him. According to his mother, ladies always wore hats. Perhaps she wasn't a lady. The notion shocked Levi.

Her hair was blond and had been drawn back into a bun falling loose from its knot. A lock of it had flopped over her brow, but she didn't brush it back. A splash of freckles across her nose looked out of place, as though they belonged on some other girl, a playful girl, a girl without this one's pride and silence. Levi glanced at Jack's horse, but couldn't tell if she might have other belongings strapped to its flank.

"Won her in a poker game off of two gents in Red Bluff," Jack announced to the gaping crowd of miners.

Levi's astonishment held him motionless and speechless for a moment. It apparently had the same effect on everyone else.

Silence as sharp as a honed ax followed Jack's statement for perhaps thirty seconds. Ben Budlow broke it at last, with three glugs from his jug as he tipped it to his lips.

"Says she does laundry, boys," Jack went on. "Reckon you fellows could use your clothes washed." Jack's dark, dark eyes glittered. There were some folks who speculated that Jack Oakes had more than a bit of Indian blood in him. He grinned at the men who'd gathered around to watch the fun.

A wag lost in the shadows and outside Levi's range of sight finally asked, "She do anything else fer money besides laundry?"

Ben Budlow choked on his last swallow. Jack's grin widened. Low murmurs began in the back of the camp and permeated the air around Levi like the smell of frying bacon on a cold Sierra morning. Although he'd been wondering much the same thing not two minutes earlier, he was embarrassed for the poor female and wished the nameless fellow hadn't implied that she was a scarlet woman. She didn't look like any loose female Levi had ever seen. Not that he'd seen many.

Jehosephat, she was young. She must have been younger even than Levi, and he was a pure baby. She didn't deserve these men gawking at her and thinking bad things about her. Even if she had fallen on hard times and turned to wickedness, maybe it wasn't her fault. Maybe she wanted to change her ways.

Levi squinted, trying to determine what dire circumstances might justify a female selling her body for money. He couldn't think of any and decided to consider the problem later.

The woman had been staring, mute, at the ground. Now she lifted her head. Levi was surprised to discover that what he'd taken for mortification in her demeanor wasn't that at all. Her eyes slitted up in anger. Contempt as thick as pea soup radiated from that look of hers and put every man in the gold camp in the place she deemed he belonged. It was several levels of perdition lower than the men had envisioned for themselves—and most of them weren't proud anymore.

In a voice low and reeking with scorn she said, "I do *laundry*."

Ben Budlow cleared his throat and tried to stop choking. Kanaka Lou had stopped whittling when Gentleman Jack rode into the clearing. Now he went back to it. Levi could barely hear Lou's knife scrape against his hunk of wood. No one else spoke for a long time.

Gentleman Jack, still grinning, shrugged. Levi hated it that he envied Jack so much. Jack had such a *way* about him, though, that it was hard not to envy him. Everyone else was just a man. Jack was special.

At last another man—Levi thought it was a fellow folks called Carolina—said, "How the hell'd you end up wagered in a poker game if all you do is laundry?"

The woman singled Carolina out from among the ragged group and eyed him as if he were even more disgusting than the rest of the men. "That's none of your business."

Jack's grin turned into a big smile. Levi silently applauded the woman for her answer. She had more grit than any ten of these fellows; he'd give her that.

After another several moments, pregnant with hostility from the woman and puzzlement from the gold-camp dwellers, she tossed her head, sending that one lock of golden hair flying out of her eye. Levi saw it glint in the almost-extinguished firelight and land in place, flat against her head, and was impressed.

"Y'all *need* your laundry done."

From the sound of her voice, which was soft and contemptuous and held a faint hint of sultry Southern summer nights, Levi could tell she'd smelled them. She was right, too. Without the civilizing influence of proper women, a California gold camp was a cheerless place, and one stinking of far too many men and much too little soap and water.

17

After another moment of silence, Gus Shackleford, proprietor of what passed for a grocery and dry-goods establishment in the camp, spoke up. "Reckon we could use us a laundress here in Christmas Gap, ma'am, but it'd help us to know to whom we was addressin' ourselves when we brung in our duds."

Jack nodded at the woman. "He's got a point there, sweetheart."

Jack's attitude obviously nettled her, and Levi's hands bunched into fists at his sides. Not that Levi Harte would dare challenge Gentleman Jack Oakes. Still, he hated Jack's knowing smile and teasing tone for the woman's sake.

Her full mouth pinched into a flat line and creases appeared in her brow. She glared at the men for a minute and then said, "My name is Meredith Wildwood." She sniffed imperiously. "Y'all may call me Miss Wildwood."

Levi, who even after a year and a half in California accepted pretty much anyone on faith, was taken aback to hear a couple of guffaws and several snickers. He looked around at the group of men, appalled that they'd doubt a woman they didn't even know, even if her arrival in camp had been unexpected and was occasioned by so unsavory an event as her having been won in a poker game. He frowned, not understanding how so superior a female as Miss Wildwood could have gotten herself into such a fix.

Gentleman Jack cleared his throat and the buzzing in the crowd stilled. His smile remained in place when he said, "And now, gentlemen, Miss Wildwood here will need a place to stay." He turned to Gus. "You got a room to spare in that saloon of yours, Gus? Or a corner she can rig up with curtains?"

"My mercantile establishment, you mean?" Gus's eyes opened wide.

Jack chuckled. "Whatever you want to call it is all right with me, Gus."

Levi was disgusted to see a lascivious grin curve the grocer's thick lips. Shoot. This wasn't fair. Without so much as thinking first, he stepped away from the fire pit and walked up to the woman. Woman, hell. She was no more than a girl, really.

Remembering his mother's lessons in manners a shade too late, he whipped the battered felt hat from his head. He could feel himself blushing and cursed inwardly. Jack's eyebrows rose over his dark eyes, giving him the ironic look of a satyr, and Levi felt like a blasted fool. He was sure Jack winked at him.

Chapter Three

December 1, 1851

Dear Mama and Papa,

Uncle George has decided it would be better if I were to settle in a place other than Red Bluff while he minds his claim. He fears the elements in Red Bluff are not edifying, and the town would be ill-fitted for a lady's dignity and reputation.

With the help of a very kind gentleman named Mr. Jack Oakes, whom I believe to be some sort of minister of the Gospel, I have relocated to a community known as Christmas Gap. Isn't that a droll name for a gold-mining camp? I trust it will live up to its propitious name. I aim to set up as a laundress here. As I may have written before, these poor men need laundry services. I fear most of them haven't seen the inside of a bath house for far too many months!

Please give my love to the rest of my family, and tell them I miss them more than words can say. I wish we could all be together at Christmas, with Jonathan back among us, and all be jolly again.

Love, your daughter,
Merry

Chapter Four

To blazes with Jack and the whole lot of them, Levi decided, and plunged ahead. "I'll help rig up a tent for you, ma'am. I've got some canvas left over from when my partner died last August."

Several men in camp laughed—amused, Levi presumed, by the way he'd phrased his announcement. He guessed it had lacked éclat. He tried to ignore their merriment.

The woman looked as surprised as he was. He shrugged, twisted his hat in his hands, and brushed his hair back from his forehead. Not that any of those gestures would do any good. He knew he looked like what he was: a young, penniless, good-for-nothing gold-camp bum.

After a moment that seemed to Levi as though it were stretching out into centuries, the woman said in her low, pretty voice, "Thank you very much, young man." She skewered the company with a scathing glance. "It's nice to know there's at least one gentleman in this pernicious place the United States government has seen fit to allow into the Union as a sovereign state.''

No one spoke. Levi guessed they were as cowed as he by the young woman's cold assessment of them and their new home.

Potter, a shy, mousy man whom most of his fellow gold-camp dwellers generally disregarded, walked up to stand beside Levi. "I'll help you, Levi." He blushed violently and nodded at the woman. "Miss Wildwood."

Levi could hardly believe his eyes when Miss Wildwood smiled at the two of them. Her smile broke out like the sun from a cloudburst and left him breathless. She was a lovely woman. Girl. Even if she hadn't been the first female he'd seen in upwards of three months, she'd have been beautiful.

"Thank you, gentlemen. Thank you both very much."

It didn't take long for Levi and Potter to rig up a tent for Miss Wildwood. They set it up near the river and behind some syringa bushes, at Potter's suggestion.

"Give her some privacy, don'tcha know, and the flowers'll smell nice come spring," he'd said, and blushed again.

Levi found no fault with Potter's suggestion, although he did wonder if Miss Wildwood would be there come spring. He didn't ask her, because she didn't appear as though she'd welcome questions. She stood to one side as they worked, hugging herself and shivering in the evening cold. She eyed the both of them as if she worried that they were up to something. Levi considered asking her if she'd like to use his spare jacket, another legacy from his deceased partner, but she made him nervous, so he didn't.

He and Potter worked like two devils as the rest of their gold-camp companions chortled and tossed suggestions at them, many of them lewd. Miss Wildwood ignored the comments with what Levi thought was magnificent disdain. He and Potter did their best to ignore them, too, although Potter's blush seemed likely to burn his cheeks off. Levi grinned at Potter and kept working, trying to emulate Gentleman Jack, whom he figured was never embarrassed by anything. Jack treated the world and everything in it as a joke designed for his own personal amusement.

The tent went up in a very few minutes. Then Levi and Potter gathered pine needles for the floor, spread them out, and laid an oilskin over the needles. Levi had learned a long time ago that pine needles made pretty fair flooring. They also made a tolerable mattress, and they didn't stick a body any more than the ticking they used back on the farm.

When they finished building her house, Levi realized that Miss Wildwood had brought over a very small leather satchel. She stood there, watching them, holding the bag in front of her, almost blue with cold. Levi noticed that her hands appeared to be chapped. Maybe she really was only a laundress.

Potter spotted her, immediately bobbed his head like a chicken diving for corn kernels, and darted off into the trees. Miss Wildwood watched him go, a puzzled expression on her face, then turned to Levi.

"Potter's a little shy, ma'am," said Levi, feeling a little shy himself.

"I see. Well, I appreciate the work you two fellows did for me. If I had cash money, I'd pay you for it."

Dismayed by her suggestion, Levi waved his hand. "No, ma'am. We don't want you to pay us. It was a favor. For a lady."

Her expression seemed to soften, and Levi could have sworn he saw tears shine in her eyes. "Thank you," she murmured. "Thank you very much."

"You're welcome."

She swallowed, and the hint of emotion passed. "And whether you want me to or not, I aim to do your laundry free for a month. Both of you."

"No need for that, ma'am. Honest."

Her gaze traveled from his mud-caked boots to his dirty hair, and Levi had no doubt she was taking note of every filthy inch of his person. Blast.

"Oh, I think there is. And may I know your name, young man?"

He didn't appreciate being called "young man" by her. It sounded as if she considered him a kid—which she probably did, even though he figured he was older than she was. He winced inside, but didn't show it. He saw Gentleman Jack out of the corner of his eye and stood up as straight and as tall as he could. He might be young, and he might be more innocent than he wanted to be, but he was taller than Jack, and built bigger too, dad-blast it.

"Levi Harte, ma'am. From Ohio." Shoot. Why did he have to go and add that? It was stupid. Her smile told him so.

"Well, Levi Harte from Ohio, I do thank you. My name is Meredith Wildwood. From Maryland."

He nodded, hating the note of teasing in her voice.

As if she sensed his humiliation, she said softly, "You saved my life, Mr. Harte. I'll always be grateful to you."

Although he knew she didn't really mean it, he enjoyed her saying so. "I'll give Potter your regards, ma'am."

"Tell him about the free laundry, please, Mr. Harte."

"I will, ma'am." He shuffled his feet uncomfortably, wondering what he was supposed to do now.

Gentleman Jack solved the problem for him. He walked up to stand beside Miss Meredith Wildwood and smiled at Levi as if he knew he was the boy's idol. "Reckon it's time for you to hit the hay, Levi. Gotta get up early in the morning if you're aiming to scare those gold nuggets out of the river."

Levi wished Jack hadn't said that; it made him feel like a child. Since he knew taking exception would only make him appear more foolish than he probably already did, he said, "Right. G'night, Mr. Oakes. G'night, Miss Wildwood."

25

Emma Craig

" 'Night, son.''

Levi loathed being called "son" by Gentleman Jack Oakes, especially in front of Miss Wildwood.

She held out her hand. "Thank you again, Mr. Harte. I meant what I said.''

About what? Levi couldn't remember, and he didn't ask. Instead he shook her hand, which was very cold. It also felt rough and smooth at the same time—again, Levi suspected, from doing laundry. "G'night, ma'am." He left, wishing he could stay and listen to what Jack and Miss Wildwood were going to say to each other.

They began talking before he was out of earshot. Levi turned around, realized he was hidden from their view by a big fir tree, and decided to listen. He knew he was doing something his mother would disapprove of, but he couldn't seem to help himself. Besides, his mother wasn't there. Bracing himself on the rough trunk of the fir, he peeked around it and watched Miss Meredith Wildwood and Gentleman Jack Oakes.

He saw Miss Wildwood shake Jack Oakes's hand. "Thank you again, Mr. Oakes. I suspect you saved me from—''

Jack held up a hand. Levi blinked in astonishment. For a split second there, he could have sworn he'd seen light emanating from Jack's hand and what looked like a halo around his head. He must be even more addled than he thought.

"There's no need to thank me, Miss Wildwood. You'll be doing me a favor, though, if you treat Levi Harte kindly. The poor boy's about at the end of his tether.''

Levi frowned into the gathering darkness. Blast it, what did Jack Oakes know about Levi Harte? Was his impoverished condition *that* obvious? Could anyone who looked tell that Levi was past his last hopes? The notion curdled in his stomach like sour milk.

"I already told him I'd do his laundry free for a month." Her tone was tart.

The older man's smile was much more gentle and soft than

Levi would have expected. In fact, it made Levi think of his home and his family and the little church they used to go to on Sunday mornings. Sometimes Levi thought he missed that church and the pretty songs they used to sing in it almost more than he missed his family. His overall state of missing things was so acute, he couldn't really tell what he missed most, although as Christmas approached, he ached with memories and longings.

"He'd appreciate a kindness from you more than clean clothes, I reckon," Jack said, his voice quiet.

The girl stiffened up like setting cement. "If you or anyone else in this stupid place thinks I—"

Jack held up a hand that again appeared to glow in the twilight. The phenomenon unnerved Levi, and it evidently had the same effect on Miss Wildwood, whose sentence broke off as if she'd chopped it with a hatchet.

"I'm not implying anything, Miss Wildwood. I'm only saying that Levi could use a kind word every now and then. The boy's had quite a run of bad luck."

Miss Wildwood sniffed. "Yes, well it looks to me as if a lot of the men out here in California should have stayed home."

Jack twinkled in the darkness. Levi could see his eyes from where he stood behind his tree. "Reckon that could be said of some women out here, too."

Miss Wildwood's hauteur collapsed like a popped balloon. Levi was astonished to see her face crumple. She began to sob. Gentleman Jack Oakes put his arms around her and patted her on the back. Levi wished he could do that, although not in the fatherly way Jack had about him.

"There, there, Miss Wildwood. Everything will turn out all right. You'll see."

Levi thought he heard her say, "How can you know that?" but he wasn't sure.

"I just know, Miss Wildwood," said Jack in the most

soothing tone Levi had ever heard. "I just know. Trust me about this one."

Listening to the poor girl cry was too hard on Levi, who wished he had the freedom women enjoyed to burst into tears any old time they felt like it. He also felt like an eavesdropper—which he was—and that made him feel guilty. So he turned and slunk away to his own tent, and wished things could be different for Miss Meredith Wildwood. And for Levi Harte, too.

Chapter Five

"Miss Wildwood?"

Levi heard a quick intake of breath from inside Meredith Wildwood's tent and then some scuttling noises, as if she were moving about rapidly. He stood at the tent's flap, holding two blankets and a sheepskin jacket and wondering if he'd lost his mind. He might as well have; the good Lord knew, his mind hadn't been any good to him for months now. It was also about all he had left to lose.

"Who is it?" Her voice was hard, suspicious. Frightened? Levi couldn't tell.

"It's Levi Harte, Miss Wildwood."

"What do you want? I'm trying to write a letter to my parents."

"I was trying to write one to mine, too, ma'am, earlier this evening. Didn't get very far."

"I'd get farther if I had more paper. But I'll never get anything finished if I don't get some peace and quiet."

Levi frowned, annoyed by her show of temper when he

was here as a gesture of good will. Marginally daunted but still game, he tried again. "I didn't mean to disturb you, ma'am, but I have something here that you might be able to use."

"I don't need anything."

Her voice rose in pitch. Now she really did sound scared. Levi didn't understand why she should be scared of him. He might be big, and he might be strong, but he was about as harmless as one of the squirrels that scolded the miners from the trees. "Just give me a minute, ma'am. I won't hurt you."

"I have a weapon, so don't you try anything!"

Levi sighed. "You won't need a weapon, ma'am."

"That's what you say. How do I know that?"

Good question. Levi wished he had an answer.

"Er, I don't mean to bother you none, ma'am, but it didn't look to me as to how you had much by the way of bedding or warm things to wear. It gets mighty cold at night here in the Sierras."

A pause. Another shuffling noise, as if she were positioning herself to ward off an attack. "Do you think I don't know that?"

It was Levi's turn to pause. He even scratched his head. "As to that, I couldn't say, ma'am, but it didn't look like you had much by way of keeping warm with." What in blazes did she expect from him, anyway?

"If you're going to offer to keep me warm at night, Mr. Levi Harte, you can just take yourself off. I'd rather freeze to death."

Keep her warm at night? Levi stared at the tent flap, dumbfounded. He'd never do such a thing! Offended, he said, "Say, what do you take me for, ma'am? I'm not any blasted reprobate or anything."

"Hmph."

"And I resent you implying that I am. Drat it, I'm trying to do you a good turn here."

"I'm fine," she snapped. "I don't need your good turn."

"Horse feathers! If all you have is that dress you had on, you sure do need my good turn."

"Well, I don't want it!"

Greatly peeved, Levi barked, "Listen, I don't know anything about you, but my folks taught me to look out for my neighbors, and that's what I'm trying to do here."

"My folks taught me the same thing, Mr. Harte, but I haven't met up with too many like-minded people in California so far."

Levi huffed out an impatient breath. This woman was so exasperating, he had an urge to walk away and leave her to her own devices. He even turned around, intending to stomp off. He caught sight of Gentleman Jack Oakes, though, sitting on a log in front of the fire pit and grinning at him, and he thought unaccountably of Christmas.

Blast it, this was the season of good will. Levi couldn't let that girl's fears and foolishness be the death of her, no matter what she thought of him or how she treated him. He turned back to Miss Wildwood's tent, sucked in a breath of icy air, chuffed it out again, and told himself his parents would expect no less of him. They might even be proud of him if they knew he was persisting in spite of Miss Wildwood's misguided efforts to rebuff him.

It galled him, but he kept his voice from sounding sarcastic when he said, "Just in case you get cold—in spite of all the warm clothes I'm sure you have packed in that little leather satchel of yours—I brought you some things, ma'am. My partner—the one who died last August—he left this sheepskin jacket and a couple of blankets. I don't think they're contagious."

Her startled laugh caught him off guard.

"In other words, you don't want to sleep with me. You only want me to die of the fever and ague."

"No!" Levi glared at the tent flap. He guessed he hadn't explained himself very well, but that was no reason for her to laugh at him. *It's the Christmas season,* he reminded him-

31

self. He refused to allow her to rile him. "I mean, I washed the blankets, ma'am, and aired the jacket out. He wasn't wearing it when he got sick, 'cause it was hot back in August."

Levi pondered his fumbling words and muttered a soft, "Blast!" He didn't hear a thing from the other side of the tent flap, and he considered dropping his bundle and taking off when Miss Wildwood's voice, sounding much less hostile and even slightly emotional, came to him again.

"I, ah, probably can use some warmer things. Thank you, Mr. Harte."

Relieved, Levi said, "Yes, ma'am."

"I'm sorry I was unkind to you. I—I've learned to be careful since I came to California."

"That's all right, Miss Wildwood. I understand."

She made no move to come out of her tent. Levi stared at the flap and wondered what she was waiting for. Then it occurred to him that, in spite of her apology, she still didn't trust him. He guessed he might be leery, too, if he'd been staked in a poker game, but still, her lack of trust galled him.

He thought of something else that she might appreciate, and took the folded sheet of foolscap out of his shirt pocket and eyed it critically. It wasn't too smudged, he reckoned. Females were more sentimental than men; she probably needed it more than he did. He couldn't think of anything to write home about anyway. "I'll leave you a sheet of paper, too, ma'am, so you can write a longer letter to your folks."

Silence. Then, "Don't you need it? To write to your own folks?" She sounded puzzled.

Levi shrugged before he remembered she couldn't see him. "It don't matter, ma'am. I don't have anything to tell 'em that I haven't already said a million times before."

"Really? I should think there would no end of things to write to them, since you're living in this strange new place and all."

This time it was his own laugh that caught Levi off guard.

"California's pretty strange, all right." He hadn't meant to sound so wry.

Another hesitation on her part. "Don't you miss your family, Mr. Harte?"

Didn't he miss his family? He'd kill to get back home again for Christmas. He shrugged again. "Yeah, I miss 'em."

"Well, don't you want that paper for yourself then?"

Aw, cripes. Why was she so dead-bang set on arguing with him over everything? Her contentiousness made Levi mad. "Listen, Miss Wildwood, I don't really want to fight with you about it. I'm giving you the paper, and you can use it or throw it away or burn it. It's all the same to me."

Shooting a glance over his shoulder, he again caught sight of Gentleman Jack Oakes, barely illuminated by the almost-extinguished coals still smoldering in the fire pit. Once more, Levi thought of Christmas, and of the three wise men who had left gifts for the baby Jesus. He had an unhappy suspicion that he was making too much of this errand of his, and he turned back to Miss Wildwood's tent.

"I'll—er, just leave everything right here, ma'am. Outside your tent. They're right here, beside the flap. To the right of it. On the ground." He took a deep breath and told himself to stop babbling. "But you'd better get 'em soon, because somebody else might come by and take 'em if you don't. I don't think any of the fellows here in Christmas Gap are dishonest, but none of 'em have much by way of money, and they might be tempted."

"Thank you very much, Mr. Harte. That's two months' worth of free laundry I owe you now."

"No, ma'am. I don't want pay for those things. I just— well, I didn't know what to do with 'em anyhow. You might as well use them if you can."

Miss Meredith Wildwood didn't argue with him, but when she said, "We'll see," Levi got the distinct impression that she wasn't going to back down.

Well, good. He wouldn't argue either. He could stand to have his laundry done free for a couple of months. Hell, he hadn't been able to afford laundry services for a year or more. Besides, anything free was all right with him at the moment.

"Well, good night, then, ma'am."

"Good night, Mr. Harte."

Levi strolled over to the fire pit and saluted Jack Oakes, who gestured at the log adjoining his. "Have a seat, Levi. Fine night."

"Thanks." A fine night, was it? Levi decided to reserve judgment on that issue. He sat, though, and watched Miss Wildwood's tent.

Minutes passed, and she didn't emerge. He muttered, "Blast it, she needs those things. I know she does."

Jack's chuckle was low and cheery. "I know it, too, son. Try to be patient with the girl. She's been through a lot lately."

Levi squinted at Jack and wished he'd elaborate, as Levi was exceedingly curious to know how Miss Wildwood had managed to get herself staked in a poker game. Jack didn't elaborate, and Levi decided he'd be hanged if he'd beg for information about Miss Meredith Wildwood.

He pulled his furry collar up around his ears and tugged his hat lower on his brow. Good Glory, it was cold. If that girl didn't fetch those things soon, Levi'd just march over there and toss 'em into her tent. That'd teach her to doubt his motives.

The tent flap lifted, and Levi squinted hard at Miss Wildwood's tent. Her face appeared, and she looked around cautiously. Levi shook his head. What was she afraid of? Shoot, if she so much as said boo to most of the men in Christmas Gap, they'd scatter like geese.

Jack Oakes nodded toward her. "Looks like your good intentions are paying off, Levi."

"Hmmm." Levi wasn't sure about that. Miss Wildwood

hadn't yet deigned pick up the bundle he'd left. Instead, she took one wary, gingerly step out of her tent. She still wore that calico dress. She'd tossed a thin cotton coat over it, but she must have been near to freezing. If Levi'd been her, he'd have snatched up those blankets and that jacket and had himself bundled up in all of them by this time.

Not Meredith Wildwood. When she finally emerged completely, Levi saw that she was carrying that leather satchel of hers as if she intended to bash someone with it. Was that the weapon she'd threatened him with? Fat lot of good that thing would have done her.

She glanced around as if she suspected that bad men were lurking just out of sight, ready to pounce on her. Then she squinted down at the bundle of blankets and jacket Levi'd left. It looked to Levi as though she were inspecting it for hidden mousetraps or something. He didn't know whether to be amused or offended.

"Jehosephat," he muttered. "You'd think she didn't trust anyone."

"I don't expect she does," Jack murmured, cradling a mug in his gloved hands as if to keep them warm that way.

Levi glanced at him out of the corner of his eye. "How come?"

Jack shrugged. "If you'd been wagered in a poker game, you might be a little skittish around your fellow man, too."

Watching as Miss Wildwood finally condescended to kneel beside his bundle, Levi scowled. She kept her head up, and jerked it back and forth as she scanned the area around her tent. She looked to Levi as though she expected some trick and aimed to be ready for it when it was sprung on her. She didn't seem anywhere near willing to let down her guard for anything, not even for Levi Harte's dead partner's sheepskin jacket, no matter how much she needed it.

Levi tried to remain huffy about her mistrust. His heart ached a little bit, though, and he wondered what would make so young a girl that fearful.

He didn't want Gentleman Jack Oakes to think him soft-hearted—or soft-headed—so he made his voice gruff when he asked, "Well, what in blazes did she do to get in with such rough company in the first place? That's what I'd like to know."

Jack's grin was as white as pearls in the light from the dying fire. "You'd have to ask her that, Levi, my boy."

His pa would tan his hide if he ever asked a female such a question, but Levi didn't say so to Gentleman Jack. "Maybe. But it seems to me she's awfully nervous. Shoot, I was only trying to be nice to her."

"I know that, Levi." Jack's voice was gentle. "And I'm sure she will, too, someday. In the meantime, it's probably better to cut the girl some slack. She's had a hard time of it since she came to California."

Levi grunted humorlessly. "Haven't we all?"

Jack laughed much more heartily than Levi thought his comment deserved.

Chapter Six

December 2, 1851
Dear Mama and Papa,

A very kind man named Mr. Levi Harte, from Ohio, and another gentleman named Mr. Potter, who is very shy, helped set up a tent for me in Christmas Gap. Although it is wintertime and the weather is chilly, you need not think that I am cold or that I do not have the necessaries of life. The men in this gold-mining camp seem to be friendly, and they like to share their goods with each other in a fine, Christian manner. Mr. Harte even gave me this sheet of paper to write home with. He also lent me a sheepskin jacket to wear. It is as warm as anything, and keeps me very comfortable.

Perhaps tomorrow I can begin my laundry business. These men can certainly use my services!

I do not want to fret you, and I do not mean to complain, but I must say that I do pine for the communion of another female. These gold camps can be such ugly, masculine places, even though they are set in some of the loveliest forest land I have ever seen—and I have now been clear across the country! Please tell Aggie that I wish she were here, and that I appreciate my little sister now more than I ever believed I would. Please tell her, too, that I am sorry that I used to be cross with her.

Oh, dear. I did not mean to fall into a melancholy. In truth, life is fine here in Christmas Gap. I suppose that, as Christmas approaches, I am missing my family more than I expected to. Of course, I expected that Jonathan would be with me in California, too, and I am ever so sorry that he is not.

I have not heard from Uncle George since I left Red Bluff. I trust that his claim is working satisfactorily.

Please give my love to Granny Wildwood, and remember me to my cousins.

Your loving daughter,
Merry

Chapter Seven

The first person Levi Harte saw when he staggered out of his tent the morning after Miss Meredith Wildwood's arrival in Christmas Gap was Gentleman Jack Oakes. Jack sat on a log beside the fire pit, much as he had the night before, only this time he was facing Levi's canvas abode. His grin widened when he spotted Levi.

Levi knew it was an illusion created by the cold morning sunlight filtering through the fir trees that made it appear as if Jack had an aura of light surrounding him. Levi rubbed his eyes to clear them of their morning fog.

"Morning, Levi!" Jack sounded as jolly as Saint Nick. Something in Levi's chest perked up a mite. Even the growling of his stomach didn't quench it.

"Morning, Mr. Oakes."

"Come over here and have some biscuits and bacon and coffee."

That sounded mighty good to Levi, who hadn't expected to eat breakfast until he'd either shot something or begged

39

some bread or cornmeal from Gus—and Gus wasn't known for his charitable leanings. Levi's stomach gave another fierce growl in anticipation.

"Thanks," he said. "That's mighty kind of you, Mr. Oakes."

Gentleman Jack winked at him and patted a rock next to his log in invitation. "Call me Jack, son. Everyone does."

Levi said, "Jack," and sat on the rock.

"Miss Merry should be joining us any minute now. She cooked up this fine meal." Jack gestured to the bounty before them, and Levi saw a mess of biscuits and a stack of thick bacon slices. His mouth watered, and he took a biscuit and tried not to stuff it into his mouth whole. It was delicious.

After swallowing his first bite of biscuit, Levi took the tin cup of coffee Jack held out to him and cocked his eyebrow. "Who's Merry?" Criminy, was there another female come to camp after he'd gone to bed? He devoured the rest of his biscuit, licked his fingers, and reached for a rasher of bacon.

"Miss Wildwood."

"Oh, I understand." Levi nodded. "Merry's short for Meredith, I reckon." He decided to stop playing coy, folded the bacon in half, and popped the whole rasher into his mouth.

Jack laughed as if he'd already guessed that Levi was on the growly edge of starvation, in spite of his efforts to hide his condition. "I reckon."

Frowning, Levi sipped his coffee and shuddered. It was stronger than he was by a far sight. His stomach was already beginning to feel full, though, so he didn't repine.

"That stuff'll put hair on your chest, Levi." Jack gestured with his own tin mug.

"I expect so." Levi wasn't sure why he felt funny about Gentleman Jack Oakes calling Miss Meredith Wildwood by a nickname, but he did. He grabbed another biscuit, bit into it, and chewed thoughtfully. Before he could sort out his odd reaction in his own mind, Jack spoke again.

"You know, son, Merry's going to need your good will and help here in Christmas Gap."

Levi downed another swig of coffee and considered inspecting his chest for new hair growth. He grimaced. "Yeah? Well, I'll do my best."

"I expect you will. I told 'em so."

Levi squinted at Jack while trying to ignore the bitterness of the brew in his mug. "You told who so?"

Jack shrugged. "Slip of the tongue, lad. I meant I expected no less of you."

"Oh." Whatever in blazes that meant.

"And here she is now."

Jack rose from his rock and swept his black hat from his black hair. Levi noticed that Jack's reputation for dudery remained unsullied this morning. His grooming was impeccable. How anyone could look that tidy in Christmas Gap, especially on a morning that was cold enough to freeze a man's butt to a log, was an enigma to Levi. He'd done his best to clean up—because he wanted to make a good impression on Miss Wildwood—using icy water from the river before he went to bed last night, but he knew his clothes were filthy and so was he. Some kind of impression that would make.

Well, never mind. He rose too, trying to tug his ragged clothing into some kind of order, and turned to greet the newcomer. His jaw dropped, and he almost spilled his coffee. He was glad he didn't; it might have eaten a hole in his stone seat.

Merciful heavens, she looked like an angel—an angel in rags and a sheepskin jacket ten sizes too large for her. Not caring to be judged a nitwit by her or by Jack Oakes, Levi clanked his teeth together. Then he opened his mouth in a less awe-stricken fashion and managed to mutter, "Good morning, Miss Wildwood."

She had her little freckled nose in the air, but she unbent enough to nod and say, "Good morning, Mr. Harte." Unbending slightly further from her regal posture, she added, "Thank you very much for the use of those blankets and this jacket. They served me quite well last night."

Levi realized his head had begun bobbing up and down, and he forced himself to act civilized. "You're welcome, Miss Wildwood. Thank you very much for this delicious breakfast."

"You're welcome. I fear I made the coffee rather strong. We used to use chicory back home. I'm not accustomed to real coffee."

So that was it. Levi peered into his coffee mug and wondered if it was strong enough to crawl out of the cup by itself. "The biscuits and bacon are mighty tasty, ma'am. Miss Wildwood." He decided not to mention the coffee at all. Shoot, until he came to California, he'd never even tasted coffee.

Gentleman Jack's soft laugh brought the attention of both young people to him. "My, my. Aren't we both formal this morning?"

Levi smiled. Merry didn't.

"Reckon we are," Levi said, glad Jack had pointed out the obvious and, as it were, broken the ice.

"We don't know each other."

Hmmm. Perhaps Jack hadn't broken the ice, after all. Levi countered, "Life's pretty casual in a gold camp, ma'am. Reckon we aren't generally as formal out here as folks are back east."

Merry eyed him up and down, and Levi became acutely aware of his sartorial shortcomings. Had he combed his hair this morning? He couldn't remember.

"I don't see that because folks in Christmas Gap have no manners is any reason for the rest of the world to sink to its uncivilized level."

Jack chuckled again. In spite of his full stomach, Levi grew indignant. "If you'll pardon me for saying so, Miss Wildwood, I don't see as how there's any reason for you to be getting uppity with me. I haven't done anything that you need to insult me for, I don't reckon."

Merry flushed. She was mighty pretty when her cheeks got pink like that. "I beg your pardon, Mr. Harte. I didn't mean to sound uppity. You've been very kind to me, really. But a female's reputation is a fragile thing, and one has to guard one's dignity or lose it entirely."

Levi pondered her comment, frowning. "Beg pardon again, ma'am, but I don't see how a lady who got herself staked in a poker game has much cause to worry about her reputation." He regretted the words as soon as they left his lips.

The flush in Merry's cheeks drained away as quickly as it had bloomed. She looked sick and as pale as one of Levi's ma's white leghorn chickens for a second or two. Levi mentally marched himself out to the woodshed and gave his behind several salutary whacks with a hickory switch. Jack tutted at him, and Levi felt even worse.

"That was unkind of you, Mr. Harte," Merry said, her voice quivering. "I had begun to believe that you were a considerate person—not like the rest of the men in this place, who judge a person by what they perceive her circumstances to be, even though they don't know the half of it. I see I was mistaken."

She began to remove the sheepskin jacket. Levi had a feeling she aimed to fling it at him. Even if he didn't already regret his hard words, and even if he didn't already kind of like her for her spunk and her cooking, he wouldn't have taken the jacket back. He held out a hand to stop her. "I'm sorry, ma'am. I didn't mean to say that. It just slipped out."

Her hands stilled on the buttons of the jacket, and she peered at him through slitted eyes. Levi stammered on. "I mean—I mean, I'm sorry. That was a rude thing to say. Besides, you need that jacket, ma'am. You can't have packed enough warm things into that little leather satchel of yours to keep you from freezing up here in the mountains. I won't

43

take the jacket back. It's yours now, and you have to keep it.''

Levi could tell that emotions were waging a war within Merry. He could almost see defiance and indignation do battle with common sense and the reality of winter, and he regretted having put her through such turmoil. He was heartily ashamed of himself, in fact.

"I'm really sorry, ma'am. My pa would whup me for saying anything like that to a lady. I reckon my manners haven't improved much since I came to California."

She eyed him again, her expression severe, but Levi was relieved to see that her hands dropped away from the jacket. He also noticed that her woolen mittens had holes in them. Criminy, the weather was as cold as a witch's heart these days, and would soon be well below freezing at night. If all she had was that flimsy blue dress and those holey mittens to wear, she'd never last here. If she didn't freeze to death, she'd catch the pneumonia and die. The men who claimed to know such things had been predicting snow for days now.

"Well . . ." Merry wavered uncertainly.

Levi knew exactly what she was going through. *Should I maintain my pride and throw this jacket into that fellow's face, or should I save my life and keep it?* Levi'd been in much the same sort of dilemma himself a time or two. He'd already decided to sacrifice his own pride. He hoped Merry would, too. He really didn't want her to die.

"Please, ma'am?" He smiled at her, hoping his Sunday-school teacher, Miss Fincher, had been right when she'd told him he had a smile that could melt a heart of ice when he set out to wheedle a body.

"I have an idea."

Levi and Merry both started in surprise and turned to look at Jack, who was grinning at them as if, together, they were the funniest joke he'd ever beheld.

"I think you should accept Levi's apology, Merry. He's only a young man yet, and he isn't used to sweet-talking the ladies. It's been a couple of years since he's had access the benevolent influence of his mama's good teachings. I do believe a lady ought to make allowances for such things.''

"Well . . .''

Merry squinted at Levi again, and Levi felt his own cheeks heat up. He'd be willing to wager he didn't look nearly as charming when he blushed as Merry did. He wished Jack had kept his mouth shut and not called him *only a young man*. On the other hand, Jack was right. He nodded. "That's the truth, ma'am. My ma would be ashamed of me.'' He elected not to admit that he was only twenty-one years old. A mere baby, in fact.

Merry nodded as if she were ashamed of him, too. Levi felt a spurt of indignation. After all, he might be starving, and he might be young, he might be socially inept, he might be a fool for ever having chased his golden dream to California, but *he* hadn't got himself wagered as a stake in a poker game.

Jack laughed again. Levi got the oddest impression that the man could read his mind—and that he considered his thoughts wildly amusing.

"I think,'' said Jack, "That Levi here—and maybe his friend Mr. Potter—should set up a laundry tent for you, Miss Merry. I'm sure they could find some big tubs or old hogsheads around here somewhere so's you could begin washing these men's dirty duds.'' He winked at them both. "And they can dig you a fire pit inside your tent to heat the wash water and keep you warm. It'd serve two purposes that way. Then you could start your business in Christmas Gap and maybe make the upcoming Christmas season a little brighter for these men here.''

"Christmas?'' Levi wondered what Christmas had to do with anything. He didn't know who had named this community Christmas Gap, but in Levi's opinion, whoever it was had possessed a mighty unpleasant sense of humor.

"Christmas?" Merry echoed, as if she'd never heard the word before.

"Christmas." Jack agreed and laughed again, obviously finding their joint incredulity hilarious. "You two remember Christmas, don't you? Family? Fruitcake? Good will to all mankind? Presents? Carols? Those three wise fellows following a star and traveling all the way to Bethlehem to honor a poor baby's birth in a manger?"

Levi swallowed, Jack's humorous recitation of Christmas traditions having reminded him all too well of Christmases back home in Ohio. Lordy, he wished he could be spirited home again, if only for that one day. Or for Christmas Eve. At Grandma and Grandpa Harte's house, with the whole family gathered around, and his cousins and his sisters and his—

He commanded his brain to cease its fruitless reminiscences. Christmas back home was too painful to contemplate. He couldn't bear to dwell on it, or his state would seem even more pitiful than it already did.

When he glanced at Merry, her eyes were glittering suspiciously, as if she'd remembered too and was now on the verge of tears. Levi's heart lurched, and he took a step toward her. She backed up an equal distance and tossed her head. Levi got the impression that she regretted her momentary failure of composure and was now trying to prove to him that she was as tough as any California gold-miner. Her show of bravado only enhanced his impression of her as a vulnerable young girl whom he wished he could somehow protect. Foolish, foolish Levi. Shoot, he couldn't even take care of himself. He sighed and faced Jack again.

"Yeah," he said. "I remember Christmas."

"Wouldn't it be a fine thing if you and Miss Wildwood here managed to spruce this place up some? And maybe get Potter to help you? Clean clothes and a tidy camp for the upcoming festive season couldn't hurt Christmas Gap any, I don't reckon."

"I don't reckon they could." Levi grinned, suddenly finding the notion of sprucing Christmas Gap up for the season a comical one. In fact, it appealed to his sense of the ridiculous, which used to be acute, and which had been sliding downhill at a precipitous rate in recent days.

"What about it, Miss Wildwood?" he asked her. "I'd be happy to fetch Potter, and we can set up a laundry tent, get you some tubs, build a fire to heat water, and have your business going in a couple of shakes."

Her narrowed eyes and suspicious expression exasperated him, but he endeavored to hide his reaction. He expected any female who'd been staked in a poker game—and he'd sure like to hear the story behind *that*—had a right to be suspicious.

"Well . . ."

He threw out his arms. "I'm not up to anything, ma'am. Honest. I only like the idea of spiffing up the place for Christmas. For the festive season." Jack's description of the season tickled him, and he couldn't stop the chuckle gurgling up in his chest from escaping.

Jack joined him, laughing as if this were the drollest proposition he'd heard in a long time.

Merry frowned at the two of them for a moment before she said, grudgingly, "Oh, very well."

Chapter Eight

Merry Wildwood had been in Christmas Gap for a week when the first of four curious events transpired. Levi had just arisen on a cold and frosty morning. He was staring up into a sky so gray, it reminded him of the sheets of metal his uncle Luther used to prop against the wall in his tin-smithing shop back home. As he gazed, he contemplated the merits of making one last futile attempt to work his worthless claim, or of asking Gus Shackleford for a clerking job in his dry-goods store, when Potter rushed up to him.

"Levi! You hear about Miss Wildwood and Clyde?"

Seeing Potter rush was surprising. Hearing him speak without having been spoken to first was an event of such astonishing uniqueness that Levi at first didn't believe it had happened. He looked over Potter's shoulder to see if another fellow was standing behind him. No one was there. It must, therefore, have been Potter who'd spoken. He'd done it loudly, too, and with much emotion.

Levi shook his head. "Miss Wildwood and Clyde?" Now

there was a combination fit to make a strong man blanch.

Clyde was about six feet, four inches tall, nearly as big around, and as shaggy as a bear. He smelled like one too, if what Levi'd heard about bears was true. Clyde would make six of Merry Wildwood, with a couple of large feet left over.

He frowned at Potter. "Clyde didn't do anything to her, did he?" Lordy, he hoped not.

Potter shook his head, reminding Levi of his cousin Leo's old spaniel who had a penchant for leaping into streams. "No. He tried to, though."

Levi felt his eyebrows arch. "What do you mean, he tried to?" If Clyde tried to do anything to anyone, Levi couldn't imagine him not succeeding. Sheer size alone would ensure his triumph. "Shoot, he didn't hurt her, did he?" Levi's hands bunched up into fists at the thought. Blast! He should have given her his gun to use or something.

Again, Potter's head wagged back and forth as if he were attempting to shake off water. "She bashed his haid."

She bashed his haid? What did that mean? Levi didn't have to ask, because Potter rushed on. This behavior on Potter's part was so unlike him that Levi could only stare at him, marveling.

"I heard it, Levi. I heard every word. Clyde went into her laundry tent, stinkin' like he does, y'know."

Levi knew. He nodded.

"I mean, he ain't never had them duds of his washed once since he come here, I don't reckon."

Levi didn't doubt it.

"Anyhow, Clyde, he told Miss Wildwood that he'd pay her." Potter's Adam's apple bobbed up and down when he swallowed. He turned crimson. "You know what fer."

Levi knew. "Yeah," he said, frowning heavily. "I know what for. Did she understand what he wanted?"

Potter's head looked as if it might detach itself from his skinny neck if he nodded it any harder. "I reckon she understood, all right, because she hollered at him to get out of her tent."

"And did Clyde get out?"

"Not then, he didn't. He said she waren't foolin' him none. He said she might be able to put one over on you, Levi—"

"Me?" Levi stared at Potter, aghast.

More nods. "Yup. Clyde, he said she might be able to put one over on you, but he—this here's Clyde talkin', you understand."

"I understand."

"But he—Clyde—says he knows better. He says he knows she's a doxy and a tart underneath."

"He used those words?" Good grief, maybe it was a good thing Levi hadn't given her his gun. She'd probably have shot Clyde dead for saying such a thing to her, and then she might get into trouble. Miss Wildwood didn't strike Levi as the tolerant sort.

"He shore did. And you know what she done?"

"No, Potter, I have no idea."

"Well—I was standin' outside her tent, you see, and I was tryin' to figger out what to do. I didn't much want to tangle with Clyde, don'tcha know."

"I understand." No one wanted to tangle with Clyde. He was too big. Besides, if you got into a tussle with Clyde and survived, you'd probably end up smelling like him, and that might well be a fate worse than death.

"Well, I stuck my haid in the tent to see if I could help her. And I seen her stick her nose in the air and say, real haughty-like, 'I am a laundress. That is the *only* thing I do for money.' She said it just like that, too. Then she stares at him real mean-like, sniffs the air like she was some kind of princess or something, and says, 'You *need* your laundry done. And a bath.' "

Levi's sudden grin caught him by surprise. "She really said that to Clyde?"

Potter's nod was so loose, Levi wondered if he had a medical problem. "She said that. And y'know what Clyde done then?"

Levi shook his head.

"He says, 'Are you a-tellin' me I stink?' He was lookin' real bug-eyed when he says it, like he couldn't decide whether to be mad or not. And y'know what she says?"

Levi sighed and shook his head again.

"She says, 'That's *exactly* what I'm tellin' ya!' And then, y'know what Clyde does?"

Levi didn't bother shaking his head this time.

"He lifts his arm and sniffs his pit! Then he wrinkles his own nose up like he'd smelt a skunk!"

"Ha! Then what happened?"

"Then she picks up this big stick she had propped beside her laundry tub and, whilst Clyde's sniffin' his other pit, she whups him over the haid."

"I don't suppose that hurt Clyde much."

"Hurt his pride, mebbe, but didn't hurt his haid none. You know how much hair he's got. Prob'ly matted up like a cushion by this time."

"I expect."

"Clyde gets this expression on his face then, as if she's done hurt his feelings and says, all hangdog-like, 'Why'd you have to go and do that fer?' And she says, 'Cause you insulted me, is why.' And she's still standin' there like a queen, only holdin' that log like she expects she'll have to use it again."

"Then what?"

Potter shrugged. "Then Gus comes in the tent and tells Clyde to stop botherin' Miss Wildwood. He tells him to bring in his clothes for her to wash, too, 'cause he needs it."

"Well, I'll be dipped."

Potter smiled a smile bigger than any Levi'd ever seen on his thin face. "Ain't that somethin'? I thought that was really somethin'."

51

Emma Craig

"It's really something, all right, Potter. Thanks for telling me about it. Think I'll stroll over to Miss Wildwood's tent. I have something I have to ask Gus, if he's still there."

"Oh, he's still there, all right. This just happened a minute or two ago."

Levi and Potter parted company, and Levi hurried to Merry Wildwood's laundry tent. He'd taken to going there to greet her in the mornings anyway, and to ask her if he could help her in any way. She never took him up on his offer, but a smile from her seemed to start his day off right somehow.

When he neared the tent, however, he was disturbed to hear loud voices emanating from within. He glanced around to see other men staring at the tent. Some of them had grins on their faces, as if they were enjoying the entertainment. Others looked uncertain, as if they didn't know if they should interfere or not. If the Christmas Gap rumor mill was running true to form, Miss Wildwood's encounter with Clyde was common knowledge by this time, and they probably didn't trust her with that club.

Levi wasn't sure what to do himself, although he was ready to slay dragons—or even Gus Shackleford—on Miss Wildwood's behalf if it proved necessary. This sudden realization unsettled him. He paused outside Merry's tent, listening hard.

"I already thanked you, Mr. Shackleford. What more do you want from me?" Levi couldn't tell if Merry sounded more angry than worried, or the other way around.

"I already told you what you can do for me, *Miss* Wildwood. You can thank me in private." Levi imagined the leer on Gus's face and went cold all over. "Hell, I aim to pay you. It ain't like I'm asking nothing for free."

"How *dare* you!"

Levi heard a wet plop and then Gus's gurgly, "Hey! Dammit, what'd you do that for?"

"Why do all of you awful men think I'm a loose woman? I'm *not*, blast you all! I'm *not!*"

"The hell you're not! Nobody but a whore'd ever get herself staked in a poker game, and you know it!"

"How *dare* you!"

Levi thought it was time for some discreet interference. Since he didn't much want to be battered to death by Miss Wildwood's cudgel, he eased himself inside her tent. He was in time to see her stagger up to Gus Shackleford, a laundry tub full of soapy water and wet clothes in her hands, and then heave the tub over Gus's head. Water splashed everywhere, including on Levi, who jumped backward. So did Merry.

"Hey!" Gus shrieked. His shriek was muffled inside the wooden tub.

Trying like mad not to laugh out loud—Levi sensed that neither Merry nor Gus would appreciate him laughing—and since he needed Gus, he waded through the muddy water to the grocer's side and eased the tub from his head. Because he wasn't sure Gus wouldn't be mad enough to lunge at Merry Wildwood, he gripped him by the shoulder as soon as he'd set the tub down.

It didn't appear that Gus was in any condition to lunge at anyone. He was scrubbing wildly at his eyes, which were evidently stinging with soap bubbles. He was soaking wet and looked pathetic. When Levi glanced from Gus to Merry Wildwood, he saw her standing back, her hands pressed to her flaming cheeks. He couldn't tell if she was still mad or not, but she certainly looked disconcerted.

"I'll take care of Gus, Miss Wildwood. Don't you worry none."

She nodded and whispered, "Thank you." Levi heard her suck in a deep breath. "Did you hear what he said to me?" She sounded mortified.

"Yes, ma'am. I'm truly sorry."

53

Her hands dropped and clenched at her sides. "He deserved it! He deserves worse than that!"

Gus bubbled something incoherent.

Levi tried not to laugh. "I expect you might be right, ma'am."

"I *am* right!"

She was getting indignant again. Although Levi didn't see any other laundry tubs she could use on him, he wasn't keen to experience her cudgel. He thought it prudent to agree.

"I'm sure you are, ma'am."

"Just because a lady falls on hard times doesn't mean she's not a lady!"

"I'm sure that's true."

"Bullshit!" The watery expletive came from Gus, and was accompanied by a fine series of soap bubbles. Levi's levity threatened to overcome him.

Merry hollered, "Don't you dare swear inside my place of business!" She darted to the corner of her tent, and Levi saw her pick up a big, heavy, knobby stick. That must be the one she'd used on Clyde. He thought he'd better get Gus out of there.

"Come on now, Gus. Let's you and me get you to your place and cleaned up. I'll help you get dried off and you can warm up beside that stove in your store. I'll fix you some tea and that'll help thaw you out, too. And it'll take the taste of soap out of your mouth."

The last sentence came out wobbly, because he was losing his battle against hilarity. Levi hoped neither Merry nor Gus would object to his finding this situation funny. He was trying to help here, after all.

"Yes!" Merry cried. "Get him out of here before I bash him!"

"No need for that, Miss Wildwood," Levi said, striving for composure. "I'll come back and help you as soon as I get Gus settled. Help you get those duds wrung out and bring more water and so forth. And you'll need to spread some pine needles on that mud puddle, too.''

She sniffed. ''I don't need help!''

Levi rolled his eyes. ''Maybe you don't need it, but I think you deserve it.''

''Well, if you put it that way . . .''

Thank God. Levi grinned, nodded his head, and led Gus out of her tent. He saw Gentleman Jack Oakes watching him, leaning against a large, elegant incense cedar tree. Levi smiled and inclined his head in greeting. He couldn't very well tip his hat at the moment since his hands were full with Gus. Jack pushed himself away from the tree.

''Let me fetch Miss Wildwood some more water and mop up some of that mud in there, Levi. You take care of Gus.''

Levi guessed Jack must have heard everything from that cedar tree and understood what Merry had done. He was grateful he didn't have to rush back to her tent, because he really wanted to smooth Gus's ruffled feathers. If he could soften the grocer up and make him grateful for Levi's help, it would be easier for Levi to ask him for a job.

Chapter Nine

December 10, 1851
Dear Mama and Papa,

I must say that I didn't anticipate some of the things that have happened to me since Uncle George and I separated in Red Bluff. I greatly fear that living here in California, away from the influence of their families and churches and the like, has not had a beneficent effect on some of the men who reside in Christmas Gap.

Now, I recognize that perhaps it is unusual for a young woman to live alone, without a male family member to protect her, even in California. I also recognize that rumors, based on nothing more than one person's false assumptions about another person, can begin and spread like wildfire. This is why you used to scold me when Jenny Mae and I set to gossiping, Mama, and I thank you for it today. I understand now, as I never did before, how a person, in all innocence, can become the brunt of vicious gossip and rumor.

You needn't think that anything bad has happened to me, for Mr. Levi Harte, Mr. Jack Oakes, and Mr. Potter (I really expect I should learn his Christian name) have helped to still everyone's wagging tongues. I am telling you this mainly so that I can thank you for the proper upbringing you gave me.

The weather remains clear, but very cold. I appreciate the sheepskin jacket Mr. Harte gave me more than words can say, for we are in the mountains. Some of the men are predicting snow soon.

You would laugh to see the community of Christmas Gap today, Mama and Papa, for its residents have decided to tidy it and themselves up for the holidays. It is very amusing to see fellows sweeping the paths in front of their tents with pine boughs because Mr. Shackleford, who operates the only store in Christmas Gap, has never stocked brooms! I must tell you that Mr. Shackleford and I exchanged a few hot words yesterday, but all is well now. He is one of the men who had misunderstood my circumstances and believed me to be something I am not. Mr. Harte spoke to him, though, and corrected his impression.

All is well, that is, except that I do miss you so! I know you will not receive any of these letters I have been writing until long after Christmas has passed, but I can't help but send you my best wishes for the holiday anyway. I wish I could be with you, and that we could be together as a family, with Jonathan still among us, on December 24 and 25.

Except for missing my family terribly, I am quite well, and my business is thriving. I love you all very much.

Your loving daughter,
Merry

57

Chapter Ten

The second of the four unusual events to transpire in the weeks before Christmas, 1851, took place several days after Merry Wildwood's encounter with Gus Shackleford. It was occasioned by the arrival of a small Indian boy to Christmas Gap. His entry into the camp passed unnoticed at first. It wasn't until he entered Gus Shackleford's mercantile establishment, and Gus spied him, that his presence was discovered, and events moved forward.

Levi had gone to Merry Wildwood's tent that morning to get his usual wake-up smile from her. He'd found her looking glum, and his heart immediately executed several sickening swoops and began to thud with dread.

"What is it?" he cried, making her jump. He rushed up to her and almost grabbed her hand until he remembered they were virtual strangers to one another—and that she apparently wanted to keep them that way.

She pressed a hand to her bosom. Levi tried not to stare, as he'd been thinking about her bosom a good deal too much lately and needed no further encouragement in the pursuit.

"Oh, Mr. Harte! You gave me such a turn."

"I beg your pardon, ma'am." Levi cleared his throat, feeling foolish. "I saw you looking unhappy, and I was worried that something bad might have happened."

"Oh."

His eyes thinned as his frown deepened. "None of the boys have been making any improper suggestions, have they, ma'am? Because if they have, you just tell me who they are, and I'll talk to 'em." Since he continued to think of himself as a young man who had yet to secure the respect of Miss Merry Wildwood, he added sourly, "And I'll tell Gentleman Jack, too. The boys'll listen to him."

She gave him a smile, and Levi knew he'd make it through the day. "That's very kind of you, Mr. Harte, but I haven't been bothered by any insults recently. Not since last Saturday, anyway."

Her expression darkened, and Levi knew she was recollecting her encounter with Ben Budlow. As a rule, Ben was a mild-mannered, polite fellow, but he was given to an excess of hard drinking occasionally. Last Saturday Ben had encountered Miss Wildwood while he was under the influence. She'd had to wield her cudgel rather forcefully to dissuade him from his advances. Levi was pleased that no one had bothered her since. They'd better not. She was doing a booming business in Christmas Gap, since the fellows had decided to tidy up for Christmas, and she'd soon be able to afford to purchase a more formidable weapon than a cudgel.

"I'm glad of that, ma'am," said Levi. "But you did look worried. Is anything the matter?"

She sighed and held up her hands. Levi blinked at them, sorry to see that they looked raw. "It's my hands," she said. "They're so dreadfully chapped from being in soapy water all day long and exposed to the bitter winter air all night. They're even beginning to crack and bleed, and they do hurt awfully. It's difficult to work with my hands so sore. I need some lanolin to rub into them, but I don't know where to get any.''

Levi wanted to take her poor hands in his and tend to them himself. To pamper them and heal them and see that they'd never be chapped again. Since he figured she'd belt him a good one if he tried, he didn't. However, since he had good reason to know such things, he said, "Gus has some lanolin ointment in his dry-goods store, Miss Wildwood. You can get some there." It crossed his mind to offer to secure her some, but Levi had learned his lesson well regarding Miss Merry Wildwood. She refused to accept anything from anyone. She called it charity and said she hadn't sunk that low yet.

"Yes. I wondered if he might carry lanolin ointment."

She sounded uncertain, and Levi wondered why that should be until he recalled her encounter with Gus Shackleford the week prior.

"Um, are you reluctant to go into Gus's because of—you know." He didn't want to say it. His mother and father would be horrified that he even knew that such things as men propositioning young women went on in the world. They had no idea what California was like, his parents. Levi aimed to keep it that way.

She cleared her throat, and her cheeks colored. Levi's breath caught in his chest.

"Well—yes, actually, that's why I haven't been into his establishment." Her blush faded and she scowled. "I do need some supplies, but I don't care to be insulted again."

Levi thought for a moment, then came up with what he thought was a brilliant suggestion. "Tell you what, Miss Wildwood. I'm clerking for Gus now, and I'll walk you over there and stay with you while you buy the things you need. Gus won't say anything rough while I'm with you."

"Will you, Mr. Harte? That would be very kind of you!"

Her smile was so glorious, Levi nearly fainted. His heart flipped over like a trapeze artist in the circus. "Glad to help,'' he said breathlessly. "Happy to help." Ecstatic, even.

So Merry Wildwood put on her enormous sheepskin jacket, and Levi walked with her from her laundry tent to Gus Shackleford's mercantile establishment. Gus's store was the only decent-looking building in Christmas Gap, Gus having eschewed canvas and hammered it together out of lumber. He said, undoubtedly with much justification, that his business would be around long after most of these men gave up, abandoned their claims, and went home again, poorer and not necessarily wiser.

Levi held the door for her, and Merry sailed into the store with her little freckled nose in the air. Levi had begun to recognize this attitude as a manifestation of her state of nerves. When she was relaxed, she never put on airs. When she was uneasy, she gathered her dignity around her like a cloak and all but dared anyone to ill-treat her. He admired her for it, too.

Gus was there, and he appeared disconcerted to see Merry Wildwood in his store. He said, "Good, Levi, you're here. You mind the counter and sweep the floor. I've got me some things to do out back." And he retreated without waiting for Levi's reply.

Since Levi now worked for Gus, he did as Gus had bade him. He felt ridiculous when he donned the big white apron Gus made him wear and picked up the broom. Shoot, he was a man, not a farm wife! Still and all, he was gainfully employed and finally earning some money. He guessed that counted for something, even if he did have to wear an apron.

Merry's haughty demeanor evaporated as soon as Gus left the room. Levi thought he heard her sigh with relief, but he wasn't sure. Since there was no help for it, he left her to browse while he started sweeping out the store. No matter how often he did it, it always needed to be done again. Miners were forever tracking in mud, pine needles, and so forth. A California gold-mining camp was not an immaculate place.

He kept an eye on Merry as he swept, not because he

didn't trust her, but because she fascinated him. He wanted to know all about her—especially how such a seemingly superior female could have gotten herself into such a humiliating predicament as being used as a stake in a poker game. He was far too polite to ask.

While Merry looked around and Levi swept, a young boy entered the store. Levi knew from his dark complexion and his features that he was an Indian. Some of the miners said mean things about the local Indians, but Levi, who figured he was in no position to despise anyone, smiled at the boy. The boy, wide-eyed and obviously uneasy, didn't smile back, but gazed in amazement at the variety of goods on display at Gus's.

Merry had just set a jar of lanolin ointment, a box of cornstarch, and a bottle of Dr. Rosewater's Tonic on the counter of the mercantile, when Gus's loud voice startled her into a squeak and Levi into dropping his broom.

"Hey! Hey there, you! What the hell do you think you're doing?"

Levi whirled around and saw the Indian boy, frozen with terror, staring at Gus as if he expected to be shot any second. Gus stormed into the room, and the boy shrank back, trying to hide against a shelf.

While Levi was still wondering what Gus was mad about, Merry spoke.

"Why are you shouting at that poor lad, Mr. Shackleford? He isn't doing anything wrong."

Levi gaped at her, amazed. She sounded like the preacher back home, Mr. Granger, when he spotted an injustice and was endeavoring to right it.

Gus gave Merry a black look. He obviously hadn't forgiven her for dumping her laundry tub over his head. "This is none of your business, *Miss* Wildwood. That there boy's an Indian, and I don't like Indians."

Merry's spine was as straight as if she'd strapped a poker to her back. "Mistreatment of another human being *is* my business, *Mr.* Shackleford. That boy was doing nothing to earn your ill temper. He was merely looking at the merchandise.''

"God dammit, he's an Indian!''

"So what?''

"So I don't like Indians!''

"And why not?''

"Because they're savages, is why not!''

Gus's face was getting redder by the second. Levi hoped he wouldn't go off in an apoplexy.

"They're no more savage than most of the so-called civilized men who live in Christmas Gap! I defy you to tell me that boy is any less deserving than that awful man, Clyde, or Ben Budlow, or any of the other drunken louts who live here!

"Dammit, Clyde and Ben're white! This boy's an Indian!''

Merry's lips pinched up like prunes. She squared off for a fight, leaning toward Gus as if she was ready to continue this discussion until nightfall. She even shook her finger at him.

"Of all the hateful things to say! Especially now, in this season of goodwill to all mankind, it's vile. You make me ashamed to call myself a Christian woman, Mr. Gus Shackleford! Indeed, you do!''

"God dammit, he's an *Indian!*'' Gus yelled, as if that explained everything.

"And Jesus was a Jew!'' Merry yelled back. "What does his being an Indian have to do with anything?''

Gus sputtered something incomprehensible. Levi could tell it was because he was now so mad, he couldn't form words. Levi's respect for Merry Wildwood soared. He took a step toward Gus and put a comforting hand on his back. As much as he agreed with Merry, still less did he want Gus to suffer a spasm.

"I think Miss Wildwood's right, Gus. The boy was only

63

lookin' around. It's not like he stole anything."

Gus turned on Levi with a look that plainly called him a traitor. He opened his mouth—to fire him, Levi presumed—when Gentleman Jack Oakes, as smooth as silk, spoke from a corner of the store. Shoot, Levi hadn't even seen Jack enter. The man was as quiet as smoke.

"There you go, Gus," said Jack in the good-humored tone he always used. "The children are right, you know. Unless the boy's stolen something, there's no cause to be upset."

Gus sputtered some more.

Merry nodded firmly. "There! You see? And the boy wasn't stealing." She turned suddenly to face the boy, who gasped and would have stepped back still farther except that he was flat up against a shelf now. "Were you?"

He shook his head, clearly petrified with fear. Levi watched Merry's expression soften, and his heart went mushy. As Levi continued to console Gus, she knelt before the boy.

"What's your name? My name is Merry. Merry Wildwood."

The boy swallowed and whispered, "Joe. Folks call me Red Joe."

Merry's lips pinched again. Levi got the feeling that she didn't care for the lad's white nickname. "Well, Joe, do you have your family nearby, or are you alone?

Joe cleared his throat. "Alone. Need work."

"Ah, I see. You need a job, do you?"

The boy nodded again.

"Well, Joe, I'm alone, too. And if you're willing to work, I do believe I can offer you a position."

Levi gaped at her. So did Gus. When Levi glanced over at Gentleman Jack, he saw Jack smiling like an angel at Merry Wildwood and Red Joe.

"I won't be able to pay you much, you understand," Merry went on. "But my business has been pretty good lately, and I could certainly use help hauling water. It's awfully heavy work. Do you think you can help me, Joe?''

The boy stared at Merry as if she were his salvation. He nodded. ''Carry water?'' he asked in a small voice.

''To my laundry. You see, I wash clothes for a living.''

Gus snorted, and she shot him a scathing glance that shut him up like a clam. Joe nodded again.

''Well, then, Joe, if you're done looking at Mr. Shackleford's merchandise, why don't I pay for my things here, and I'll take you to my tent and show you what needs to be done.''

She adopted her queenly attitude when she straightened and walked to the counter. ''Can you give me my total, please, Mr. Harte?'' She opened her little handbag and reached in, prepared, Levi supposed, to retrieve the appropriate number of coins.

Levi had been standing as if in a trance for several moments, pounding Gus on the back. At Merry's request, he jerked away from Gus and dashed to the counter. ''Yes, ma'am.''

He added up her purchases, told her what she owed, and accepted her money. He was so astonished by what had recently transpired, that he couldn't find any words to say to her except those associated with his job.

She inclined her head and gazed critically at him. Levi hoped he'd shaved that morning. He was so rattled, he couldn't remember.

''You know, Mr. Harte, even though I can't approve of Mr. Shackleford's general disrespect for God's creations—''

''Hey!'' Gus said.

She ignored him. ''—I must say I admire you for securing a position in his mercantile establishment. I think you're very wise to have done it. Perhaps one of these days you can open your own business here in California. The good Lord knows, the place needs more people with your charitable instincts, because there are far, *far* too few of them here at present.'' She offered Gus Shackleford one more look that showed exactly what she thought of him—very little—and turned to smile at Red Joe.

The boy gazed up at her in awe. She shifted her bundle to her other arm. ''Shall we go, Joe?''

The boy nodded numbly. Merry left the store, as regally as she had entered it, Joe trotting behind her like a royal attendant.

Levi looked at Jack, who looked back. He was twinkling like a star, Levi noticed, and wondered how he did that.

Gus grumbled something Levi didn't catch, and stomped into the back room.

Jack tipped his hat at Levi and said, ''Well done.''

Levi didn't have any idea what he was talking about.

Jack was laughing when he left the store, and Levi decided he'd probably never understand anything.

Chapter Eleven

December 17, 1851
Dear Mama and Papa,

   You will be pleased to learn that my business has become so profitable that I have taken on an assistant! This isn't just any assistant, either, but a young Indian lad named Joe. There are a number of Indians in these parts. They aren't generally savages, although the miners seem to view them as objects either of fear or of ridicule.

   Personally, I find most of the miners much more savage than poor Joe, who is an orphan and a very hard worker. He carries water from the river for me, and heats it up so that I may launder these men's clothes (I should think they'd thank Joe for doing this, since, heaven knows, they need clean linen!) I am able to get much more work done now that Joe's come to help me, because I don't have the back-breaking task of hauling water in between batches of laundry.

Emma Craig

Mr. Levi Harte has been very kind and attentive to Joe. He brought the boy some warm clothes to wear, since the lad was almost naked and totally without resources. Mr. Harte's partner died last summer, and Mr. Harte has been very generous with his late partner's leftovers. As he says (quite modestly, I think), someone might as well benefit from them. I still believe him to be a warm and generous man, an anomaly, in fact, in this dreary state of California, where greed seems to be the overriding motivation among its citizens.

As Christmas approaches, and especially with the arrival of little Joe into my life, I have become acutely aware of my own prejudices and judgments. You have always told me not to judge others before I know them, yet I have done that far too often in my life. I see how the miners in Christmas Gap treat Joe, and it is clear to me now what you were trying to teach me.

Joe is a good boy. He can't help being an Indian. I'm sure our Lord loves Joe as much as he loves any of these other fellows, who certainly look like sinners to me, although that, too, is a judgment. I sometimes find being good a sore trial!

I'm sure you are both tired of reading these lines, but oh, how I do wish we could all be together for Christmas! The community of Christmas Gap is ever so much more cheerful now that the men who live here have begun tidying it up, but it's nothing like home, believe me.

Please give my love to everyone.

Your daughter,
Merry

P.S. I have not heard a word from Uncle George. I hope his claim is prospering.

Chapter Twelve

The third of the four curious events to transpire in Christmas Gap during December of 1851 occurred several days after Red Joe began working for Merry Wildwood in her laundry business. Right about the middle of the morning of December 22, a Dancer's Freight carrier drove his team of mules into Christmas Gap. His arrival in the tiny community sparked much excitement, especially when the miners learned that Gentleman Jack Oakes had ordered all the ingredients for a Christmas feast as a treat for the residents of the gold-mining camp.

"By damn," Kanaka Lou exclaimed, goggle-eyed. "Looky there, Ben! If that ain't a barrel of oysters, I'm a rich man!"

Ben Budlow looked and confirmed Kanaka Lou's observation. It was a barrel of oysters all right, and Kanaka Lou was decidedly not rich. Ben himself had been forced to shut down his sluice box due to the cold weather and now spent most of his days sprawled beside Gus Shackleford's potbellied stove, playing cribbage with anyone who'd play, and wishing he could afford another jug of whiskey.

Levi, clad in his big apron and carrying his broom, ran outside. He scratched his head as he stared at the bounty being unloaded before Gentleman Jack. "How'd you get an order placed and delivered so fast, Jack?"

Accepting, in his usual unhurried manner, a barrel of potatoes from the Dancer's man, Jack gave Levi a sly nod. "I have my methods."

Levi was reminded of the jack of hearts Gentleman Jack could produce any time he wanted to, out of seemingly thin air, and nodded. "Reckon you must. Here, Jack, let me help you there." He set his broom against the wall of Gus's mercantile and went to assist Gentleman Jack.

The Dancer's man unstrapped a barrel of onions from one of the mules and heaved it at Levi, who staggered under the weight of it. His admiration for Gentleman Jack grew another foot or so. Gentleman Jack hadn't seemed to notice the weight of his own barrel, yet potatoes must be as heavy as onions.

"Hams," barked the Dancer's man.

Levi set his onions down and held out his arms to accept two twenty-pound hams, cured in salt, and sent via ship from Virginia to San Francisco, and from San Francisco to Christmas Gap. Virginia ham for Christmas! Levi's mouth watered just thinking about it.

"We'll save all this, boys," said Gentleman Jack with a cheerful chuckle. "And have us a regular feast come Christmas Eve."

Out of the corner of his eye, Levi saw that Merry Wildwood had forsaken her laundry business to investigate the commotion. Red Joe hurried behind her, trying to hide himself from the gaze of the miners. Poor little guy. He wasn't but about ten years old and an orphan—and an Indian, to boot. Levi felt a rush of compassion for him.

Merry clutched that old sheepskin jacket around her, and

Levi experienced a sudden compulsion to buy her a new jacket, one that fit. And a new dress or three. Not that she'd accept them from him. He sighed and walked over to her.

"Good morning again, Miss Wildwood." He'd already visited her once this morning, to get his daily smile. She gave him another one now, and he felt doubly blessed.

"Good morning again, Mr. Harte. What's going on out here?"

"Dancer's Freight. Gentleman Jack ordered some stuff for Christmas." He lifted the hams, and was pleased to see her blue eyes go as big and round as saucers. She had very pretty eyes.

Jack looked over his shoulder and gave Levi a big grin. He nodded at Merry. "Maybe you can help cook up some of these potatoes and onions, Miss Wildwood. For Christmas Eve dinner in Christmas Gap."

Merry blinked at him. "For Christmas Eve? You mean, you ordered food for Christmas Eve? For the whole camp?"

Jack shrugged, and his white teeth sparkled in his dark face. "Sure. Why not? I'm in favor of celebrating the birth of our Lord, aren't you?"

"Why, of course, I am," said Merry. She sounded bewildered. "But I didn't think anyone else in Christmas Gap was."

"Why, sure they do!" Jack grinned at the miners who stood like a pack of wolves around the Dancer's mule team. "Don't you, boys? You all want to celebrate the birth of our Lord, don't you?"

Considerable shuffling of feet greeted Jack's question. Kanaka Lou finally muttered, "Why, surely, Jack. I surely do think it's a good idear to celebrate Christmas." He turned toward his companions. "That's why we was cleanin' up the camp, waren't it, boys? For Christmas?"

Apparently, when it was put to them that way, the miners saw the justice of Jack's observation. Levi grinned to himself, wondering if "celebrating the birth of our Lord," hadn't

71

been a little too big a bite of holiness for some of these hard men to swallow. Several of them nodded, and Levi heard a few of them mutter, "That's right, ain't it? It's fer Christmas?"

"I'll be happy to help cook the food," Merry said, surprising Levi, who had believed her to despise all of her fellow Christmas Gappians.

"And I'll warrant Levi there'd be happy to help you, too," said Jack with another broad grin for Levi.

Levi decided to ignore Jack's grin. "Yeah," he said. "Sure. I'm not much of a cook, though."

"That's not a problem," said Jack. "There's not much a body can do to hurt a cured ham, I reckon. And you can roast the potatoes and onions over the fire. And the oysters don't need to have anything done to 'em."

"Joe said he knows where we can get some yams," Merry said. Every man in the camp swiveled his head to gape at her. She blushed and said defiantly, "Well, I like yams. I think they go very well with ham." Then she tossed her head, and her nose went into the air, and Levi's heart turned to slop on the spot. He noticed Joe trying his best to look even smaller than he already was.

"Reckon I can donate some beans, boys."

Heads swiveled in the other direction, and all eyes now focused on Gus Shackleford. To the best of Levi's recollection, Gus had never offered anything to anyone for free before. He wondered if Gus was sick.

The question of Gus's health remained moot, but Gus did look slightly sheepish when he shrugged and said, "Well, hell, I got sacks and sacks o' dried beans in the back of the store. I reckon they'd cook up pretty good with a little salt pork and an onion or two."

"That's a very kind thought, Mr. Shackleford. Thank you. I'll be happy to fix the beans."

Heads swiveled back again, and Merry blushed once more. It was a fact well known in Christmas Gap that she and Gus

Shackleford had been at outs ever since Gus's ill-mannered proposition of her, and their animosity had intensified over the issue of Red Joe. Her nose inched higher into the air. Levi loved that freckled nose of hers. He intervened before anyone could say anything to sour the festive mood.

"That's right nice of both of you. I'll do anything I can to help, too." There. That should ease the atmosphere.

It did. All the miners turned to gape at Gentleman Jack and the Dancer's Freight man, who remained doggedly unloading his cargo, impervious to in-camp tensions. He said, "And here's some tins of English peas. Don't know where they come from. Ain't seen no English peas since before I left Vermont."

"English peas," spoken in awed whispers, erupted from several of the men. Levi wondered if civilization was finally sneaking its way into Christmas Gap.

A line of men had formed to convey the bounty from the Dancer's mules to Gus's grocery, where it would be stored until used. Levi wasn't sure how this line-forming operation had been decided, but it seemed to have come about through some tacit understanding among the assembled men. Gentleman Jack passed the tinned peas to Levi, who passed them to Kanaka Lou, who passed them to Ben Budlow, who passed them to Carolina, who passed them to Potter, who passed them to Gus, who set them on the counter in his store.

Several small wooden crates, the contents of which remained a mystery, were unloaded, as well as barrels of beef, strings of garlic, and several pumpkins. Bags of salt, cases of lard, and sacks of flour, sugar, and cornmeal were unloaded, along with tins of sardines.

It took an hour to empty the Dancer's Freight mules of everything Jack had ordered. The miners were gape-mouthed with wonder as the process continued. If they were anything like Levi—and Levi knew they were—most of them hadn't seen such Christmas fixings in years, not since they'd left their homes in various parts of the eastern United States.

When the last barrel of beef had been set against the wall in Gus's store, Gentleman Jack dusted his hands together and grinned at the miners. "There, boys. That should make as fine a dinner for Christmas Eve as any you ever ate back home. Any one of you men play the fiddle?"

The fiddle? Levi turned to scan the men in the crowd, who were doing likewise. After several silent moments, the man whom Levi considered the least likely to display musical talent, Potter, took a step forward. Blushing brightly, he said in a small voice, "I took me some fiddle lessons back home in Georgia."

"And do you know any Christmas tunes, Potter?" asked Gentleman Jack in a hearty voice. He didn't sound nearly as surprised as the rest of the men looked.

Potter cleared his throat. "Reckon I could practice up on a couple."

"Fine. That's fine, then!"

"You have your fiddle here, Potter?" Levi asked, astounded.

Potter dug his toe into the earth at his feet. "Reckon I do, Levi. I been keepin' up practicin', too."

"How?" asked Levi. "Where?" He'd never heard any fiddle music in Christmas Gap in the year and a half he'd been here.

Potter hung his head. "Well, I was right shy about playin' in front of the boys, Levi. I took my fiddle to the woods to practice, where nobody could hear."

"Shoot, Potter, I'd love to hear some music in camp. Might make the place less dismal." Levi glanced at his gold-camp companions, most of whom were nodding vigorously. "There," he said. "See? Everyone would like to hear you play."

Potter's blush deepened. "Well, all right then," he muttered, sounding not entirely pleased.

"Wonderful!" Gentleman Jack turned to Levi and Merry, who stood together at the front of the gaggle of miners.

"And now, I think it's time for you two to head off into the woods and fetch some pine cones and boughs to decorate the camp. Now that the place is all spiffed up for the holidays, it'll look right pretty with some pine boughs hung up here and there. I've got some red ribbon in one of those crates in there." He shrugged in the direction of Gus's store.

Spiffed up, was it? Levi scanned the community of Christmas Gap, expecting to view it through the eyes of a jaundiced, half-starved miner who'd given up the struggle. To his surprise, the place didn't look half bad to him today. In fact, it looked almost pretty, sitting as it did among the evergreen trees in the the northern California mountains, and all raked and orderly. Even the river, which Levi had, not many days ago, thought of as an enemy, mocking him with its merry music, sounded pleasant as it rushed down the mountainside. The sun filtered through the pine and fir branches and dappled the community with light. Why, old Christmas Gap looked as attractive as anything this morning. He was impressed.

"By Jupiter, it's kind of nice here," he said, flabbergasted.

"Yes, it is," agreed Merry at his side. "It's beautiful."

He glanced down at her and noticed that she appeared to be as amazed by the sight as he was. He grinned at her. "How did that happen?"

She grinned back. "I don't know. When I first came here, I thought this was the ugliest place I'd ever seen."

"Me, too," admitted Levi.

"Well," said Gentleman Jack in a loud voice, startling Levi, who'd forgotten anyone but he and Merry existed on earth, "why don't you two fetch some greenery? We can rig up a space in the middle of camp and celebrate Christmas in style."

Levi, peering down at Merry, lifted an eyebrow in question.

Merry turned to Joe, who had been marveling at the activities from behind her skirt. "Can you handle the laundry for an hour or two, Joe?"

Levi was pleased to note that she spoke to the boy with respect and affection. Joe drew himself up and squared his shoulders, proud, Levi suspected, to be offered this responsibility. "Sure," he said. "I can do it."

Merry gave him one of her beautiful smiles. If she'd directed that smile at Levi, he might have fallen over from the sheer glory of it, but Joe seemed less pervious to her charms than Levi. The boy only smiled at her and trotted back to the laundry tent, full of importance and energy.

"There," said Merry, sounding happier than Levi'd heard her sound so far. "I won't have to worry about my business while we gather pine boughs."

"Good," said Levi. He suddenly recalled that he, too, had a position in the world. "Let me ask Gus if it's all right for me to take off for a couple of hours."

Gus said it was, much to Levi's surprise, and he and Merry set off into the woods. As he guided her over a fallen log, it was natural for him to take her by the hand. It was also natural that he forgot to release her hand when they'd overcome the obstacle.

When they came to a huge cedar tree, hung with mistletoe and berries, Levi was happy to cut several bunches to take back with them to Christmas Gap. By this time, he and Merry were as easy with each other as friends who'd known each other for decades.

What Levi Harte felt for Merry Wildwood was far from friendship, however. Although he didn't have any idea what she thought of him, he felt bold enough by this time to hold a branch of mistletoe over her head. She blushed and turned her head away, but Levi did not desist. Instead, he dropped his branch of mistletoe and took Merry into his arms.

He was ever so pleased when, after resisting for only a moment, she kissed him back.

Chapter Thirteen

December 22, 1851
Dear Mama and Papa,

The most unexpected thing happened today! Mr. Jack Oakes, of whom I have written before, surprised us all by having delivered all the trappings for a wonderful Christmas celebration! It was very kind of him to do so, as most of us here in Christmas Gap miss our families deeply at this time of the year. His generosity will at least give us a small celebration with which to console ourselves. We even discovered that the very shy Mr. Potter plays the violin! He has agreed to serenade us with Christmas carols on Christmas Eve after dinner.

Mr. Harte and I gathered pine boughs and fir cones with which to decorate the camp. He is a very nice man, and not at all like most of the rough fellows living here, who have been hardened by the difficult time they've had in the gold camp. In fact, Mr. Harte has shown the good sense (uncommon here, believe me) to secure a

Emma Craig

position in Mr. Gus Shackleford's dry-goods store.

I believe Mr. Harte feels his lack of success as a gold-miner keenly, but I do not fault him for that. After all, Uncle George, Jonathan, and I all believed the newspaper accounts of gold finds in California, too.

Mr. Harte hails from Ohio originally and comes from a farming family, as we do. It has been pleasant to discuss life back home with him, as his experiences, even though he comes from the North, have been similar to my own. I feel as though I have met a kindred spirit here in this unlikely place, and it makes me miss Jonathan less sharply.

Although it appears that Christmas will be brighter than I had formerly anticipated, I do miss you all very much and wish that we could be together. One day soon, I hope to see you all again. I still have had no word from Uncle George. I hope he is well.

Your loving daughter,
Merry

Chapter Fourteen

Levi felt like a racehorse straining at the gate when he arose on December 23 well before dawn. He and Merry had talked long into the night the previous day, sitting beside each other on a log near the fire pit. She hadn't objected when he'd laid his hand over hers as it rested on the log between them. Even through the darned wool of her mitten, Levi had felt the warmth of her skin, and it had thrilled him. Before he led her to her tent and gave her a chaste good-night kiss, he'd

Chapter Fourteen

Levi felt like a racehorse straining at the gate when he arose on December 23 well before dawn. He and Merry had talked long into the night the previous day, sitting beside each other on a log near the fire pit. She hadn't objected when he'd laid his hand over hers as it rested on the log between them. Even through the darned wool of her mitten, Levi had felt the warmth of her skin, and it had thrilled him. Before he led her to her tent and gave her a chaste good-night kiss, he'd come to a decision. It was a major decision and Levi, being a prudent young man in spite of his circumstances, had decided he'd best sleep on it.

Sleep hadn't diminished his determination. He loved Merry Wildwood, and he aimed to ask her to marry him. He didn't know anything about her except that she was a good-hearted, hardworking young woman of firm principles. If she had a shady past, she'd evidently changed her ways. There was nothing in the least unsavory about her today.

Marriage was a huge step in a young man's life. Levi was,

after all, only twenty-one years old—twenty-two come the end of January. That was old enough. Shoot, his mother and father had wed when they were both but nineteen, and they'd had a long and happy life together. They'd taught him that marriage was a commitment and a joy, and sometimes a sore trial. Levi was ready for it. By gum, he'd weathered California, hadn't he? Surely marriage couldn't be any worse than that.

The hardest thing was waiting to find out if Merry would have him. Since he'd risen before the sun was up, he had to wait until he saw Merry stirring before he could rush over to her tent and pop the question. He was as nervous as a cat as he stalked back and forth in front of his tent.

"You look like you're on a mission this morning, Levi."

Gentleman Jack Oakes's voice startled Levi in mid-prowl. He swung around to find Jack sitting on the log Levi and Merry had shared the night before. Although his nerves were jumping almost out of his skin, he responded to Jack's friendly grin. "Reckon I am, Jack."

Jack tipped his hat. "Good luck to you, Levi. You deserve it."

"Thanks, Jack." Levi wondered if his purpose was plastered on his face for all to read, or if Jack was merely a perceptive fellow. On the other hand, Levi'd told Jack that he was on a mission. Surely any man would wish another man good luck if he knew he was on a mission.

Too edgy to stand still and ponder the matter, Levi started pacing again. When he finally caught a glimpse of Merry, walking straight-backed and determined—as ever—to her laundry tent, he stopped and sucked in an enormous, pine-scented breath of frosty air. Red Joe trudged behind her carrying a tub full of water. Levi frowned, wondering what to do about Joe. Well, he'd just ask to speak with Merry outside.

He took another breath and stared hard at Merry's tent.

This was it. Now was the time. He was going to do it. It was now or never.

"Go on, boy."

Levi was so shocked by Jack's voice in his ear and Jack's gentle nudge on his shoulder blade that he cried out. Then he felt really stupid. Shooting a grin over his shoulder, he lurched forward and said, "Thanks, Jack."

He heard Jack's gentle chuckle at his back.

Merry looked up from where she'd been bending over a huge pile of what looked like shirts and dungarees. She gave Levi a big, surprised smile. "Good morning, Mr. Harte." She blushed then, and Levi knew she was remembering the two discreet kisses they'd shared yesterday.

He whipped his hat from his head and held it in front of him. His heart battered at his ribs like a sledgehammer. "Good morning, Miss Wildwood. Merry. Miss Wildwood." Shoot, he was nervous! He sucked in another breath and told himself to calm down. He wouldn't impress the woman if he fainted or appeared addled, now would he?

She tilted her head to one side and gazed at him quizzically. "Is there something you need, Mr. Harte? Can I help you in any way?"

Could she help him? Oh, Lordy! Levi licked his lips. "May I speak to you for a minute, Miss Wildwood?"

Merry looked around, evidently searching for impediments that might prevent him from speaking to her right then and there. "Certainly you may."

She gave him an encouraging smile. At least, Levi was pretty sure it was meant to be encouraging. Whatever its intent, it hit him like a load of bricks in the solar plexus and rendered him breathless. He managed to gasp, "Outside? Please?"

"Outside?" Merry stared at him hard for a moment, then turned to Joe. "Do you mind if I step outside with Mr. Harte for a minute, Joe?"

"No, ma'am." Joe smiled at her from the fire he was tending. "I'll keep heatin' the water."

"Fine. Thank you."

Merry appeared worried when she wiped her hands on her apron and walked outside with Levi. He tried to keep his breathing under control, but he felt lightheaded when he finally led her to a cedar tree some distance from her tent. He didn't crave an audience for this.

"What is it, Mr. Harte? I have to get back to work. There's lots for me to do today, and I have to get it all hung up before noon, or it'll never dry before evening." She was getting impatient; Levi heard it in her voice. He didn't really blame her.

"Yes'm. I don't want to interfere with your work, only—only—Oh, hell." Levi turned and slammed his fist against the trunk of the cedar tree. He was going about this all wrong; he knew it.

"Whatever is the matter, Mr. Harte?"

He turned around again. His hand hurt, and he shook it. "It's about yesterday, ma'am."

Her eyes opened wide, and her face paled. She turned away from him. "Please, Mr. Harte. If you're going to apologize for yesterday, there's no need, really." Her voice sounded stifled, as if her throat were tight.

"Apologize? No, ma'am. I'm not going to apologize. What I wanted to know was—well, you see, it's this way." Blast! What the devil was the matter with him? Then he remembered what was expected of a fellow in this circumstance. Levi lowered himself to one knee and took Merry's hand. She stared at him as if he'd lost his mind—which he might well have done.

"Miss Wildwood. Merry. Miss Wildwood, what I wondered was if you'd do me the honor of marrying me, ma'am. Merry. Miss Wildwood. I love you, you see, and I want to marry you."

Her mouth dropped open to form an *O* that went rather well with her round eyes. "You what?"

Levi cleared his throat. "I love you, ma'am. I want to marry you, if you'll have me." It was awkward, saying all this stuff on one knee, so Levi got up again. Good Glory, the ground was cold. He lifted her hand to his lips and kissed it.

"I know I don't look like much, Miss Wildwood, but I'm not a loafer, and I'm not a shifty character. I'm a farmer, ma'am, back in Ohio, and I'll do pretty much anything I can in order to support you. You deserve better than breaking your back washing all these men's duds all day, every day."

"But—but, we hardly know each other, Mr. Harte. I mean—I mean, I know you're a good man and all, but—but—but this is all so sudden."

Sudden, was it? Well, Levi reckoned it was. He knew his own heart, though, and he knew he'd never find another Merry. "It's not that sudden," he said. "Ma'am, I've known for days now that you're the only girl in the world I've ever loved. It's blamed certain I'll never want to marry anyone else."

It occurred to Levi that Merry might be concerned about her unsavory past. He said, "Listen, Miss Wildwood, I don't care what you did before you came to Christmas Gap. If you hit some hard times and had to do some things you regret, well, that's all right with me. I know you're a good woman now, and that's all that matters."

He didn't like it when her eyes narrowed. "I'm not sure I take your meaning, Mr. Harte."

He didn't like that hint of hardness in her voice, either. Blast! This was all so difficult. He shrugged uncomfortably. "Well, you know, like when Gentleman Jack won you in that poker game and all. It don't matter to me if you had some rough times, is all I'm saying, and had to do some things you didn't want to do. I don't care about that."

She withdrew her hand from his and propped it on her hip.

83

"And just what sort of rough times do you think I've had, Mr. Harte? Are you of the opinion—as the rest of the men in Christmas Gap seem to be—that I am, or was, a loose woman?"

Frustrated, Levi held out his arms. "Well—well—well, yes, I guess that's what I'm saying. I don't care about that."

Merry propped her other fist on her other hip. She looked angry now, and Levi didn't understand. "And if I tell you that I've never done one single solitary thing in my whole life for which I have any reason to be ashamed, what would you say about that, Mr. Levi Harte?"

Levi was beginning to feel helpless. "Why, sure, ma'am. That's fine with me, too."

"But would you believe me if I told you that?"

Levi was about to offer a quick affirmative, when he realized he wasn't sure if he'd believe her or not. He said, "Er, why, I guess I would. I mean, I think so."

Her brow furrowed. She looked really mad now. "I'm not sure I believe *you*, Mr. Harte. But let me test you here and now. I have never, in all my life, done anything unsavory. Do you believe me?"

Levi shrugged. "Well, hell, ma'am, I reckon I do." He held his breath for a moment, and then burst out, "But glory, Miss Wildwood, what about getting yourself staked in that poker game? I mean, that doesn't happen to very many pure ladies, you know. I mean, it's sort of a strange thing to happen, don't you think? I mean, it makes a man wonder. But that's what I'm telling you. I'm telling you it doesn't matter to me what you've done before you come here. Blast it, ma'am, I love you!"

"It seems to me, Mr. Harte, that your love doesn't go very far, if you're not willing to trust what I say. How can I marry a man who doesn't trust me to tell him the truth? Do you think that's a very firm foundation for a marriage?"

"Yes, drat it! I mean, I think it's as firm as any foundation. I don't care what you've done."

"I haven't done anything!"

"Well, then, that's fine, isn't it? I haven't done anything myself, so we're even."

She glared at him for a moment. "All right. I believe you when you tell me you haven't done anything you're ashamed of—"

"Well, except for coming to California and making a hash of looking for gold," Levi cut in.

It looked for a second that she might smile, but she didn't. "Yes, I understand that, believe me. I'm not proud of coming to California and making a hash of things, either. But what I want to know is if you believe me when I tell you I've never done anything immoral."

Levi squinted at her and guessed she deserved his honesty. "Listen, Miss Wildwood, it's fishy, you getting yourself staked in a poker game. I mean, look at it from my point of view for a second. Don't you think anyone would wonder about a girl who got herself staked in a poker game?"

She sniffed.

"Well, he would, believe me. I mean, you've never told anyone what happened. Maybe if you'd explain it all to me, then I'd understand."

"What happened to me in Red Bluff is no one's business but my own, Mr. Harte. I won't tell you what happened. You'll have to take my word for it that I did nothing to deserve what befell me there."

Genuinely puzzled and more than a little annoyed himself, Levi cried, "Why not? Why won't you just tell me what happened? Then we'll both know, and you'll never have to worry about me or what I think of you again!"

"I can't tell you!"

"Why not?"

"Because it's not my story alone! It involves other people, and I will not, ever, drag their names in the mud!"

That stopped him cold. It involved other people? Other male people? Levi guessed so. "Well, then," he said, his voice gone soft, "we're kind of back to the beginning again, aren't we?"

"Are we?"

"Yes, ma'am. You won't tell me what happened, and I'm going to have to tell you that it's all right. I don't care what happened."

Merry whirled around and pressed her hands to her cheeks. "Oh, you don't understand! I love you, Levi Harte! But I'll be diced and fried before I'll marry a man who won't trust me!"

"It'd be a whole lot easier for me to trust you if you'd trust me, Merry—if you'd trust that I'd never tell anyone your secret."

"I can't." She had begun to sob, and Levi felt terrible. "I can't."

He put a hand on her shoulder, but she shook him off. "Please? Believe me when I tell you that I love you, Merry. I love, blast it all. I'd never hurt you. Won't you please marry me? I promise I'll do everything in my power to take care of you."

"Except trust me."

"I *do* trust you!"

She turned around again and wiped her fingers under her eyes to catch the tears. Levi's heart ached. "No, you don't. You're willing to forgive me, but you aren't willing to believe I've done nothing to be forgiven for, are you?"

"I—I—" Levi hadn't any idea in the world what to say. "Blast it, Merry, how can I believe you when you won't tell me anything?"

"I've told you I've done nothing to be ashamed of."

"All right. That's fine, then."

She gazed at him, her big blue eyes swimming, a sorrowful expression on her face. "No, Levi. It's not fine. Thank you for your offer, but I can't marry a man who doesn't trust me."

"But—"

"No!" Merry dodged the hand he held out to her, and ran clear back to her tent without stopping once.

Levi watched her go, his heart heavy, his brain in a muddle, and he recalled his cousin August telling him once that women were the oddest, least-intelligible critters in the whole wide world. For the very first time, he understood what Cousin August meant.

That night, as Levi endured a fitful sleep, he had a bizarre dream. In it, Gentleman Jack Oakes appeared, garbed all in white, with a golden halo encircling his head. He even had wings, and an aura of shimmering light surrounded him. It was about the strangest dream Levi had ever had.

"She's right, son," the angelic Jack told him in his dream. "Trust is the best foundation for a marriage. If you can't trust her now, you'll never be able to trust her."

"But I do trust her," Levi cried out in his dream, feeling sorely beleaguered.

Jack's smile was as tender as any Levi'd ever received. It was an angel's smile, and it made his heart hurt. "I know what you mean, son, but that's not good enough. If you want Merry Wildwood as your wife, you're going to have to believe what she told you, without proof. If you can't do that, if you can't trust her, she'll never be yours. You have to take things on faith sometimes, Levi, my boy. Faith and trust."

"But she won't tell me what happened."

"She told you that what happened concerns others, Levi, and that she's trying to protect them. What do you want? Solid proof? In order to have solid proof, you'd have to have been there."

"You were there."

"Yes, I was."

"Why can't you tell me what happened, then?"

Jack's grin was astonishingly devilish for someone in an angel suit. Even in his dream, Levi frowned.

"It's not my story to tell, Levi. It's Merry's."

There he was again. Back at the beginning. If Levi'd been awake, he'd have pounded his fist against something. Fortunately, he was asleep and dreaming, so his fist remained undamaged.

Jack shook him gently. "Do you believe that Jesus was born in Bethlehem, Levi?"

Levi scowled at him. "I reckon."

"Did you see it happen?"

"No."

"Do you believe the Gospels?"

"I reckon."

"Well, then, think about it, boy. If you can believe what some folks wrote two thousand years ago—folks you didn't even know and who lived in a foreign country—what's so difficult about believing Merry Wildwood, a woman you claim to love, when she tells you she's done nothing to be ashamed of?"

In his dream, Levi scratched his head. Before he could think up a good answer, Jack faded into darkness, taking his wings, his halo, and his angel suit with him.

Chapter Fifteen

December 23, 1851
Dear Mama and Papa,

I wish I'd never come to California. I hate it here. Everyone is detestable and awful. This is a horrid place, full of mean spiteful people.

First Jonathan died, and then Uncle George took to bad company and drink. He staked me in a poker game, Mama and Papa. Your own brother did that to me, Papa! I've never been so humiliated in my entire life. If it hadn't been for that kind Mr. Oakes, the good Lord alone knows what would have happened to me—and I'm sure the good Lord doesn't care any more than Uncle George does. I haven't heard from him since. I'm sure he doesn't even remember me by this time.

And now the one person whom I believed I could trust, Levi Harte, thinks that I am a scarlet woman because of what Uncle George did.

I wish it had been I who'd died of that wretched fever

instead of Jonathan. I wish he were here now, and I were dead!

Merry

Chapter Sixteen

The fourth and final curious event to take place in Christmas Gap during the winter of 1851 occurred on Christmas Eve.

All day long, Levi had been wondering how to approach Merry with an apology and a renewal of the proposal he'd botched so badly the day before. When he'd gone to her tent in the morning, she hadn't wanted to talk to him. He'd lifted the tent flap to discover her, eyes puffy and red, tearing up what looked like a letter she'd written. Red Joe was nowhere in sight. Levi assumed he was fulfilling some task Merry had set for him.

When she lifted her head and saw him, she glared with patent hostility. "What do you want?"

"I—ah, would like to talk to you for a minute."

"I don't want to talk to anyone, especially you." She sounded very bitter.

Levi sighed. He gestured at the paper. "What's that?"

She sniffled miserably. "I wrote a letter to my parents, but I tore it up. I'm not going to post it."

"Why not?"

"Not that it's any of *your* business," she said nastily, "but I finally wrote them the truth." Her eyes filled with tears. Levi felt perfectly dreadful. "But I don't want them to know the truth."

Levi wrinkled his brow. "I don't understand, ma'am."

Tears leaked from her eyes. Levi wished he could hold and comfort her. "I've been lying to them. I've been telling them how fine everything is here in Christmas Gap. I've been keeping the truth from them—haven't told them how awful everyone's been to me—because I love them."

Levi hesitated, not sure he should say what he was thinking. Then he decided, *To hell with it.* "Don't you think they deserve the truth, ma'am?"

She looked down at the shreds of paper in her hands. "It would hurt them," she whispered. "I couldn't bear to hurt them." Then she squared her shoulders and turned on him. "I don't want to talk to you, Levi Harte. If there's anything I don't need right now, it's someone who doesn't believe anything I say telling me to break my parents' hearts! They've had enough to grieve over lately."

Levi held out his arms. "Damnation, that's not true, Merry!"

"Don't you dare use profanity in my tent, Levi Harte. Get out of here! I have a meal to cook!" And with that, she picked up her cudgel and threatened him with it.

Now, it is true that Levi Harte stood a good solid six feet tall. It is also true that he was well-muscled and strong, and that he could easily have overpowered little Merry Wildwood, who stood all of five feet, two inches in her heavy-heeled work boots. The truth that held Levi motionless, however, was that he loved her more dearly than life itself, and that he would never, if it was within his power, do anything to hurt her. He decided to tell her so.

"I'm sorry I hurt your feelings yesterday, Merry. I still need to talk to you."

She sniffed. Levi couldn't tell if it was a weepy sniff or an angry one.

"I'll leave you now. I have things to do, too, to get ready for the celebration tonight. But I'm going to talk to you one of these days, Merry, whether you want me to or not, because I love you, and I still want to marry you—and I *do* believe you."

She sniffed again. This sniff sounded more like defiance than either anger or tears, but Levi acknowledged to himself that he wasn't much of a judge. He repeated, "I love you, Merry."

And he left, unsatisfied but willing to wait until hell froze over for the Merry he wanted in his life.

He went out of his way to help her that day, just as she went out of her way to avoid him. He noticed several of the miners, also scurrying about, tacking pine boughs to walls and hanging streamers from tent poles, eyeing the two of them askance. He didn't enlighten anyone as to why he and Merry seemed to be estranged today when they'd been hand-in-hand yesterday.

No one's opinion mattered but Merry's. Not a single one of the men watching them knew what had transpired between them, but they were all drawing conclusions. And the conclusions were undoubtedly all wrong. Levi's understanding of her position regarding her reputation deepened as the day went on.

Every time he caught a glimpse of Gentleman Jack, who was supervising activities from a rocking chair on the front porch of Gus's grocery, Levi remembered his dream. Once, when the sun was just right, Jack appeared to have a halo surrounding him. Levi knew it was a trick of the light, but it made him stare until Potter bumped into him.

"Oh, Lordy, Levi, I'm sorry."

Levi turned and smiled at poor, shy Potter. The fellow was in a perfect dither today, the knowledge that he was going to have to perform that evening having rendered him a bun-

93

dle of nerves. "My fault, Potter. I shouldn't have stopped so suddenly."

"Kin you sing, Levi?" Potter asked anxiously.

"Can I sing?" Levi scratched his chin. "Reckon I can hold a tune. Don't know if—"

"Good, good," Potter muttered, hurrying away without listening to the rest of Levi's equivocation. "Good. Got to have folks to sing whilst I play, or I'll faint dead away."

Levi chuckled, forgot about Gentleman Jack's halo, and went back to work. At present, his work consisted of hammering together a small stage, upon which Potter would fiddle and Kanaka Lou would play his harmonica after the Christmas Eve feast Merry and Gus were preparing. The miners had already built two long pine tables upon which the feast would be laid. The meal would be served, buffet-style, on the miners' own tin plates.

Levi noticed that Merry and Gus seemed to be getting on fairly well today, and was glad of it. They didn't speak much, but Merry at least deigned to smile at Gus from time to time, and Gus didn't growl at her. Neither did Gus growl at Joe, who was being as efficient as he could be while trying to appear invisible. Levi grinned. It wasn't much, but it was an improvement.

Along about sunset, Gus shooed Merry out of his store. "You get along now, Miss Wildwood, and spruce yourself up. Joe and I can set out the food."

Levi looked up from where he was nailing the last pine bough over Gus's front door. He'd already tied a big red bow to it. By God, Gus had sounded almost kind about Joe. Levi was pleased.

"All right, Mr. Shackleford." She turned to Joe. "You do whatever Mr. Shackleford asks you to do, Joe. All right?"

The Indian boy nodded and slanted a wary glance at Gus.

Merry turned to the grocer. "And I expect *you* to treat Joe with politeness, Mr. Shackleford. There isn't a person alive who doesn't respond better to kindness than to meanness."

She said it with a smile, but Levi saw Gus stiffen momentarily. Then his shoulders relaxed, and he smiled.

"Reckon you're right, Miss Wildwood. I'll keep it in mind."

Incredulous, Levi stared at Gus, waiting for the punch line. It didn't come. Apparently, he'd meant what he'd said. Well, glory be.

Levi gave Merry enough time to wash up and brush her hair; then he hurried to her tent. He stood outside, feeling nervous. "Merry?"

A few seconds passed. Then Merry lifted her tent flap and peered out. "Oh, hello, Levi."

He licked his lips. "May I talk to you now, Merry?"

She took a step outside, stood up, dropped the tent flap, and sighed. "I suppose so. Do we really have anything to talk about?"

"Yes. Yes, we do. I need to tell you that I was flat-out wrong yesterday. I do believe you, and I trust you when you say you've never done anything to be ashamed of. I guess I can understand wanting to protect others at the expense of yourself. I know for sure that I'd die for you if I had to."

Her blue eyes blinked and opened up wide. "You would?"

"I would. I know you're a good woman. The best. That's what I've come here to tell you. And I wanted to ask you to please forgive me. I understand what you were trying to tell me yesterday."

"You do? Honest?" She looked suspicious.

Levi gave her a mock frown. "*Now* who's not believing whom?"

She lowered her head. Levi thought he saw the edges of her pretty mouth quiver, as if she were trying not to smile. He took heart.

"Listen, Merry, I know I'm not much of a bargain right now. I've made a hash of everything I tried to do here in California. But I've been talking to Gus. He says he's been thinking of taking on a partner. I never much thought about being a grocer before I come here, but it's a good business, and I could do a lot worse. Shoot, I could support you easy if I owned half of his grocery business.''

Eyeing him narrowly, she said, "What about the rest of his business? The saloon part? I don't hold with liquor, Levi Harte. It does evil things to people.''

"I don't drink, Merry. Honest." He held up his right hand, palm out, as if swearing an oath. His brow wrinkled slightly. "Well, I admit to getting drunk when I first come to California, but that was only an experiment, to see what it was like.''

"What was it like?"

Levi shuddered, the eighteen-month-old memory still clear in his mind. "Horrible. Awful. Disgusting.''

Merry's lips twitched into a tiny smile. "I'm glad you don't drink, Levi. I really hate it.''

His heart swooped. "Does that mean you'll have me after all?'' Remembering protocol, Levi dropped to one knee, as he'd done on his first attempt. He didn't feel quite as foolish this time, probably because he knew both Merry and himself better today than he had yesterday.

She gazed down at him, her heart in her eyes. Levi swallowed hard. "Oh, Levi, I—''

Suddenly a great commotion arose from the direction of the camp. Levi sprang to both feet just as Red Joe darted around the side of the tent, his eyes as round as platters.

"Good heavens, Joe, whatever is that awful racket?''

"It's some men come to the camp, Miss Wildwood. And they've brung a whole bunch of stuff with 'em. One of 'em claims he knows you.''

"Some men?'' Levi and Merry looked at each other. "And one of them knows you?''

Merry shrugged, obviously bewildered.

So Levi took Merry by the hand, and they followed Joe back to the center of Christmas Gap. It looked quite festive now, with Christmas decorations hung everywhere, the stage ready, a feast set out, and the miners all scrubbed and polished and eager for the party.

"Who are those guys?" Levi asked, not expecting an answer.

He was taken up short when Merry, scurrying behind him, suddenly stopped dead in her tracks. Since she didn't let go of Levi's hand, she nearly pulled his arm out of its socket. He turned, puzzled, and saw her gawking at the two men who had driven a wagon into Christmas Gap.

"What is it, Merry?" He turned and squinted at the men. "Do you know those fellows?"

He was distressed to see her lower lip begin to tremble. He took her in his arms. To hell with what folks might think. "What is it, Merry? Tell me, please."

"It's my Uncle George."

Levi wasn't sure he'd heard her right. He held her at arm's length and stared down into her face. "Your uncle? One of those men is your uncle?"

She nodded.

He tilted his head to one side as he considered this information. "Aren't you glad to see him?"

She nodded again. "Yes. Oh, yes, I'm so glad to see him! I was afraid I'd never see him again."

"You don't look to be all that happy, Merry," Levi told her honestly, wondering if this was going to be a big secret, too. He guessed he could tolerate it, but he'd really like it if she'd trust him enough to confide in him.

Merry gulped a big breath of ham-and-fir-scented air. "He's the one who got drunk and staked me in that poker game, Levi."

This time it was Levi's eyes that popped open wide. He dropped Merry's shoulders like two hot rocks and whirled around. "He did *what?* Your own *uncle?*"

He didn't wait for an answer, but lit out for the two men hefting cartons down from the wagon. He heard Merry cry,

"Levi!" but he didn't stop. He heard her pelting after him, and still didn't stop.

He skidded to a halt in front of the two men. "Which one of you is Miss Merry Wildwood's Uncle George?"

A twinkle-eyed man, in his mid-thirties, with a red beard, turned and grinned at Levi. "Reckon that'd be me, young feller. And who might you—"

Levi didn't give him a chance to finish his question, but socked him, hard, in the gut. George folded up like a concertina.

"That's for staking your own niece in a poker game, you damned skunk!"

George looked up at Levi, his eyes watering. Levi punched him in the jaw, and he went down like a gaffed trout. Levi swooped down, grabbed him by his red muffler, and hauled him to his feet. "And that's for me, because I don't take it kindly when folks hurt the people I love!"

He drew his fist back, prepared to launch another blow at George, and was taken up short when Merry grabbed his fist in both of her hands. He dropped George with a plop.

"Levi, don't!" Merry knelt beside George and helped him to his feet. "Oh, Uncle George, are you all right?"

Except for a cut lip and no breath, George looked as though he'd survive. He staggered to his feet. "The boy's right, Merry," he said when he could draw breath. "He's damned right. I'm a skunk, and it'd serve me right if you never spoke to me again in your whole life."

He held out a big hand to Levi, who gazed at it angrily. "I'm tryin' to make it up to her, boy. Ain't no way to do it, as I well know, but I'm tryin'. Won't you shake a fool's hand, boy, and tell me your name? It appears to me that our Merry has found herself a right good champion. It surely does."

Several of the miners had gathered around Levi and George. They stared in amazement. Levi had never been known as a violent man; in fact, he'd been called upon to mediate disputes in Christmas Gap more than once.

Gus Shackleford, his big white apron streaked with food stains, goggled at both men. "Who's that, Levi? What'd he do?"

Levi gazed down at Merry, who gazed up at him. She smiled at him and kissed his fist. "Thank you, Levi," she whispered. "No one's ever tried to protect me before." She lifted herself on her tiptoes and kissed him on his lips.

Levi's heart softened and started beating out a strong tattoo in rhythm to the words running through his mind: *I love you.* His hand unclenched and gripped hers. He turned to Gus.

"Reckon that's Miss Wildwood's business, Gus. If she cares to share, it's up to her." He reached out to Uncle George. "I'd take it kindly if you'd shake my hand, sir. My name's Levi Harte, and I aim to marry your niece here."

Uncle George left off rubbing his sore chin and shook Levi's hand. Then he threw his arms out wide. Levi felt momentarily bereft when Merry left his side and flung herself into them.

"Will you give me away, Uncle George? Will you? That would make me so happy."

Tears began to leak from George's eyes. "Reckon I will, Merry gal. I don't know how you can ever forgive me, but it'd be the greatest honor of my life if you'd let me give you to young Levi here. He seems like a fine man. A fine man."

"He is, Uncle George."

Uncle George and his partner, William Benedict, a Methodist minister from Kentucky, stayed to partake of Christmas Gap's Christmas Eve feast. Then, with Mr. Benedict presiding, Gentleman Jack acting as Levi's best man, and Joe serving as ring-bearer—where Gentleman Jack had managed to secure two gold wedding bands, Levi never did know—Levi Harte and Merry Wildwood were united in holy matrimony. Fortunately Potter was in practice, and he provided a stunning musical accompaniment to the wedding and ensuing Christmas festivities.

The feasting and celebrating continued far into the night. When Merry and Levi finally retired to Merry's tent, they did so amid much friendly teasing.

"This is the happiest Christmas of my life," Merry murmured into Levi's ear as she walked into his arms.

He held her tightly, his heart almost too full for words. "Mine, too. Merry Christmas, Mrs. Harte."

"Merry Christmas, Mr. Harte."

They didn't get out of bed until past noon on Christmas day.

Ernest Oakes

···································
···································
···································
···································
···································
···································
···································
With much love, ... your son

Seventeen

Christmas Gap, California
December 25, 1851

Dear Mother and Father,

I am writing to you this fine Christmas day with some good news for a change. I am now a married man! I was married to the loveliest girl in the world, Miss Merry (short for Meredith) Wildwood, from Maryland, only yesterday. Her uncle, George Wildwood, stood up with her and gave her away.

Merry and I aim to stay here in Christmas Gap until the springtime. I have a good job now, in Gus Shackleford's grocery store. Merry and her partner, a small Indian boy named Joe, run a profitable laundry business here. Come spring, we aim to settle near Sacramento, on some rich farmland.

I've been told that farming is good in California, because both the soil and the weather are suited for growing crops. Jack Oakes, a very fine fellow who stood as my best man, says the real riches in California are in her soil! I hope he's right. We're both eager to get back to the work we know. Joe has said he will be very happy to come with us, which is a good thing, as life is difficult for him, what with him being an orphan and an Indian and all. Merry and I both like him very much.

It is my great hope that you can meet my Merry soon. I am the happiest man in the world.

> With much love from your son,
> Levi

Epilogue

Saint Peter looked up over his half-glasses from where he'd been entering names in a huge book, and frowned at the guardian angel of Christmas Gap. "You took your sweet time," he growled.

Gentleman Jack Oakes shrugged, fluttered his wings, and grinned at the grouchy older man. "It worked, though, didn't it?"

It looked to Jack as if Saint Peter were trying not to smile. "I suppose it did." Peter bent over his golden quill for a moment before peering up again, his white eyebrows drawn down over his eyes. "I don't know why you had to name that horse of yours after me, though."

Jack's grin broadened. "Saint Pete's a good horse. He deserved a good name."

"Humph. At any rate, I'm glad you got those two together, and taught them a lesson. And that wretched uncle of hers, too." Saint Peter snorted. "Waging his niece in a poker game! I've never heard of such a thing!"

"Guess he slipped a little there. He's sorry about it, and he's doing his best to make it up to her. Gave the happy couple two hundred acres of prime farmland near Sacramento that he won in another poker game."

"Poker! Bah!"

Jack lifted his halo down and buffed it on his white robe. "Well, there weren't any jars of myrrh handy, I reckon. He felt he had to give 'em something as a wedding gift."

Peter looked up sharply. He sagged a little and sighed. "You're right, of course. Even if you are rather unconventional in your approach. Goodness knows, I did my share of failing in life." His eyes took on a sad cast for a moment.

"That's why you got this job in the great everlasting, Pete. It's because you understand people trying and failing and picking themselves up and trying again."

Another great sigh gusted from Saint Peter's lips. "Yes. I understand failure and redemption better than most, I suppose." He gazed pensively out over the feathery clouds, and Jack got the impression he sort of appreciated being reminded of his own shortcomings. "But I wish you'd name that blessed horse after someone else next time."

"Hmmm." Jack replaced his halo and turned to leave. "I might try Balthazar next."

Saint Peter rolled his eyes. Gentleman Jack Oakes strolled away from Saint Pete and the Pearly Gates. He had more interference to run in the California gold-mining camps. It was his job, after all. He looked forward to it.

THE SHEPHERDS AND MR. WEISMAN

ANNIE KIMBERLIN

*To Paula, who every year wraps Christmas lights around
her antique gas pump and puts presents under it.
In honor of Ch. Nab's Ace of Spades,
"Ben," my geezer dog who spends 99.9 percent of his life
asleep. Thanks as ever to Laurie, and to Mark.*

A portion of the author's royalties supports THE
COMPANY OF ANIMALS, a nonprofit agency that
distributes grants to animal welfare agencies providing
emergency and ongoing care to companion animals
throughout the United States.

Write to Annie at P.O. Box 30401, Gahanna, OH 43230

Many years ago, three journeying kings invited elderly Francesca Epiphania to go with them to bring presents to a little baby. The old woman told the kings she couldn't go because it was her cleaning day. Besides, she didn't have anything she could give to a baby. She didn't even particularly like babies. Her own children were long grown and gone.

A short while after the kings had continued on their way, Mrs. Epiphania was visited by the Archangel Gabriel. He was not amused by her refusal to accompany the kings. In fact, he was so unamused that he sentenced her to spend eternity wandering the earth, giving gifts to deserving children. So, for the next one-thousand, nine hundred, and ninety-seven years, Mrs. Epiphania had to do just that.

But now she was even older than she was when she turned down that blasted invitation. She was bone weary. She was burned out. Gabriel, however, in the last almost two thousand years of Archangeling, had mellowed—thank goodness.

Annie Kimberlin

At the beginning of the one-thousand, nine hundred, and ninety-eighth year, Mrs. Epiphania and Gabriel came to an agreement. Gabriel gave her a long list of people. If Mrs. Epiphania could bring each of these people happiness by the end of the year, Gabriel promised her that she could buy out the rest of her sentence. She could retire. She could spend eternity with people her own age.

Now it was the middle of December, and she was down to the last two people on Gabriel's list. She was to give them love. Love for each other. Mrs. Epiphania had saved them for last because—well, because in the last almost two millennia, she had picked up a bit of magic here and there. So making two people fall in love with each other should be a piece of cake. Chocolate.

Chapter One

"You sure you don't want me to stay, Carly? Help you close up?"

Carly studied her cash-register clerk. His coat was on and he was as close to the door as he could get without actually being outside. Ah, to be a teenager again. "Nah, Richie. I'll take care of it," Carly told him. "You go on home. I'll see you tomorrow."

A relieved grin erupted on his freckled face. "Okay, Carly. I promised Megan I'd take her to finish her Christmas shopping before dinner. But she says the best present would be snow, and you can't buy that." He ho-ho-ho'd to her as he ducked out the door. The silver bells, hung by the lovely Megan, his optimistic girlfriend, tinkled merrily. It was evidently Christmastime in the city.

Bill wandered in, wiping his greasy hands on the rag that lived in his back pocket. "That's it for tonight, Carly. Mr. Paynter's truck is all that's left. You said you wanted to do that oil change yourself."

"Yeah, Bill. Thanks." But she didn't look at him. He'd known her since she was a bitty tyke. Since she'd been big enough to tell the difference between an adjustable wrench and a screwdriver. It was under Bill's direction that she'd rebuilt her first engine. She'd been avoiding him all week. Ever since she'd received The Letter.

"Say, Carly," he said hesitantly. "Is there something wrong?"

"No." She examined the little McTree, also brought in by the optimistic Megan, that stood on the worn counter proclaiming to one and all that it was Christmastime in the city. It was decorated with gaudy little balls and covered with fake snow. Carly absently wound the key. The McTree started turning around and around to the tune of "O Tannenbaum."

"You sure?" Bill persisted. "You know if there's something I can do to help, you just have to say the word."

"What? Are you gonna start singing about bridges and troubled waters now? Or that old Carole King song about summer, spring, winter, and fall?" Bill's penchant for singing was great fodder for teasing. "Megan's tree is all the music I think I can stand right now."

He grinned. "No." He twisted the rag in his hands. "You've just seemed a mite distracted lately. You're always so bound and determined to do things yourself. Shep went overboard teaching you to be self-reliant."

"I've had to be self-reliant, Bill. You know that."

"There's a time to ask for help."

"Well, when I'm there, I'll let you know." She smiled brightly, forcing the expression in her eyes to be cheerful. She didn't think he was fooled. "Besides, what could be wrong? Christmas is coming, the goose is getting fat and all that." She came out from behind the counter to give him a brief hug. "Now go home early to Marianne and those kids of yours. I'll lock up as soon as I finish Mr. Paynter's truck.

110

I don't think there'll be much business the rest of the afternoon.''

"Okay," he sounded unsure.

"Go, go, go." She shooed him out of the door. "Give Marianne my love and have a terrific evening."

"You, too, Carly."

"Yeah, me too, Carly," she muttered to herself as she opened the old-fashioned cash-register drawer and pulled out The Letter. She unfolded it and stared at it for at least the hundredth time. Maybe this time it would say something different. But no. "Dear Ms. Shepherd, We regret to inform you . . . blahdy blah blah. Sincerely, Jacob Weisman II." Sincerely. Hah! She snorted. There wasn't a nail filing of sincerely anywhere in this letter, let alone in that man. The man wouldn't know sincerity if he met it in the street.

"Magic doesn't happen, Carly my girl," she said to herself out loud. "So, your gas station'll be closed and you'll be out of a job and a home. But, hey, it's almost a new year. Time for a new beginning. Winter solstice and the return of the sun."

Ratchet landed on the counter and shoved his furry face between her and The Letter. "Hey, Ratch." She scrubbed his head. "You up for a new beginning?"

Ratchet answered her with an eyes-closed purr, shoving his head into her hand to promote more head scrubbing.

"What about you, Murph?" she called to her ancient German Shepherd. He was in his corner, behind the counter, curled up on a blanket that was almost as old as he was. "You ready for a new year?" Murphy did not stir. Murphy never stirred. Murphy spent 99.9 percent of his life asleep.

With a sigh, Carly heaved herself up from the stool and trudged into the car bay to change the oil in Fred Paynter's truck. She gathered her tools to start the job. Tools that had belonged to Gramps. Tools that she'd grown up with. Cut her teeth on. Tools that were as familiar to her as her own toothbrush. Tools that, come January 1, would belong to Mr.

111

Sincerely Jacob Weisman II, and his almighty bank. She hoped, sincerely, that they poked their eyes out with her tools. But they didn't want her tools. They didn't want her gas station. They wanted the land.

With a heavy heart she lifted the hood on the truck. This was her territory—the familiarity of an oil change soothed her like a lullaby. She could almost do this in her sleep. When she'd poured the used oil into the drum, she gathered the tools scattered around the car bay—the lubratorium, as Gramps used to call it. But now, the normally cheerful clatter of metal sounded hollow and dead.

Carly hung up the last stray Allen wrench and turned, leaning against the work table, and gazed around at her world. One of the last of the mom-and-pop gas stations in Franklin. Heck, in the whole country. A creature endangered, near extinction. Shep's Gas and Mechanic. Her life. Her love.

Jake Weisman groaned to himself for the hundredth time since he'd agreed to drive crotchety Mrs. Epiphania and her nasty little dog to the vet's office. She'd insisted the little thing was sick. It didn't look sick to Jake. In fact, the little rat dog had had the audacity to bare its teeth at him when he bent down to take a look at it. Jake liked dogs, but this wasn't a dog. This was a rat. A rat was riding in his '57 Chevy. His pride and joy had a rat in it. Jake shuddered.

"It's a good thing you could take us, Mr. Weisman," the rat dog's owner said. "I don't know what I would've done. Little Sweetcakes is much too delicate to take on the bus."

Maybe the little rat-dog would've died, Jake thought. Now there was a cheerful thought. "No problem, Mrs. Epiphania," he lied, trying valiantly to keep his voice pleasant. After all, crotchety or not, the lady was elderly and frail with a sick dog. Only someone who was a real heel would refuse to help her. There were enough heels already in the Weisman family tree.

The Shepherds and Mr. Weisman

Sweetcakes emitted a series of piercingly shrill noises. Jake mentally cringed, sure his windshield would shatter. It had taken him three months to find this one. There wasn't another tinted windshield for a '57 Chevy in the entire country. He shuddered again. Think of the positive, Jake, he told himself. She was holding the rat dog in her arms so it wasn't on the seats. And he hadn't gotten the seat covers restored yet.

"Sweetcakes says thank you, also, Mr. Weisman. I've taught him that he must mind his manners."

"Yes, well, please, Mrs. Epiphania, call me Jake. People say Mr. Weisman and I look around for my father." The thought of his father was even less comforting than the thought of Sweetcakes in his car, if that was possible. He avoided his father as much as he possibly could, but still, old habits didn't die, hard or otherwise.

Suddenly he noticed the old woman twisting around in the seat, evidently trying to look out the window at something. She muttered something, in Italian, he supposed.

"Excuse me?" he asked.

Just then his car started to putter and hesitate. He gave a few quick light whacks to the gas gauge. It read empty, but sometimes it stuck. "Damn," he muttered under his breath as his pride and joy rolled to a stop.

"What's wrong, Jake?"

"Looks like we're out of gas." He thought he'd filled the gas tank. Must've done more driving around than he'd thought. "I'll have to find a gas station that's open."

"There's one back there." Mrs. Epiphania pointed a gnarled finger. "Just across that field."

Jake looked where she pointed. Sure enough, on the stretch of old road, bypassed by the new highway, was a little gas station. He couldn't make out the name of it, but the lights were still on, so it must be open. He had plenty of gas additive in the trunk, so that wasn't a problem. That was one

113

of the many little details involved in driving an antique car. Unleaded gas, without an additive, would kill it.

"Okay," he told Mrs. Epiphania, "I'm going to go get us some gas. It shouldn't take too long. I'm sure you'll be fine."

"Of course we'll be fine, Jake," the old woman said testily. "We'll be with you. But you had better carry Sweetcakes, in case I stumble. These old legs aren't what they used to be." She thrust Sweetcakes in his face. The little dog glared at him and bared its teeth again. It made a sound that was similar to a purr, but Jake had the distinct feeling that the little rat thing wasn't expressing joy.

No way did he want to carry the little rat dog even two feet, let along across a cornfield. "It might be best if you stayed here, out of the wind. It's a cold night." Then he had an inspiration. "You don't want your dog to catch a chill."

"We can't stay here. You never know what kind of people drive along this highway. Why, we wouldn't know what to do if someone stopped. They might point a gun at us." She clamped the dog to her chest, looking totally alarmed at the thought. "We'll go with you." As if it were settled, she unlocked the door and tried to open it. It was stuck.

She sure was a stubborn one, Jake thought. As he walked around his car to open the door for Mrs. Epiphania, he flicked at an imaginary speck of grit on the hood. Imperial Ivory and Dusk Pearl. What a classic color combination.

He helped the elderly woman out of the car, holding on to her elbow to help her if she slipped. Her little-old-lady shoes were encased in clear plastic little-old-lady boots. Not the thing for cross-field trekking. She held the rat dog out toward him again. It curled its lip.

"I know what we can do," he said. "I have an old blanket in the trunk. I can wrap your—uh, dog in that, and he'll be warmer." He doubted even those sharp little teeth could bite through several layers of surplus army blanket. He dug into his parka pockets and brought out his gloves. "Here. Put these on. I know they're too big, but they'll keep your hands warm.''

"Why, thank you, Jake. That's quite thoughtful.''

No, he wasn't thoughtful at all. He didn't want her to get sick. Then he'd probably be stuck taking care of her little dog. Still, he thought of his own grandmother. How would he like her to have been treated? With a sigh, he opened the trunk and pulled out the blanket. "Here, give me Sweetcakes,'' he told her, trying not to choke on the dog's name.

The blanket weighed more than the dog.

They started off, over the frozen field. Jake held the dog-in-a-blanket firmly in one arm, his other hand at Mrs. Epiphania's elbow. It was slow going—the old lady was probably not used to trampling, whereas his work boots were made for stomping. He looked across the field at the gas station. It perched at the end of a street of elderly houses. They all, even the gas station, looked like the '30s. Probably hadn't been touched since then. Now there would be a terrific project to renovate all the houses on that street. Starting at one end and working his way down the street, it'd take a couple of years. But when he was finished, the street would look exactly as it had when it was new.

The old woman trudged over the frozen ruts in the field. She had arranged for Jake to meet this young lady. Now all they had to do was fall in love. Certainly this mechanic would see that Jake was special. After all, they were destined for each other. The old woman grinned in anticipation. She was almost home free. Besides that, she would love to win this wager. She couldn't wait to see Gabriel's face.

No sense in staying open much longer, Carly thought. No one had come in for the past two hours. No one had even driven down the street. Might as well close early for once. What difference could it possibly make now, when Shep's would soon be closed permanently?

115

Carly had just reached out to turn the OPEN sign over to CLOSED when she saw two people making their way across the street toward her. The man was tall and slender and carried a blanket. The woman looked like a little old rummage sale refugee. They both looked toward her gas station expectantly. She sighed. Gramps always taught her that excellent customer service was as important as regularly changing an air filter. She dropped her arm and, pasting a smile on her face, opened the door. "Hello. You just made it. What can I do for you?"

"Thanks," the man said as he ushered the old lady into the warmth. Carly noted the courtesy. "I ran out of gas up on the highway. I need a gas can and a gallon of unleaded."

The old lady was staring all around. Maybe she hadn't seen the insides of many gas stations before. Carly was suddenly conscious of the floor that needed a good sweeping. More than that, it needed new tile.

"I don't sell gas cans, but I'll loan you one," Carly told the man. "I keep a couple on hand back here."

"That'll be fine," he answered. He followed her into the back storage room where Ratchet suddenly appeared and leaped up onto a worktable. "Hello, kitty," the man said as he bent slightly toward the cat.

"That's Ratchet," Carly told him.

Ratchet blinked at the man.

The blanket exploded in a shrill scream. The man jerked the blanket away from the cat. "Sorry, kitty. This is Sweetcakes," he said dryly over the continued shrilling. "I guess it doesn't like cats."

Ratchet looked down his nose in a decidedly superior feline sneer. Carly resisted the urge to stick her fingers in her ears. "What's a Sweetcakes?" she asked.

"I've been told it's a dog."

"Can't you make it stop?"

"It's not mine. It belongs to Mrs. Epiphania."

"Mrs. who?"

"Epiphania. I'm taking her to the vet's. She said Sweet-cakes is sick."

"Doesn't sound sick to me," Carly muttered. "Why don't you take it—is it a boy or a girl?"

He grimaced. "It's a boy," he said with an apologetic grin.

"Well, why don't you take him into the other room and I'll be right back with the gas can."

"Good idea," he agreed. She could hear the little dog holding forth continuously for several moments. Obviously swearing a blue streak. Then there was blessed silence.

When she returned with the gas can, the old lady was holding the blanket and muttering to it.

Murphy hadn't stirred. But then, Murphy never stirred. Murphy just slept. Carly automatically watched him for a few seconds, to make sure he was still breathing. He was. She handed the gas can to the man.

"Thanks. I'll go outside to fill it up and be right back in to pay." As the door swung closed after him, the Christmas bells merrily ting-a-linged once more.

She shivered at the memory of Sweetcakes barking. At least, she supposed it was a bark. It sounded more like fingernails on a blackboard. Maybe Murphy had the right idea after all. She turned the pump on so the man could pump his gas. "I guess Sweetcakes doesn't like cats," she told Ratchet as he jumped up onto the counter. Ratchet blinked at her.

"I'm glad you were open," the little old lady said in a voice that was at once wavery and strident. "I don't know what we would have done if you hadn't been. Sweetcakes would have been terribly distressed." She peeled back a few layers of blanket and peered at the animal inside. A miniature pink tongue whipped out and flicked against the woman's chin. "That's enough, Sweetcakes," she chided. "You're sick, remember?"

The little old lady peeled back a final layer of blanket, liberating a tiny dog, profusely covered with long, fluffy

117

black fur. Tiny ears stood erect on its head but Carly had to search carefully for its eyes amid the fur.

So this was the Sweetcakes, Carly thought. Excellent customer service, she said silently to the memory of Gramps. "Hello, Sweetcakes," she said. "I hear you're sick." The little dog waved its plume of a tail. Emboldened, Carly held out her hand for a sniff. "I'm Carly. I like dogs."

Sweetcakes sniffed her hand delicately. "He likes you," the little old lady said. Carly wondered why she sounded so relieved.

The tinkling of the Christmas bells announced the return of the man. He set the gas can down while he reached into his pocket. "Thanks again," he told her. "Not a night to be stranded on the highway." He pulled a few bills out of a leather billfold. He handled the money as if he'd always had so much of it that it wasn't important to him. His jacket probably cost more than she spent on an entire year's worth of clothes, his faded jeans were well cut, and his work boots, though obviously worn, looked expensive. His hands were clean and hard, the hands of someone who worked with tools, not the soft hands of an office worker. Wealthy and working? Now there was an unusual combination.

She glanced at the meter. He'd pumped exactly one gallon. "No, sir. It isn't," she agreed. As she handed the change to the man, Carly watched him glance uneasily at the little old lady, then out at the darkening gloom of the winter evening. There was concern in his face. Carly liked him for it. She realized she hadn't really looked at him before now. She hadn't noticed that he was very good looking, a classic look, the kind that belonged on ancient Greek statues, or in an ad for a Mercedes. She was suddenly aware that she was covered in engine grease. But he wasn't looking at her. He was still watching the old woman.

"She can wait here for you," Carly said in a whisper. "It's okay. It's no problem."

He turned back and his gaze searched hers for a long mo-

118

ment; then she was rewarded with a blinding smile and a slight nod. "Thanks," he said in a voice low enough not to be overheard by the old lady.

"It might be best if you and Sweetcakes stayed here, Mrs. Epiphania, where it's warm, while I get the car."

The woman looked sharply at Carly.

"It's no trouble," Carly hastened to add. "Honest. In fact, why don't you come over here and sit down while you wait." She led the woman to the most comfortable chair in the place. It was an ancient recliner, decorated with strips of duct tape that covered the rips in the Naugahyde. "Would you like a cup of coffee?"

The woman's face cleared. "Thank you, young lady. That would be lovely. Sweetcakes doesn't like the cold. And to tell the truth, neither do I."

"I'll be back," said the man cheerfully. Too cheerfully, thought Carly.

"At least," the old lady continued, "we haven't had any snow yet."

"Don't you like snow?" Carly asked. "It doesn't seem like it could be almost Christmas yet without snow."

The old woman frowned. "Snow is pretty, but then people track it into the house. Or they track in mud, which is worse. So much extra cleaning to do when there's snow."

"I never thought of it that way," Carly admitted, keeping her amusement to herself. "I usually think about how pretty it is." She flicked a finger at the fake snow on Megan's McTree on her way across the room to the coffee pot.

"That Jake is certainly a thoughtful young man, don't you think so, missie?"

"Jake?" Carly asked, pouring coffee into a Styrofoam cup. "Creamer or sugar?"

"No, thank you. Black is just fine. Jake is the young man who drove me today. Don't you think he's thoughtful? And he doesn't have a girlfriend." Carly caught a gleam in the little old lady's eye. There was a sly quality to it. If Carly

119

didn't know better, she'd think the lady was matchmaking. What an idea! "Yes. He seemed very pleasant."

"I just moved in next door to him. My name is Francesca Epiphania," the little old lady announced.

Carly guessed it was time for introductions. "I'm Carly Shepherd," she said.

"This is your gas station?"

How did she know that? Carly wondered. "Yes, ma'am. My grandfather left it to me when he passed away."

Mrs. Epiphania nodded, a look of total satisfaction on a face that was more wrinkles than not. "Good."

"Good?"

"It's good to own your own business."

Carly grimaced. "I won't own it much longer," she found herself saying.

"Why is that?" the woman asked.

Almost without thinking, Carly found herself telling Mrs. Epiphania about Gramps's loans. How she'd paid them off one by one until there was only a final loan remaining. How the bank had decided to refuse her request for an extension and was, instead, calling the loan in. Due by the end of the year. Sincerely.

"And you see, I live next door in a house that is part of the property. So unless I can come up with twenty thousand dollars by the end of the year, I'll lose that as well."

"Maybe a miracle will happen."

"I don't believe in miracles."

Mrs. Epiphania looked at her curiously. "No? Why, Carly Shepherd, miracles have happened for at least two thousand years. I know this to be true."

Carly shoved her hands into the pockets of her coveralls. "Look, Mrs. Epiphania." She struggled with the unfamiliar name. "I don't want to put down your beliefs, but I don't believe in miracles—even at Christmastime. Or magic. Or reincarnation. Or angels. Or astrology."

120

"What *do* you believe in?" The old woman sounded genuinely curious under her gruffness.

Carly frowned. She'd never thought about it before. "I guess I believe in hard work. I belive in honesty. And duct tape as a cure-all." She drummed her fingers on the countertop. They looked as if she'd just changed the oil on an old Ford truck, which, of course, she had. "And I believe in GoJo Orange with Pumice for getting out the stubbornest automotive grease," she added, trying to bring a bit of levity to the conversation. "That's about as miraculous as anything I know."

"I'm sure those things all have their place, young lady," Mrs. Epiphania said seriously. "But magic and miracles and angels do exist. I know that better than anyone. Oh yes, I do. Believe me, sometimes I wish I didn't know." She tee-hee'd softly to herself for a moment. Carly wondered if she was—well, all there. "Magic exists, young Carly Shepherd. Believe me, in two thousand years you tend to pick up a few bits of magic here and there."

But Carly wasn't really paying attention to Mrs. Epiphania. She'd just seen a vision. She pressed her face up against the window and cupped her hands around her eyes to see it better. "It's beautiful," she breathed, watching it come closer and closer.

"What is?" Mrs. Epiphania asked.

"That '57 Chevy. It's beautiful. It's a true classic." Carly felt herself melt into a little gob of goo. The car was gorgeous. Oh, how she'd love to get her hands on that car. Run her fingers over that body, sweet and smooth and sassy. The twin windsplits on the front hood, nestled on either side of the gently concave slope that reached to the back of the hood. And down the side of the car, like silk, the brightwork molding arched delicately from the headlights down the full length of the car to separate into a *V*-shaped section of shallow horizontal flutes that proudly proclaimed to one and all that this was not merely a '57 Chevy. This was a Bel Air. The top of the line. Carly sighed with lust. A car as gorgeous as that deserved to have, *needed* to have, its original V-8 engine. Anything less would be sacrilegious. She wanted to unlatch the hood and explore its inner depths. Learn its mysteries. Turn it on and listen to it purr.

"You mean you like the car?" Still focused on the dream of a machine, Carly almost missed the surprise in the woman's voice.

"She's gorgeous," Carly breathed in awe.

Mrs. Epiphania muttered a few words in a foreign language, but Carly ignored her. The vision on wheels was turning into her gas station. And it—oh, my! Oh, no! Suddenly, thick white smoke gushed out from under the hood.

Chapter Two

In an instant Jake had the key turned off and the door opened, and was out of the car staring blankly at the steam. At least it was white. Coolant, instead of fire. But where was it coming from?

"Do you want to push her into the bay and let me take a look at her?"

It was the girl from the gas station. He looked at her in surprise. Then he really looked at her. Her jumpsuit had the name Carly embroidered over the pocket. She was a mechanic?

"I'm certified, if that's what you're thinking," she told him. "I've worked on '57s before. Do her numbers match?"

He nodded. "Engine is as original as the day she rolled off the line."

She jerked her head toward his car. "If you want to get out of the cold and open her up, I'll take a look."

He glanced once more at the steam. Then back to her. "Sure. That'd be fine."

"Okay, I'll raise that door over there and then we can push her in."

This was obviously not some shrinking violet kind of lady. This was a lady who was used to being in charge in a man's world. His thoughts were interrupted by the raucous noise of a garage door opening. He gestured to the name on the gas station sign. Shep's Gas and Mechanic. "Who's Shep?" he asked conversationally.

"My grandfather. Shep Shepherd. He died a few years back and left me the station. I'm Carly Shepherd. Is her brake off?"

"Yeah."

"Then let's get this baby inside, let her cool down, and open 'er up."

Jake reached across the front seat to unlock the passenger door and shoved it open. Then, as Carly prepared to push on the frame, Jake positioned himself at the driver's door, pushing on the frame with his shoulder and one arm as he maneuvered the steering wheel with the other. They pushed together, putting all their weight into moving the car. Like some great beached ocean creature, the car rolled slowly toward the yawning garage. "You like being a mechanic?" he asked her as they rested for a moment.

"Love it. Wouldn't do anything else"

"Isn't it unusual for a woman to like fixing cars?"

She leveled her gaze at him. "I consider myself lucky," she said in an even tone, "to be able to spend my life doing something I love."

He sent her an apologetic grin. "I'm sorry. I'm put in my place."

She turned to face him square on, over the top of the car. "Look, if you want someone else to check your car out, that's fine with me. You can call a tow truck now, or you can leave it in my garage and tow it in the morning. I wouldn't recommend leaving it outside overnight. Hawthorne Street isn't a crime-ridden neighborhood or anything—

in fact, it's very quiet. But you have one gorgeous car. If you want me to take a look at it, I'll do that. Just don't patronize me. I'm a damn good mechanic. I also happen to have experience with '57s.'' She stood for a moment, quiet and still, giving him time.

He felt his face redden slightly. He mentally squirmed as he realized he'd acted like his father, and then, like his father, expected to smooth everything over with the old Weisman charm. Except the Weisman charm didn't work on this— lady? Woman? Neither word seemed to fit her. Oddly enough, the one word that did fit her perfectly—was mechanic.

Then his time was up. "So what's it going to be?" she asked.

"Thanks," he said seriously. "I'd appreciate it if you gave her a look. It's probably nothing more than a blown hose."

She nodded. "Probably. '57s have fairly simple engines, so it shouldn't be too hard to figure out which hose is blowing coolant."

They put their combined weight into the car again. Again the behemoth rolled toward the garage. "I've spent most of my time working on the body," he told her. "The engine hasn't needed much work, so I'm not as familiar with it."

They rocked the car gently before they gave one huge heave to get her up onto the cement floor and into the garage. Carly flipped the switch and the great garage door made its ponderous way back down.

"Let's give her a few more minutes to cool down before we open her up," she said after feeling several places on the hood. "And you might want to let your friend know what's going on." She nodded in the direction of Mrs. Epiphania.

He smacked his forehead. "Mrs. Epiphania. I'd forgotten."

But the old woman wasn't the least bit upset. In fact, she seemed to be in a good mood. "Well, Jake, you just take all

125

the time in the world. This is a comfortable chair here. I may even lean back and take a little nap.''

"But—Sweetcakes? I thought he was sick.''

The little dog, curled up on Mrs. Epiphania's lap, raised a furry head. Jake expected it to growl at him, but it didn't. In fact, it flung its tail around for a moment.

"See, Jake, I think Sweetcakes is better. I guess he doesn't need to go to the vet's after all.'' The little dog yawned, showing sharp little white teeth and a miniature pink tongue. Then it curled back into a ball of fluff. Mrs. Epiphania covered the little dog with a gnarled hand, a hand that was gentle, though strangely hesitant.

"Well, if you're sure,'' he said uncertainly. "I don't know how long this will take.''

"Take all the time you need. Don't worry about me. That pretty young woman owns this garage, you know. Take all the time you need.'' The chair crackled as she settled deeper into it. "When you're as old as I am, you realize that time doesn't really matter anymore,'' she murmured, looking down at her dog.

All at once, Jake was filled with an odd feeling of protectiveness toward and compassion for this elderly woman. That little dog was all she had in the world. She'd told him her family was long gone. She was biding her time until she could retire—he'd thought retire was an odd word for her to use. Then she'd said she was looking forward to spending eternity with people her own age.

Suddenly, Jake wanted to do something to make her happy, something to cheer her up. He caught sight of a little fake Christmas tree that stood jauntily on the counter. That was it, he thought. A Christmas tree. He would get her a Christmas tree. He'd do it tomorrow. Now he crossed the worn green tiles of the gas station and stooped down in front of her. "I don't know how long this will take. I'll call a cab to take you home, if you'd like.''

She smiled at him, a smile that would have looked at home

on the Mona Lisa. "You are a nice young man, Jake. I'm glad I met you. But, no. I'll wait here. I have to make sure everything ends as it should."

He frowned. "What's supposed to happen?"

For an instant she looked startled. "Oh, you know, dear." She waved her hand vaguely in the direction of the car bay. "That pretty young Carly Shepherd needs to fix your car."

He could probably fix it himself, he thought. After all, a blown hose was no big deal. But he didn't want to tell Mrs. Epiphania that. Somehow he didn't want to tell Carly the Mechanic that either. It looked as though she could use the business. And he could certainly afford it.

Then Carly the Mechanic was there, leaning inside the door. "I think she's cooled off enough to open the hood."

Jake studied her for a moment. She was tall and slender with a strength that came from being self-assured. Her long brown hair was pulled back into a thick braid. And her soft brown eyes were calm and steady. Mrs. Epiphania was right, he realized. Carly was pretty.

Carly led him past Fred Paynter's Ford truck to the Chevy. "Have you had her long?"

"About two years."

For a moment, they stood side by side gazing at the dream of a car. "Lovely job restoring her," Carly said at last. "What shape was she in when you got her?"

"She'd been sitting in an old garage for about ten years."

Ten years? Just sitting? Poor baby, she thought, patting the front hood gently. "Out of the weather, at least. You're lucky she's not rusted through."

"She was in a couple of places. She'd been painted a screaming orange." He shuddered. "Ugly color. She belonged to my cousin, who drove her around for a few years until leaded gas got hard to find. He didn't want to bother with keeping additives on hand all the time, so he parked her in his garage, bought a Nova, and forgot about her. I discovered her a few years ago and called in a few favors. The engine was filthy, but it worked, so I drove her home. She was in bad shape, body-wise. But still, even through all the dirt and grime, I knew she would be a beaut when she was cleaned up.'' The enthusiasm in his voice was a palpable thing.

Well, Carly thought, any guy who loves his car can't be all bad. "Let's open her up," she announced briskly, "and find out why she's blowing coolant."

But there seemed to be no earthly reason why the car was blowing coolant.

"Engine's dry," he said in surprise. "With a blown hose it should be wet."

"The radiator hoses look fine," she said, puzzled. "A little worn, but certainly in decent condition." She pointed. "See the wear there, and over here." She leaned over the engine to get closer to the hoses. "I don't even see a pin hole," she told him. "Will you please hand me that flashlight. I want to take a closer look at the lower hose."

He handed her the flashlight and joined her hanging over the side of the car, their heads inside the engine compartment.

But the lower hose was also whole.

"Heater hose," she said. "Let's look at them."

"A little worn," he said. But that was all. They, also, were whole.

"Freeze plug?"

"Let me have the light," he said. "Nope," he added, a few seconds later. "Look at it. Tight and fine."

"No leaks," she agreed.

She drummed her fingers thoughtfully against the manifold. What could have caused the steam? "How's the coolant level?"

They hauled themselves out of the engine compartment and huddled together as she carefully unscrewed the pressure cap on the radiator. "Feels like the right amount of pressure here,'' she noted. As one, they peered into the radiator. "It's right where it should be," Carly said in surprise. "Two inches below the bottom of the filler neck. How can that be? It blew."

They looked at each other. They were both totally baffled.

She leaned over the front of the car so she could see the inside of the radiator. A heartbeat later, he was there too, next to her. He played the flashlight beam slowly over every inch of the radiator. "Nothing," she said. "Turn on the engine. I want to check for any restriction."

They let the car run for a few moments. "It sounds smooth," she commented. "No steam at all." They stood side by side. Out of the corner of her eye she watched him stare at his car—deep in thought. "That's enough," she ordered. "Turn her off."

He did. She firmly placed her hand at the bottom of the radiator, then at the top, then several places in between. "It fees fine," she said at last. "I can't feel any clogged sections at all." She scowled at the unoffending radiator.

Then they were underneath the car, on creepers, their heads together, studying the underside of the engine. "These are simple systems here on this baby," she said. "There's not all that much that can go wrong."

She turned her head, meaning to glance at him quickly, then back at the private parts of the engine. But it didn't work that way. She found herself gazing into his eyes, eyes that were almost closer than anyone else's eyes had ever been before. Closer than anyone else's eyes should be. Especially someone whose car she was working on. Someone who was a stranger. Someone she knew nothing about—except that he had a great car, and he was kind to Mrs. Epiphania, and he'd talked to Ratchet, but he hadn't seen Murphy—but then no one ever saw Murphy, unless they knew he was there. She knew he was on an errand of mercy to take Sweetcakes to the vet's—and that alone spoke volumes for him. Yes, she realized, she knew things about him—things that spoke to the kind of person he was inside. And those things were the important things.

Kiss him! The thought came out of nowhere. Kiss him! Obediently, Carly edged a tad closer. Hold it! She stopped. What was she doing? She wrenched her gaze—and herself—away from him and turned her attention back to the underside of the engine. Kiss him, indeed. What an absurd idea. She crawls under a '57 Chevy with a guy who is both great-looking and nice and it makes her all mushy inside. Carly, grow up, she told herself. Figure out what's wrong with this car.

"I can't find anything wrong with it," she said at last. With a great sigh, accompanied by the sound of wheels on concrete, she scooted the creeper out from under the car.

She was next to him, leaning back against the garage wall, staring at the '57 Chevy. He had his face toward his car, but he was really watching her. A few minutes ago, underneath his car, he'd had a fleeting urge to kiss her. He almost had, but he'd caught himself in time. Thank goodness she didn't know what had come over him. Right now, she was scowling at his car. Evidently she didn't like being stumped.

"If I hadn't seen it myself, I wouldn't have believed all that steam came out from under the hood," she said. "But it doesn't make sense. Your engine should be wet, but it's clean and dry. You don't get steam from nowhere."

He nodded.

"If there was something there, I'd have found it. I'm a good mechanic." She was emphatic about it, but she seemed to be trying to convince herself, rather than him.

"Yes, you are." She was. He'd known it the moment she'd opened the hood. She knew her way around the private parts of a car. In fact, she knew more than he did.

She heaved a great sigh and pushed off from the wall. "Jake, I'm sorry. I can't find anything." He watched her let the hood down carefully, then turn to face him. "Or if you

130

want to leave it overnight, I can do a more thorough check tomorrow—use a pressure gauge, pull the radiator to look for anything unusual." She shrugged. "But you don't seem to have lost any coolant. I can also recommend a mechanic over in Phillipsburg who specializes in antique cars. He might be able to figure it out."

There was a sense of competence about her that he liked. A sense of fairness, of honesty. She couldn't find anything wrong with his car, and she was willing to send his business to someone who she thought could. She had integrity. He liked that. He liked her, he realized. He cleared his throat. "I'll leave it here tonight and think about it before I make a decision."

She nodded. "Sure."

"I'd like to use your phone to call a cab."

She shoved her grimy hands in her coverall pockets. "Tell you what. It's past time I was closed and I have to go out anyway. Why don't you let me drive you and Mrs. Epiphania home?"

"I don't want to trouble you."

She shrugged again. "No trouble at all."

He searched her face for any sign of hesitancy or of ulterior motive. There was none. Nothing but straightforward what-you-see-is-what-you-get honesty. "Thanks. I appreciate it."

She nodded, as if settling a deal.

They scrubbed their hands at the work sink using GoJo Orange with Pumice. Carly smiled to herself. She always liked the scent of orange. She turned out the lights in the garage, after making sure the big doors were locked. She went into her little office and peeled off her coveralls, leaving her in jeans and a turtleneck. Then, in the storage room, she checked Ratchet's bowls for food and fresh water. Ratchet watched her with great interest but followed her into the front room where Jake was.

"Is he your cat?" Jake asked.

"I guess so. He showed up one day and liked it here, so he stayed. I feed him, get him shots. Sometimes he wanders next door, where I live, but he's happiest being right here. Maybe he was an automotive engineer in a former life." She gave Ratchet's head a thorough knuckle scrubbing. The cat arched his neck and pushed into her hand.

There wasn't enough money in the till to take to the bank, she thought morosely. So she made sure the old-fashioned cash register was locked tightly. She wouldn't be doing this many more times. How many days was it until the end of the year? Stop it, she told herself. You're being morose.

She knelt down beside Murphy. "Murph, old guy, c'mon now. It's time to wake up." She reached down to gently stroke his side, wake him up slowly so he wouldn't startle. The old dog opened his eyes. "That's it. Time to wake up. You can do it. We're going for a ride."

"Has he been here this whole time? I didn't see him earlier."

"That's not unusual. Most people don't see him until he wakes up. Which he almost never does. He's my old geezer guy," she said with great affection.

The geriatric German Shepherd stretched his long legs, then slowly and unsteadily staggered to his feet. He gave a halfhearted shake, almost losing his balance in the process.

"Good boy," she told him. "Murphy, this is Jake. We're going to take him home."

Jake reached out a hand. Murphy sniffed it, then gave a few meager wags of his tail.

"Mrs. Epiphania," Carly called softly. Like Murphy, the old woman slowly came awake. Sweetcakes, still in a ball on her lap, raised his furry little head. "Mrs. Epiphania, we couldn't figure our what's wrong with Jake's car, so it's going to stay here, and I'm going to drive you home now."

The faded blue eyes finally focused on her. "Oh, Carly, my dear. Didn't you fix it?"

"No, ma'am. I couldn't find an earthly thing wrong with it."

The old woman gave her a look of total, albeit sleepy, satisfaction. "Well now, maybe it's a little of that magic I was telling you about."

From behind her, she heard Jake snort. Carly smiled. "Mrs. Epiphania, no offense, but I don't think a car blowing steam is magic. Especially when I can't find a reason for it. I call it frustrating."

"Well, Carly Shepherd, you may know about cars, but I know about magic. Trust me. You too, Jake. I hear you over there, trying not to laugh." But there was no anger in her voice. Only tolerance, as if they were mere children.

Then Sweetcakes caught sight of Murphy. He launched himself off Mrs. Epiphania's lap and flew at the older dog, his piercing bark furious and insistent. Before Carly could react, the German Shepherd put his great grayed muzzle down to touch the little dog's nose. There was instant blessed silence. Then both dogs wagged their tails and sniffed each other. They were friends.

Chapter Three

"Tell Carly about your house, Jake," Mrs. Epiphania told him. They were driving through the Christmas light–encrusted houses of his current neighborhood. Jake was in the back seat of Carly's truck, along with Murphy, who had crammed himself into the floor space behind the driver's seat and immediately gone back to sleep.

"What about your house?" Carly asked.

"Tell her how you fix houses," Mrs. Epiphania urged.

"I buy old houses and live in them while I fix them up. Then I sell them."

"You fix them up?"

"I restore them, actually," he told her. "But with modern plumbing and electricity of course. Though I keep the feel of the period in the fixtures."

"Are you an architect?"

"No. I've studied architecture, but I'm more of a craftsman."

"You do all the work by yourself?"

"Most of it."

Carly nodded in approval. "Like your car."

"Sort of like that, but my car is for fun, a hobby. Turn left up here at the stop sign."

"Have you restored other cars?" she asked, flipping on her blinker.

"I did a '53 Ford a couple of years ago. I drove it for a while, but it wasn't practical, so I sold it. Then I found the Chevy. I expect I'll eventually sell it, too. Turn left again up here, and my house is the fifth one on the right. Just past that house with the reindeer on the roof. Mrs. Epiphania lives in the next house over. But," he added, peering through the front windshield, "it looks like you can't get in her driveway right now."

"That young man in the next apartment," Mrs. Epiphania added in a tone that was just this side of annoyed, "is evidently having another one of his drunken bacchanals." She pointed at the long string of cars that started in the driveway and dribbled out into the street.

"Go ahead and park in front of the garage."

"Nice garage," she commented. "Lots of space to work on your car."

He chuckled. "Right now it's full of my truck and building materials for the house."

As he was helping Mrs. Epiphania and Sweetcakes out of the high front seat, she plucked at his arm and said again, "Jake, why don't you show Carly your house? I'm sure she'd love to see the work you do." This time she sounded cross. No doubt about it. Sounded like a crotchety old lady.

"Oh, no, that's all right," Carly murmured hastily. "I'm sure you have other things to do." Jake thought he could see a slight tinge of red in her cheeks.

"Nonsense, young lady," Mrs. Epiphania scolded her. "You must see the kind of work Jake does. He has the good sense to take care of things that are old."

Jake had the feeling that Mrs. Epiphania wouldn't quit

until she had her way. He glanced over at Carly and raised his eyebrows. "Would you like to see my house?"

Carly shot him a resigned smile, and shrugged, as if she had come to the same conclusion. "Sure."

"Good." The old woman nodded her head briskly. "Then we'll leave you two. Say good night, Sweetcakes."

"Good night, Sweetcakes," Carly said with a grin. "I hope you're feeling better."

Jake watched, amused, as the furry rat dog swished his tail a few times.

"Let me to walk you to your door," he said, reaching for her elbow.

"Oh, no, Jake. I'll be perfectly safe. After all, I'm only going next door. You stay here and take care of Carly. Be sure you show her everything." The old woman stomped off a few yards, then stopped and looked back. She muttered a few words in that foreign language, then added cheerfully, in English, "Isn't it a lovely night?"

Nothing lovely about it, Jake thought. Any stars in the sky looking down where they stood were obscured by soupy clouds, and the temperature was bitterly cold. So what was the old woman so cheerful about?

"Yes, it is, Mrs. Epiphania," Carly called out. "A truly lovely night."

He watched for a few moments more, just to make sure she was safe, until she had disappeared into the building with her little dog.

"You're scowling."

"What?" His attention was jerked back to the woman standing next to him.

"I said you're scowling. Listen, you don't really have to show me around your house if you don't want to."

She was giving him an out. "It's not that," he hastened to reassure her. "I'd like to show you my house."

"Then why were you scowling?"

"I was wondering about Mrs. Epiphania."

"Do you think she's all right?"

"Oh, I'm not *worried* about her. She has a way of making people do what she wants them to do." He chuckled ruefully. "No, I was wondering what this whole thing was about. She said her little dog was horribly sick, but he didn't seem sick to me. In fact, she didn't seem to care much about him at all. Then when my car is at your garage, she decides her dog is fine and doesn't need the vet after all. Now she wants me to show you my house."

"It's probably her age. You know, people sometimes become a little confused when they get old. I think she's probably older than she looks."

"Why do you say that?" he asked.

"The look in her eyes." Carly leaned against the door of her truck and gazed at him thoughtfully. "She has the oldest eyes I've ever seen."

His attention was drawn to the building next door. A light had gone on in one of Mrs. Epiphania's windows. Then the blind twitched. "She's watching us," he told Carly, amused. "This is evidently important to her, so why don't you come on in and see my current project?"

Carly pushed herself away from the truck and dusted off the seat of her pants. "Okay," she agreed. "But only for a moment."

"Why don't you bring your dog in?" he told her. "It's too cold for him to stay in the truck."

He liked the way she woke her old dog gently, then physically guided him out of her truck, half catching him as he launched himself down. She wasn't the least bit impatient with the old dog. In fact, she treated him as if he were a beloved and respected elder that it was her honor to care for.

They made their way across the frost-crunchy grass, where Murphy stopped to leave a message for any passing neighborhood dog. "He's too old to lift his leg anymore," Carly told him apologetically. "So he does this leaning squat sort of thing."

He led them up the steps onto the porch, moving slowly so she could give Murphy hands-on encouragement. Jake took his keys out of his pocket and unlocked the door. He reached around the inside and switched on the light.

"Come in." He ushered her ahead of him. An old nursery rhyme flitted through his brain. *Come into my parlor, said the spider to the fly.* But he was no spider. And Carly was certainly no fly.

"I feel like Alice in Wonderland," she told him. They were in the living room, with a huge stone, not brick, fireplace, flanked by deep, built-in bookshelves that waited to be filled. The floors were gleaming, wide-planked wood.

"Just a minute," he told her, his words echoing slightly in the empty house. "I'll be right back." And he was. With an army blanket he folded onto the floor. "This is for Murphy. He looks like he could use a nap after maneuvering himself up the front steps."

Murphy settled gratefully and noisily onto the improvised dog bed and closed his eyes. After a few contented grunts and groans, he yawned widely, then put his head on his paws. Jake stooped down to give Murphy a pat, then he grinned up at her. "Come and see my house."

"I'd love to," she said, and realized it was true.

She followed him into a room he told her was the study. There were cabinets sitting on the floor waiting to be hung on the walls, and tall windows that overlooked the expanse of backyard. Jake pointed out holes in the plaster that needed to be repaired; then he took her into the dining room. It also had tall windows and recessed window seats that begged for cushions and a rainy day. This led into the butler's pantry with floor-to-high-ceiling shelves and a work counter along one side. Then into the kitchen.

"This is where we begin to look like the Before picture for an episode of *This Old House,*" he told her. "I'm going to replace the sink, and all the counters have to be redone,

138

as well as pull up that ugly linoleum from the floor. I'll put in new appliances, of course. The original cupboards didn't have doors, which seems odd at first, but I've gotten used to it. There's some more plaster patching to do in here.''

Carly let her gaze follow where he pointed, but she also noticed a plate in the sink, a jar of peanut butter on the counter, cans and boxes of food on the shelves. Half a roll of paper towels on a holder. Crumbs in front of an ancient toaster. It wasn't the kitchen of a lived-in house, but of someone who was camping out. This room was old and shabby and worn, a direct contrast to the rooms she'd just seen.

"This is what the whole house looked like? Before?" Oops. She didn't mean to sound reverent, but the difference between this room and the rest of the house was incredible.

"Yeah."

"And you did it all yourself? How long did it take you?"

"I started work on this house about a year ago. But come on, you haven't seen the rest of the house yet. Look, this door leads to a screened-in back porch. And up here, this is the upstairs.''

The stairs were wide and deep. Halfway up there was a landing, with another window seat.

"This top pane here''—he pointed—''was originally stained glass. I'm looking for a replacement for it. But I may have to commission it because it's an odd shape.''

They turned a corner of the landing and went up the rest of the stairs.

"There are three bedrooms up here, and this huge bathroom.''

Two of the rooms were finished and glorious, but the third door was closed. This one he didn't open. "That's where I live, while I'm working on the house.''

"They don't make bathrooms like this anymore, do they?" she asked, glancing through an open door. "It's huge. Oh, look at the feet on the bathtub!" She fell in love. With the most beautiful bathtub she'd ever seen. She didn't have a bathtub. She had a shower, a fiberglass job put in by Gramps himself. He was a fine mechanic, but he didn't know beans about putting showers in houses that weren't built for them. Mechanics usually came home filthy, smelling of hot car engines and grease. Carly had a very personal relationship with her shower. But she lusted after this bathtub. This was a bathtub made for bubbles. Mountains of bubbles. Mountains of luxurious bubbles. Reluctantly she pulled her gaze from the tub to the rest of the bathroom.

As in the kitchen, evidence of his camping out was scattered around the bathroom. A towel tossed over the rack, toothbrush in the holder, toothpaste tube squeezed in the middle, slight soap scum in the sink. And an untidy stack of books and magazines by the toilet. She felt as if she were seeing something intimate.

"They didn't make them like this *then,* either." He shot her a grin. "I'm not finished in here. I have to add more cupboards. They weren't here originally, but I think I can do it without compromising the integrity of the original form."

"Cupboards are useful," she agreed, lust for the tub still simmering.

"Spoken like a true female," he teased. "You want cupboards, look over here."

At the other end of the hallway he threw open a set of double doors to reveal more shelves, lined with cedar.

But he still didn't take her into the room where he lived.

They wandered back down to the kitchen. It was the end of the tour, but Carly felt loath to leave. She wanted to stay longer, in the warmth of his house, of his voice, of his eyes. Not go forth into the cold and end up at home, all alone, except for a practically comatose dog. She adored Murphy, but he wasn't much of a conversationalist these days.

"It's past dinnertime—would you like to stay and send out for pizza?" he asked.

It was an eleventh-hour reprieve.

After poring over a delivery menu magneted to the refrigerator door, Jake asked, "Does Murphy like pepperonis and onions?"

"Maybe," she answered, looking through the dining room into the living room where her dog still slumbered peacefully. "But he'd have to wake up first."

While Jake made the call, she looked around the kitchen again. The morning sun would come in those windows and hit the table just so. It would be lovely, she thought. And those shelves above the small counter were just deep enough for a jar of jelly. They were probably an afterthought, but she liked them anyway. In fact, she liked the whole house. No, she loved the whole house.

"Let's build a fire and eat in the living room," he said, interrupting her musings. "Then if Murphy wakes up, he won't have to go far for food. Besides, he might be confused if he wakes up alone in a strange house."

How thoughtful Jake was. But then, if he'd renovated a different house every year or so, he'd likely had lots of experience waking up in strange rooms. The thought of him, in bed, waking up, jolted through her, leaving a smoldering trail. It was unsettling. "Can I help you bring wood in?" she asked. She wasn't merely trying to be helpful; she needed something to distract her from images of Jake in bed.

"Nah, wood's just on the porch. Not far."

Soon there was a fire in the fireplace reflecting in the gleam of the wooden floors. He disappeared upstairs to return with an armload of cushions.

They talked until the pizza arrived, then they talked through the pizza, and after the pizza. Carly had never met anyone with whom she could talk so easily, and listen to as well. Jake was interested in everything, from global warming to Algerian drum music, to Michaelson's newest fantasy novel. Not only did he talk to her, but he asked her opinions and thoughts and listened carefully to her answers. Carly was used to being treated as an equal among men—but while Jake treated her as an equal as well, there was something more. Something new, unfamiliar. Jake treated her like a woman. It was in his eyes when he looked at her, in his voice, in the way he moved. It made her feel warm, as if she were smiling inside. Murphy, on the old blanket next to Carly's cushion, never stirred. They saved pizza crusts for him, though.

When Jake padded into the kitchen in his socked feet, to get more ice for their sodas, Carly got up to put yet another log on the fire. She glanced out the window and saw that the light in Mrs. Epiphania's window was still on.

They talked their way through another log on the fire. And another. And still another. With each log the fire burned hotter, along with their growing awareness of each other.

Murphy twitched and whimpered in his sleep. "He's dreaming," Carly whispered so she wouldn't wake him up.

"About rabbits maybe? Or great flocks of sheep?"

"Probably about taking a nap."

They talked through a quart of ice cream with chocolate sauce. When the chocolate sauce was gone and the very last log burned down to a glowing red, Carly said, with regret, "It's awfully late. I really need to go home now."

Home. She realized she hadn't thought of her gas station closing down all evening. And by now it was too late to stop by the small grocery store to pick up boxes for packing. Looking for an apartment was going to be incredibly depressing. But it was also an inescapable fact.

Together they gently woke Murphy. "C'mon, my old geezer guy, it's time to wake up so we can go home and go to bed."

Then Jake pulled her to her feet. "I thought you had some errands."

"Too late." She smiled at him, knowing it was a thin smile. "I'll do them later. Nothing important." Hah! She thought of the mountains she'd have to pack. Gramps had lived there for forty years, and then Carly had moved in on top of all his junk. Maybe the bank would agree to let her stay in her house for another month until she found a place to live. She didn't think so. Mr. Sincerely Weisman didn't seem to have a Christmas spirit. Maybe he was the prototype for Ebeneezer Scrooge. Or the Grinch.

She and Jake gathered the paper plates and napkins and empty pizza box. Murphy was finally awake enough to clamp his jaw on a piece of pizza crust. He sat down and chewed. And chewed. And chewed. "Actually, he's gumming it to death," Carly explained. "He doesn't have many teeth left."

She shrugged into her coat and reached into the pocket for her keys.

Then she realized he wasn't looking at her. He was looking up. She followed his gaze to the top of the door jamb. There, tied with a bright red ribbon, was a small sprig of mistletoe.

Mistletoe! The sight of it slugged Jake in the stomach. Where in the world had that come from? How did it get there? He glanced from the offending bit of Christmas greenery, hanging innocently above Carly's head, to Carly's eyes. She'd seen it too, he could tell. And everyone knew what mistletoe meant. He had to kiss her. To not kiss her would be rude. It would be insulting. Besides, the thought of kissing Carly seemed actually quite appealing. He liked her. He liked her a lot.

She started to move away, giving him a chance to refuse gracefully. No way was he going to refuse this opportunity. Who knew when he'd get the chance again. Magically appearing mistletoe wasn't a common occurrence in his reality.

"Ms. Shepherd, you're standing under the mistletoe," he said softly, and quite unnecessarily. Before she could answer, or move farther away, he lowered his head until his lips met hers.

He kept his arm loosely around her as he walked her out to her truck. He wanted to hold on to her, keep his connection to her, for as long as he could. As he helped her hoist Murphy into the truck—front seat this time—he glanced over at Mrs. Epiphania's window. Her light was still on. And he thought he saw her blind twitch.

Chapter Four

How many more times, she thought the next morning as she unlocked the door to her gas station, would she do this? Let's see. Today was December 22. That gave her nine more days to come up with $20,000 to save Shep's. Even if every car in town drove by for a fill-up and engine repairs, she still wouldn't have the money. It was a complete impossibility. In fact, it would take some of Mrs. Epiphania's magic.

Carly turned on the radio. She listened for a moment, then decided she didn't want to hear perky songs about Mama kissing Santa. She snapped it off. She poked at the fake snow on the lovely Megan's McTree. Probably the only snow they'd have this year.

"Morning, Ratchet." She bent down to the cat, who'd leaped up onto the counter to shove his head in her face in a purrful greeting. Face it, Carly, she told herself as she headed into the back room to scoop cat food into Ratchet's bowl. Shep's is going to close. The last of the mom-and-pop gas stations. A true dinosaur and just as extinct. But at least

145

she'd have a job; that guy over in Phillipsburg had been telling her for years that any time she wanted a job he'd hire her in an instant. Thing was, she liked being her own boss. She liked making the decisions.

"Well, my fine furry friends, you can't always get what you want." She hummed the Rolling Stones song. "And we tried real hard. Maybe the Stones were wrong. Maybe we should listen to the Beatles and sing about 'love, love, love.' "

Murphy swished his tail agreeably. Murphy would agree to anything. If he was awake. She handed him a piece of dried cat food. He swished his tail again.

She peeked in the car bay. The '57 Chevy was right where they'd left it, looking elegant and as gorgeous as a swan. She couldn't resist going over to it and running her hand down its side. It sure was a beauty. What she wouldn't give to own this car. This dream of a car. Well, that would take even more of Mrs. Epiphania's magic.

She wondered what Jake was going to do about his car. He'd have to pick it up today, or at least call her to let her know what he was going to do. Either way she'd have a chance to talk to him. The thought of talking to Jake again danced shivery steps up her insides. C'mon, she told herself. Get a grip. You don't even know his last name. So he kissed you under some dumb mistletoe. That doesn't mean anything. But in her heart she wished it did.

She headed back into the front room of the gas station to unlock the cash register and get ready for the day. The joys of being the first one in.

"Hey, where are you going?" she said to Murphy. "Your blanket is over here. Are you getting senile?"

Her geezer dog had tottered over to the Naugahyde recliner and was sniffing interestedly all around it. He seemed almost perky. Something must be truly exciting to keep him awake this long. "What did you find?" She went to look.

146

Murphy looked quite pleased with himself. Murphy had found a purse.

"How did she leave that here?" Carly asked him.

Murphy sat down, tongue lolling. He panted.

Carly opened the purse to look for identification, just to make sure it was Mrs. Epiphania's, though whose else could it have been? She found a nondescript wallet with several small bills, but no identification. There were no pictures of children or grandchildren. There was, however, a small packet of tissues, half a roll of Necco Wafers, and a pencil stub with the point rounded and smooth. There was also a piece of well-worn paper. Carly unfolded it. It was a list, written in thin, spidery handwriting. A long list of names. All of them crossed out, except the last two. Carly and Jake.

What in the world? Images of serial killers flashed through her mind. But somehow, the thought of Mrs. Epiphania as a murderer just didn't do it. Murphy shoved his grizzled head under her hand. She stroked it absently. "Yes, you're a good old guy. What a clever dog you are." She worked her fingers on his ears.

Murphy groaned in pleasure, and drooled on her jeans.

What should she do? She had to get the purse back to Mrs. Epiphania. But there wasn't a phone number. She didn't know Jake's phone number to call him either. She gently shoved Murphy's head off her knee. "Gotta call Directory Assistance. Why don't you go take your nap?"

But information didn't know any Mrs. Epiphania either.

"Guess I'll have to drive it over there later today," she told the cat.

Ratchet gave her his Egyptian cat stare.

"Maybe I'll see Jake. Maybe he'll be out in his yard raking winter leaves or something."

Ratchet blinked knowingly.

He woke late. He lay in bed, staring drowsily up at the ceiling. Images from his dream flowed through him, around him. Images of Carly, beckoning him, a seductive smile on her face. Carly with her long hair unbound and floating around her, around them as he wrapped his arms about her luscious body.

Whoo! He shook his head soundly. Get that thought out of there. He didn't have time for salacious thoughts; he had work to do. Today he was going to install those cabinets in the study downstairs. He also had to think about putting this house on the market. He'd delayed because he had developed a love for this old house. It was amazing how Carly had brought life into it. Almost as if it had become a home last night. Carly with her ancient dog had made this house into a home. How had she done that? he wondered. Suddenly he was aware of his aloneness. Aware that he'd spent most of his life alone.

Enough of this silly stuff, he told himself. This is a new day. Time to get cracking.

His first task for the day was to unload the supplies from his truck, then track down a small Christmas tree for Mrs. Epiphania. He wondered if she had any ornaments. Probably not. However, the discount stores would be crammed with half-priced Christmas decorations today.

He padded into the bathroom and turned on the water in the shower. He stepped into the warm spray and wondered if Carly had a Christmas tree. He closed his eyes and turned his face into the water. Once again, images of Carly floated tantalizingly through his mind. Images of her with him in the shower, her long brown hair, the color of rosewood, out of its long braid and streaming, like a mermaid's. He began to feel good. Whoops! He began to feel too good. He turned the water to cold and grabbed the soap.

Carly raised her hand to knock on Mrs. Epiphania's door. Then she stopped and listened. Voices. Mrs. Epiphania had company.

"You promised, Gabriel." That was Mrs. Epiphania. Waspish rather than whining.

"The deal isn't finished until they have their gift." It was a man's voice, slightly amused, deep and rich. The kind of voice that came with a new luxury car.

"Let them do the rest of it on their own," she snapped. "After two thousand years, I'm tired."

The old woman glared at the archangel in front of her. She'd known him far too long to be intimidated by him any more.

"The young people today use the phrase 'burned out,' I believe." The amusement in his voice was as unmistakable as the twinkle in his eyes. If he were human, he'd be dangerous. "Besides, it's only been one thousand, nine hundred and ninety-eight years."

Her shoulders sagged and she sighed a deep sigh that seemed to come from the center of the earth. "Gabriel"— she tried to keep a whine out of her voice—"I just want to be around people my own age."

"Francesca, no one is your age. I, of course, don't count." He stroked Sweetcakes, who was curled in his arms.

The old woman forgot to feel sorry for herself. "Thank you very much for bringing that up," she said, bristling. "You know what I mean. I thought you had mellowed out sometime around the Middle Ages. For a while there you were a little bit kinder. What happened?"

"I'm sorry I'm not as kind as you thought I was." He grinned his oh-so-charming grin.

"You're just as irritating, though."

"You're the same persnickety Mrs. Epiphania you always were. Still, I have to admit, you've done an excellent job this year. In fact, you've been a godsend. The dog was a stroke of genius." Gabriel fondled the little dog's ears. Sweetcakes flicked out his tongue and licked the archangel's nose. "As soon as these last two are taken care of, you'll be ready to—"

"I'll be ready to buy out my last two years. You promised. As soon as this one is finished, I'm out of here and don't you dare forget it."

The archangel chuckled. "I'm not likely to forget it. You keep reminding me."

Bang! Carly jumped, guilty at being caught listening at doors. But it was only the front door slamming shut. A young man sauntered down the hall toward her. He nodded to Carly, the king deigning to recognize the peasant, then passed on to the last apartment. Probably the young man of last night's party. Carly shifted, the purse bumping her hip. She knocked on Mrs. Epiphania's door.

She heard—what was it? Nothing she'd ever heard before. The fluttering of wings was the closest she could come to a description.

Then Mrs. Epiphania's door opened.

"Carly," the old woman said in surprise. "Come in."

"No, that's okay, Mrs. Epiphania. Um, there was a break at work, so I just came by to return your purse." She held it out. "I guess you left it at the station last night."

"Why, thank you. That was very thoughtful of you." Mrs. Epiphania took the purse without so much as a glance at it. "But please, do come in. I have some cookies straight out of the oven." She muttered something softly.

"Excuse me?"

"What?"

"Did you say something?"

"Why, no. I just said I had cookies straight out of the oven. So please come in and have some."

"I don't want to intrude."

"Nonsense. I'm an old lady living alone. I enjoy company."

"But . . ." Carly hesitated. Then decided to go for it. "I thought you already had company."

150

"What made you think that?" The old woman almost scowled.

"I—I thought I heard voices," Carly said, puzzled at her attitude.

The old woman's face cleared up. "You must have heard the television. One of those odious soap operas. They keep me company. So. No more about voices. Come in and have a cookie. What's your favorite kind?"

"Chocolate chip," Carly said promptly.

"You're in luck. That's the exact kind I made." Without waiting for an answer, the old woman turned and, muttering to herself, led the way.

Carly stepped into the apartment, expecting the smell of cookies. But all that wafted past her was the faint scent of burning candles.

"How is Sweetcakes this morning?"

"Who? Oh. You mean the dog. He's just fine." Mrs. Epiphania waved Carly to a threadbare couch and settled herself in the elderly rocking chair next to the window.

"Is he here?"

"Here? In my apartment?" Stark terror flashed across the woman's face for an instant, then was gone. "Of course. Where else should he be? I'll go get him." She heaved herself up out of her chair and disappeared down the hall, talking to herself all the while in that funny foreign language. Suddenly, there was the glass-shattering sound that passed for a bark. Sweetcakes came scampering into the living room and jerked to a stop. He shrilled at Carly.

"Hello, Sweetcakes. Remember me? We met last night."

The little dog went silent for a moment, then crept cautiously to Carly until he sniffed her fingers. His guard went down and he started into the best-friend's routine. Well, anything was better than his bark.

"You certainly look like you feel fine, don't you?" Carly asked him.

The little dog pranced and danced. The bright black button

151

eyes flashed in excitement. Carly was afraid he'd bark again, so she picked him up and settled him on her lap.

"You like dogs." It was a statement rather than a question. But it was said with approval. "You like dogs and old cars."

"Why, yes, I guess I do." The little dog weighed next to nothing. "How much does this guy eat?"

For a moment the old woman looked flustered. Then she caught herself. "One scoop."

Carly stared at her.

"A little scoop. Very small scoop." Then Mrs. Epiphania got to her feet again. "Speaking of food, let me get you a plate of those cookies. Would you also like a cup of tea?"

"I don't want to put you to any trouble," Carly protested.

"It's no trouble at all. You sit there and wait. Hold Sweetcakes and wait."

Carly absently petted Sweetcakes as she looked around the living room. There was nothing personal on the walls, no photos—no bits of projects. The couch, the rocking chair, a lamp—very minimalist. The thought that someone could live in these stark surroundings was very depressing. She was used to her own house, with the carnage and clutter left from Gramps that still littered the place. But wait. Jake told her that Mrs. Epiphania had just moved in. Maybe she wasn't unpacked yet. Yes, that was it. Carly relaxed.

Hey, wait a minute, she told herself. Something was missing here. There was no television.

Chapter Five

There was a knock on the door.

Before Carly could leap to her feet, Mrs. Epiphania was in the living room, handing her a tray with a platter of cookies and two cups of tea. Carly set Sweetcakes on the floor and took the tray from the old woman.

Sweetcakes scurried after his mistress, shrilling all the way to the door. What a horrible sound, Carly thought. Then she chided herself. He can't help it. He's little.

"Why, Jake. Come in."

Carly felt the blood rush to her face. What if he thought she had come here hoping to see him? What if he thought—

"Carly," Mrs. Epiphania said, sounding almost jovial. "Jake is here. Oh, and see what you've brought. Come in, do come in. Carly and I are just sitting down to tea."

Then he was there. In front of her, with a small Christmas tree in one hand and a large plastic bag in the other. And a smile in his eyes, directed decidedly at her.

"I was picking some things up at the store," he said to

Mrs. Epiphania. "I saw this little tree and thought you probably hadn't had time to get a Christmas tree. So I got it for you." He held out the other bag. "And in here are some decorations." He looked quite pleased with himself.

"Why, Jake," the old woman's voice quavered, and Carly could see that her eyes were suddenly wet. "That is the most thoughtful thing."

"Where do you want it set up? Carly," he added. "How about an impromptu tree-decorating party?"

Carly glanced at her watch. She had about an hour before she had to get back to the gas station. "I'd love to decorate a tree," she said.

She looked around the bare apartment. Where could they put it?

"Do you have a small table we could set it on?" Jake asked. "It *is* a rather short tree."

"Short it may be," Mrs. Epiphania said. "But it's perfectly shaped. I have a small table in the other room. I'll get it."

"No, let me." Carly leaped to her feet. "Where is it?"

Mrs. Epiphania muttered words again. Carly frowned. She wondered what language it was.

"In the bedroom, dear, at the end of the hall."

Soon Carly was back with a small table.

They set the Christmas tree up in front of the living room window, the one that overlooked Jake's backyard, the one with the twitching blinds. They spent a delightful hour arranging ornaments, and icicles, and garlands of glittery stuff. And for the top of the tree Mrs. Epiphania produced an angel—a small angel all glittery and sparkly and dressed in white. Carly hadn't decorated an actual tree for many years.

"Have you decided what to do with your car?" Carly asked Jake when they'd stepped back to admire the tree.

"You know," he said thoughtfully. "You couldn't find anything wrong with it. You're the mechanic. I guess I'll trust your judgment. If it starts shooting off steam again, I'll bring it back to see you. But until then, I'll have to assume that it was some anomaly."

Carly shook her head. "I don't believe in anomalies."

Mrs. Epiphania joined in the conversation. "You say you don't believe in magic either, or miracles." She shook a bony finger under Carly's nose. "You have a lot to learn, missy." But it was said without rancor.

"Yes, well . . ." Carly hedged. "I have to get back to work now. I just wanted to return your purse. Jake, would you like a ride back to pick up your car?"

The ride to Hawthorne Street was too short, Jake thought when they neared the gas station. He had to do something quickly, or he'd be left to drive away, with no reason to see her again. "I don't know what your plans are for the rest of the day, but I plan to put up some cabinets in the study, then some other little jobs. Would you like to go out to dinner with me tonight? Something more than pizza."

Her open smile was like a reward.

This certainly was more than pizza, Carly thought that evening, glad she'd worn a skirt. One of the few she owned. It was also much more pleasant than packing, or apartment hunting. She'd go through the for-rent listings in the paper tomorrow. Then she'd get lots of boxes and start packing up. But tonight was not going to be spoiled by thoughts of Shep's going under. The restaurant was in a restored Victorian mansion. Their table was set up in what had probably been the living room. The fireplace boasted a cheerful fire. The other four tables in the room were all mismatched, the chairs equally individual, which gave the place a quaint charm.

"Jake, how good to see you again!" The hostess hurried over to their table, a warm smile on her friendly face. "It's been too long!"

Jake stood to greet the woman with a hug. "Marnie," he

said, "I'd like you to meet my friend Carly. Carly is a top-notch mechanic. Carly, this is Marnie Maxwell, who owns this lovely establishment." He said the words with great sincerity and affection.

"Hello, Carly," the woman said warmly. "If this place is lovely, Jake is one of the folks I have to thank."

Carly looked a question at Jake. It was caught by Marnie. "Yes, he worked on the restorations. One of the first places he did. I like to think that my restaurant got him started in his business."

"I worked on this place part-time while I was in school," Jake added. "Marnie's right. It was my first experience with restorations. I learned a lot from it. The guy who was in charge of the project taught me a lot."

"He taught you the mechanics, dear boy, but you already had a feel for the artistry involved. No one can teach you the intuitive part." The woman chuckled. "It's like cooking. You can learn the mechanics, but you can't learn the art."

"You, Marnie, are a great artist," Jake teased.

"You are a flatterer," the woman said with a broad grin and a sparkle in her eyes. "However, you are right. Carly, it is a pleasure to meet you. My Christmas gift to you both this evening is dessert on the house."

The next day, when Carly got to work, there was an elderly Oldsmobile Delta 88 waiting for her. "Mr. Kent dropped off his land yacht for an oil change and a check-up," Bill said as she looked at the appointment book. "He said he'd already talked to you about it."

Carly nodded. "Yeah. Last week. I guess I forgot to put it in the book."

Bill looked at her sharply. "I guess you were thinking of other things?"

"Guess so," she said. Other things, she thought, like the sincerity of Mr. Jacob Weisman II. She had to tell Bill that Shep's was closing. She was not looking forward to that.

Not a bit. Bill was as much a part of Shep's as Carly was. Now she pointed to the Olds and shrugged apologetically. "Sorry, Bill."

"No problem. I figured that we'd be able to squeeze Mr. Kent in. We have room. Most people don't do big stuff this time of year. Sort of like elective surgery, I guess."

The Christmas bells on the door tinkled merrily. Carly looked up. It was Mrs. Farragut dropping off her car for a new muffler. It was Monday morning at Shep's. Maybe Keith over in Phillipsburg would be willing to take Bill on, also. Bill was a good mechanic, steady and reliable. And as honest as the new day. Of course, Bill had worked under Gramps. Gramps was a stickler for doing what needed to be done for the car, not for the till.

Carly settled Mr. Kent's Olds on the rack to change the oil. She'd been thinking of herself all this time. Wondering what *she* would do when Shep's closed. What about Bill? He had a wife and two kids. What about Richie? He was saving for college, and he had his optimistic girlfriend to squire around town. This might not be important in the big scheme of things—but to a high school senior, a good part-time job was important. And Tom, who worked the cash register during the day. He went to night school and needed a day job where he could study when business was slow.

She gathered tools for changing oil and headed under the Olds. She pulled the plug on the old oil and watched it drain out. Good color. Not corrupted by coolant. She replaced the plug and poured the used oil in the holding drum. Not only Bill and Richie and Tom, but what about Mr. Kent? He'd been coming to Shep's for forty years. Every week for a fill-up, and every six months for an oil change, right as rain. And Fred Paynter with his old Ford truck, and all the other regular customers. Shep's was the only gas station in this neighborhood. Who knew what Mr. Sincerely Weisman wanted to do with this land. Hawthorne Street wasn't exactly prime real estate. Hawthorne Street was on the edge of nowhere. Still, the new highway that surrounded Franklin was right across the cornfield, so there would be easy access, if there was something to have access to. No, Hawthorne Street was part of a fading neighborhood of mostly elderly residents and blue-collar families with young children. Most of them Carly knew by name. She was one of them. So was Bill; so was Richie. They liked coming to a gas station where everyone knew their names.

Something pushed against her legs. She looked down.

"Hello, Ratchet, old guy. How are you this morning?"

Ratchet assumed his Egyptian Cat pose and stared at her, unblinking. Ratchet was a survivor. He'd arrived at Shep's one winter evening long ago, dirty and hungry. She'd fed him and he'd stayed. There were dozens of gas stations in Franklin, but Ratchet had chosen the one where he was loved and appreciated.

The thought hit her like a bolt. Yes, there were dozens of gas stations in Franklin. There were also dozens of banks. All right, maybe not dozens, but at least sixes. She'd banked at Weisman's forever because that was where Gramps had started their account. But that didn't mean she couldn't apply to a different bank for a loan.

Excitement surged through her. She could do this. She could apply to some other bank for a $20,000 loan. Take that! Mr. Sincerely Weisman. A plague on all your houses. She'd been rolling over and playing dead. She'd given up without a fight. But she didn't have to. She could find a bank that would feed her—as she'd fed Ratchet.

But first, she had to finish changing the oil on Mr. Kent's Olds. His old Olds, she joked to herself. She patted Ratchet on his furry head, picked up her filter wrench, and turned back to the underside of the car. "Hey, Bill," she called. "I need to go out for a bit this afternoon. Do you think you could close for me today?"

* * *

Hawthorne Street, Jake thought to the accompaniment of the scritching of the sanding block. He was repairing the plaster. The houses on Hawthorne probably had plaster walls also. What would it take to restore an entire street? He'd need more help, of course. And money. The city had other gentrified areas, why not Hawthorne Street? Plans and possibilities whirled and danced in his mind as he worked on the plaster.

First thing would be the gas station. It could be so charming, the steeply pitched roof and the window boxes. He wondered what had been planted in them originally. Petunias maybe? Window boxes on a gas station. He chuckled to himself. We'd certainly come a long way, baby. But we'd also lost something on the way. Why shouldn't we have flowers in a window box at a gas station?

He had just finished sanding down the last plaster patch in the study when there was a knock at the front door. He jumped lightly off the step stool into a splash of early afternoon sun and dropped the sanding block onto the pile of rags. He brushed his dusty hands off on his jeans, though they were covered with so much plaster dust already that he didn't think it did much good. Then he went to answer the door.

"Hello, Jake," said Mrs. Epiphania brightly.

He thought her brightness was a little forced. "Come in."

"I just dropped by to see how you're doing. I brought you some gingersnaps. You said they were your favorite kind of cookie." She held out a plate. Jake took it. The plate was still warm and the fragrance of ginger wafted enticingly around him.

"Thank you," he said, closing his eyes to take in more of the gingery scent. "They smell wonderful."

"Put them in the kitchen so they can cool off. They're too hot to eat just now," Mrs. Epiphania ordered.

She followed him into the kitchen.

"You've done an excellent job here, Jake. But it's a big house for just one person."

"Oh, I'm not keeping this house, Mrs. Epiphania," Jake hastened to say. "I'm going to put it on the market and sell it."

She looked at him steadily for a moment. Jake squirmed. His parochial school teacher, Sister Mary Margaret, used to look at him the same way. It wasn't a lie, he told himself. Not exactly. He intended to put the house on the market, he really did. He should have listed it before now. It was just that he liked this house. He liked it more than any other house he'd ever worked on. He'd even imagined living here permanently. But he couldn't. Mrs. Epiphania was right. It was too big for one person.

"I don't think so, Jake," Mrs. Epiphania said. "You have a lovely backyard, perfect for children to play in. I think you should stay here. Right here in this house. You should get married."

Jake rubbed the wood of a kitchen shelf. It was worn and old, yet as warm and friendly as wood could be. It felt right in his hand. He leaned against the old painted iron sink, stuck his hands in his pockets, and faced the old woman. She was staring intensely at him, as if willing him to accept her words. Well, the best way to deal with difficult people, he'd learned from dealing with his father, was if you couldn't avoid them, then agree with them. "You may be right," he said making his tone as agreeable as he could. "This is a wonderful house. The backyard is perfect for children. Maybe I should get married. I'll think about it."

She snorted. "Don't try to brush me off, young Jake Weisman," she snapped. "I know that trick. I've even used it a few times myself." She fixed him with her eyes. "I've lived longer than you'll ever live. And I tell you that you need to get married and have children. In this house." She thumped the heel of her hand on the table. "And what's more, I think you should marry Carly Shepherd."

Chapter Six

Marry Carly Shepherd! The thought swirled around and around in front of him. Like a blizzard of swirling snow and wind. He looked over at Mrs. Epiphania. She was sitting peacefully, innocently, at his table, as if she'd not just detonated a bomb.

"Marry Carly Shepherd?" he asked her, incredulous. "I barely know her."

"Nevertheless," the old woman said calmly, "she is the person you need to marry." Then her shoulders sagged, and suddenly Mrs. Epiphania looked as old as time itself. "Please, Jake, take my word for it. Marry the girl. You will be very happy together."

He moved over to the table, crouched down in front of her, took her hands in his, and looked into her eyes. Carly was right, he realized. Her eyes did look ancient. He wondered why he hadn't noticed it before.

"Mrs. Epiphania," he said gently. Then he stopped. What could he say to her? She was obviously off her rocker. Still,

161

she did have an odd sort of charm. He didn't want to upset her.

"Mrs. Epiphania," he began again. "I appreciate your interest in my life, but I simply can't go up to a woman I barely know and ask her to marry me."

"Why not?" she asked him. "She might say yes, and then you'll be all set."

"Because . . ." he said kindly. "Because I just can't. These things take time. It takes time to get to know if you're suited to someone, to know if someone is suited to you."

"But you *are* suited, and time is something that I don't have," she whispered, her voice stark and pained.

She didn't have? Was she dying? Was this some sort of strange deathbed wish? He was becoming decidedly uncomfortable with the whole thing. "Look," he said at last, "I'll think about it. All right? I won't make promises, but I'll think about it."

Her gaze searched his, piercing, probing, peeking into the corners of his intentions. "Well then, I guess I'll have to be satisfied with that."

By late that afternoon, slumped on a park bench, all Carly's enthusiasm had drained away to despair. She'd visited every bank in Franklin, filled out more forms than she'd ever known existed, and been turned down over and over and over. Evidently banks didn't like female mechanics, even though, thanks to GoJo Orange with Pumice, she'd gotten every smidge of grease off her hands. She'd even worn a skirt. Sure, it was out of style, but at least there weren't any runs in her stockings. Still, the loan officers she'd talked to weren't impressed. So much for trying to play the femme fatale.

And so much for putting things off. She would tell Bill and the others tomorrow. She heaved herself up off the park bench and shoved her hands into the pockets of her parka.

Slowly she trudged back down the street to the small grocery store.

She ordered a double-dip chocolate ice cream cone and then wandered over to the newspaper rack and picked up today's edition. Holding the paper under one arm and the cone in one hand, she wrestled with her unfamiliar purse and finally came up with her money.

Five minutes later she sat in her parked truck with the paper, her ice cream cone, and Murphy. Of course, Murphy was asleep. She got a pen out of the purse. Here goes nothing, she told herself. She opened the paper to the classifieds and found her way to the for-rent section. It looked dismally meager.

The old woman sat in her rocking chair and rocked. And thought. And rocked. And thought. And rocked some more. Her time was almost up. She had only a handful of days to help Jake and Carly fall in love. It should have been so easy. Surely people believed in love at first sight nowadays. Of course, neither of them was exactly looking for a soul mate. Carly was worried about her gas station and—That was it! Mrs. Epiphania stuck her foot out and stopped her chair in mid-rock. Get rid of the gas station problem and Carly would have no reason not to fall in love with Jake. After all, he was good-looking, had a job, and he was nice. Besides, she was supposed to fall in love with him.

So, how to go about fixing the gas station problem? She couldn't make the gas station itself disappear. She was only able to do magic things directly related to Carly and Jake's falling in love. Making a car appear to run out of gas, making steam come out of it, even conjuring up a little dog—those were needed to get them together. But making something as large as a gas station disappear was something else. It would affect too many people. Besides, Carly would probably be upset if her gas station went *poof*. Even if one were able to do great magic like that, it wouldn't be approved. Magic running rampantly amok in the world would not be a pretty sight. Why, it would be anarchy. It would be chaos. No, there had to be reason to any magic that was done. It needed to be tidy. Mrs. Epiphania had always liked things reasonable and tidy. This was what had gotten her into this whole mess in the first place.

Mrs. Epiphania started her rocking again. She didn't have much time left. The old woman rocked. And thought. And rocked. And thought.

Evidently, thought Carly, the landlords of Franklin were, down to the last lord, engaged in a plot to deny residence to any tenant with a cat and a dog. Even a geezer dog like Murphy. She refolded the rustling newspaper. There was no apartment she could rent. No room at any inn.

Her spirits at an all-time low, Carly turned the key in the ignition. The truck came to life. She turned to look over her shoulder out the back window as she clutched and shifted into reverse.

She had fully intended to go home, to start packing. To call the guy over in Phillipsburg to ask if he needed a couple of good mechanics. But somehow she found herself pulling into Jake's driveway.

He heard a car pull up into the driveway. He glanced out the window. It was Carly. A strange sort of contentment surged through him as he watched her help Murphy out of the truck. He felt he could watch her forever.

He got to the front door before she had even gotten Murphy across the lawn. Not difficult to do, since Murphy moved at geezer speed. Ignoring the fact that the temperature was hovering around the freezing mark, he went outside into it.

He leapt down the steps to join her on her way up the walk. "Hi." Brrrr—he wrapped his hands around himself. The weather forecasters were wrong again. It was colder than freezing.

"Hi."

Then he noticed her face, and all thoughts of being cold were forgotten. Her face was drawn and tired. He wondered if something was wrong. What a dumb question, he told himself. Of course something was wrong, or else she wouldn't look like that.

"I wondered if you might like to go out for a burger or something," she asked before he could speak.

"Sure," he agreed. "What's the occasion?"

"No occasion. Just supper." But she kept her eyes on Murphy, who was investigating a low branch on a bush. The dog decided to leave his own message. "I've been out doing business stuff all afternoon and didn't have the energy to go home and cook. So I thought you might like to go out for a burger with me."

He looked at her carefully, for any cracks that might let some light into her mood. He couldn't find any. She was as closed as an oak door.

"It'll take me a few minutes to finish what I'm doing, then I need to change clothes so you're not embarrassed to be seen in public with me. Come on in."

He helped her shepherd Murphy up the steps. "You can do it, old guy," they said to bolster his confidence. It did take him a few starts, but finally he was wagging his tail at the top. No Everest climber had ever looked more proud.

He led her, with her dog, into the house. She smelled the fine-old-house scent again. The smell of well-taken-care-of wood. She entered another world, a world of family and security. Except that this world was not hers.

After his great climb up the steps, Murphy wandered into the dining room and around it until he found the heating vent. "Wait a minute, Murphy," Jake said.

Murphy raised his head, his old eyes looking around in the direction of Jake's voice. But Jake was there with the old blanket, which he folded and put on the floor by the vent. "There you go, old guy."

165

Murphy huffed and slowly waved his tail in thanks; then, with a great groan, he sank down onto the blanket. He closed his eyes.

"He's going to take a nap," Carly told Jake unnecessarily.

"After such exertion he probably needs one," he agreed. He helped her off with her parka and hung it in the closet. She wasn't used to men helping her with her coat. She liked it. She also liked the care he took with Murphy. "Thank you for being so considerate," she told him.

He smiled slightly. "It's no big deal."

"It is a big deal. And I—we—appreciate it. Now, what are you doing today?" she asked, more to make conversation than anything else. She didn't want to be alone with her thoughts right now. There was so much to do, so many decisions to make, that she needed some time away from it all before she was ready to sit down and face it.

"Working on plaster." He gestured to his jeans.

"Dirty work?" she guessed.

"The worst." But his grin was like a sun shining on her gloomy day.

"What do you do with plaster?"

"Lots of things. Cracks have to be repaired before I can paint. I like to do one room at a time; then I don't get bored doing the cracks in an entire house."

He led her farther into the dining room. "See here." He motioned her over to the wall. As he pointed out the patches he'd done, she was conscious of his nearness. She had the sudden urge to kiss him. That would be dumb, she told herself. Sure, he kissed you once, but don't think that means he is ready to jump your bones every time he sees you. Don't think that means he even wants to jump your bones at all. After all, mistletoe at Christmas is so common it's a cliché. It doesn't mean beans.

At least, that was what she told herself.

"Then you have to sand it down so it's smooth."

She wrenched her thoughts back to his explanation.

166

"Here, feel this patch. It's as smooth as silk."

She reached up a hand to feel the patch on the wall. It was cool and hard and smooth—yes, it was as smooth as silk. She thought of something else that was hard and smooth as silk.

"It's ready for the next step," he told her.

Where was her mind today? She cleared her throat. "What's that?"

"Coat of primer, then paint. But I usually don't paint until I've finished the whole house."

"Why is that?" she asked, struggling to keep her mind on his explanations and out of his pants.

"Sometimes I sell a house before it's painted. Then the buyers can choose their own colors." Was that a bit of wistfulness she heard in his voice?

"It's too bad you have to sell this house," she said. Then she realized she'd matched his wistful tone. "It's lovely. If I ever have a million dollars fall into my lap, I'll buy a house just like this." She laughed at herself. "Of course, I don't believe in magic or miracles, so—" She shrugged. "I guess it's just a dream."

"But a nice one," he said. His voice was warm, even though his hands continued to stroke the silky patch on the wall. "It's a nice dream. There's a big backyard for Murphy to explore. If he woke up."

"And those cupboards in the hall upstairs," she added. "And that glorious bathtub." She caught a vision of Jake with her in that bathtub. "Not to mention the fireplace," she hastily added. But the fireplace also had sensual visions attached to it. "And the window seats." Window seats were probably safe. At least with window seats she didn't have any lascivious images of Jake dancing in her mind. "Window seats are always great for a rainy day. At least, that's what I've always imagined." Reminded of the other things she'd just imagined, her face felt hot.

"You've imagined exactly right," he said, grinning at her.

167

"Window seats are a good thing to have on a rainy afternoon."

There were any number of things that would be good on a rainy afternoon, she thought as she looked into his grin. Then the grin turned to something else that would be good on a rainy day. And even on a day when it wasn't raining. He came closer and closer to her. Oh-so-slowly closer. Carly felt her eyes widen, her breathing deepen, her pulse quicken. She leaned toward him to meet him halfway. And meet they did. Their lips first, then their hands and arms, then their whole selves. They met and greeted, welcomed, with great joy.

Suddenly, there was a knock on the front door. Murphy, from his spot next to the heater vent, did not stir.

"Who could that be?" Jake asked. "It's been like Grand Central Station around here today."

It was a very distinguished-looking gentleman. A regular suit. A Fleetwood Brougham Cadillac, she bet herself. She fought an urge to peek out the window into the driveway to see if she was right.

Then she caught sight of Jake. Though he stood at the door, he did not look pleased to see this man. His posture had stiffened noticeably, and much of the life in him had gone to some hidden place.

"Hello, Dad." he said.

Dad? she thought. Evidently Jake did not like his father.

The suit turned his gaze on her and she was confronted by eyes of ice. She did not like Jake's father either.

"Father," Jake was saying. "I'd like you to meet my friend Carly Shepherd."

The suit nodded distantly at her. Carly felt suddenly conscious that her skirt was ten years old. But Jake was still speaking.

"Carly, this is my father, Jacob Weisman."

Jacob Weisman? Carly almost gasped. The Jacob Weisman who wrote her The Letter? This was the Jacob Weisman who was responsible for her losing Shep's? And he was Jake's father? Jake, short for Jacob. It hit her like the first stone.

Chapter Seven

"Your last name is Weisman?" she asked. Jake watched her face go white and still.

"Yes. I'm a third. My father is a second."

She didn't move for what seemed like an eternity. Then she said, "I'm sorry, Jake. There's something I really must do." She turned slightly to his father. "It was sincerely nice to meet you, Mr. Weisman."

Before he could react, she'd roused Murphy, quickly for once, and was opening the closet door to find her coat. In two strides Jake was at her side, his father forgotten. "Are you all right, Carly?" he whispered. "Is something the matter?"

"No," she muttered to him as she yanked her parka off the hanger. "I'll see you 'round. Let's go, Murph."

Then she was gone. Leaving him, bewildered, holding the door open.

"For goodness sake, Jake." His father's tone was strident. "Close the door. You don't live in a barn, you know."

"Yes, sir," he answered automatically. He closed the door and leaned against it. What had just happened?

"Who was that strange person?" his father asked. "And what was she doing here?"

Jake noticed that his father particularly ignored the fact that Murphy had been here too. His father had always ignored dogs and cats, as if they were beneath his notice. No. Not as if. His father felt cats and dogs *were* beneath his notice.

"Father, remember the summer I wanted a puppy?" Jake was still leaning against the front door. "More than anything else I wanted a puppy. Do you remember that?"

"Of course. You drove us all mad with your begging." His father was walking around, surveying the room. Jake felt he was looking for some sign of a shoddy job.

"And you wouldn't let me have one," he said. "A puppy. Even though Mom would have."

"You wouldn't have taken care of it." His father peered closely at the wood surrounding one of the window seats. "Nice wood. Besides, animals don't belong in the house. They make too much mess."

Jake decided he'd get a dog. Tomorrow. Maybe tonight. Maybe a German Shepherd like Murphy. Except younger. That wouldn't be difficult. In all probability every canine on earth was younger than Murphy. Yes, a dog was exactly what he needed, and was something he'd always wanted. But there was time to get a dog. Right now he had to deal with his father. He shoved away from the door.

"So, Father, what brings you out on a cold night like tonight? Certainly not to see the house." He congratulated himself for keeping all traces of sarcasm out of his tone.

"Your mother wants to see you."

But you don't, Jake added silently.

"She is having some sort of party for New Year's," his father continued. "When we get back from our trip. She would like you to attend. You're to dress appropriately."

171

Jake would have bet any amount that the last command was not from his mother at all. "I'll call Mom tomorrow and discuss it with her."

His father caught sight of Murphy's blanket. "What did you say that person's name was?" he asked.

"Carly Shepherd."

"Carly Shepherd. Carly Shepherd." He nodded. "Ah, yes. Now I remember. She runs a dilapidated gas station by the old road."

"Hawthorne Street," Jake corrected. How did his father know where Carly's gas station was? "She owns the gas station. She inherited it from her grandfather." Why did he always feel that he was on the defensive when he talked to his father? Probably because he was.

"Not for long," his father said, gazing into the butler's pantry, up all the rows of shelves. "Hawthorne Street will be turned into something else. Quite different."

"How do you know?"

"I'm a banker, Jake. I know these things. You would too if you'd joined the bank instead of playing craftsman. Put that expensive education of yours to work."

It was a longtime point of disagreement between them. But today, Jake didn't want to play. "What do you mean about Hawthorne Street?" he persisted.

His father turned a cold stare on him. "I have plans for Hawthorne Street. Plans that I am not at liberty to discuss. With you." He dusted his hands, which had not touched a thing. "Well, I've delivered your mother's message. Be sure you are dressed appropriately for your mother's party."

Jake was only minimally aware that his father was leaving. He was, however, very aware of the kinds of plans his father made. They usually included demolition equipment and parking lots. The thought of Hawthorne Street's quaint houses and tall trees meeting the wrecking ball sent rivers of resentment raging through him. This was everything he was

172

struggling to correct. Ripping out the old and putting up the new. Not a better new, either.

Take this house. It had been a rental property for several years. It had been abused by a series of revolving tenants. Consequently the selling price had been low. The house that had been next door, a house with a similar history, had been torn down and a small apartment building put up in its place. This house had been on the same path when he'd found it. Poor old abused, mistreated house. So much work to do to fix it up. But now he was returning it to its former beauty and elegance.

The houses on Hawthorne Street would be torn down without a chance. Not only the houses, he realized. The gas station. Shep's. Did Carly know this was happening? Was that why she'd bolted when she met his father?

He had to find her, explain to her.

Jake grabbed his coat out of the closet, slung it over his shoulder, and hurried through the house to the kitchen, where his keys hung on a hook by the back door.

Outside was bitter cold. He shoved his arms into the sleeves of his coat as he hustled out to the '57 Chevy. As a car it was impractical, he supposed, but he was fond of it.

"Jake, there you are."

"Oh, hi, Mrs. Epiphania. I'm in kind of a hurry."

"You are on your way to see Carly?" she asked. "I have something I must tell you first."

He really didn't have time for her now, he thought in irritation. "What is it?"

"I can't talk to you here," she said. "It is too cold. You come into my apartment. I will tell you there."

No. At least he wanted to tell her no. "All right," he found himself saying. Somehow he couldn't manage to pull himself away from the elderly woman.

"Your Carly," she started. "Your Carly is in a bit of

173

trouble. She told me about it the other evening, when you were getting gasoline.''

''What trouble?'' Jake began to have a very bad feeling about this.

''Her grandfather borrowed some money from your father's bank for some machinery. Now the bank wants the money back. If Carly does not give it to them by the end of the month, they will take her gas station.'' She frowned. ''Why would a bank want a gas station?''

Suddenly it was all clear. Carly knew his father's name because she owed the bank money. His father knew who she was because he wanted her land. Not the gas station itself, but the land. Well, Jake wanted the gas station also. Not for the land, but for the building itself. Why, it was practically a historical landmark. It should be restored.

''How much money does she owe the bank?'' he asked. ''Do you know?''

Mrs. Epiphania looked very earnest. ''Twenty thousand dollars.''

Jake's shoulders slumped. That was more money than he could put his hands on right now. Still, there had to be another way.

''Jake, you are thinking of helping her?''

''Not only Carly, Mrs. Epiphania. I've been thinking of renovating the whole street. Starting with Shep's.''

''But how will this help Carly?'' the old woman persisted.

''If I can come up with the money, I can pay off my father's bank. Then the gas station will stay in business. And I can renovate it.'' It was the obvious solution. There was only one flaw. ''All I need to do is find the money.''

The old woman rocked in her chair and smiled serenely at him. ''This is no problem. You will sell me your car.''

He frowned. ''My car?''

''Yes. It is an antique, is it not? What would be more fitting for an antique like myself than an antique car? Is not twenty thousand dollars the right price for a car such as yours?''

''Well, yes, it would be about right.'' He thought for a moment. ''Of course, the seats haven't been restored yet, and the—But Mrs. Epiphania, do you know how to drive?''

''No. But I could learn. Even at my age one can still learn a thing or two. These new cars, bah. They are ugly. Your car is a true classic. I would like to drive around in a true classic.''

''I can't let you buy my car.''

''Why not? You said yourself that you restore cars and then sell them. Like you do your houses. Why not sell this car to me?'' She thrust out her pointy chin, looking for all the world like the Wicked Witch of the West wearing clothes from a thrift store.

''Because an antique car requires special maintenance.''

''You can do the maintenance. Or Carly can.''

''It requires special gasoline additives.''

''You have such additives. I can have them too.''

He stared at her. ''You're serious.''

She smiled back. It was a tense smile. ''You don't know how serious I am.''

''You really have twenty thousand dollars?''

''I will get it.'' She stood up.

''No, wait.'' He held up his hand. ''I have to think about this. You have to think about this. People don't go around just buying antique cars on the spur of the moment.''

Her eyes looked suddenly very old. ''Jake. Dear Jake. I have been thinking of nothing else for a very long time. Now, finally, what I want most is so close, I can reach out and almost touch it. Please. Please don't take it away from me now.''

Jake had the feeling she was talking to someone else, not to him at all. ''This car means that much to you?'' he asked at last.

She nodded slowly, as if she were so tired that it was all

she could do. "Yes, Jake. It means that much to me."

He searched her eyes for any hesitancy, any at all. He could find none.

"All right, then. I'll sell you my car, my '57 Chevy, for twenty thousand dollars."

The old woman closed her eyes and nodded again, slowly, the ghost of a smile on her lips. "Thank you, Jake." He thought he could see tears under her eyelids. "There is only one condition."

"What's that?"

"You must use the money to pay off Carly's loan." Her eyes jerked open. "Promise me this," she said solemnly. "That the money will be used to pay off the loan."

"I promise," he said matching her solemn tone.

"Good. Then wait here. I will get you the money."

Jake reached out to help her out of the rocking chair. "Thank you, Jake," she said. "You are very considerate of an old woman." She disappeared down the hall muttering to herself.

Jake wondered if he was doing the right thing. He wondered if Mrs. Epiphania would even be able to get a driver's license. He had no idea how old she was. What if she had trouble driving the car? What if she were in an accident because she was too frail to steer the car or something? He was just about to follow her to call off the deal when there was a glass-shattering blast of fur hurtling down the hall toward him.

"Sweetcakes."

The little dog came to a stop in front of him, fixed a beady black eye on him, and stared.

"How are you today, Sweetcakes?"

Sweetcakes came a step closer, then another. Then another. Finally he was close enough to sniff Jake's work boots. Evidently he passed muster, for the little dog threw himself at Jake with great glee. Jake discovered that the little guy really was sort of cute.

"You think I'm some sort of long-lost best friend, do you?"

"Sweetcakes knows a good person when he meets him," came Mrs. Epiphania's voice. Jake looked up, and there was the old woman in front of him holding out a stack of green bills.

"Twenty thousand dollars."

Jake gasped. "You keep that kind of money just lying around your house?"

The old woman chuckled. It was a sound that needed oiling. As if she hadn't laughed for a very long time. "I would hardly say it was just lying around. Still, if I kept my money in a bank I would not have had it to give to you now, would I? Go on. Take it. In payment for the car. Remember?"

"Yes," Jake said, uncertainly. "I remember." He tentatively reached out and took the money. Twenty thousand dollars was a very thick wad of bills.

"You'd better count it. Make sure it's all there."

He looked down at the bills. They seemed to all be hundreds. This would take a few minutes. He looked up again at the old woman.

"Go on. Count it."

He did. Sure enough, it was twenty thousand dollars.

"Oh dear. I almost forgot," she said when he was finished counting. "You were on your way to visit Carly when I interrupted you. You were going to drive your car. Which is now my car."

Jake nodded.

"I will tell you. Since I interrupted you, why don't you go ahead and use the car tonight. You can give me my first driving lesson tomorrow."

For a long moment, Jake stood, staring at the money in his hand. Then a thought occurred to him. "What if Carly won't take it?"

The old woman smiled a mysterious smile. "She wants

177

her gas station. You must give the money to her in a way that she will accept it. Now go. My Sweetcakes and I must go to sleep if we are to be rested for our driving lesson tomorrow.''

Chapter Eight

Carly sat all scrunched into the corner of her sagging couch, staring morosely at the cheerfully blinking Christmas lights that festooned her antique gas pump. So Jake was Jacob Weisman III. The son of her all-time greatest enemy. And she'd started to fall in love with him, too. Had his father sent him to seduce the owner of a piece of land? Was she just so much meat to him? Unlike his father, Jake had seemed so sincere. His father—now there was a trip of a man. Like solid ice. And she'd been right about the Fleetwood Brougham Cadillac. It had been parked in the driveway, some distance from her truck and the Chevy. As if it, too, were snubbing her, looking down its long nose at her. Hah! Well, it could look down its nose all it wanted. She knew what its engine looked like on the inside.

From beside her on the couch, Murphy lifted his head. "What's the matter, guy? What's gotten you all excited?"

Then she heard it. The purr of a '57 Chevy. Pulling up in front of her house. She heard a car door thunk shut. She heard steps coming up her sidewalk. Steps made by work boots. No. She didn't want to see him. Not now. Didn't want him to see her. Not in her oldest comfort clothes. But it was too late.

Murphy managed to clamber off the couch and totter over to the door, where he stood swishing his tail. Waiting to see someone he liked. How could she disappoint Murphy? She couldn't.

She took a few deep breaths. Steadied herself. When the knock sounded on the door, she was ready. She was composed. She was calm.

She opened the door. "Hello, Jake." It was almost the same tone his father had used.

"Hello, Carly." His voice was almost as formal. "May I come in?"

"I suppose so." She pretended she didn't care one way or the other. She stood away from the door, not exactly inviting him in, but not preventing it either.

He came in.

"What is that?" he asked, pointing, forgetting to be formal.

She was used to that question. She'd heard it ever since she could remember. She didn't forget to be formal. "It's a Christmas gas pump."

"A Christmas gas pump?"

"Yes."

"Instead of a tree?"

"Yes."

"You even put presents around it?"

"Yes. I do every year."

She wasn't going to make this easy for him. Even if she really had died inside, she wouldn't let him see it.

"Carly . . . um, could we sit down, or something?" Without waiting for her answer, he moved into her small living room, toward her sagging couch. He settled in and bent down to pet Murphy. "Hiya, old guy. How are you, hmm?"

Murphy drooled on his pants leg. Jake didn't seem to mind.

Carly perched on the edge of a straight chair she'd pulled over from the dining room table. She didn't utter a word. He was the one who had come to her. Let him say what he wanted to say. She wouldn't give him anything else.

But Jake was looking around her home. He cocked his head to try to read the titles of the books crammed into the small bookshelf. They were engine manuals, mostly. But then his gaze left the books and went up the walls to the ceiling. She watched as his gaze moved on along the ceiling over to the dining room, then down the walls, where it was snagged by the table. The dining room table was covered with parts to an engine she was rebuilding in her spare time. Then he leaned slightly so he could see into her kitchen. Her supper, barely nibbled at, on a plate she'd left on the counter, the curtains at the small window. But he seemed to be looking at the floor. Then he leaned back to move his gaze to her. She waited. She didn't have long.

"I guess you were surprised by my father today," he said apologetically. "I mean, I guess you were surprised to learn that I'm a Weisman."

She stopped herself from cringing at the name. "Yes." She'd give him that small answer. He already knew it anyway.

He continued to scratch Murphy on the head, gently, rhythmically. "When I was little I wanted a puppy. More than anything I wanted a puppy. But my father wouldn't let me have one. All the time I was growing up, I had to do what he wanted me to do. I didn't dare show rebellion. He bought me a car, I drove it. He chose my college, I went. I even majored in business, like he wanted me to." He shot her a shy smile. "But by majoring in business I was able to stay in school and study what I really wanted to learn. When I graduated I had a terrific education. He expected me to join the bank. But I didn't. I went to work for a building company. He threatened to cut me out of his will. But I had an inheritance from my grandmother that he wasn't able to touch.'' His grin was a bit more secure now. ''It was with another bank. Father was livid. My grandmother had bested him and he knew it.''

''What does this have to do with me?''

The grin left his face. Now he looked sober and solemn. ''I want you to know that I'm not like him. I care about things he doesn't even see. I look at buildings and I see what they are, how I can make them better, not how much money I can make by tearing them down and putting up movie theaters.''

''What about your mother?'' She almost bit her tongue off for asking, but she was curious.

''She's never stood up to him overtly. But I think she approves of me.''

How sad, she thought, that he didn't *know* of his mother's approval. She realized that her formality was slipping. She hiked it back up to where it belonged. ''Still, what does this have to do with me?''

He looked down at Murphy's head on his knee, continuing to pet the old geezer dog. Murphy's eyes were closed and he was breathing heavily. Maybe he was asleep standing up.

''I know that you owe my father's bank twenty thousand dollars and that my father has called in the loan. I also know that you have until the end of the month to repay it or your gas station is forfeit.''

She startled. How did he—? But of course, it must be easy for him to find out information from his father's bank.

''Mrs. Epiphania told me a little while ago. She said you'd told her.''

Oh, Carly told herself. So this is what comes of telling complete strangers your business.

''I have a business proposition for you.''

''For me?'' Again she was startled into forgetting to be formal.

"Yes." Now it was his turn, evidently, to wait her out.

She counted to ten before she absolutely had to know what it was. "So what is your business proposition?"

"I will lend you twenty thousand dollars to pay off that loan. You will repay me according to a schedule and at a rate we'll come to by mutual agreement."

"And?" There had to be more than this.

His eyes twinkled merrily. "And you'll stop giving me this ice maiden treatment."

She could only stare at him. "Are you serious?"

He grinned. "Yes. I don't like the icy thing at all. Doesn't suit you."

"No, I mean serious about lending me the money?"

"Serious as I can be."

"Why?" She was baffled. People didn't go around lending people twenty thousand dollars for nothing.

"I don't want your gas station to end up as a parking lot to an upscale shopping center with a million-plex movie theater. I happen to like old buildings. I want to keep them around. I like your gas station. I also like the other houses on your street. Look." He stood up and moved over to the window to point. "Come here. Look. C'mon. Look."

She got up, reluctantly, and moved closer to him. But not too close.

He grinned at her, knowingly. "C'mon over here. I won't bite."

She moved closer, but she still kept her armor on.

"Now. Look at your gas station. What do you see?"

She frowned. Was he being a comic? "I see Shep's."

He smiled in triumph. "What that is, my friend Carly, is an historical building. From the '30s. One of probably only a handful of gas stations left with that design. You know why the roof is pitched so steeply?"

She shook her head.

"That kind of roof was only built in northern climates, so snow could fall off more easily. Of course, this year we'll

183

be lucky if we see snow at all by Christmas. And this year they can't blame it on El Niño." He paused, giving her the chance to catch his joke. She gave him a tiny smile. Evidently, it was enough for him.

"We have here an example of a type of architecture that is long gone. I want to restore your gas station."

If he'd said he wanted to fly to Mars, she couldn't have been more surprised. "What?"

"I want to restore your gas station. Look." He hurried back over to the couch to the books he'd brought in. He flipped through one of them until he found what he was looking for. Then he looked up at her, his eyes gleaming with excitement.

"After my father left, I talked to Mrs. Epiphania for a while. She told me about your loan. Then I went to the library and stayed until they were closing. I checked out some books. Look at this." He held the book out to her. "This is a history of gas stations. Look at this one. And this one on this page. And"—he flipped some more pages—"this one also. This is what your gas station used to look like. This is what it could look like again."

Carly looked at the photographs in the book. Yes, it did look like Shep's. A sudden longing tore through her, longing for Shep's to be like that again. She looked up at him. Was this guy for real?

He smiled sincerely, angelically. "Carly, think. We can restore your gas station, make it a landmark."

Carly turned back to the photographs. "Flowers in the window boxes? Did they really have flowers in the window boxes?" She ran her finger over the photograph in the book. "Gramps once told me they used to. But I didn't believe him."

"Why not?"

"It seemed so silly. So frivolous. You have flowers in your home, not at a gas station."

He pointed to the book again. "A long time ago, gas stations were built to be part of their neighborhoods. To blend in with the houses. We can do that with Hawthorne Street.''

But she wasn't looking at the book anymore. She was looking at him. With a thrill of hope, she said, ''You're really sincere.''

He didn't answer her for what seemed like a long time. Then he did. ''Yes. I am.''

She believed him. She sincerely believed him. Her weary soul rejoiced.

Jake could tell the moment she let down her reserve. Love and joy came to him. Along with an elderly German Shepherd, who stuck his head in between them, promoting himself another round of head scratching.

''Hey, Murphy, you're still awake,'' Carly said, her voice colored by amazement.

Jake wanted to give her something to be really amazed about. He drew her attention away from her dog. To him. When he had her full attention, he lowered his lips to hers and proceeded to amaze her. Thoroughly. As she amazed him.

At last they rested, her head under his chin, their hearts beating together.

She raised her head. ''One question.''

''Okay.''

''Where did you get the twenty thousand dollars?''

''I sold my '57 Chevy to Mrs. Epiphania.''

She jerked her head up so she could look him in the eye. ''Are you serious?''

''You have to quit asking me that question. I'm just a serious kind of guy.'' He countered her look of disbelief with a grin. ''I'm giving her driving lessons tomorrow.''

''Mrs. Epiphania driving around in a '57 Chevy.'' She sounded amused by the thought. ''Now, if we only had snow for Christmas, this year would come to a perfect end.''

*   *   *

Annie Kimberlin

The next morning, while he waited for Mrs. Epiphania to join him in the car, Jake sang about a white Christmas. Something the forecasters said they wouldn't see this year.

She came trudging across the frozen grass. Funny, Jake thought. She looked years younger. Not only that, but she looked happy. He realized he'd never seen her look happy.

"Buying a car must agree with you," he teased her as she opened the door and slid behind the wheel.

"That is a compliment. Thank you," she said. He realized that until this moment, he'd never seen her smile before, either. "Have you heard from Carly? Did she take the money to the bank?"

He nodded. "She called a few minutes ago. She said she handed them the money and asked for a receipt. I only wish my father had been there to see it, but he and my mother left for Europe this morning." Still, he thought, probably that was for the best. When his father found out that Carly had paid off the bank, he would not be pleasant to be around. Jake didn't wish that on anyone, least of all his mother.

"So the gas station is all hers?"

Jake nodded. "Yup. All hers." And Carly was all his. But there was no need to share that bit of information with his neighbor. She might be shocked at how much *his* Carly had become last night. And would be again, tonight. "She said if we only had snow, this would be a perfect Christmas."

"Yes." The old woman nodded thoughtfully. "I seem to remember that she likes snow. Do you like snow, too?"

"Love it, Mrs. Epiphania. It doesn't seem like Christmas without the white stuff, all deep and crisp and even."

"Deep, hm?" Then she clapped her hands. "Well, then," she stated. "It is time for this driving lesson. What do I do first?"

"You sure you've never driven a car before?"

"Never."

Mrs. Epiphania liked driving the car. It gave her a feeling of freedom. They had some nice cars back in the forties, all

186

rounded and balloony, but she'd never had the opportunity to drive one. And not one of them was as fine as this one was. This car had character. It was too bad she couldn't take it with her. She'd have loved to show it off. Still, she couldn't wait to get wherever it was she was going, to spend eternity with people her own age. One other thing she couldn't take. Sweetcakes. Even though she had never truly liked the furry little creature, she couldn't just make it disappear. This would not look good, and she had to stay on Gabriel's good side right now. She'd have to find some other home for it.

That afternoon, after Ratchet was fed and the gas station was closed—early because it was Christmas Eve—Carly helped Murphy clamber into her truck. On the way through town, something white caught in her headlights. Then another white something, floating gently down.

"Murphy," she gasped. "It's snow."

But Murphy didn't answer. He was asleep.

Carly cranked down her window to stick her hand out. Sure enough, a snowflake landed on her hand. A great big white snowflake that melted when she drew her hand into the heater-warmed truck.

Jake heard a truck door slam, then heard her calling his name. He looked out his bedroom window and there she was, in the yard below, her arms outstretched and her face up to the sky. "Snow," she was calling. "Jake, it's snowing!"

In his socked feet he ran downstairs and outside to see the snow with her. He hopped from one foot to the other as the snow melted on his socks, leaving his feet wet and cold. He wouldn't have missed it for the world.

"Not enough to make a snow fort," she called joyously. She bent down to scoop up some snow. "Not even enough for a snowball yet, either." She threw the bit of snow into the air. "But it's here!"

187

"If it keeps up like this, there'll be more than enough by tomorrow."

"What a terrific Christmas present! How could snow like this escape the weather forecasters? Maybe Mrs. Epiphania was right. Maybe magic is real."

Before he could answer, his gaze was snagged by a tiny movement. The blinds in Mrs. Epiphania's living room were settling back.

This was where he lived, this room was his, Carly thought as she looked around the large room. There was an old dresser, well polished with deep drawers, a bookcase filled with books, a caned rocking chair. Under the window on one wall was a long work table that held papers, drawing pencils, rulers. And against the opposite wall was a large, inviting bed. A bed of many pillows.

She felt him come up behind her, slip his arm around her, press a kiss against her hair. "Did you have enough to eat?" he whispered in her ear.

She nodded, her eyes closing at the pleasure of his nearness.

"Look up," he whispered.

She looked. His hand held, over her head, a sprig of mistletoe. "This means you have to kiss me."

"Yes," she agreed, matching his whisper. "It does." She rose on her toes to meet his kiss.

"You know, I was thinking." His voice sounded warm and velvety. They were in the middle of the pillows on his bed. "If we started the renovation work with your house, you'd need some other place to live."

"I looked for an apartment in the paper when I thought I was going to lose Shep's. But no one wanted to rent to someone with a geezer dog."

"What if you didn't have to rent?"

"I can't afford to buy a house."

"What about this one?"

She was silent for a moment. Her head was on his bare chest. She didn't want to move it to see his face. She was too comfortable. "Where would you live?"

"Here. With you."

This time she did raise her head. "Are you asking me to come live with you?"

"Yes. And Murphy, of course." His voice was calm and sure, but then he continued in a teasing tone. "I like the idea of living with a mechanic. For someone like me, with a thing for antique cars, it could be a smart move."

"What about Ratchet?" Carly's heart had started to pound rapidly. She tried to keep her voice light, so it wouldn't betray her. "He won't like the construction work going on at the gas station, all that noise and commotion."

"Ratchet as well." His heart thudded against his chest, against her ear. "And maybe even, sometime down the line, after we get married, a couple of kids."

"Kids? Where do we get kids?"

"We make them."

"Make them?"

"Yes. Like this." He reached over to switch off the light. Then he showed her.

The old woman released the window blinds and grinned with satisfaction. She'd done it. Piece of cake. "Well, Gabriel," she said out loud. "It's time for your part of the bargain."

Gabriel was there, with her. "So you did it, did you, Francesca?"

"You know I did it, so don't try to weasel out of it."

The angel threw back his head and laughed heartily. "I've not been accused of weaseling out of anything for a very long time."

"So keep your part of the bargain and no one will this time, either." The old woman reached for her old purse and pulled out the long list. She took up the pencil with the dull point. "See here. I'm crossing them out."

His mirth under control, he looked down at her. He was a very tall angel. "I'll miss working with you, Francesca. You've been an asset."

The old lady looked pleased with herself. "Yes, I have, haven't I?"

Sweetcakes hurtled into the room, his shrilling loud and insistent. Gabriel scooped him up and settled the little dog against his chest. "So what are you going to do with this little creature?" he asked.

The old lady looked thoughtful. "Murphy likes him," was all she said, a faraway look in her eye. Then she briskly rubbed her hands against each other. "I have one more thing to do here. Follow me." It was an odd thing, for her to command the angel. Still, she wasn't going to stand on convention at this point in their relationship. She patted her pocket to make sure the note she'd written was still there, scooped Sweetcakes out of the angel's arms, and headed for the door. "Oh dear. I almost forgot those keys." Keys in hand, she led the angel out into the silent night.

She set the parking brake on the car, set the key and the note on the dash, and arranged the blanket for Sweetcakes. "There, you little dog. This will keep you warm," she told him.

The dog regarded her with his beady black eyes.

"You'll be just fine. They're good people."

The little dog curled up on the blanket and closed his eyes. She was actually going to miss him, the little rascal.

Mrs. Epiphania turned to the angel. "Well, don't keep me waiting, Gabriel. I'm ready."

The noise beat against his mind. Shrill, persistent noise in short bursts. Jake reluctantly opened his eyes. The first thing he saw was Carly's hair, spread over the pillow. She was still asleep. The shrill sound came again.

He groaned. Only one thing in the world made such a sound. Sweetcakes. He glanced at the clock. It was almost midnight. Sweetcakes shrilled again. Maybe something had happened to Mrs. Epiphania. Trying not to disturb Carly, Jake slipped out of bed and into his bathrobe.

He padded downstairs to find Murphy standing at the back door, total bewilderment in his great old eyes. "So you're awake, are you, guy?" he said. He turned on the outside light and shoved his bare feet into his work boots.

Jake guided Murphy down the steps into the still falling snow. If it kept up like this, Carly would have her snow fort tomorrow. Murphy found his way to a bush. The noise came again, reminding Jake why he'd come downstairs. There in the driveway was his '57 Chevy, with Sweetcakes inside, peering out the window and barking for all he was worth, which wasn't much.

Jake waded through the snow to the car and opened the door. Sweetcakes launched himself into his arms. "What are you doing here, little guy?"

Then he saw the key and the envelope. Written on it in a spidery hand, in pencil, the lines thick and soft as if the pencil point was well worn, were two names. His and Carly's. He turned it over and over, then slipped it, along with the key, into his bathrobe pocket.

He put Sweetcakes down to decorate some snow, then helped both dogs up the steps and into the warm house where he had to towel them dry.

He found Carly, as he'd left her, asleep. He glanced at the clock. It was ten minutes after midnight. It was Christmas.

"Merry Christmas," he whispered, kissing her on the cheek.

She stretched luxuriously before opening her eyes. For a moment he felt like drowning in her eyes again, in her body again. But then her eyes narrowed.

"Why are you holding Mrs. Epiphania's dog?" she asked in a voice that was heavy with sleep. "And why is it still

191

dark outside?'' She covered her eyes while he turned on the dim bedside lamp.

He told her about the car and the note. She took the note from him and patted the bed for him to sit next to her. Then she read,

Dear Jake and Carly,
I am giving Sweetcakes to you both. He is a good dog, when he doesn't bark, and I know you will be good to him. Please consider the car as payment for his care. You will not see me again, but I will remember you both, always.

Sincerely,
Francesca Epiphania
P.S. I hope you enjoy the snow.

They got out of bed to look out the window down at the driveway. There Carly saw her truck, and nestled beside it, at the end of a trail of tire tracks in the new snow, was the '57 Chevy. They saw the tracks from Jake's work boots leading from the yard up to the car, and back to the house again. Yet, there was something missing. Carly looked carefully for a moment before she realized what it was.

"Look," Carly whispered to Jake, pointing to the driveway below. "Where are Mrs. Epiphania's footprints?"

"I don't know," Jake said lightly, a puzzled frown on his face. "Maybe she was a magician after all."

He set Sweetcakes down next to Murphy. As if on cue, the two dogs curled up together for a nap. Then Jake took Carly in his arms to show her a little magic of his own.

NAME: _____

ADDRESS: _____

_____

_____

TELEPHONE: _____

E-MAIL: _____

_____ I want to pay by credit card.

__ Visa   __ MasterCard   __ Discover

Account Number: _____

Expiration date: _____

SIGNATURE: _____

*Send this form, along with $2.00 shipping
and handling for your FREE books, to:*

Love Spell Romance Book Club
20 Academy Street
Norwalk, CT 06850-4032

*Or fax (must include credit card
information!) to:* 610.995.9274.
*You can also sign up on the Web
at* <u>www.dorchesterpub.com</u>.

Offer open to residents of the U.S. and
Canada only. Canadian residents, please
call 1.800.481.9191 for pricing information.

If under 18, a parent or guardian must sign. Terms, prices and conditions
subject to change. Subscription subject to acceptance. Dorchester
Publishing reserves the right to reject any order or cancel any subscription.

THE
YULETIDE
SPIRIT

KATHLEEN
NANCE

For my Mom, who shows me every day what courage, hope and the spirit of Christmas mean. Although I must admit, I never decorated cookies like this.

Chapter One

She would make this the best Christmas ever.

Noelle Melancon stood in the aisle of the Christmas in New Orleans store and gazed wistfully at the three-hundred-dollar talking Christmas tree complete with twinkling lights and batteries. Way beyond her budget, but wouldn't the residents of Shady Magnolia Seniors Home love it? She waved her hand in front of the tree's motion sensor to activate the voice.

"Look, a Vulcan."

Noelle blinked; that line wasn't part of the tree's repertoire.

It was the shrill voice of the freckled terror who'd spent the past fifteen minutes knocking over an artificial tree, smudging dirt on a white felt angel, and breaking a glass ornament. Fifteen minutes during which every clerk seemed to have vanished, along with most of the other customers.

"Hush, Timmy," hissed the child's harried mother. "He's not a Vulcan."

"Is too. He just beamed down. Look at his ears."

Curious, Noelle looked around and spied the man who'd caught Timmy's attention. A clerk! Where had he come from? And how had she missed seeing him?

Not many men could carry off the holiday color scheme, but on him a red V-neck tunic and green tights somehow looked natural. And very appealing. The air in the overheated store seemed to shoot up another ten degrees while Noelle hurried over, her sights fastened on the clerk.

With a graceful but impatient gesture, the man raked a hand through the spikes of his short blond hair.

"Look, Mom," Timmy crowed. "He's a Vulcan. He's got pointy ears."

The clerk's motion—and Timmy's words—drew her attention to the man's ears. Noelle squinted as she closed in. Nah, they weren't pointed. Just an interesting bump, a charming quirk to an intriguing face. A face that fit the rest of the package. His height lent him dignity, the muscled legs in those tights were to die for, and the long, loose shirt couldn't hide the masculine power in his shoulders and chest.

Get a grip, Noelle! Keep your mind on your business, not on a hunk dressed like an elf.

The clerk was looking around, frowning. Hands on hips, he muttered to himself, "Saskatchewan. Why couldn't he have sent me to Saskatchewan? There's *snow* there. It's quiet. It's cold." He fanned himself with the collar of his red shirt and looked skyward. "How am I supposed to find the Yuletide spirit in this heat?"

Noelle halted. Maybe now was not a good time to approach the clerk.

Timmy had no such qualms. "Are you a Vulcan?" he asked, looking up at the tall man.

The clerk looked down at him. "No, I'm an elf, a high elf."

A rather disgruntled elf, thought Noelle. And no elf in her picture books ever looked like that!

The clerk crouched down until he was at eye level with Timmy. "I work for the Holly King," he said in a conspiratorial whisper.

He had a magical voice, a voice that seemed to hold the ring of silver bells within it. A fluttering started in the pit of Noelle's stomach.

"The Holly King?" Timmy's voice held curiosity, not demands.

The self-proclaimed elf nodded. "He's gone by many names over the years. Wodin, St. Nicholas, Father Christmas, Kris Kringle. You probably call him Santa Claus, but I call him by his original name: The Holly King."

"Then that's what I'll call him," Timmy answered with a firm nod of his head. "My name's Timmy. What's yours?"

"Keldan. Keldan Winterfall. Do you have a Yuletide gift to be fulfilled?"

"Yeah! I want a MarioKart 64 game and a 56K modem and a Gateway—"

Keldan pursed his lips and shook his head, cutting off the litany of greed. "Not material goods. The Holly King gives only gifts of the heart."

Timmy looked at him, puzzled.

A fleeting sadness crossed Keldan's face. "I didn't think it would be that easy."

"Could you check me out?" Timmy's mother thrust an armload of Christmas purchases at Keldan. "Before he destroys something else?"

"Mom says I'm gonna be the next Bill Gates," Timmy proudly told Keldan. "If I don't land in prison first."

Noelle felt the mother's wince.

Keldan looked at Timmy. "Boundless energy, you have. Think on the magic it can do." He whispered something to Timmy, and then rose, an easy, fluid movement that entranced Noelle. His fingers dipped into a leather pouch that hung from his silver chain belt. "There is the place for check-out," he told the mother.

197

Noelle glanced to where he pointed. To her surprise, a clerk stood at the cash register, and, wonder of wonders, there was no line. The grateful mother ran over, Timmy in tow. The child stayed right at her side, a thoughtful look on his face, and not once did he reach for the fragile ornaments they passed.

Noelle returned her attention to Keldan. "You're a miracle worker."

Keldan, who was watching the two, dusted his hands and shook his head. "That was not a true Yuletide miracle."

"It was in my book. I thought that child would add at least three more broken articles to his mother's purchases before they got out of here."

" 'Twas no miracle in the Holly King's—" He stopped abruptly as he finally looked at her. His gaze swept down the length of her and then back to her face, where he studied her eyes. His hand reached out, as if to touch her, then dropped. "Are you an elf?"

The unusual question gave Noelle an inordinate shot of pleasure. She'd always adored Christmas, despite the utilitarian holidays she'd had in the orphanage and foster homes of her youth, and she now tried to share that incredible joy of the season with others. To be called an elf suddenly seemed the sweetest compliment she'd ever received.

She smiled. "An elf? Not by a long shot."

Keldan gave a regretful shrug, though his gaze stayed warm. "You have the eyes of a woodland elf. Brown with a slight tilt at the corners."

"You've seen a woodland elf?"

"Many."

Noelle started to laugh, before she realized that he must be staying in character while working, like those people who reenacted the Battle of New Orleans each year. "Then I guess that makes you the authority." She returned his frank gaze, and slowly her humor faded.

His eyes were those of the warrior and the poet, Noelle

198

thought, bemused. Old eyes, wise eyes. Gray, more silver than pewter. Clear and honest.

His face intrigued her. Very masculine in its planes and angles, in its firm chin and narrow nose, yet tender when he had looked on the child. And his ears did have the hint of a point.

He tilted his head, and his gray-eyed gaze held hers. For a sharply-defined moment all the clamor and crowding, all the confusion faded along with Noelle's capacity to breathe. It was a moment of recognition, where inexplicable ties are knotted.

Fingers shaking, she tucked a strand of blond hair behind her ear and shook off the strange link that ran between her and the erstwhile elf. She'd come here for a purpose. *Focus on that.*

"Maybe you can help me," she said. "The manager promised to donate a box of ornaments to the Shady Magnolia Seniors Home, but I haven't been able to find anyone who knows where they are, and the manager is gone today. Have you seen the ornaments?"

Keldan blinked, as though startled. Had he too felt the connection?

"Ornaments?" he questioned. "Yes, ornaments." As he peered around, his hand dipped briefly into the pouch again, and then he opened a door beneath one of the display cases. From its depths, he pulled out a huge box and peeked inside. "This is what you want."

A sparkle dusted the air. Noelle stood on tiptoe and looked over his shoulder. Keldan opened the box, and she gasped.

The ornaments were beautiful—spun-glass balls filled with delicate angel's hair, glittering icicles, tiny figures dressed in rich brocade and velvet. The ornaments shone and shimmered and gleamed. Several even played soft tunes.

"There must be a mistake," she whispered.

"No mistake." Keldan turned. Hand-lettered on the side

of the box were the words, "Shady Magnolia Seniors Home."

"I can't believe the store donated such beautiful things."

"Last year's models."

Noelle touched one of the ornaments, a cat made of calico. "Mr. Brandenburg will love this one. He misses his cat, Spicy." She smiled at Keldan. "Thank you."

He tilted his head. "My pleasure."

Noelle took the box. She shifted her weight from foot to foot, hitched her purse higher on her shoulder, wanting to say something else, not wanting to leave, but her mind stayed blank. In the end, she repeated her thanks, settling for safe and cowardly, and then left.

"What do you want for Christmas?" asked the tinny voice of the three-hundred-dollar, talking Christmas tree when she passed it.

Noelle paid it no attention. A long time ago, she'd stopped asking for Christmas gifts for herself.

An unexpected thrill sparkled through Keldan while he watched the sway of the woman's hips as she walked away, carrying the ornament box. He watched until she disappeared around the end of the aisle. She had a nice walk. Great pair of legs, too.

At first, he'd thought she was another elf. Her face was pretty with its kindness and soft, brown eyes, and she had the smile of a pixie, a smile that hovered around the edges of her mouth. He'd soon realized his mistake, yet he couldn't deny he'd felt some link between them.

Keldan rubbed a hand across his chest, savoring the glow she'd left inside him. He'd almost given in to the temptation to smooth the windblown, shoulder-length tresses of her hair and see if they felt as smooth as the gold they mimicked. She—

His thoughts were cut abruptly short. *She!* He didn't even know her name, didn't know where to find her. He took a step down the aisle, ready to chase after her, and then stopped.

What was he thinking? Had this hot, bright place scrambled his brains? He was an *elf,* a Yuletide elf. He could locate anybody he wanted. Grinning, Keldan reached for the waist pouch that held his magic dust.

Gone!

Suddenly all sound, all movement around him halted, frozen between moments of time. A blast of frigid, pine-scented air swept around him.

"Looking for this?" boomed the Holly King in the silence, holding up the pouch. His red cheeks glowed even amongst the multitude of decorations. The snow on the hem of his green robe began to melt.

Keldan crossed his arms. "You didn't say anything about not using magic, sire."

"I've changed my mind."

A surge of satisfaction coursed through Keldan. "You need me back." He *knew* the Holly King couldn't do without his chief elf for the three weeks right before Christmas.

"Yes, but I need you to regain your Yuletide spirit more. You're a leader; you're supposed to inspire. Instead, I have a bunch of elves going around muttering 'Bah, humbug.' You never should have shown them that video, Keldan."

Keldan shrugged. "Inspiration's your job, sire; mine's organization. I can get the work done."

He would; he was good at organization. He'd worked hard, harder than most since he was half human, to become chief elf. In the ten years since he'd earned the job, he'd streamlined operations, cut waste, improved efficiency. Last year they'd fulfilled 10 percent more Yuletide wishes.

"The work will get done," answered the Holly King. "You've had the timetable laid out since August." His voice softened. "What's important now is getting my chief elf's spirit back."

Keldan stared back, not letting his frustration show. What

201

could he tell the Holly King? That every year there were more letters written in childish scrawls, and the magic only went so far? That he doubted what good one gift, or a hundred gifts, did when there were still hundreds more unfulfilled?

None of that mattered, he'd decided. What mattered was getting the job done. He didn't need to care to do that.

He hooked his thumbs in his silver-chained belt. "I'm ready to come back. You're the one who banished me on the three busiest weeks of the year when you need me most. You're the one who told me I have to find my Yuletide spirit by bestowing one special Yuletide gift. One gift for one person I truly believe makes a difference. Now you tell me I can't use magic?"

"You need to replenish your spirit on your own, not with magic. Yuletide is in the heart, Keldan, not the mind or eye."

"Spare me the lectures." Keldan swept his hand through the air, encompassing the mass of shoppers. "I won't find the Yuletide spirit here. Just let me come back to do my job."

The Holly King rubbed a hand down his white beard. "You might be surprised at what you'll find here."

Obviously the Holly King wasn't going to change his mind.

"So, I'm stuck here until Christmas morn, without my magic. What if I don't find my Yuletide spirit? What if I don't find one worthy person to bestow my gift on? Am I banished from the North forever?"

The Holly King's eyes grew sad. "You will always have a place in my realm. The North is your home. It always will be." The pine-scented wind rose. "Remember, one gift for one person you truly believe makes a difference. For one person who holds true Yuletide in his or her heart. I want you back, Keldan, but I need you back whole."

The Holly King disappeared, taking Keldan's magic dust and leaving only a puddle of melted snow.

"In other words," Keldan muttered with a trace of bitterness, "what use is a Yuletide elf without the Yuletide spirit?"

Time restarted. A customer jostled by, apologizing with a cheery "Sorry" when she stepped on Keldan's toe. The tinny carols on the loudspeaker grated on his ears, for Keldan was used to the songs of the wind and the elves. White lights twinkled in annoyingly random patterns. He was surrounded by the Yuletide spirit, and it didn't make a bit of difference.

If he went back without bestowing his gift, though, he'd no longer have any claim on the position of chief elf. To disappoint his sire, to fail before the other elves was unthinkable. They'd lose all confidence in him.

He wouldn't go back under those conditions.

The Holly King was wrong. It didn't take a Yuletide spirit to fulfill the dreams of Yuletide. It took planning, attention to detail, and the ability to figure out what each person needed.

"Yuletide spirit?" muttered the elf. "Bah, humbug."

All he had to do was bestow one gift, and he'd be back where he belonged. Shouldn't be too hard.

Except the Holly King had added stipulations. Someone with Yuletide in his heart. For those who asked, Keldan found the needs of the heart all the time. Finding someone who made a difference would be tougher. One person's efforts didn't change a thing. Didn't he have the years to prove it?

Ah well, he'd manage to give the gift somehow, and not by caring again.

Keldan grimaced. If he was going to be here without his magic, he had to find the necessities of food and shelter, and in this society, that meant money. *I doubt the Holly King's plan includes me starving.* Keldan speared his fingers through the short strands of his hair and glanced around.

A thin man in a dapper suit scurried up to Keldan. "There you are," he fussed. "We need you over at Santa's Village."

He sped back up the aisle. When Keldan didn't immediately follow, he glanced over his shoulder. "Well? Do you want the job or not?"

The Holly King's magic at work. That answered the question about survival.

A thought struck Keldan. At least now he had time to find the woman with the elfin face and a huge box of ornaments. Anticipation brought a smile to his face. Whistling "Santa Claus Is Coming to Town," Keldan prepared to bestow a gift and search for a woman who stirred his soul.

The Holly King carefully placed Keldan's leather pouch in a small cedar box. On top of it, he put a brittle, yellowed letter—written on notebook paper in neatly printed letters—and then closed the lid. He held the chest to his heart.

He was taking a big risk. He might lose Keldan forever, and that loss was unthinkable. Keldan had cared once, cared very deeply, but over the years he'd protected himself and his big heart, burying his love in organization.

For the magic only went so far. And each unanswered letter or request was remembered.

Like this letter.

It had come too late one year, and by the next year she no longer asked, no longer held that glimmer of belief or hope needed for the magic. The Holly King rested a hand on the smooth wood of the box. "Twenty years I've saved this letter," he whispered to himself, staring at the crackling fire in the fireplace, "for I've never forgotten." Never forgotten he'd failed Noelle Melancon when she was seven.

The Holly King just hoped he wouldn't fail her again, because he wouldn't get a third chance.

Chapter Two

Closing time at the Christmas in New Orleans store drew Noelle as surely as tinsel attracts a cat. After stashing the ornaments in her car, she'd shopped and browsed, watched the Tarot readers around Jackson Square, and generally wasted time while the sun set and the air dropped to a New Orleans–chilly 52.

Hunching her shoulders against the damp wind off the river, she ambled up Decatur street toward the store, pretending nonchalance, feeling her stomach knot.

"What do you think you're going to do, Noelle?" she muttered, clutching her shopping bag. "Follow him home like a lost puppy?" She stopped. "This is nuts."

The wind whistled about her, and a sharp gust at her back set her moving forward again. She could ask him to the decorating party. An excuse, she knew, but some compelling need drew her back the store. Noelle rarely indulged her own desires, but this one sang inside her with an urgency and excitement she couldn't deny.

There he was, standing on the street corner in front of the store. Easy to spot, his blond hair gleamed in the fading light. He hadn't bothered to change out of the red-and-green costume, but in the French Quarter of New Orleans such oddities were rarely noticed. Despite the falling temperature, he didn't wear a coat, but the chill didn't seem to affect him. He was looking around, as if deciding what to do next.

"Hi," she said, coming to his side. "Remember me? I'm—"

"The lady with the ornaments," he finished. "I remember you." He looked at her with pleasure and welcome and a hint of male interest no female could resist.

At least Noelle couldn't. She took a deep breath, remembering her excuse for returning. "We'll be using the ornaments to decorate Shady Magnolia this weekend. I thought maybe you, or a representative of the store, would like to come by and help. If you're free," she added hastily, then held her breath, waiting for his answer.

"Will you be there?"

The simple question pleased her. "Sure, I wouldn't miss a decorating party. Besides, I'm in charge."

"Then I shall come. What time?"

"Two o'clock. Sunday. Let me give you the address." She scrawled it on a scrap of paper. "It'll be fun. We'll have all kinds of food. You can bring your family." Noelle gave a surreptitious glance to his left hand. No ring.

"I have no mate," he said softly, "and no family here. And you?"

"Me, too. Single." Noelle handed him the address. "I'll see you Sunday, then." She hesitated, then, unable to think of an excuse to delay, stepped away to leave.

"Wait!" he called.

"Yes?"

He gave her a half-grin. "You haven't told me your name."

Her heart picked up its pace. If Keldan were ever photo-

206

graphed with that grin, he'd be a shoo-in for Hollywood stardom. That grin packed more pure energy and sex appeal than one man had a right to. And when his knowing gray eyes focused on her—as though she were the only sight that existed for him in that moment—well, she was surprised the damp air didn't sizzle off her skin.

What had he asked? Noelle shook her head. Her name. "Noelle. Noelle Melancon."

"Noelle Melancon," he repeated, using the French pronunciation. "A pretty name. It suits you." He picked up her hand, kissed the back of it, then loosened her fingers. "*Enchanté*, Noelle."

The glow inside her, lit by his grin, turned to wildfire with his kiss. Geez, what was happening to her common sense? She barely knew the man.

Keldan nodded toward the crowds gathering along the river. "Is there something special going on?"

Noelle nodded enthusiastically. How had she forgotten? "It's the night they light the bonfire!"

"The bonfire?"

"Bonfires along the river are a Cajun tradition. They light the way for Papa Noel on Christmas Eve. It's not Christmas Eve, but Algiers, the neighborhood across the river, adopted the tradition for tonight. They build a huge bonfire made from the wood of dismantled crack houses. It's incredible to see."

"Lots of people? Filled with the Yuletide spirit?" Keldan rubbed his chin. "Perhaps this I should see." He fixed her with that warm, intent look. "Would you like to come with me? I would guess you know the best place to watch."

"Sure!" Noelle grinned, glad for the excuse to spend another hour with him. She threw some coins into the kettle of a bell-ringing Santa and fell into step beside him. "You've not heard about the bonfires? Are you new in town?"

"I arrived today."

She stopped and stared at him. "And you already started on the job? That was fast."

"My choices were limited," he said drily.

He must be very short of funds or very eager for a job. Noelle tried to think of something to say, but chitchat had never been her strength. She worked in a nursery around plants most of the time and spent her free time at either the seniors' home or with the children at the orphanage. The young and the old. Much safer than an attractive man whose smile stirred the ashes of forgotten dreams.

She couldn't think of anything to say, but maybe she could think of some way to help him. After all, this was Christmas.

Fortunately, Keldan had no trouble with conversation. As they resumed their walk, he seemed entranced with the river, asking her about the passage of large cargo ships and barges and the sound of the calliope on the steamboat. He listened with rapt appreciation to the music of one of the street saxophonists, and the musician responded with an unfamiliar but complex and stunning melody that brought tears to Noelle's eyes.

They wound through the crowds to Woldenberg Park beside the Mississippi River. The chill was no deterrent to New Orleanians determined to celebrate. Street mimes, jugglers, and a clown making balloon dachshunds all plied their trades, while the Navy Brass Band played "We Three Kings." Keldan whistled along, the low melody apparently second nature, since his attention was focused on the kaleidoscope of revelers.

They found seats on a crowded wooden bench. Just as they settled down, a preadolescent boy whizzed by on his in-line skates, did a tight circle, and then dropped onto the bench. His mother shoved her ample hips to the side to give him room.

Noelle, no match for the large woman, was shoved against Keldan. She ended up half-sitting on his lap, squeezed between his chest and her neighbor's shoulder. His thigh was strong and warm beneath her leg.

"Sorry," she said, laughing.

He grinned that lethal grin. "Pleasant as this is for me," he murmured, "I imagine it's not too comfortable for you."

She wasn't complaining.

Keldan shifted anyway and laid his arm across the back of the bench in an effort to give Noelle more room. Now, instead of sitting on his lap, she snuggled into the crook of his shoulder, her shopping bag resting on her lap. He smelled fresh, like pine, and radiated a heat that negated the brisk wind off the river. This was very nice place to be, she decided.

She settled in to wait for the bonfire.

A woman, holding shut her trenchcoat with one hand while she gripped a small boy with the other, approached them. The night breeze fluttered the scarf covering her dark hair. "Excuse me, Señor Elf?" Her soft voice held a strong Hispanic accent.

"Yes?" answered Keldan.

"My son, he saw you at the store. He wanted to speak to you, but the crowds were too great."

"Didn't he talk to the Santa?"

The woman shook her head. "He said he would speak only with you. He would ask only you. Would you talk to him?"

Keldan's lips tightened, and a flash of something that seemed almost like pain crossed his face. "I can do nothing. Unless—" For a brief moment, he stared at the woman expectantly; then he shook his head. "I'm out of the elf business for now."

The words could have sounded short and cruel, but instead they were suffused with sadness and a hint of anger.

"*Por favor*," said the mother. "One listen, if you would."

The boy looked at Keldan with wide, dark eyes.

The muscles in Keldan's forearm tightened as his fist

clenched and the silence grew deeper. Then he relaxed and gave a small sigh. He leaned forward, robbing Noelle of his warmth. "I can listen."

The boy began to speak, halting and low. Keldan said something to him in Spanish. The boy's eyes lit up, and he straightened. A spate of Spanish poured from him, and he gestured wildly with his hands. Keldan glanced once at the mother, who nodded back, and then he answered the boy. The boy's face beamed.

"*Gracias, gracias,*" enthused the mother, taking her son by the hand. "*Adios.*"

The boy waved as they walked away.

Noelle cast Keldan a curious glance. "What was that about?"

Keldan gave a negligent shrug. "They'd just moved here from Honduras. The boy was afraid the Three Kings would not come here, since no one seems to speak his language. His mother's reassurances didn't help. Hearing me speak Spanish did."

Noelle was reminded of one of her favorite movies, *Miracle on 34th Street*. She wrinkled her forehead. "But why you? They didn't know you spoke Spanish, did they?"

Keldan gave her an even look. "Children can often see the magic of a Yuletide elf."

Noelle blinked. He'd said that as if he believed it.

"What did you purchase?" Keldan asked, nodding at her shopping bag and interrupting her thoughts.

Excited, Noelle reached into the bag past her purse, and held up a red-and-green-velvet angel fish. It was soft and plush, perfect for cuddling. "It's for Adam. He's a little boy at the children's home where I sometimes help. He doesn't talk much, but he's fascinated by fish." She rubbed a hand across the velvet. "He'll love it," she said softly, her thoughts turning to the silent child.

Didn't talk much was an understatement. Five-year-old Adam rarely strung more than two words together on the rare times his voice was heard. Losing his family—except for his older brother Jordan—in a car accident two years before, followed by the numerous hospitalizations needed as a result, had left Adam silent and withdrawn. Only fish seemed to draw him from his shell, although Noelle thought she had begun to reach him.

She put the fish away and dug into her shopping bag again. "I also got this fabric that I can use to make a pretty chain for the tree at Shady Magnolia and some Christmas napkins that were on sale and a vinyl Santa that attaches to your lampshade so the light makes him glow."

"*You* glow when you talk of these things." Keldan leaned back and shoved up the sleeves on his shirt.

"I love Christmas," Noelle said simply. "It's my special day." She'd made it her special day, made it hers because no one else did.

And she was determined that no one around her would have the barren Christmases she'd experienced as a child.

"Yuletide is work, not fun," Keldan said. From the look on his face, he didn't share her love of Christmas.

"Oh, come on. How can you say that? Look at this." Noelle held up a plastic elf—pointed shoes, tall hat, stumpy legs—that was attached to a spring and suction cup. She bobbled the elf back and forth and a bell rang inside. "Isn't he cute? One of the ladies at Shady Magnolia collects elves."

Keldan burst into laughter. The rich sound drew smiles from those surrounding them. "That's not an elf! That's a gnome!"

"It's an elf!"

"High elves are not chubby, and we do not wear silly shoes."

Noelle shivered in a gust of cold air and crossed her arms. A light drizzle started, dampening her cheeks and hair, robbing her of heat as she stared at Keldan.

The guy couldn't still be playing a role, could he? "How do you know?" she asked warily.

"Because I am one," he answered.

"You're an elf. Who hates Christmas."

Keldan nodded.

"A real, North Pole, Christmas elf?"

Keldan nodded again.

"Aren't you a little tall to be an elf?"

"I'm a high elf. Our race is taller, plus I'm half human."

"You're joking."

"Why would I joke about who I am?"

He believed it! Stunned, Noelle turned to face forward. He truly *believed* it. The first guy who had attracted her in a long time, and he believed he was an elf.

She gave him a sidelong glance. Maybe she'd made a mistake. Maybe this guy wasn't altogether *normal*. Dang, but he looked too good to have one light out in the string.

The crowd oohed and aahed and clapped as the bonfire sprang to life in a column of yellow flames. For once, the impressive Christmas sight failed to stir Noelle. She was intensely aware of Keldan beside her, watching her instead of the fire.

"I thought, perhaps, you could believe," he murmured.

Noelle shot to her feet. "I have to go now," she muttered, heading for a break in the crowd. Keldan followed.

Away from the heat of the massed bodies, the cold drizzle slapped at her cheeks, and the wind drove frigid air through the fabric of her coat. The temperature had lost another ten degrees since the sun set. Streetlights glinted off the wet streets.

She lifted her hood and pulled on gloves, not looking at the man standing beside her, then hesitated before leaving. He might be a little odd—okay, a lot odd—but he was a stranger to New Orleans. It was a town easy to get lost in. "Do you know how to get back to your car from here?" When he looked at her puzzled, she added, "Did you take the bus? The streetcar? You live close enough to walk?"

He hesitated. "I haven't yet found a place to stay."

She gaped at him. "You just arrived; you started work; and you don't have a place to live?"

Keldan shrugged, seemingly unconcerned about his lack of shelter. He dug into his shirt pocket and pulled out a fistful of bills. "I received this in payment today. It will be enough to obtain lodging." He glanced around. "And I observe I will need different clothing."

Suddenly, Noelle felt a tug on her shopping bag, and then it was ripped from her arm. A man took off running through the darkened eve. "My purse!" shouted Noelle. *Adam's fish!* She scrambled after the thief, slipping on the slick sidewalk.

A blur, then a gust of pine-scented air blew past her. The next thing she knew, Keldan had drawn even with the thief and stopped him with a tackle that would have made a Saint proud. Noelle skidded to a halt beside them.

How had Keldan gotten there so fast? He'd been behind her, and she was no slouch in the speed department.

The strong sinew and muscles in his forearms bunching, Keldan pulled the thief to his feet. "You have something that belongs to the lady." Hands on hips, he waited. Lamplight dappled across his face and glinted on his pale hair. Drops of rain beaded on the silvery dusting of hair on his arms. Despite the glow, he suddenly looked very forbidding, dangerous almost.

The would-be thief cast one scared glance at Keldan, threw down Noelle's shopping bag, and took off.

Keldan glanced skyward. "Yuletide spirit, sire? Yuletide greed, I think."

Her heart still pounding from the surge of adrenaline, Noelle drew a shaky breath. "How did you catch him?"

The lines of irritation in his face softened. "Elves are noted for speed, even without magic. And I have won a few races," he added with a note of pride. He dusted his hands on his shirt. "Now, I must find a place to stay. Do you have any suggestions, Noelle?"

A ten-dollar bill rolled down the sidewalk, blown by an

icy gust. Keldan snagged it. "And do you see any more of my money?" he asked ruefully, looking around.

He must have dropped the cash he was holding when he'd tackled the thief on her behalf. Keldan, a man who took a job before he found a place to live, had lost his funds helping her. Noelle picked up a lone bill and handed it to him.

He was alone in the city, with not even a place to live, while her garage had an empty apartment attached to it. She didn't know anything about this man, except that when she was with him—and even when she wasn't—an excitement she'd never felt burned through her.

That, and he claimed he was an elf.

Neither was conducive to inspiring deep trust.

But if there was anything Noelle was a sucker for, it was a lost soul at Christmastime.

He'd been gentle with Timmy at the store, he'd cheered the boy from Honduras, and he hadn't harmed the thief. Keldan might be nuttier than a pecan pie, but he wasn't dangerous. Not to her, not physically. That she knew down to her bones.

Her emotions? Ah, there he might be very dangerous, but she was very good at protecting them.

"You can stay with me if you like," Noelle heard herself say. "I've got a little apartment attached to the garage."

"*Merci*, Noelle Melancon."

Keldan's smile set her heart spinning and chased away the chill of the December drizzle.

She loved Christmas. Loved everything about it.

How could she resist a man who claimed to be one of the Holly King's high elves?

While Noelle rummaged through a drawer in her kitchen, looking for the apartment key, Keldan studied her tiny house.

"You have a lot of decorations," he said with understatement.

"I've been collecting for years. Since I was seven."

The Yuletide Spirit

No doubt about it, the woman loved Christmas. Decorations adorned every flat surface. A doorstop covered with a needlepoint wreath braced open the kitchen door. Christmas china rested in a drainer by the sink. Her curtains were made with a holly-patterned fabric. Cinnamon potpourri simmered in a pot, which she'd turned on in an unthinking gesture that spoke of habit.

Red, green, silver, and gold battered his eyes from every direction.

The Holly King had a wicked sense of humor. All Keldan wanted was to get away from Yuletide gaiety. Instead he found himself working in a Christmas store and living with a woman who adored Christmas.

Two glaring omissions in the nonstop festal cheer jarred him. Surprisingly, she had no Christmas tree. In this culture, didn't most Christmas celebrants use trees? Perhaps she hadn't had time to get one. No, the festooned rooms were evidence that there was no tree by choice. Or perhaps she would put it up on the Holy Eve.

Then there was the barren brick fireplace, which lacked the traditional stockings. Instead only a single, faded ornament hung there, its isolation strange among the sequins, felt, glitter, and velvet. It looked homemade—two circles cut from Christmas card pictures and laced back to back by a strand of ragged green yarn.

Why? Why those two omissions—tree and stocking? Perhaps, one day, with luck, he would know her well enough to ask.

"Ah, here it is." Triumphantly, Noelle held up a key. "C'mon, I'll show you the place. It's not big, but it's clean." On the way out, she picked up a paper sack filled with clothes.

The apartment was as she had said: small—bedroom, bath, and a kitchenette along one wall of the main room—but scrupulously clean. Her Christmas exuberance had spilled into here, too, with a wreath on the wall, lights in the windows,

215

and a jar tied with a gold bow and filled with peppermint candy.

She gave him a cheerful smile. "I've got a few more decorations I can bring out. Some candles—"

"No." Quickly he stopped that idea. "This will be fine. Thank you." He smiled at her and was gratified to see a flutter in the vein at her neck and a glow in her cheeks. They reflected the flame her mere voice had started within him.

Keldan took a step closer. An urgent need to touch her caught him by surprise, yet that seemed the necessary response to the yearning that unfolded deep inside him.

Her skin would be soft, that he could tell just by looking, and her hair shone like a candle flame. Would her spell over him melt when he touched her, as snowflakes melted on skin, or would it stay as fresh as pine?

He waited.

She swayed toward him, a slight movement, yet Keldan took it as an invitation. Lightly, he touched her shoulder, the fleece of her sweatshirt soft beneath his fingertips. She was not a tall woman, not as tall as he, and her hair and face gave her a delicate look, yet she had strength to her bones. For a brief, mesmerizing moment, Keldan savored the willowy feel of her, the apple cider scent of her, and then he stepped back and took a stabilizing breath.

Those thoughts were not for now, and should not be for her. He had one goal: to bestow his gift and go home. No chaos, no involvement, no caring. Within three weeks, he'd be back in the North, doing his work without aching for all the lost dreams he could not fulfill.

He could not give this woman anything but the promise that he would be gone in three weeks.

He would not complicate this time with dangerous emotions.

The spell broken, Noelle also took a step back and thrust the paper sack toward him. "These are clothes I collected for Shady Magnolia. Maybe you could find something to change into, at least until you have a chance to go shopping.'' Her voice raced. ''Here's the key; you can come and go as you please.''

He took the key, careful not to let his fingers brush her hand, careful not to touch her again. He did not want her to fear him or to be wary of him. To walk out that door and then avoid him. Though there could be nothing between them, the thought of not seeing her at all over the next three weeks was a lonely prospect. Congenial neighbor and pleasant companion would be his role.

Keldan watched as Noelle fled from the apartment.

Too bad he'd always been lousy at acting.

Chapter Three

The next afternoon Noelle took advantage of the cool temperatures and sunny skies left after the rain swept through, and set out her lighted crèche lawn display.

"Would you like to put the manger and the sheep in place, while I handle the wise men?" she asked Adam, who was helping. The small boy nodded and trotted off, silent as usual.

His silence left her too much time to think as she dragged a five-foot plastic camel over to the stable. Last evening, Noelle admitted, there was no denying she'd wanted Keldan to kiss her. A man she'd just met. A man she'd lent an apartment to. A man who claimed to be an elf. She loved Christmas, but this was a new one, even for her.

None of that had mattered later, in the dark of the night. Vivid memories of light on blond hair, desires smoldering in gray eyes, and a single touch that kindled unwanted needs had replaced sleep. Her sheets had become hot and tangled, until finally she'd gotten up and, in desperation, made batches of chocolate fudge.

Too bad she'd devoured half of it before packaging it for the children's home. The sugar high only fueled her imagination. What would it have been like if he'd kissed her, if he'd given in to the desire she'd seen on his face? Or if she'd been bold enough to claim what she wanted? How would his kiss be?

Noelle rested her arm on the back of the plastic camel, surrendering to the moment of fantasy. His kiss would be sure, not hesitant, and as sweet as ribbon candy.

She gave herself a mental shake. This time of year, she was too busy for such nonsense, and these fantasies were more dangerous to her peace of mind than Keldan's elf fantasy could ever be.

For she'd decided one thing last night, after about her fifth piece of fudge: Keldan's was a harmless fantasy. He was matter-of-fact, not insisting anyone believe but himself. His wise eyes and his flair for languages spoke of intelligence, and there was a charm about him that radiated good will and drew people to him with trust.

If Keldan wanted to believe he was an elf, fine with her, as long as she didn't have to buy into it.

Adam placed a sheep outside the stable, then tugged at her sleeve and pointed. Keldan, coming home from work, trudged up the sidewalk toward his apartment. Brittle, brown leaves crunched beneath his feet, and the fitful breeze ruffled the papers he carried. He wore a pair of soft, faded jeans, their hems frayed, and a khaki shirt with the sleeves rolled up. She hadn't realized there was anything in the sack of clothes that looked quite that breathtaking and masculine.

His blond hair stood in short spikes, as though he'd run a hand through it numerous times in exasperation. Weariness and irritation etched his face. When he caught sight of her, though, he grinned—that dang lethal grin—and splintered her early-morning resolve to ignore him.

"I see you have a helper, Noelle." Keldan shifted direction and strolled over to them.

"This is Adam."

Adam tugged her sleeve again.

"That's my new renter," she said, answering the child's silent question. "His name's Keldan Winterfall."

Keldan had reached the stable. He hunkered down until he was at eye level with Adam and smiled at him. "What's your name, young man?"

A sucker for kids, thought Noelle. *Geez, why couldn't he have just stuck to being as handsome as the devil? Why does he have to be a sucker for kids?*

"Adam," whispered the child. He reached out one finger and touched Keldan's hair. "Glows."

Keeping an eye on the two, Noelle hauled a wise man over and batted down a traitorous twinge of jealousy. It had taken her weeks to get Adam to speak aloud to her.

Adam, with his dark, unruly hair and wide, wary eyes, had tugged at her heart from the first, and the feeling had grown when she met his fifteen-year-old brother, Jordan, who tried so hard not to care. The children had stirred her long-buried memories of being alone, of hoping so hard for a family that she ached with need, of pretending she didn't care when none came forward.

She had decided she would try to keep the children together and give them the family they deserved, something she'd stopped asking for herself twenty years ago.

She'd applied to adopt them, but had been turned down. Noelle's stomach clenched in remembered frustration. The anal-retentive social worker had cited numerous spurious reasons, but the most hurtful has been her contention that Noelle's fascination with Christmas made her unstable. Noelle had protested, but her letters were buried somewhere in the bureaucracy, and her phone calls never got beyond voice mail.

So, she'd started foster parent training, hoping the boys would be allowed to stay with her. By year's end, she should know. While she waited to hear, she refused to hope or even think about becoming a foster parent, for fear it would disappear as surely as unmet Christmas wishes.

Setting the wise man in place, Noelle glanced at Adam, who stared raptly at the self-proclaimed elf. "Glows," he repeated.

What had taken her weeks had taken Keldan one look. What kind of magic did he have?

"How old are you?" Keldan asked Adam.

The child held up five fingers.

"Five? That's a good age. Almost grown-up."

Adam nodded, then pointed at the sheep.

"Did you put that there? Good choice. Maybe that baby lamb would like to go right by the manger."

Adam looked from the lamb to the manger, then nodded and ran to set the scene. Keldan rose and retrieved the papers he'd laid on the lawn, straightening them into a neat pile.

"Are you bringing work home already?" Noelle nodded at the papers.

"Their scheduling is inefficient; I found a way to improve it. They'll implement my suggestion next week, but I need to draw up the schedule. I didn't have time today."

"Busy day at the store?"

Irritation darkened Keldan's face. "Crowds, noise, heat, 'Have a Happy Holiday,' repeated endlessly, and incessant carols. If I hear 'The Twelve Days of Christmas' one more time—"

"Christmas spirit a little frazzled?"

"Yuletide spirit is no longer my concern. What I need is order. And silence."

"Everybody needs holiday cheer."

"You're as bad as the Holly King." He spaced the words

221

with a quiet tension. "I do not need the Yuletide spirit."

Noelle opened her mouth then, shut it. The Holly King bit again. What could she say to that?

Keldan watched her, the muscles in his face tight, as though he expected an argument. When she stayed silent, he relaxed and nodded in satisfaction, briefly tousled Adam's dark hair, and then strode toward his apartment.

Noelle looked after him thoughtfully. Why would he claim to be a Christmas elf—not that she believed that part—and then be so anti-Christmas? He had, apparently, once believed, but something had soured Christmas for him.

Not need the Christmas spirit? She hoped the day never came when *she* felt that way.

She and Adam finished setting up the crèche. Noelle stowed the boxes in the garage, then gave Adam a regretful smile. "I have to walk you back."

Adam's bottom lip stuck out. "Keldan."

"Keldan is right there." Noelle pointed to the apartment. Adam shook his head.

"You want to see Keldan before we leave?"

Adam stubbornly crossed his arms. "Keldan."

"I don't understand."

Adam's jaw worked a moment. "I want . . . Keldan to go with us." His voice sounded rusty.

It was the longest sentence she'd ever heard him say. "Would you like to go ask him?" Noelle said, almost breathless. Would the allure of Keldan be enough to tempt shy, withdrawn Adam from his shell?

Adam hesitated, then nodded. "I'll ask."

Two sentences. Two whole sentences. Tears of joy welled in her eyes, and Noelle swallowed against the expanding lump in her throat. At last, Adam was talking.

She wanted to shout the news, hug Adam, run and hug Keldan, but she was afraid to break the magic of the moment.

"Can we—?" Adam took a deep breath. "Jordan can meet."

He wanted his older brother to meet Keldan, too. "I think we can manage that," Noelle promised. "Now, go ask."

She watched Adam, blossoming from Keldan's magic, skip away.

Long ago, Noelle had vowed that no one she knew would ever suffer the utilitarian Christmases of her past. Not if she could help it. For this gift to Adam, she would make sure *this* Christmas brought Keldan back his Yuletide spirit.

Somehow, she would make this Christmas the best one Keldan had ever had.

Keldan stared at the empty interior of his refrigerator, the cold and white reminiscent of his homeland.

A day in the Christmas in New Orleans store had snapped any vestiges of his remaining Yuletide spirit. The endless cycle of five carols; every time "On the first day of Christmas" bellowed out, he'd itched for his magic dust to melt the speakers. The grabbing, the strident demands, the general air of hurry had only confirmed what he knew. His years of miracles hadn't made a bit of difference. One person's efforts didn't mean a thing. It was just a job to be done as efficiently as possible.

And now, he didn't have that job. He wouldn't have it in the future, either, if he didn't bestow his gift, because he would not go back a failure. He had more pride than that. He'd worked long, hard hours and overcome the small biases against his half-human side to earn the chief elf position and the respect of the Holly King and the other elves. He would not go back to anything less. If that meant bestowing one gift, then bestow it he would.

Unfortunately, in the throngs he'd faced today, he hadn't found one person who made a difference.

"Five golden rings," he whistled, then stopped in disgust when he realized what he was doing. Keldan slammed shut the refrigerator door.

Maybe Noelle had some food. No, he had to stay away

223

from Noelle, he'd decided, though all day his unruly thoughts refused to follow the decision.

Then, when he'd seen her outside, other parts of him had joined the rebellion. She had looked like a woodland sprite with her green sweatshirt, her cheeks red from the chill, her fair hair windblown and appealing. Despite his fatigue, he'd wanted to find out just how she tasted when kissed.

A faint knock on the door roused him. Noelle! He flung open the door. Not Noelle. Adam.

The child tugged at his pant leg, soundlessly urging him to follow.

For the moment, Keldan resisted the plea. He bent down to meet Adam's eyes. "Do you want me to come with you?"

Adam nodded.

"Where?"

Adam pointed down the street.

"Why?"

That gave Adam pause. "I hafta go back," he answered finally, his voice low and ragged. "To the home. I want you to meet Jordan."

"Who's Jordan?"

"My brother. He's fifteen."

Keldan remembered that Noelle had said Adam lived at the children's home, although when he'd first seen them, woman and child, he'd thought their closeness resembled that of a mother and son. Apparently there was an older brother in the mix as well.

A wave of loneliness struck him with surprising clarity. He'd felt loneliness before, but the edge of envy piercing it surprised him. He'd long since given up the notion of a family of his own. He was one of the few high elves in the northern compound of the Holly King, and most of the others of an age to join had already chosen their mates. Being half-human didn't help; even elves had their prejudices. Besides, his work kept him too busy.

"Will you go with us?" Adam's hesitant question brought Keldan back.

"I'd be glad to."

A shy smile, one that seemed little used, crept onto Adam's face. "Are you magic?"

"I'm an elf." Keldan tilted his head. "Do you have a dream for Yuletide? A gift you'd like?"

Silent again, Adam nodded.

"Would you like to tell me?"

After a moment, Adam shook his head.

"Some things are hard to put into words, aren't they? Remember, you have to ask somehow, so the Holly King can listen to here"—Keldan touched briefly above the child's heart—"as well as to the words."

"That's why kids write letters to Santa?"

"And why stores have Santas in them." Keldan rose. Just as well Adam hadn't asked him, for it would be the Holly King and his new assistant—probably Verlan, an able elf—handling the Yuletide wishes this year. A sudden twinge of longing, of lost purpose, sped through him, but Keldan quickly squelched it.

This year, he wouldn't concern himself with dreams and hopes. Next year—just get the job done the most efficient way he could.

As long as he gave out his gift.

He took Adam's hand. "Let's go."

George Washington Carver Johnson, GW for short, lowered his bulk onto the Shady Magnolia porch swing, stuck his thumbs in his suspenders, and gave Keldan a suspicious look. "You a friend of Noelle's? Cause Fred and I think she's a right special lady."

"And we wouldn't want someone trifling with her, if you catch my meaning," added Frederick Douglass Johnson, aka Fred. He hitched up his baggy pants before sitting stiffly on the swing beside his brother.

After leaving Adam at the children's home, Noelle had detoured to the Shady Magnolia Seniors' Home on the walk back, saying she needed to check on arrangements for the decorating party. The red-brick building on a quiet side street boasted a wrought-iron fence, a porch with the requisite swing, two magnolia trees, and three geriatric owners—two of whom waylaid Keldan while Noelle, with a jaunty "Be back in a flash," disappeared inside with their sister.

Black eyes and dark faces examined him with unwavering intensity. "So, why you seeing Noelle?"

It seemed his day to attract suspicion, Keldan thought with some amusement. Adam's older brother Jordan had been skeptical as well.

Arms crossed, Keldan leaned easily against the newel and gazed back at the elderly men. "I'm just renting her apartment." *Liar,* returned his innate honesty. "Have you known her long?"

GW rubbed his grizzled cheek, the slight scratching noise sounding loud in the silence. " 'Bout five years, I'd say." He looked to Fred, who nodded in confirmation.

"She does a lot for us," continued GW, " 'specially at Christmas. Last year, when my heart was actin' up, she drove me to the doc's regular-like. Every week."

"And always so cheerful," put in Fred.

"She's got no family, so we figure it's up to us to watch out for her."

"Make sure no one takes advantage of her. If you catch my meaning."

"Your meaning's caught," said Keldan.

GW nodded. "Just so's you know. Fred don't talk much, but I wouldn't want to get on his bad side, no siree."

Fred preened, rubbing a hand across his bald head, and shot Keldan a fearsome look, oblivious to the fact that he probably didn't weigh but a hundred and thirty pounds and didn't look as though he'd squash a cockroach.

"Are you boys giving the youngster a hard time?" Harriet

Tubman Johnson—Hattie to her friends—scolded as she bustled out, Noelle trailing behind.

The three—Hattie, GW, and Fred—were triplets and never separated a day in their seventy-plus years, "except when GW was taken with that sick spell with his heart," Hattie had informed him. Triplets they might be, but they didn't look a thing alike. Hattie was rotund and short, Fred was nearly as short but scrawny, while GW surpassed Keldan in height and size. They did share a common concern for Noelle.

"Just having some conversation," Keldan answered.

Hattie thrust a sack into Noelle's hands. "Now here's those pecans I shelled."

"Oh, I couldn't—" protested Noelle.

"Trees had a bumper crop this year; cook can't use 'em all. I don't want them going stale."

"Thanks. I'll sugar them. I'll bring some to the party—you know how Mr. Brandenburg likes sugared pecans—and there's a new worker at the children's home I don't have a gift for yet."

Hattie threw her an exasperated look. "They're for *you*."

"And I'll put them to good use."

Noelle had no idea Hattie meant for her to eat them, not give them away, Keldan realized. For a woman so fired up about Christmas, Noelle didn't know much about receiving.

"We'll see you on Saturday," Noelle called as they walked down the brick walkway.

"You comin', too?" GW asked Keldan.

"Yes, he is," Noelle answered for him. "He's from the store that donated the new ornaments."

"Remember what I said," GW warned Keldan. "Remember Fred, here."

Fred hitched up his pants and glared at Keldan. Keldan bit back a laugh, yet the thought that Noelle had such staunch defenders pleased him, too.

The sun lowered in the winter sky while Noelle and Keldan strolled back, chatting idly. Keldan's eyes, accustomed to the long winters of the north and the shadowy glades inhabited by his ancestors, had no trouble adjusting to the indistinct twilight, but Noelle stumbled on the uneven pavement. He used the excuse to touch her, steadying her with a hand at her waist. His arm felt so right there, resting against the curve at the small of her back, that when she made no move away, he left it there.

This close, he could catch her unique scent of fresh outdoors and apple. Beneath his fingers, he felt the warmth of her sweatshirt and the subtle movements of her walk. Desire flared in him like a newly lit candle, but the peace and serenity that came from having her close kept it banked and in control.

Too soon, they reached her house. Her outside lights were on, a rainbow of red, green, blue, and yellow bulbs outlining the roof and windows and strung through the bushes. A spotlight highlighted the newly added crèche, while a mischievous-looking artificial Santa pretended to crawl down the chimney.

Keldan had never understood where *that* particular fiction had originated.

"Your house reminds me of the aurora borealis," he said. "Streams of light brightening the sky, although yours are more colorful."

"You've seen the northern lights?" She held up a hand, forestalling his answer. "No, wait, of course you have. You're an elf. And what do elves think about nature's wondrous display?"

He could tell from the way she said it that she didn't believe he was an elf, but at least she was teasing him, not running in terror. He grinned at her. "Elves think it's a damn nuisance, shining in their eyes when they're trying to sleep."

Noelle laughed. "I never thought elves were bothered by such things."

"Even magical beings need nourishment and rest."

"Nectar and ambrosia and beds on dewdrops?" she asked.

Keldan laughed. "Do I look like I could sleep on a dewdrop? You're thinking of fairies. I'm no fairy."

"Thank God," she muttered. "That *would* be a disappointment."

At her dry tone, his gaze traveled inexorably back to her. He should stay away from her, for her sake and for his. He should be seeking to bestow his gift, not standing here thinking she was prettier than nature's lights and fresher than an arctic breeze.

The colored lights shimmered across her bright hair and gleamed on her fair skin. It was a picture that suddenly appealed to him. Banked desire turned to hot blue flame.

Keldan shoved his hands in his pockets, unable to force himself to take that first step away. He wasn't strong enough to be sensible and say good night.

"I also need more nourishment than dew drops." He gave her an expectant look. "And my cupboard is bare."

Noelle laughed. "I might be able to rustle you up a bowl of chili." She took a deep breath. "I planned to make cookies for the decorating party tonight. Would you like to help?"

His desire was not for making cookies; it was for Noelle. Noelle with flour on her nose and flushed with the heat of the oven. Noelle laughing. Noelle tasting of sweet treats.

His decision to stay away from her vanished as thoroughly as wood smoke in a freshening wind. He could no more ignore her than he could stop being an elf.

It was just making cookies. It didn't have to go any further, he rationalized. "Cookies? Love to."

Keldan in her kitchen was a disturbing, disrupting experience for Noelle. His presence stole both space and air, leaving her light-headed. Yet, because of his quick grace, they rarely bumped or collided—except by design—while they worked. The lack of touch, however, did not cool her tingling

229

skin or burning cheeks. The oven said 350 degrees. The room felt like 500.

While they made the cookies, she discovered two new facts about Keldan. He automatically took charge, and he was a fanatic for organization. Every ingredient was lined up in order before they started, every box and bag returned to its place immediately after use, every measurement precise.

She'd tolerated it long enough. Catching Keldan eying the food coloring she planned to add to the frosting, Noelle snatched it from his reach. "No. You won't measure this. You won't count the drops. Coloring frosting is an art, not a science."

She squeezed the bottle, and dark green coloring spurted into the bowl. Noelle mixed it in with vigorous strokes, then held it out, ignoring how dark green the frosting had turned. "Ready to decorate."

Keldan gave her a masculine look of disbelief. "You used too much green. It looks black."

"It's perfect." She smiled innocently, then scooped a dab of frosting with her finger and decorated his nose with it. "Keldan the green-nosed elf."

A pause, and then he burst out laughing in a full, rich belly laugh. Noelle grinned back. She'd finally gotten him to laugh. Could the Christmas spirit be far behind?

A dangerous, teasing glint narrowed his eyes, though his lips still twitched with mirth. Wordlessly, he scraped a large dollop of frosting from the bowl, then advanced toward her.

Noelle backed away. "Oh, no, you don't." She feinted left, but Keldan was quicker. Soon, he cornered her against the counter. Noelle squirmed, trying to escape, but she was laughing too hard to accomplish much.

"Not green noses," he corrected. "Green cheeks." He easily held her trapped between his legs while he painted two streaks of frosting on her cheeks.

In retaliation, Noelle reached into the bowl she still held and added frosting to his smooth chin. "How about green

230

beards?'' He laughed again, and while he was distracted, she tried to duck beneath his arm.

"You'll not escape me that easily." Keldan wrapped an arm about her and pulled her flush against him. He plucked the bowl from her hands and set it on the counter.

Noelle twisted and turned, continuing the game of catch, but his grip was strong and the giggles left her weak. She reached for more frosting, and then stroked the sweet icing across his lips. His tongue darted out to catch the frosting from her finger. She stroked his lips again, this time with no frosting.

With that one stroke, the warmth of her laughter changed to the heat of desire. And, pressed against Keldan as she was, she had no doubt that he felt the same arousal.

Keldan stilled, and his gaze caught hers. He gave her one moment, one moment for escape, for sanity. When she didn't move, he tightened his arm around her. The gray in his eyes turned dark and turbulent.

He bent his head, but instead of taking her lips, his mouth traced the line of frosting on her cheek. With each bit of frosting his lips captured, he captured more of her breath and her reason.

"Sweet," he murmured.

"My turn," Noelle breathed, nipping at the frosting on his smooth chin.

Soon, the only frosting left remained in the bowl, and Noelle felt softer than melted chocolate. She laced her fingers through his silky hair and sagged against Keldan. He turned, deft and sure, leaned her back against the counter, and then finally took her mouth.

His customary finesse and grace seemed to desert him, as he pulled her between his legs with an urgency that matched her own. She opened for his searching tongue.

Oh, she had been so right in her fantasies. His kisses were sweeter than frosting and very, very dangerous to her turbulent emotions.

Flames licked deep in her belly. She moaned softly and heard an answering growl low inside him. His fingers danced across her back, sending shivers to her nerves.

This felt so *right*. So real. His embrace felt like coming home and Christmas Eve all wrapped into one.

Buzzzzzz! The alarm rang on the oven, jerking Noelle from her passionate haze. "The cookies," she rasped. "They'll burn."

"Let 'em," he muttered against her lips. "I already do." He turned his head to settle into another scorching kiss.

"I can't," Noelle said weakly. "The party . . ."

Keldan lifted his head and gazed at her, his hands softly massaging her back.

Whatever he saw in her face—a return of reason, a wariness for the suddenness of it all, a fear at the closeness—banked the passion on his face and in his eyes. He took a deep breath, his hands stilled, and then he moved away from her.

"I'd better leave," he said, running a hand across his hair, his voice unsteady. "We both have other things we must do." He stepped toward the door, then halted, pivoted, strode back to her, and pulled her into his arms for one last, seething kiss.

"I shall see you Sunday," he promised, then left.

The cookies were charred and dry before Noelle remembered to take them out of the oven.

Chapter Four

Keldan lugged a huge bowl into the common room at Shady Magnolia. Those residents who could help were spreading snacks and sweets out on long tables decked with red paper tablecloths and cut holly leaves. He set his bowl at the end of one table, and Hattie began pouring in ingredients to make the punch.

"Do you have a recipe?" he asked, curious, as she seemed to pour at random, without measurement.

"Of course, but I never look at it." She held out a dipper. "Here. Taste."

It was sweet, with an edge of cranberry tartness. He smacked his lips. "Good."

"Hey, Kel! Where should I put these?" The teenaged boy—baseball cap on backward, black T-shirt hanging out, baggy pants dragging over his unlaced sneakers—held up a tray of cookies.

"Over here, Jordan." Keldan cleared a place on the table.

Jordan set down the tray, then delved under the plastic wrap to filch three cookies.

"There are still some residents who need help getting down here," Keldan told him. "Can you help GW by lending an arm and giving a wheelchair a push?"

"Sure." Jordan gulped down the cookies, then hesitated. "You know all that crazy stuff Adam talked about the other day, the day he met you? The elf stuff and you glowing and all that?"

Keldan nodded.

"Well, I don't believe none of that and I wasn't too sure what I thought about Adam believing, but he's talking now. Not a lot, but he's talking." Jordan jammed his fingers into the back pockets of his jeans. "I don't know what you said or did, but I just want to say thanks."

"You're welcome."

Jordan gave him a fierce look. "Just don't disappoint him, okay? I—he—he's had too many already."

Disappoint another child? Keldan forced away the thought, numbing himself to its sting. He would not start caring again. "I'll try not to."

Jordan eyed him carefully, then gave a short nod and ambled away, calling to a friend to come push a wheelchair.

Noelle had invited other children from the home, those who'd earned enough points for good behavior to merit the outing, to come to the decorating party at Shady Magnolia. At first the children were too cool, or too wary, to show enthusiasm, but Noelle's infectious cheer soon had them unloading her carful of food and unpacking stored ornaments from the nursing home attic, while Hattie and some of the more mobile residents of the home added to the feast. The room filled with the chattering of children and the smiles of the elderly.

Keldan leaned one shoulder against a door jamb and sipped punch, resisting the lure of the festivities.

Around him, the old and the young strung lights on the

tree, hung garlands of greenery Noelle had gotten from the nursery where she worked, and sprayed fake snow on the windows. Someone had brought a portable CD player and the carols sent feet tapping, although Keldan thought it might be the first time these rooms had heard a rap version of "The First Noel."

Hattie, assisted by Adam, arranged food on the tables, while GW and Fred hammered nails, twisted wire, and moved chairs. Jordan balanced on a ladder, straining to reach a string of lights around the back of the tree.

Keldan tried to ignore it all; his focus was on Noelle.

Between his work at the store, his search for a way to grant his gift and get home, and her avoidance of him, he'd seen little of Noelle these past five days. Apparently that scene in her kitchen had shaken her as much as it had him. Only because she wanted help with loading and unloading her car had she knocked on his door early this morning.

Unfortunately, the separation had not quelled his need for her. It had planted it more firmly.

Noelle was everywhere, her face shining, her smile reaching all, her touch evident in the pockets of color blossoming around the room. As Keldan watched her bustle about, her excitement increasing as the decorations went up, a sense of peace stole across him. Once he'd found that same contentment in the sounds and scents of the Holly King's workshop. His peace and his joy had slipped away so gradually, he'd not even been aware of the emptiness. Now, with the return of this tiny measure of spirit, he felt their loss keenly.

Keldan straightened. Aloofness no longer held the appeal it once did. With elfin quickness, he moved to the tree. "Let me get on the other side and pull that string around," he told Jordan, stopping the teen before he fell into the tree.

"Thanks, man."

Thus, Keldan rejoined the noise, the confusion, and the gaiety. He worked, he talked, and, most of all, he shared the pleasures of celebration. His Yuletide spirit, which had never left but had been merely bruised and in a healing sleep, stirred to renewed life.

After he finished helping with the lights, he draped a silver garland over the door. Others hung up ornaments and tinsel. One white-haired woman in a wheelchair held on her lap a tiny girl, her hair in neat cornrows, and together they decorated a reachable segment of the massive tree.

Jordan nudged Keldan. "Where should we put this?" He held up a green sprig of mistletoe.

"How about there?" Keldan nodded toward the silver garland he'd hung over one of the hallway doors, and soon the two of them had the mistletoe in place.

Jordan eyed a blond teen with a lot of eye makeup and a skirt that barely reached her legs. "See that girl over there? Now, that is one hot babe. I sure would like to have her under this mistletoe with me."

Had Noelle ever been kissed under the mistletoe? Keldan's glance searched her out and at once found her holding Adam up to add a fish ornament to the tree. She glanced over her shoulder at him, as though she, too, was unable to keep from watching him. Her hand betrayed her thoughts when she touched a finger to her lips in memory. She blushed and returned her attention to Adam.

Still watching her, Keldan shoved his hands into his jeans pockets. Noelle under the mistletoe. The idea held appeal, and Noelle would never refuse such an honored tradition.

For he was tired of only stolen glances and remembered touches. These days of separation hadn't lessened his desire for her. His heart twisted with longing and need. He wanted Noelle.

Jordan saw the direction of his gaze and gave him a very grown-up sidelong look. "Don't tell me you'd complain if you found Noelle standing there."

Was his desire for her that obvious? Keldan gave a rueful grin. "I wouldn't complain."

Jordan loped away to try to persuade the blonde to stand

under the newly hung mistletoe. Keldan aimed for Noelle.

She and Adam were loading cookies onto a tray. Adam looked up and smiled.

"Are you taking those cookies somewhere?" Keldan asked.

"Some of the residents are bed-bound, so we're going to take the party to them," Noelle explained. "I've got some little gifts to give them, too."

"I'll go with you."

"The more the merrier."

While the three of them distributed the cookies and gifts to the half-dozen residents too infirm to rise, Keldan was struck by what a difference Noelle made.

When she walked into each room, her smile and chatter made the sometimes Spartan quarters brighter. The four women and two men they visited were eager to talk, and Noelle never rushed them, listening patiently to their talk of Christmases past. She gave each a gift, something to add year-round cheer to the room, and he noticed that the cookies she brought were mostly low in sugar and without nuts. One woman, who'd been lying and staring listlessly out the window, struggled to a sitting position to eat her cookies.

Noelle made a difference in these people's lives. She couldn't do something for all—she was only one person— but those she did touch had better lives for knowing her.

Noelle made a difference.

One person who made a difference.

As he followed her back down the stairs, Keldan stared at her back, stunned. He had been so angry at the Holly King for banishing him, so distracted by his own desires and red-hot need for her, that he had missed it.

Noelle was the one he'd been sent for.

He should have realized it. The Holly King rarely worked by chance.

His sire had known that her endless joy in Christmas and the many who surrounded her would reignite the embers of

Keldan's Yuletide spirit. Would help him believe again.

What did Noelle want? He just had to find out, grant it, and he could go home.

Home. A place of peppermint and snow, of whistling winds and singing elves, of magic and belonging. A beloved place. A week ago, he had wanted to return immediately.

He still did, he told himself, but this gift needed to be perfect. He needed to find out exactly what Noelle wanted, what gift her heart asked for. A special gift for a special woman. It would take time. He didn't need to go back yet; he had two more weeks.

Would that be long enough? Would that be enough time to spend with Noelle? He had an uneasy feeling that no amount of time would be long enough.

When they returned downstairs, Adam scampered ahead, eager to see the lit tree. Before Noelle could follow, Keldan stopped her with a hand to her arm.

"You're standing beneath the mistletoe," he said. "You know the penalty for that."

She glanced up, startled, then back at him with a slow smile. "Who put that there?"

"Jordan. For the hot babe with the blond hair."

Noelle laughed. "Jordan's hormones are in control these days."

"But I was in complete accord," Keldan added softly. He tilted Noelle's chin up with one finger, just enough to make it easy for him to bend down and meet her lips.

The kiss wasn't the passion-driven one of the kitchen, nor the frustrating near-touch from his apartment. It was light, yet that one touch was sweeter than a candy cane and stronger than magic.

Noelle's fingers gripped his arms, and she moved restlessly against him. She smelled of powdered sugar and cinnamon.

She kindled a blaze inside him, even as he refused to

deepen the kiss, preferring to savor the taste and feel of her lips.

Slowly he lifted his head, then dipped down for just one more taste before releasing her. Her wide eyes stared back.

"Tell me, Noelle," he whispered. "Tell me what you ask for this Yuletide."

The light in her eyes faded. "Not a thing. I have all I need," she answered with false gaiety.

"Noelle," someone called from the common room.

"I—" Her gaze darted from him to the party, then back to him. "I have to get back." She whirled on one foot and sped back into the distraction of the party.

As he watched her go, Keldan took a deep breath, steadying his jumbled senses. Then he frowned. Giving her a Yuletide gift was going to be more difficult than he had first assumed.

His throat tightened, and his heart thumped against his ribs. Always, when he listened, he had known what had been asked for and what Yuletide gift was needed. For the first time, however, he heard only silence.

Noelle was an expert at giving, but she voiced nothing—no needs or wanted gifts—for herself. Her deeds were directed toward helping others, and she expected nothing back.

Noelle Melancon asked for no gifts. Not one.

It was only a kiss under the mistletoe. For the rest of the afternoon, Noelle tried to convince herself that the kiss had been just a kiss. Just because her blood felt like part of the Indy 500, hot and racing, or because her heart had pounded and swelled, didn't mean Keldan's did, too. *A Christmas tradition.* That's all it was.

Except Keldan didn't believe in Christmas traditions.

Thoughtfully, Noelle loaded the last of the trays into her car, leaving the leftover food with Hattie. With Keldan sitting beside her, she waved at the bus carrying the children back to the home, then pulled away from Shady Magnolia. The brief ride home was silent, Noelle deep in her own thoughts, while Keldan rested one foot on the dashboard and braced his hands on his knees. Occasionally he threw her a puzzled, sidelong glance, but he said nothing.

Something had changed in Keldan today. Even before that mistletoe kiss, something had changed.

When they'd visited the residents upstairs, he'd spoken easily of Yuletide, as he called it. He and Mr. Brandenburg had reminisced about the traditions of the "old country," often lapsing into German—another language which Keldan appeared to speak fluently. He told another resident an amusing story about elves and reindeer, putting twists on the old legends that even Noelle hadn't heard.

Afterward, after they'd kissed, he'd returned to the festivities with an enthusiasm, a glow, she'd not seen in him before. He'd drawn out the shyest child, brought a sparkle to the dull eyes of the most silent adult. Even Jordan had behaved himself, except for that one moment when he and the blonde had tried to move from the mistletoe to one of the spare rooms upstairs. Yet Jordan had taken Keldan's mild rebuke with good-natured aplomb.

Noelle pulled into her driveway. Still in silence, Keldan helped her haul the party debris into her kitchen. He leaned one hip against her counter. "I'll help you wash those."

"You don't need—"

"I'll help," he interrupted, gently but implacably.

Who was she to refuse a man offering to do the dishes?

Apparently Keldan had gotten back his Yuletide spirit. It was what she wanted, yet, oddly, it left her feeling sad, abandoned almost. For the more this magical Keldan emerged, the more untouchable—different—he seemed to her. A glow, a charm, a sensation of good will and cheer seemed to surround him like an invisible mist.

In other words, he seemed like the elf he claimed to be.

Who was this man who had appeared so suddenly in her

life and lit a candle in shadows she preferred to keep forgotten?

She didn't want to care. In Noelle's life, people you cared about—foster families, child-care workers—always left.

But she wanted to know. Wanted to know when he would be leaving. Wanted to protect herself.

Noelle tossed more dishes into the hot, soapy water, then washed and rinsed them. "I had someone ask about the apartment," she said, "wanting to know if it would be available after the first of the year. Are you planning on staying?"

His silence told her what she needed to know, even before he answered. "I will be gone by Christmas morn."

Noelle swallowed hard against the lump of tears that collected in her throat. She gripped the slippery dish, beating back the traitorous emotion that left her weak. She'd known not to care, not to hope.

It was better to know ahead of time that he was leaving. So why did it hurt so?

"Who are you, Keldan?" she whispered. She spun around, holding a glass candy dish. "Where are you from?"

Calmly, Keldan took the dish from her hands. "I told you. I'm from the North. The realm of the Holly King. I am—was—will be his chief elf."

Loss turned to anger. Time for a little reality check. "If you're an *elf,* then why aren't you up there in the candy cane workshop, making toys for all the good little girls and boys? After all, this is your busy season."

"We *are* busy, for our magic is Yule magic, but we don't give toys. We give gifts for the heart, like self-respect or joy. We work through means such as a helping hand from a neighbor or encouragement from a friend."

This was ridiculous. "Then what are you doing here?"

"It's a long story, one I doubt you'd believe."

"If it involves Santa Claus, you're damn right. Look, Keldan, no excuses. Just honesty. I know I go overboard at Christmastime, but you don't have to say you're an *elf* to

241

humor me. I learned a long time ago that there's no Santa Claus and Christmas only comes through someone's hard work.''

Keldan braced himself against the table. "I'm not humoring you. How old were you when you learned there was no Holly—no Santa?''

So much for a rational discussion. "It doesn't matter.'' She tried to leave.

"It does to me.''

The soft answer stopped her. She leaned against the counter and crossed her arms. "If I tell you, will you tell me the truth about who you are?''

"I already have.''

She threw him a disgusted look. "Don't forget to lock the door on your way out.''

"Tell me,'' he repeated. His voice grew more musical, almost painful in the beauty of it.

Noelle let out a puff of air. "It's no big deal. I was seven.'' She had made an ornament, hung it up in her room as a gift to Santa, and then written a letter, a letter containing her heart, her dreams of a family. She still remembered the lined paper, the big block letters she'd used.

"A young age.''

"Not so young. I grew up early. That year I decided to give Santa one last chance. He blew it. So then I knew, Christmas would be what I made of it, nothing more, nothing less. And I decided I could make it as good as he could.'' She shrugged. "No big deal.''

"What did you ask for?''

"Doesn't matter.''

"I think it does,'' he said.

"I assure you, it doesn't. Because I've forgotten what it was.'' She straightened. "Now, I'm tired and need some sleep. I think you'd better go.''

Keldan hesitated, then nodded. He dropped a swift, hard kiss on her lips. When he left, he disappeared so fast, she'd have thought it was magic if she believed in that kind of thing. Only a lingering breath of pine remained.

Reluctantly, Noelle walked into the living room to the lone ornament above the fireplace. Her talk with Keldan had stirred memories she wanted erased and hopes she'd long since denied.

Growing up, she'd wanted only one thing—a family. A place where she belonged, with people who cared, who couldn't be taken away by a new job or a court order. With her last vestige of childish belief, she'd made this ornament for Santa Claus and poured out her heart in a letter. She'd even snuck out Christmas Eve, risking a spanking, to mail the letter.

The ornament was still hanging above her bed the next morning.

She'd gotten the answer to her letter in the new year, when Social Services had located her mother. The mother who'd abandoned her baby because she couldn't be bothered to take care of a "whiny brat." The mother who, though she wanted nothing to do with Noelle, had perversely refused to relinquish her parental rights. By the time the paperwork had made its slow way through the courts, forcing the issue, Noelle had been too old, too long in the system, for anyone to want to adopt her.

She'd abandoned hope for unflinching reality.

That was why, with Jordan and Adam, she ruthlessly refused to think about her lost dreams. For Jordan and Adam, things would be different. She'd applied to adopt, then, when that fell through, to foster the boys so *they* could stay together, be a family. She didn't hope, didn't think about it, didn't ask for it in her heart. It was for them, not her.

Noelle looked out the window and saw the lights wink on in Keldan's apartment. Apparently he wasn't going to get much sleep right away either. Her pensive mood switched, with disconcerting abruptness, to one of heated longing. Resolutely, she closed the holly-patterned curtains and resisted the urge to cross the space between the two homes.

Noelle shook her head. How could she even think about it? The man swore he was an elf! That he would be returning to the realm of the Holly King on Christmas morning!

If that wasn't a recipe for a disastrous relationship, she didn't know what was.

Her fingers trailed along her lips. Ah, but for an elf, he sure did know how to kiss.

And he made her feel as though there was something deep inside her, something special that only he could see.

He had gotten Adam to talk.

He was charming, full of laughter, kind, and sexy.

And his grin was darn-near irresistible.

Who was she kidding? Despite her caution, despite his nutty fantasies, Keldan attracted her more than any other man she'd met. More than any other man she could imagine meeting.

She wanted to see more of him, much more, and she had two weeks left. If she got any further involved, though, she'd do it with her eyes wide open, protecting her heart, knowing he'd soon be gone.

She knew better than to hope for more.

Chapter Five

How was he supposed to grant a Yuletide gift to a woman who wanted nothing, asked for nothing?

One week later, as he whistled "The Little Drummer Boy" and rearranged a display in the store, Keldan still hadn't found the answer.

He'd spent time with Noelle over the past days: quiet times while she made gifts of flavored oils and vinegars and he worked on a plan to inventory stock; fun times while they helped her neighbors add outside lights and a wreath; tasty times when he treated her to one of the hotel's special Reveillon dinners.

Always between them was the desire. It hummed, a low, thrumming counterpoint to the conversation, and formed the melody of their relationship. The occasional hug became harder to break, and the never-missed good-night kiss grew more scorching each day.

Other feelings bloomed, too, feelings they never voiced.

A need to be together. A contentment in the small pleasures. A fascination with each other.

Every day, Keldan was painfully aware that his time was limited.

A clerk interrupted him to ask about pricing. When a customer asked about fresh-cut Christmas trees, Keldan recommended buying one at the library tree sale fund-raiser, located across the river, only a ferry ride away. Pleasure and a certain rueful amusement at the unlikely manner with which he'd regained a chief elf position—only here they called it a manager—stole across Keldan. All it took was a little organizational ability.

Must his time here be limited?

If he didn't grant her gift, he'd vowed not to return to the North. Could he stay here? Be a part of human lives in a way he'd only observed before? Maybe he could make a good life here. The human part of him longed to do just that.

The elf part of him knew these dreams were impossible. His renewed Yuletide spirit cared too much to abandon his work. It was just too important, and the Holly King needed his special skills. He must be content knowing that.

Content, yes, and filled with purpose, but he would always yearn for Noelle at his side.

Whoa, where did that thought come from?

Keldan added more glitter to the display. *Noelle.*

The more time he spent with Noelle, the more he watched her gaiety and her giving, the more convinced he became that she needed *something.* Some very special gift that she was too afraid to name. Everything that was a Yuletide elf in him shouted that, though she was a woman who celebrated Christmas for others, who reveled in the traditions of the holidays, she was missing the true spirit.

He wanted to give her that gift, that something.

Whatever it was.

"Hey, Kel!" Jordan bounded up beside him holding Adam's hand.

Keldan dusted glitter from his palms. "Hi. What are you two doing here?"

"Adam wanted to come. Noelle was busy, and I was off from school, so I brought him. Ready, kid, to talk to Santa?"

Adam tugged on the edge of Keldan's red tunic.

Keldan crouched down and looked Adam straight in the eye. "Have you decided to ask the Holly King for something?"

Adam shook his head. "You."

"You want me?"

"Can I ask you for my gift?"

Keldan shook his head. "I wish I could give your gift, but I can't. Not this year." This year, he could only grant one gift, and that was Noelle's.

Adam stuck his chin out in five-year-old rebellion.

"Remember?" Keldan said softly. "I explained how I'm out of the chief elf business for this year."

Adam's lids half closed, and he nodded. "The Holly King tooks your magic so you could learn to like Christmas again." He gave Keldan an earnest look. "But you learned, didn't you?"

"I did, but I have to wait until the Holy Day to return to my work. Why don't you ask the store's Santa? Perhaps the Holly King will hear. For his magic to work, you know you have to ask and to believe."

Adam chewed on his lip, not trusting an unknown Santa.

"You can tell me what you want, too, if you like. Sort of like a practice telling."

Adam leaned forward. "I want Jordan and me to get 'dopted together with Ms. Noelle as our new momma. An' I want her to find someone so I can have a daddy like you."

A daddy like you. Keldan's throat tightened. A plea, like so many of the pleas he'd fulfilled over the years and so many of the ones he'd been unable to answer. He couldn't answer them all, but those he could did make a difference;

247

he saw that now. It would make a difference to this very special little boy.

A daddy like you. A husband for Noelle? Another man in her life? Was that what she wanted? The thought was an icicle to his gut.

Keldan ran a hand across Adam's soft, dark hair. "You ask Santa. We'll see what we can do."

"Hey, Adam," said Jordan, "go look at those angel-things for a minute, will you? I gotta talk to Kel."

While Keldan rose, Adam skipped over to the display.

Jordan fixed Keldan with an even stare. "I figured it out. You're not going to be sticking around, are you? That's what all that elf stuff is about, isn't it? Getting him ready for when you go." Jordan didn't wait for an answer. "That's okay, the kid can handle it. It's when people skip out after saying they'll stay that it's tough."

Jordan obviously had experience with broken promises. Keldan remembered Noelle mentioning families who'd thought to adopt one or the other of the boys, then backed out when the brothers refused to be separated. Keldan touched Jordan very lightly on the arm. It didn't take an elf to know, despite the boy's bravado, the one thing that Jordan wanted: someone who wouldn't break a promise.

Oh, how Keldan ached to give him that promise, but it was not his place. Not this year.

Jordan dragged the toe of his sneaker along the floor. "Noelle, now, she's different. She's always around. Didja know she wanted to adopt Adam and me, but they turned her down? Now she's put in for foster care. Maybe you can talk to someone or do something. Make sure she gets it. That way Adam gets his gift."

"How do you know all this?"

Jordan flashed him a grin. "Once, I was in the director's office, just waiting, you know. See, I'd—Well, that's not important. There happened to be these letters on the desk—"

Keldan raised a hand. "I get the picture."

"You gonna help Adam, Mr. Elf?"

"I'll try."

Jordan studied him a moment. "Well, if I believe anyone's an elf, I can believe you would be. D'you think Santa would bring me a Harley?"

"Doesn't work that way, Jordan."

"I didn't think so, Jordan said, then turned toward Adam. "Hey, c'mon, kid. Let's go see the fat guy."

Keldan bit back a chuckle as the two strolled away. He looked Northward. "I hope you heard those two wishes, sire."

A woman beside him froze in midair as she reached for a dropped Christmas stocking. That, and the pine-scented wind, gave him about two seconds' warning.

"Well, Keldan, I see you've put your time to good use." The Holly King's voice boomed across the aisles. "Got the store running in peak form."

Keldan crossed his feet at the ankles and rested against the display counter. "Good to see you again, sire."

The Holly King rubbed his beard. "We miss you, Keldan. We need you back."

A sudden clutch in his stomach felt suspiciously like panic, but Keldan didn't let it show. "You said I had to get my spirit back. That I had to bestow one gift."

The Holly King glanced at Adam and Jordan, motionless in the doorway. "I think you've found your spirit again. You wanted to fulfill those two boys' dreams, didn't you? You cared." He laid a hand on Keldan's shoulder. "I have my chief elf back. It's time to return, Keldan. I need you in my realm."

"No!" Keldan thought furiously. "I haven't given the gift, yet. You said I couldn't return until then. There is someone who needs a gift from the Holly King. Someone who makes a difference."

"Noelle."

"Yes."

249

"Now that Adam has asked, I can give his gift and give Noelle something she wanted long ago. A family."

Keldan didn't understand; he only knew he couldn't leave yet. "One more week. 'Til Christmas morn."

The Holly King's wise eyes narrowed. "Why do you wish to stay?"

"Noelle. It's not enough, sire. I feel it. She needs something else."

"Then why not bestow your gift and be done?"

Keldan raked his hand across his hair. "Because I don't know what she wants. She doesn't ask for anything. Her *heart* asks for nothing."

A thought struck him. "She doesn't ask, because she doesn't believe," he said slowly. "She loves and creates gifts for others, but deep down, she doesn't believe in the gifts of the Yuletide. Not for herself. She does not hope."

That was why she had no tree. On Christmas morn she would be alone, while others enjoyed the presents she had made and collected and distributed. But there would be no surprises for Noelle.

His heart ached for her. The woman who created Christmas for so many others had no Christmas for herself.

If he could just make her believe, get her to ask for her heart's wish, he could grant her that special Yuletide gift.

"I *have* to stay, sire. If I don't, she'll haunt me. The way that old letter you've never let me see haunts you. I have to try."

The Holly King grew as still as those frozen about them. Normally there was constant motion about the Holly King. Faint puffs of air ruffled his beard, or his robe shook from the jiggle of his laughter, or his hands cherished a letter or a gift. Yet, for one brief moment, Keldan's words brought him to marble solidity.

Then he gave a long sigh. "Will you promise to return?"

"I will."

"Stay until Christmas morn, but you must come back after

250

that. Right now, you are straddling two worlds, Keldan. You belong in only one. Mine. Remember, you're a Yuletide elf.''

The last words faded on the pine-scented breeze following the Holly King's disappearance.

A Yuletide elf. Once those words had been his whole world. Now they made him feel restless.

He didn't have time to worry about that now. He had to teach a woman who made miracles for others, that miracles were possible for herself.

The Holly King gazed pensively at the letter and the pouch of magic dust in the cedar chest. He had thought Noelle would give Keldan back his spirit and that Adam and Jordan would provide the family Noelle had asked for so long ago.

He'd forgotten something, something he hadn't planned on.

Love.

Keldan was a Yuletide elf, a superb elf with a kind and wise heart and a talent for gifts. The Holly King did not believe Keldan would be happy doing anything else.

Unless he had found love—and she loved him back.

Did Noelle love Keldan with a love as powerful as Yuletide? Love him enough to overcome her fears? Love him enough for a lifetime? Important questions as yet unanswered.

Thoughtfully he set the chest aside. He would not use his magic to interfere with or alter Keldan's remaining time in the human realm. Only their hearts could write the answers.

Noelle sniffed as she came in her back door. Pine? She didn't use pine potpourri. No, it was fresh pine, but her wreath and garland had been up for a couple of weeks.

And was that hot popcorn? A ding from the microwave told her where the popcorn scent came from. A thump from the living room followed by a low, musical masculine voice

251

whistling, "Oh, Tannenbaum," hinted at the source of the pine.

The whistling stopped. "Hold it straight, Jordan, while I tighten these bolts," she heard Keldan say.

"Got it."

"I know where Ms. Noelle keeps a watering can." Adam's voice. "And I'll get the popcorn."

Adam bounded into the kitchen. "Hi, Ms. Noelle. We got a surprise for you." He sniffed. "Mmmm, popcorn."

Adam had changed so much in the two weeks since Keldan had joined them, Noelle thought as she poured the popcorn into a bowl and followed Adam. His silence seemed a thing of the past. Oh, he still had trouble pronouncing words and he occasionally lapsed into silence, but didn't all kids his age?

She stopped short at the entry to her den.

A massive Christmas tree filled the room. Redolent of pine sap and fresh-cut wood, it brought the scents of an old-fashioned Christmas to a tiny city home.

"But I don't want—" Noelle bit back the protest, seeing the eager looks on Jordan's and Adam's faces. Faces that, before this Yule season, had held only detachment or wariness. How could she tell them she didn't want a tree? That Christmas trees only made her lonely?

Bottom line? She couldn't.

"I don't have any decorations," she said lamely.

"I brought some from the store," Keldan said with that irresistible grin. He came over, hugged her, and gave her a chaste kiss on the cheek. From the look in his eyes, she figured he would have liked much more.

"Where did you get such a beautiful tree?"

"The Holly King left it with Keldan," explained Adam. His lip jutted out. "How come the Holly King says you gotta go back, Keldan?"

Keldan's arm around her tightened. "Because that is

where I belong, where my work is. I must return to the Holly King's realm on Christmas morn.''

Noelle laced her fingers through Keldan's hand, holding tight. The magnificent tree, Adam's matter-of-fact belief, the miracles Keldan had worked with Jordan and Adam—she could almost believe that he *was* an elf.

The elf was, apparently, being recalled. Whatever his true reasons, Keldan definitely would be gone on Christmas morning. She knew that, but every reminder still filled her with the desperate ache of longing.

Noelle fought back against the hurt. People left; she was used to that. As long as she was very careful not to hope for more, for a future, she would be fine.

The stunning tree filled her house with its Christmasy pine fragrance. She leaned against Keldan's lean strength and watched the excited expectation in Jordan's and Adam's faces. For the first time in twenty years, she found she wanted a tree. She wanted *this* tree, decorated in its finest.

She smiled. ''What are we waiting for? Let's decorate.''

After they'd decorated the tree, eaten several bags of microwave popcorn, and downed fresh-squeezed lemonade, made from the lemons in Noelle's backyard, Noelle and Keldan walked the boys back to the home.

Noelle hugged Adam, clinging to him for one timeless moment, before she tweaked his nose. ''Be good in school tomorrow. It's your last day before the holidays.''

She looked at Jordan.

''Don't even think about it,'' he warned. ''Thanks for having us.'' He ambled away, shoelaces dragging. Adam swaggered after him in five-year-old imitation.

Keldan's arm wrapped around her shoulders. ''Let's go home.''

Home. It had a nice ring to it.

At her driveway, when they would have parted—she to

her house, he to the apartment—Noelle paused. "Would you like to come in and . . . admire the tree?"

Keldan grinned at her, a heating grin that reminded her hormones that he might claim to be an elf, but he was very much male. "I need to get something from the apartment first. Then I'll be over in a flash. Turn on the tree lights. Leave the others off."

He loped away. Noelle stared after him, bemused, then turned and did exactly as he had suggested.

It was slightly longer than a flash, but not much, before he returned holding three packages. One was about five inches square and exquisitely wrapped in glittering silver paper and a bright red bow. The other two were larger and more clumsily wrapped, one in brown paper inked with blurred fish stamps and the other in Christmas paper decorated with a motorcycle-riding Santa. "These are for you. This one's from me," he said, holding up the silver box, "and the other two are from Adam and Jordan. I think you can guess which is which."

A soft thrill spread through Noelle. Three presents? For her? She reached out her hands. "Thank you. And I'll have to thank Adam and Jordan when I see them."

Keldan refused to hand over the packages. "Uh-uh. You were going to open them right now, weren't you? Don't you see the tags? They say, 'Do Not Open Until Christmas.' "

"I can't open them now?"

"Nope. I need your solemn, never-to-be-broken promise that, if I leave them, you won't open them. You won't even peek until Christmas morn."

Noelle eyed the packages, then Keldan's implacable face. "I promise."

"Solemn? Never-to-be-broken?"

Noelle nodded, a smile stealing across her face, and her soul. "I promise—solemn, never-to-be-broken—that I won't open them before Christmas."

"All right, then." Keldan set the packages under the tree

and then stepped behind Noelle and wrapped an arm around her.

Noelle leaned back against him. His warm hand splayed across the side of her rib cage, the tips of his fingers just below her breast. The room was dark, lit only by the tree lights and the rainbow of reflections in the silvery tinsel. Pine mixed with the scent of cinnamon potpourri. The new-age carols she'd put on played a soft counterpoint.

The moment of Yuletide peace created its own Yuletide bustle inside her. The weight of Keldan's arm, the strength of his body, the light touch of his breath upon her hair, the unique masculine scent of him wove about her a bright ribbon of sensations that set her heart pounding. Anticipation made her fingers tingle.

Noelle's glance stole toward the three packages. Waiting, waiting for Christmas morning. Waiting for her to open them. Waiting for Keldan to leave.

A single tear slid down her cheek. Joy and loss. Two sides of the same coin. Without joy, the loss wouldn't be so keen. Yet, without loss, the joys would never seem so sweet.

Keldan's finger brushed against her nape, moving aside the wisps of hair. His kiss followed his touch, so light she thought it must be an angel's wing, yet so powerful that she felt it to her toes. His hand slid from her neck to her shoulder, then down her arm until he laced his fingers with hers. His lips and tongue and teeth worked their magic against her neck, behind her ear.

She lifted her chin, allowing him greater access. Inside her, a flame she'd thought long extinguished flickered to life.

She reached back and let her fingers trail across his face, trying to memorize each contour, each detail. His hair was silky and lush, his face smooth and powerful.

He loosened their entwined hands. Noelle turned in his arms, then lifted her face to his. "Kiss me, Keldan."

He bracketed her face with his palms and dropped tiny kisses on her nose, her cheeks, her chin before settling on her mouth with a light kiss that sprinkled glitter throughout her.

It was not enough. She found herself greedy for more.

"Again," she whispered. "More."

He rubbed his cheek against hers. "Ah, Noelle, I want you so much. I don't understand it; it frightens me. You kiss me. Let me know you feel this same mad Yuletide gift. Let me hear your heart."

That small admission of vulnerability from Keldan, who was usually so self-assured, exploded inside her, a nova of light and need.

Noelle wrapped her arms about his neck and stood on tiptoe. She pressed against him—lips, chest, groin, knees—needing to savor every inch. His mouth opened in invitation, and she accepted.

He tasted of butter, salt, and chocolate. He had such a sweet tooth; he never could resist filching Hershey's kisses.

An evergreen-scented breeze seemed to whirl about them, leaving her breathless and giddy.

Keldan's arms tightened around her, and he lifted her until her toes left the floor. His hand cradled her head, and he deepened the kiss.

"Now," she whispered.

He lifted his face from hers. His gray eyes seemed lit with an inner candle. "Are you sure?" His voice was hoarse with the need that burned through her. "We have so little time left."

Yes, she was sure. She wanted these five days and nights until Christmas. Her hands ran across the tops of his ears, caressing the elfin points muted by his human side. "I'm sure."

Again, he kissed her.

The sudden ringing of the telephone jarred Noelle from the mindless, breathless tornado. "The answering machine will get it," she murmured against his mouth.

Yet they both paused, listening for the message to be left.

"Hey, Noelle, pick up. Is Keldan there?" It was Jordan.

Keldan sighed and loosened her. "I'd better answer," he said reluctantly, stepping away.

Noelle nodded and shivered at the loss of his warm body. While he spoke to Jordan on the phone, she drank in the sight of him. He rubbed a hand across the spikes of his hair and scratched the point of his ear.

The point of his ear.

In one shattering instant her world shifted, and she looked at him with new eyes. Pointed ears. The stories, the unshakable insistence of his elf status. As she watched, a light seemed to grow about him, a shimmering aura of magic. The charm, the glow. Adam had seen it, and now she did, too.

Yes, he would be gone by Christmas morn, for he *was* a Yuletide elf. She knew that now, just as surely as she knew her own name. Not from facts, but from faith.

On Christmas morning, he would leave her forever.

People she loved always left. *Love?* Oh, dear Lord, not that, too.

She bit her lip against the well of tears she'd vowed never again to shed, against the sudden stark truth. She'd fallen in love with Keldan. How ironic. She, the woman who lived for Christmas, had fallen in love with a Yuletide elf. An elf who would leave in just five short days.

Keldan hung up, and she stared at him. Her insides churned—with desire, with shock, with wonder, with confusion. The rapid emotional shifts left her exposed and vulnerable. It was too much to deal with in these brief moments. She had to think; no, she couldn't think.

As if sensing her withdrawal, Keldan made no move to close the gap between them. "I promised to take Jordan and his friends to a Brass hockey game tomorrow. Some of the other boys are giving him a hard time, claiming they should go in his place or that I'll back out. I think he just wanted to be reassured that I was going to keep the promise."

She could manage no response, her throat too clogged with emotion.

Keldan eyed her with concern, taking a step forward. "What's wrong, Noelle?"

"You're an elf," she rasped.

He stilled, then nodded

"You *will* be leaving Christmas morning."

"Yes." He took another step toward her, his hand outstretched. "Noelle, please—"

She lifted her hand, stopping him. "I can't—" She took a shuddering breath. "I need—"

Keldan shoved his hands into his jeans pockets. "You need someone who will stick around."

She'd been about to say she needed more time, time to think and to understand the dual shocks she'd been given, but time was what they didn't have.

Keldan didn't wait for her answer anyway. He took in a deep breath. "I'd best be going." He waited a moment, giving her a chance to stop him.

She didn't. She couldn't, not right now.

"*Adieu*, Noelle."

Noelle looked past the Christmas tree to the window and watched Keldan walk to his apartment, head bowed, hands thrust in his pockets. Despite the glow that seemed to shimmer about him, he did not look happy. He looked . . . resigned. Noelle fought the urge to call him back.

He was the man she loved.

He was an *elf*.

Before she took that next step, she had to be very sure.

She watched until he disappeared into his apartment. Could loving him, then losing him, hurt any worse than this?

For a long time, Noelle stood motionless; then her gaze went back to the tree, to the three presents that rested beneath it.

Step by slow step, she moved forward, her eyes never wavering from the silver and red and tan paper. She dropped to her knees. One finger reached out and touched the motorcycle Santa package. Her hands picked it up. Squeezed it. Gave it a shake.

What was it?

The damnable phone rang again. "Hello?"

"Uh-uh." It was Keldan. "Remember, do not open until Christmas. You promised. Solemn. Never-to-be-broken."

Noelle laughed. "Ah, but I never promised not to snoop."

Once more she knelt beside the tree and looked at the packages, this time with bittersweet longing. What she wanted wouldn't be in them.

"I want more Christmases like this one," she said in a low voice, "with a family and someone who's there for me, helping me celebrate in a very special way. Is that too much to ask?"

The faintest whisper of hope flickered inside her.

Keldan stood in the darkness, gazing out the window, his hand on the replaced receiver. Noelle knelt beside the Christmas tree, gazing at the packages beneath as though they were a once-in-a-lifetime miracle.

Because she spoke, oh-so-faintly and tentatively but still out loud, he now knew what she wanted. She would have her family with Adam and Jordan, but she also needed someone who would be there for *her*, a husband who would not be leaving.

His hand knotted into a fist. He had to leave; he'd made a promise. He had compelling responsibilities calling him back. He couldn't abandon the children who would need him next year.

But not yet. *Not yet.* He had five days. Tomorrow he was going to a hockey game. The next day was caroling in Jackson Square. Two more nights followed; then it would be Christmas Eve. He was greedy; he needed those days with her.

On Christmas morn, he'd grant Noelle her gift: her family,

another man. His heart thudded against his chest in painful denial. He would give her that gift, and then he would leave. Forever.

How ironic. A disgruntled elf had regained his Yuletide spirit by falling in love with a very special woman. And now, because of that spirit, he would give her up to a life he longed for but could never have.

In shadow, he walked over to the window. He rested one arm along the frame and stared out into the night. The air-conditioning clicked on, for in typical New Orleans fashion, the cold weather had not lasted. Lights from the decorated houses hid the starlight and the moon. The jolly plastic Santa on the roof of Noelle's house beamed in an electric glow.

Over the long hours of night, Keldan watched, alone.

Chapter Six

From the edge of Jackson Square, Noelle peered anxiously down the street. Where was Keldan? He'd agreed to meet her here for the annual candlelight caroling on the Square. The small area, enclosed by a wrought-iron fence, was filling up.

Then, just like the night they'd first met, when she'd sought him outside the store, she spied his pale blond hair in the streetlights. He wove through the crowds with the effortless grace of an elf. When he spied her, he lifted his hand in welcome. Before she could draw two breaths, he was at her side.

He'd changed from his work tunic and tights into jeans and a plaid shirt with the sleeves rolled up. He looked wonderful.

And she was a damn fool. She'd wasted one entire day, and she had only four left.

"Hi, handsome. Merry Christmas." Noelle grabbed the front of his shirt in one fist and tugged lightly, bringing his face closer to her level. Then she rose on tiptoe and kissed him. The kiss of a woman for the man she loves.

Obviously startled, Keldan remained quiet beside her for a moment. But his response, when it came, was all she'd hoped for—enthusiastic, muted only by the fact that they were in a very public place.

When he drew back, Noelle was breathless.

Ah, well, breathing was optional.

She stood on tiptoe, ready to claim him again, but Keldan lifted his head, although his hips stayed flush against her.

"Do that again, and we might as well forget about caroling. Because I won't be able to sing a note." He rocked his hips against her. "We males tend to lose the power of speech in this condition."

"Well . . ." Noelle drawled.

Around them, carolers were lighting their candles. From the microphone set up by the organizers near St. Louis Cathedral, someone announced, "Let's start with 'Jingle Bells'."

Keldan smiled at her. "Be true to your name, Noelle, and sing tonight. First sing the songs of Yuletide." He leaned closer. "Then sing another song with me tonight."

Noelle nodded, her throat so dry, she wondered how she'd manage a note.

But sing she did. With Keldan's arm wrapped around her shoulders and his lean strength at her side, she sang from the heart.

The anticipation, the eagerness that had simmered, then bubbled, then boiled through Keldan during the endless carols turned into to apprehension as he and Noelle neared her house, walking from the streetcar stop.

She always turned her display lights on at dusk, but tonight her house was dark. Completely dark.

"Did you turn on your lights before you left?" he asked.

Beside him, Noelle stilled. "Yes," she said in a faint voice. "A power failure?"

All around them other lights burned merrily.

"A fuse?" he suggested.

"Probably."

The logical suggestion did nothing to dampen the frisson of unease that crept up his spine. Hands on hips, eyes narrowed, Keldan studied the house before him. What was it? What else was he seeing? Then he spied it, or rather missed it. The Santa on the top of her roof was gone.

By this time, Noelle had reached the side of her home. When she pushed at the door, it opened easily.

"Wait! Don't go in," Keldan warned.

She shook her head. "I wasn't."

"You can call the police from my apartment."

"My thoughts exactly." She started, then stopped and shook a finger at him. "Don't you go in there either, Keldan Winterfall. You may be an elf, but that's no protection against guns."

Actually, it was. Except for the human half of his genetics. Nonetheless, he pushed open the door and peered in.

The interior was dark and silent. Not a breath, not a heartbeat could be heard. Whoever had been there was gone, of that Keldan was sure.

He slipped inside and turned on a single light.

It was too much light. It revealed too much.

"I told you not—" Noelle hissed behind him. "Ohhh." Her low moan told him that she'd seen what he had.

She set down the hammer she'd picked up from somewhere and walked around in a daze, touching a curtain ripped from its hooks or the fluffy cotton stuffing plucked from a pillow. Her footsteps crunched on the potpourri leaves strewn about the floor. She knelt and picked up a wire angel, its halo bent backward. Her fingers stroked it, and her eyes glistened with unshed tears.

The shambles looked as though a williwaw, that violent

polar wind, had been trapped inside the house.

All the gifts were gone. All the gifts she'd collected over the months, the gifts she'd labored to make, the gifts for the children's home and for the residents of Shady Magnolia were gone. The three gifts he'd given her were gone, too.

"Who could have done this? Why?" Disbelief and shock threaded her voice.

Keldan knelt beside her and put an arm around her, but she refused to lean against him.

"I should clean up." She looked around, as though unsure where to start.

"After the police come. Did you call them?"

"What? Oh, yes."

At that moment, they heard the wail of the siren. Noelle rose to her feet, dusting her hands, withdrawing from his comfort. She looked around, swallowed. "Merry Christmas," she said faintly.

It was past two AM when they finished cleaning up after the police left. Noelle was exhausted, drained of energy and emotion.

Heaving a large sigh, she hung up her dust cloth while Keldan emptied the final dust pan into the garbage. He wrapped it up and took it outside. When he returned, he handed her retrieved mail to her.

"Thanks." She handed him a glass of wine she'd poured. "I thought we both could use this."

Absently, she sorted through her mail while she sipped her wine. Silence sat between them, but Noelle could think of nothing to say and Keldan seemed content just to share the quiet.

Much of what had seemed like total destruction at first had simply been items strewn around. Those could be cleaned up or repaired. Some things, however, had broken in the careless treatment, and other things were missing, stolen along with the gifts. With each shattered decoration, each collected me-

mento that had not survived, each missing item, bits of her had died. Bits of spirit and hope.

She'd spent months and hours on those gifts. How was she ever going to replace them all in just three days?

Her eye caught on the return address of the top envelope. Social Services. The answer to her request to be a foster parent to Adam and Jordan. She set the glass of wine down with a thunk.

Please, if there were ever a Santa Claus, or a Holly King, let this be one Christmas wish he didn't ignore.

Unable to stop the sudden trembling in her limbs and the roiling in her stomach, Noelle slit open the envelope. Her fingers felt so cold, she could barely grasp the paper inside.

Please.

She opened the letter. Only one word jumped out at her, but it was enough. *Denied.*

Denied. Denied. Denied.

She'd been turned down as a foster parent.

The letter fluttered to the counter, and Noelle gave a hollow laugh. She took a large gulp of wine, then another.

"Your Holly King is a real jokester, Keldan. This year, I almost believed." She turned her eyes skyward. "I wanted to believe." She beat back the tears. "Well, I've got my answer. Ho, ho, ho."

Keldan had picked up the letter and read it. Shock stamped its mark on his face. "This can't be right. He said—"

"Spare me. I don't want to hear about your stupid Holly King or your northern realm or your elf cousins. I don't want to hear one more thing about Christmas." She turned her back to him, braced her fists on the counter, and drew in gulps of air.

"I have the power to grant one gift. Let me—"

"No!" she bit out, pain beating at her insides. How had she been such a fool? How had she forgotten that it *hurt* to hope and then learn Christmas wishes were dross? *"I don't want anything—except to be left alone."*

265

"But—"

"Please."

She felt a wisp of breeze, caught a faint scent of pine, then stillness and silence. Keldan stood behind her, his hands resting on her shoulders. He didn't urge her to lean against him, just offered her the warmth of human contact.

"You do not need to be alone," he said in a low voice. "But neither do you need the pressure of aught else. Go to bed, Noelle Melancon, get what sleep you can. I shall watch from out here, make sure the hooligans do not return."

She was too weary to argue. Without a word, without looking at him, she trudged to her bedroom, alone, and shut the door.

The vandals had stolen presents and destroyed ornaments, but the Christmas tree still stood. Keldan stretched out on the sofa, head resting on his stacked hands, and gazed at the colored lights and shimmering tinsel while he berated himself.

The Holly King had expected *him* to handle this. If he had done his job and given her her gift, if he had not tried to grab a few hours for himself, this wouldn't have happened. Oh, he couldn't stop the vandals, but the blow of the theft would have been tolerable if she'd had that family to soften the pain.

His selfish absorption had denied her that.

Never again, he vowed. Never again. He'd be the perfect Yuletide elf, fulfill as many dreams, give as many gifts as he could, and care nothing about the cost to himself.

He had tried to fix it, tried too late to grant her that gift. But the magic hadn't worked. Her heart had closed again. She no longer had that glimmer of hope.

Well, he had two days. Two days to help Noelle Melancon regain her spirit.

She might not have family, but, by Holly, she had friends.

She had her goodness.

She had his love.

She'd have her Christmas.

Noelle finally fell into a fitful sleep about five in the morning, resulting in her oversleeping and waking up feeling off-kilter and out of sorts. She threw on a pair of jeans and a yellow T-shirt—not a speck of green or red anywhere. If her nose served her right, Keldan had started a pot of coffee.

Yes, there was brewed vanilla-flavored coffee, but Keldan was nowhere to be seen. Just as well. She didn't know if she could handle his potent presence this morning. Not when she felt so empty herself.

A knock on the door startled her. Who would be here this early? Keldan, she suspected, would just barge in.

It was Jordan and Adam. Adam's hands were behind his back. Jordan studied his toe bouncing against the cement instead of looking at her. "Kel told us what happened," Jordan said.

"He shouldn't—"

"It was some guys at the home," he continued, the words rushing as if he were afraid to stop. "They were mad because they couldn't go to the decorating party or the hockey game." He swallowed. "They threw all the stuff into the river."

Noelle took a deep breath. She hadn't really expected to get anything back.

It didn't matter anyway.

"So we brought you this." Jordan nudged Adam.

Adam reached from behind his back. He held two pine cones. Glitter and sequins were glued to the ends. "They're dec-rations," Adam said proudly. "Since you lost yours."

Noelle's throat closed, making words difficult. The gaudy pine cones were beautiful to her. "Thank you, Adam."

"Can I find a place to put 'em?"

"Sure, come on in."

Adam raced inside when she held open the door.

Jordan scuffed his toe some more. "Some of the other guys—well, since you've been nice to us, and since it happened 'cause Keldan took us to the hockey game and 'cause the guys were talking about you two and how you were— um, going caroling so the others knew when you were gonna be gone, well, we decided we had to do something. One of the guys wanted to beat them up, but I figured you wouldn't go for it. Even though I wanted to, too, and we coulda won."

"I appreciate your restraint," Noelle said drily.

"Well, anyway, so we went to where the guys had thrown the stuff in the river." He reached down and pulled on a wagon handle. The toy wagon had been on the side of the house, so she hadn't seen it before. "We found these at least."

Inside the wagon were a dozen soggy packages—their paper ruined by the Mississippi but the jars of flavored oils inside still intact—and the plastic Santa.

"Guess the fat guy floats," joked Jordan.

"Come see, Ms. Noelle," shouted Adam.

He had placed the two pine cones upright, so they stood like trees, next to a window. The curtains hadn't been replaced yet, because the rod was bent, so the morning light glistened on the shiny sequins. A large crystal bead on the top caught a beam and a tiny rainbow appeared on her table top.

Noelle touched a finger to it, and her hand warmed in the sun. "Thank you, Adam. It's beautiful." She gave him a big hug, which he returned enthusiastically. Jordan tolerated his hug, but at least he didn't shrug her off.

"The vandals left some cookies. Would you like one?"

Jordan shook his head. "Keldan said we were supposed to bring you to Shady Magnolia."

"Why?"

"Surprise," said Adam, his eyes dancing.

Curious, Noelle followed the boys' eager steps to Shady Magnolia.

268

Hattie bustled up and enveloped Noelle in a huge hug. "You poor dear. When Keldan came by this morning, we were shocked."

"Shocked," echoed Fred.

GW patted her on the shoulder. "Boys aughta be whooped," he muttered.

"It makes me shudder, positively shudder, to think what might have happened if you'd been home," Hattie continued.

"Your gifts, the children's gifts, they're all gone," Noelle said. "I'll try and replace—"

Hattie reared back. "Oh, hush, girl. This isn't about gifts. This is about you. Don't you know? It's not the gift, the giving or receiving that's important. What's important is the spirit of Christmas, things like sharing and hope and love."

The spirit of Christmas. The words echoed like a gentle wind.

"Now, you just come in here and set. You've been giving and giving, and now it's our turn to give to you."

Inside the common room, Noelle looked around. The residents of Shady Magnolia were assembled, but Keldan was nowhere to be seen. Where was he?

"Keldan had some errands to run," Hattie said, as if reading her mind.

Errands? What else was he up to? Questions fled as an old woman tottered up and handed Noelle a hand-tatted doily. "For you," she whispered. "To decorate."

Others followed suit. A red and green crocheted pot holder, a box of homemade pecan pralines, a candle, a tray heaped with shiny holly leaves, a kiss on the cheek. Small gifts that were the biggest gifts of all. Gifts of the heart.

Soon Noelle's hands and lap were overflowing, matching the tears on her cheeks and the fullness in her heart. She choked out her "thank yous," inadequate words for the feelings inside.

Hattie brought her cranberry punch in a to-go cup, while GW sliced turkey and wrapped it up for a dinner sandwich.

Fred offered to come sit a spell with her, vowing he'd keep her safe. Noelle refused with a smile. She bundled up everything, repeated her teary thanks, and headed home. When she got inside, she discovered Keldan had been busy there, too.

A large rectangular package, about four feet high and wrapped in shimmering, glittering white paper, stood under her tree. A floppy red-and-green bow graced the top.

Noelle looked at the tag. It was unsigned, but she recognized Keldan's scrawl. "Do Not Open Until Christmas," she read. She laid a hand over her heart. "I promise. Solemn and never-to-be-broken."

The only thing missing from the day was Keldan. But like the elusive Holly King he served, Keldan was nowhere to be found.

Chapter Seven

The next day, and the following one, Noelle discovered more of Keldan's work. A reporter for the Times-Picayune ran a feature in the paper about the stolen gifts. Channel 4 highlighted "The Christmas Lady," as she found herself dubbed in a "special at 6 and 10." And the news spread.

A first-grade class at one of the schools adopted gruff GW as their Christmas grandfather. Another school used their Giving Tree donations for gifts for the children's home. The bell choir from a local church performed at Shady Magnolia. Corporate gifts for both elderly and young poured into Noelle's mailbox. Gifts from families, gifts from children for other children, gifts from seniors for those not blessed with local family.

Others sent decorations. A boy scout troop replaced the broken bulbs in her outdoor lights. A huge wreath arrived from the nursery. None quite captured her heart the way Adam's two pine cones had, but all came with a story or letter she cherished.

Kathleen Nance

Noelle wrapped and packaged the gifts, spread the decorations between Shady Magnolia and the children's home, ate some of the cookies, fudge, fruit, and nuts, and gave the rest to shelters.

The generosity and the outpouring of concern overwhelmed her. This—this was Christmas. As Hattie said, as Keldan said, not the giving, not the receiving, but the love and hope, the spirit behind each.

Only one thing marred her joy. Keldan was avoiding her.

She caught glimpses of him coming and going from work, but every time she tried to corner him, he vanished, using his elfin quickness to speed elsewhere.

Even today, Christmas Eve day, she had thought she would see him at Shady Magnolia or the children's home, when she'd taken over the collected gifts and left them under the trees to be distributed tomorrow morning. But the elf had become more spirit than man.

Enough was enough.

It was Christmas Eve. Tomorrow Keldan would be gone, but tonight, for once, she would not spend Christmas Eve alone. Tonight would be hers.

The store closed early today, she knew, and when Keldan came home he would find an early Christmas present.

Noelle tied the red ribbon about her throat and smoothed her sweaty palms down her white dress, studying her reflection in the mirror, suddenly nervous.

What if he wanted nothing more to do with her after she had rejected him the other night?

She shook her head. No, a discouraged suitor didn't do what Keldan had done these past few days. Noelle put her hands to her flushed cheeks and took a deep breath. He'd be home in a few minutes, and she would be waiting.

For she had love, and she had hope.

Yes, Keldan would be gone tomorrow morning, but tonight she would love him, and tomorrow she would face the future with hope.

272

When Noelle let herself into Keldan's apartment, the changes he'd made during his days of residence surprised her. This place had been barren for a long time, but just during the past week he'd thrown a cloth—a green-and-red plaid woven with gold threads—across the back of the sofa. A collection of scented candles, each a different height and thickness, graced his dinette table. A wind chime made of brass bells tinkled when she pushed it.

A leather pouch lay on top of the counter. Unable to resist, Noelle peeked into it. It appeared to contain some kind of fine, glittery powder, but when she touched it, she felt nothing.

One of Adam's pine-cone trees sat in a place of honor on the windowsill. She sat next to it, her legs tucked beneath her.

In a few minutes Noelle heard Keldan whistling, "It Came Upon the Midnight Clear," then his key scraping in the lock. He came in, spied the leather pouch, and pounced on it, wrapping its belt twice around his waist. He gave a satisfied sigh and then stretched, muscles as sleek and graceful as a large cat.

He stilled in mid-stretch and pivoted toward her, as if he had suddenly detected her presence. By sound, by scent, by that instinct that always told her when he was near? It didn't matter.

His hot gaze—from her legs to her hips, lingering on her breasts a moment before reaching her face and halting—erased all her doubts, all fears, all insecurities. Noelle lifted her chin. "I have a package under my tree, wrapped in white and red. I thought I'd give one to you."

Keldan knelt beside her and fingered the red ribbon around her neck. Silently he moved to her lips and traced the curve of them. His touch was gentle, yet the merest brush sent flames licking across her.

"You have found your lost Yuletide spirit," he said.

"It wasn't lost, just temporarily misplaced."

273

"I'm glad. Now I can give you my gift."

She stopped him with a finger to his lips and a shake of her head. "No, you told me my gifts were for Christmas morning. I gave a solemn promise, never-to-be-broken. You wouldn't ask me to break a promise, would you?"

He smiled. "No."

She grinned at him. "You, however, made no such promise." Her smile grew serious. "Will you unwrap your gift tonight?"

Desire flared in his eyes, but he made no move toward her. "Are you sure, Noelle? You know I cannot stay."

"I know. Give me tonight, Keldan. A gift not from an elf, but from a man."

"Tonight is ours." He surged to his feet, pulling her up and into his arms. Almost before she could blink, they were at her door.

"I hope you don't do everything that fast," she murmured.

Keldan tilted his head back and laughed, pure and spontaneous. "Elves can be very, very patient," he promised.

"I assume elves can, ah . . ."

"Yes, we can."

"And with humans?"

He threw her a disgusted look. "*I'm* half human."

"Which half?"

"My mother."

"Why did we come back to my home?"

"Did anyone ever tell you, you talk too much?"

She lifted one brow.

"We came back here because I'm going to unwrap my present by the Yule tree. Because I want to see the lights reflected on your naked skin. Because that's where I'm going to make love to you. The first time."

Noelle heated up, head to toe, at his words.

And his kiss effectively silenced any further questions.

Inside he headed unerringly toward the den and tree, pausing only long enough for Noelle to switch on the cinnamon potpourri.

The only lights they needed came from the tree. While red, green, and blue twinkled about them, Noelle ran her hands across Keldan's cheeks, through his hair, over his broad shoulders, memorizing the masculine feel and scent of him.

Oh, how she would treasure this memory. His body was hers for tonight, his lips hers to taste, even as she offered him mastery over her.

He undid the red ribbon first, tugging on the end, drawing the satin across her neck. The sensuality of the simple act made her feel like smooth, hot wax.

Instead of immediately unwrapping the rest of his "present," however, Keldan followed the path of the ribbon with a series of kisses that left her weak and wanting. Her fingers fumbled for the buttons on his shirt. He shrugged off the garment, and Noelle stroked the sleek muscles on his chest.

"I always thought elves were supposed to be frail, delicate people. And short."

"Some are. My race is not, perhaps because we have interacted with humans for so many years. My human genes make me bigger than most."

"Was it difficult? Growing up as an elf, yet half human?"

He shrugged. "No more difficulties than others have experienced. My mother is popular amongst the elves."

She suspected he glossed over some of the problems in his typical don't-dwell-on-the-bad attitude. Keldan seemed to glow with good cheer.

She rubbed her finger across the bump on his ears. "You have pointed ears, you know?"

He gave her a mock offended look. "Doesn't everyone?" He laced his fingers through her hair, cradling her head. "Your ears are very beautiful. And your cheeks. And your chin. And your nose." Each place he named, he kissed, making her feel as beautiful as his words. Slowly he lowered the zipper at her back. "Enough talk of childhood and the past. It's tonight that matters. Tonight, and you."

"And you."

With rapid efficiency, Keldan stripped off her dress, leaving only the lacy strips of her bra and panties. Noelle stretched back on the carpet in a silent invitation for him to join her. Eyes never leaving hers, he dispensed with the remainder of his own clothes, then hers, in a blur. He lowered himself beside her, that shimmering bond from him to her almost palpable in its power, and he gathered her into his arms. Kissed her. Stroked her. Loved her.

Never in her life had Noelle been the focus of such single-minded attention, such overwhelming masculine determination. It was magic, pure magic. She gave herself up to him, to the swirling, glittering snow of desire, to the hot-scented candle flames igniting all her senses, to the sweet taste of his skin and his lips, sweeter than the richest chocolates.

Her hands moved over his sleek skin, seeking a gift only he could give. The gift of himself.

"Noelle," he groaned, for once inarticulate as she kissed his shoulder. "I . . . can't . . . wait."

"Then don't." Her hips arched to meet him.

With one powerful thrust, he was inside her, part of her. Noelle held on. She wrapped her arms and legs about him, moving in concert to his long strokes.

This was what she had longed for. This was what she would cherish. This closeness, this loving.

She exploded, light and glitter and sparkles. With an exultant shout Keldan joined her, filled her. For one timeless, breathless moment they were one; then slowly, gently, they separated. Keldan shifted, taking his weight from her, but cuddling her close to his side.

Her limbs were too satisfied, too warm to move. Instead, Noelle basked in the comfort of Keldan beside her, the weight of his arm and leg across her, the tickle of his breath on her hair.

"Best present I ever had," he murmured.

Noelle laughed. "I think I could lie here all night."

Keldan bent his elbow and propped his head in his hand to look at her. Idly, he ran a hand up her thigh, around the dip at her waist, across her ribs, and up to her breast, which he held for a light kiss on the tip. He reversed, then repeated the motion. Rainbow lights twinkled in his fair hair and reflected off the gleam in his gray eyes.

"Yes, lie there, Noelle," he said, his voice a low growl. "Let me give you this gift."

Too languorous to move, too submerged in the maelstrom of sensation his touch drew forth, Noelle lay there and watched the rainbow of desire etched in his face.

Keldan surged to his feet. He gathered Noelle into his arms, collecting the leather pouch in the same movement.

"Where are we going?" she asked.

"To bed. To celebrate."

Noelle's arms wound about his neck, and she leaned against his smooth chest. The erratic thump of his heart matched the pounding in her own chest. "I liked the colored lights."

"Then lights you shall have."

He reached into the pouch and pulled a tiny pinch of dust from it. Noelle heard him mutter some strange words; then he tossed the dust before them.

The short hallway disappeared behind a multitude of colors and lights, and, when he turned into her bedroom, the same display greeted her.

Noelle peered down at the pouch. "What *is* that stuff?"

"Magic dust."

"What else can it do?"

Keldan gave her a very masculine, very anticipatory grin. "Why don't I show you?"

At midnight, Keldan rose from the bed and dressed. Noelle lay on her stomach, sleeping, the sheets wound around her hips. Lightly, so as not to awaken her, he smoothed her hair from her face. The strands, as smooth and soft as gold, clung to his fingers, enticing him back to the bed. How he ached to lie down beside her again, to bury himself in her softness and her light.

A pine-scented breeze wafted through the room and set a distant silver bell chiming. It was time to go.

He sprinkled the magic dust about her. "This gift I give thee," he whispered, barely able to form the words through his tightened throat. "Family. Children. A husband should you but ask. For your happiness, let the memory of me fade, as the snows melt under the spring sun." He hesitated, his hand hovering above her cheek, then his fingers convulsed, and he withdrew without touching her. "Good-bye, my love."

Keldan crossed the snowy barrier at the boundary of the Holly King's realm and found his sire waiting for him. For once, the Holly King did not greet him with a jolly laugh.

"It's good to have you home, Keldan."

Keldan took a deep breath of the dry, clear air. The magic here filled him, replenished his soul—all but the large part that belonged to Noelle. "It's good to be home, sire."

"You might trying saying that like you mean it."

"Was this Yuletide a success?" Keldan asked, ignoring the question in the Holly King's voice.

"Yes. Thanks to your plans, we were able to fulfill many of the requests this year. Very few went unanswered."

"I'm glad." And he was. His renewed spirit rejoiced that they had given to so many. "I have some ideas for next year."

The Holly King laid a hand on Keldan's shoulder, stopping him. White brows knit over his wise black eyes. Sadness and resignation wrote their tale on his face. "You needn't pretend with me. I wanted you back whole, but you're not. Much of your heart was left in New Orleans."

"I love her," Keldan admitted.

"You loved her enough to give her the gift she needed, even though it meant losing her."

Keldan gazed off at the snow-capped gray mountains of ice, at the lower level of dark pines. "I had to," he said simply. "My place is here."

"Is it?"

"Where else would I be?" Keldan looked at the Holly King in surprise.

"We'd be more efficient if we had someone in the human realm full-time." The Holly King's wise eyes held Keldan. "Is her love strong enough to overcome all her fears and doubts? Only a love that powerful can replace your purpose, your place, here. Does Noelle love you like that?"

"I don't know." The wind picked up and swirled glittering flakes of snow about his ankles. He felt very much at home in the cold.

"All she needs to do is ask, and her Yuletide gift will be granted," the Holly King continued. "But she has only today before the magic ends, and by next year her memory of you will have faded. Does she love and believe that much? Does she hope?"

"I don't know," Keldan repeated.

Noelle opened one eye, instantly aware of three facts. It was Christmas morning—very early, judging by the pale light—and someone was banging on her back door. And Keldan was gone.

She rubbed her hand across the sheet, trying to find some warmth left by his body, by his passion, but the sheet was rumpled and cool.

And covered with glitter. She lifted her hand. No metallic bits dotted her palm or fingers, yet her hand glittered with pinpricks of silver and gold.

Magic dust. Her hand tightened around it, but when she opened her fist it was gone. Gone, as surely as Keldan.

The pounding at the door continued. "I'm coming!" Noelle dragged herself from bed. After the vigorous night, a few muscles she didn't realize she owned protested the movement. She donned her robe and knotted the belt at her waist. "I'm coming," she called again to the insistent pounding and rubbed her scalp.

Jordan and Adam stood at the door, Jordan holding Adam aloft so he could pound the door. He almost hit Noelle in the face.

"Whoa, there." She stopped his hand just in time.

"Merry Christmas, Ms. Noelle."

"Merry Christmas to you. Come on in."

She had almost closed the door when she spied a tall man dressed in an overcoat, hurrying up her sidewalk. At the sight of his blond hair, her heart sped up and she clutched the door jamb. Keldan!

The man looked at her then, and she realized her mistake. This man was a stranger to her.

"Noelle Melancon?" he called, drawing up to her door.

"Yes."

"I'm Nicholas Houston from Social Services."

Social Services? What more damage could they possibly do? She shoved her hands into her pockets. "What do you want?"

"This letter was supposed to be mailed to you earlier this week. It got lost in the holiday chaos, so I decided to deliver it to you personally."

Reluctantly, she took the envelope he held out.

"I'm the boys' new case worker, so I expect we'll be seeing more of each other." He gave her an engaging grin that held a shade more warmth than bureaucratically necessary.

Three weeks ago she might have found that grin appealing, might have wanted to see more of him. Now, all she knew was he had blue eyes, not gray, and he didn't shine with magic.

"Merry Christmas, Noelle." He tapped his finger to his brow in a quick salute and then left.

Noelle closed the door behind him. Unwilling to spoil her Christmas with another blow from Social Services, she shoved the envelope into her pocket, then stared at the pocket edge. Glitter dusted her robe.

Family. Children. A husband should you but ask. The faint words echoed through Noelle. A memory? A dream? She reached into her robe pocket. The letter burned her fingers.

"Why is Social Services writing to you?" Jordan asked.

She pulled the letter out, mesmerized by the drifting glitter. Her heart tattooed against her ribs as she slit open the envelope and then pulled out the letter and tried to read. Tears stung her eyes, welling up until the words became near impossible to fathom. "Here." She thrust the paper at Jordan. "What does it say?"

Jordan cleared his throat. " 'The caseworker who handled your adoption request has been reassigned due to irregularities in her case management, and we have reexamined your application. Your petition to adopt Adam and' "—his voice stumbled—" 'Jordan Cheramie has been approved.' " He looked up, hope etched across his face.

"If you agree," she said softly.

Jordan gave a whoop of glee, picked her up and spun her around, and then set her on her feet.

"I take it that's a yes," Noelle said breathlessly.

"Hey, kid." Jordan picked up Adam and ruffled his hair. "Noelle's gonna be our mom."

One of the bells on her tree chimed softly. A family. She'd gotten her family. She'd finally gotten that long-ago Christmas wish.

Yet something was missing. Or rather, someone.

"And Keldan's gonna be our daddy!" Adam exclaimed, looking around. "Hey, where's Keldan?" He turned to race out to Keldan's apartment. "He must be asleep. I'll wake him up."

281

Noelle grabbed him by the waist before he could leave. "Keldan's gone, honey. Remember? He's with the Holly King now."

"He was always straight about that," Jordan added.

Adam's lip thrust out. "He was *supposed* to be my daddy." Then his shoulders slumped. "Phooey. I guess I said someone *like* him."

A husband should you but ask. For your happiness, let the memory of me fade.

Although her body still felt the touch of Keldan's, and her heart still beat with love for him, already snippets of memory were fading. Did his eyes hold the patina of silver or the heat of smoke?

No! She couldn't forget! She wouldn't!

Always her heart would know: someone was missing.

Adam's head tilted, and he eyed Noelle. "Didn't you ask for Keldan to stay?"

"I—"

Adam gave her a disgusted look. "You mean you didn't *ask?*"

"I thought about it. I wanted him to stay."

"Did he know?" added Jordan.

Noelle blinked. Had she ever told him she loved him? "If I say something now, do you think he will hear?"

"You gotta ask Santa," said Adam.

Ask Santa? What if she asked and it took another twenty years? She had her family. Could she risk asking for more? What if she asked and was ignored? That loss of faith and hope was a pain she'd endured for so long, she couldn't face it again.

Yet, wasn't her love for Keldan strong enough to overcome any doubt?

Even if it meant risking and losing, she had to ask.

"Let me put on some jeans, and then we—"

Jordan shook his head. "I think you need to do this alone. Me and Adam will wait for you at the home."

She nodded, then watched them leave.

It was time to go find Santa.

There was one place in New Orleans that was open 24 hours a day, 365 days a year, even in the early hours of Christmas day. The Cafe du Monde, situated along the river at the edge of Jackson Square, served an unchanging menu of beignets with chicory coffee, hot chocolate, milk, or orange juice.

Noelle hopped on the streetcar to Canal Street, then walked the remaining blocks into the French Quarter and the Cafe du Monde. A light mist rolled off the river, muting further the quiet streets and bathing the old buildings in eerie white. The weather had turned cool again. Noelle buttoned up her jacket and turned up her collar against the ever-present damp.

At first the outdoor cafe looked empty. Noelle sat at one of the tiny round tables. "One cafe au lait," she ordered when a waiter appeared from the mist. In a moment, her order came, and Noelle leaned back, looking around and sipping the strong brew.

Santa just had to be here.

A freshening breeze swirled leaves through the cafe, and the mist parted. At a table in the corner, she spied an old man hunched over a plate of beignets. His white beard curled to his waist. His traditional red suit looked plush and new.

Noelle pushed to her feet and walked over to him, feeling both silly and determined. What was the worst that could happen? He could say no.

No, the worst was, he would say yes and nothing would happen.

But she could live with that now. She had her family and her friends, and she had remembered how to hope. She cleared her throat.

The Santa looked up at her. His dark eyes gleamed. "Yes?"

"I want to ask you something. Ask *for* something. Someone." She dropped into the chair beside him.

"It's already Christmas," he said. "I'm done 'til next year."

"I still want to ask. I want to hope."

The stranger leaned back. "Go ahead."

Noelle drew a deep breath. "I'm in love with someone. One of your elves. I know you need him, but we—my sons and I—need him more. I haven't asked you for anything for twenty years, but I'm asking now. I want Keldan. I love him."

In the ensuing silence, Noelle knew she'd just made an utter fool of herself in front of a stranger, but she didn't care. It felt too good to tell someone of her love.

"It's time to go home," Santa said.

Noelle nodded and rose to her feet.

"Are you going to ask me if I'll grant your Yuletide wish?"

She looked at him. "No. I have faith. And hope. And, most important, love."

The lone Santa watched her turn and walk away. "Go in peace, Noelle Melancon," he whispered when she was out of hearing. "And take care of my chief elf."

Her house was as silent as a late Christmas Eve. Noelle started the potpourri simmering, turned on the lights of the tree, and sat beside it. In a moment she would call Adam and Jordan. Their new gifts from her, and theirs to her, still rested under the tree to share.

This moment was for her. She pulled the white-and-red package from Keldan toward her. Carefully, savoring each moment, she unwrapped it, then gave a delighted laugh.

It was the talking Christmas tree she'd wanted the day she met Keldan. Noelle righted its stocking-cap topper, then waved a hand in front of the motion sensor.

"I'm glad you like it," said a husky, musical voice.

Noelle blinked; that line wasn't part of the tree's repertoire.

It was the voice of the man she loved.

Noelle whirled around. Keldan stood in the doorway, smiling, his silver eyes alight with joy. In a moment, he was at her side, taking her hands in his, lifting her to her feet, pulling her into his embrace.

He kissed her, his lips moving on hers, his arms tight about her. Her nerve endings fluttered to life, replacing the peace of the morning with the excitement of him.

Here was her gift. This strong, caring, magical man.

"You asked. You believed." His voice was muffled against her hair as he held her close.

"I loved," she corrected. She lifted her gaze to his. "I love you, Keldan. Will you stay with me? With us? I know your work is important, but—"

He laid a finger to her lips, then followed with his mouth for a brief, searing kiss. "There are other elves there. I can train someone. The Holly King and I decided we needed an envoy on earth. Someone to keep us up to date. I can do that here, although it may require some travel. And the days right before Christmas I must be in the North. Would you like to go with me? Meet my parents and visit the Holly King's realm?"

Noelle lifted one brow. "Would the Christmas Lady like to see Santa's North Pole? Just say the words."

"The words? Love me, like I love you." Keldan framed her face with his hands. "Will you marry me, Noelle?"

"Yes, with all my heart."

"And with your Yuletide spirit?"

Noelle lifted her face once more to his kiss. "And with my Yuletide spirit."

TWELFTH KNIGHT
STOBIE PIEL

To my new critique group, Yvonne Murphy, Kathy Emerson, Kelly McClymer, Sylvie Kurtz, and Lynn Manley. For catching all the things I wouldn't, for sharing wonderful talents with me, and for being friends.
Thank you!

Chapter One

Tutbury Castle
Staffordshire, England
First Day of Yule, 1335

"Alfred! Position yourself at the hall's end, and see that no one passes this way." Dera waved a fierce command to her servant, then crept farther down the stone-walled corridor of Tutbury castle. She glanced back to be sure Alfred had obeyed her instructions.

He was a huge, hulking man of uncertain heritage. He had dark red hair and a full beard like a Scotsman, but he had no brogue, and his skin was darker than a Celt's. Dera didn't know where he came from, or how her father had arranged to purchase him, but he made an impressive guard.

Alfred was adequately positioned by the gate, where he could see anyone passing through the first bailey. If an unsuspecting knight happened upon the scene of Dera's impending crime, Alfred would thump him once on the top of the head with his fist, and the knight would be no further trouble. Buoyed by this certainty, Dera made her way down the corridor, then positioned herself by the fourteenth stone on the left.

She ran her hands over the rough rock wall, seeking an indentation. She found nothing. She puffed an exasperated breath, then pulled the well-worn map from her pack. She held it up to the sconce on the wall and examined the cryptic messages. ''Ah, it's the twelfth stone. Of course!''

She was seeking a mysterious artifact known as the Twelfth Night, an object rumored to bestow great treasure upon its owner. Penn of Llangollen, the only father she had ever known, had given her the torn map when she last saw him. Only on the twelfth night of Yule could this artifact be seized. Though many had tried, no seeker had found the mysterious passages that led to its secret crypt.

She had two weeks to find the treasure. She had done well so far. Dera had feigned her way into Tutbury Castle during the First Night celebration—perfect timing. The first stage of her journey had reached its culmination, and she was determined not to fail. She had taken great care infiltrating the inner keep of the castle, waiting until the gatehouse guards began imbibing ale, toasting each other in a festive spirit.

Dera studied her map, but she had very little time to find the secret crypt. According to the map, she was near the entrance to a long-secret dungeon, where nobles were once held for ransom. She took two steps backward and examined the wall again. A suspicious bump caught her attention, and she shoved at the wall. Nothing happened, but she felt certain the knob indicated her destination. She pushed again, then again with all her might.

Unfortunately, she was a small woman, with slight bones and less than impressive musculature. Her cleverness and skill with both lock pick and bow made up for any physical deficiency, but at times, her lack of strength proved frustrating.

"Alfred!" Her whispered command sounded like a shout in the silent castle. She expected to hear knights thundering on the gallery above, charging down the spiral staircase to apprehend the invader, but she heard no sound.

Apparently, Alfred hadn't heard her either. Dera seized an impatient, annoyed breath. "Alfred! Present yourself at once!"

Alfred lumbered slowly down the narrow passageway to answer her summons. Penn had assigned his new servant to Dera for the duration of her quest, but beyond his bulk, Alfred offered little companionship. He simply obeyed orders, slowly and methodically, and broke down walls.

Perhaps that was for the best. Dera didn't need a partner questioning her decisions. As much as she loved her father, his constant advice could be irritating when they engaged in a mission together. Alfred positioned himself at her side. He was several heads taller, and three times as broad as she, but Dera never doubted her innate superiority.

"Alfred. This wall is in my way." He nodded, but took no action. Dera rolled her eyes. He had to have every order spelled out in exact form. "See to this bump. Quietly."

She stepped aside. Alfred thumped the knob and the door scraped open, leaving just enough room for Dera to enter. "You wait here, Alfred."

She slipped into complete darkness, but she knew what she was looking for, and she didn't have to see it. To center her concentration, she closed her eyes. Three steps forward. Two steps sideways to the left.

Something moved ahead in the blackness. Dera stopped; her heart slammed in her breast. It had to be a rat scurrying across the floor. She waited a moment, heard nothing, then proceeded onward.

Five steps forward. Two steps angled right. Stop. Dera drew a long breath. According to the map, as she remembered it, she had avoided one ominous pit and one jagged rock.

She started forward, but the tiniest sound met her ears, as if small pieces of metal had touched each other. Dera froze, not breathing, not moving. If a knight were in the room with her, guarding the treasure perhaps, he would certainly apprehend her. Knights weren't a sneaky lot.

She contemplated summoning Alfred again. But he wouldn't fit through the passage without shoving the door wider, which would alert more guards than even Alfred could handle. Dera waited, but she heard nothing more. Perhaps it was her imagination, or the pounding of her heart beneath her leather breastplate.

Where was I? Two steps angled right. She had done that. She should be within reach of her destination. She edged her foot forward until it met a smooth surface, then placed herself before what should be a large, square crypt. It would be open. She felt for the top. It was open. Good.

She knelt before the crypt, then reached in. Smooth objects met her seeking fingers, some temptingly cold and hard, such as a gem might be. Dera seized a rock-sized object and shoved it into her side-pack, then reminded herself that jewels weren't the subject of her theft tonight.

She felt around to the left, then the right. She pushed one round object aside and it offered a dull clank. She felt cool metal against her fingers. Gold. She sensed it in the dark. It had to be the circlet she sought. Dera bit her lip to contain her glee as she gripped it tightly.

"This is it!" she whispered in excitement.

She tugged at the circlet.

It tugged back. Hard.

Dera pulled harder. It pulled back. She yanked. In return, it jerked out of her grasp, accompanied by the sound of a soft, low chuckle.

Surprise outweighed fear. She shoved herself to her feet, then recognized her danger when someone else did the same. "Alfred! Help! And bring a torch!"

The door ground inward as Alfred burst into the room. His

dim torch sent blinding light into the darkness and Dera winced.

"Hair as black as a raven's wing, emerald eyes . . . Well met, my lady thief."

A teasing voice, low and masculine . . . Dera opened her eyes and stared at the most beautiful, sensual, and annoying face she'd ever seen. Alfred's torch light glinted on her adversary's pale golden hair, gleaming in eyes the color of a storm. The glow illuminated the man's full lips curved in a mocking and self-satisfied smile.

He was a Saxon pirate by the look of him—tall, light-haired, too pleased with himself. In his hand was the golden circlet that should be hers. *Not a pirate. A thief.*

Dera felt supremely confident as Alfred took up position beside her. As usual, he didn't take the obvious action of defeating her enemy, but waited for her order to do so.

The Saxon's blue eyes widened at Alfred's looming presence, but he drew no sword in defense, though Dera spotted a fine specimen at his belt. The jeweled hilt in particular intrigued her. It would fetch a good price for her when Alfred had deposed her opponent.

"Alfred. This person has apprehended my circlet. Relieve him of it."

She felt smug, but the Saxon laughed. Alfred proceeded dutifully around the crypt, and the Saxon moved to the opposite end. Alfred stopped and turned back the other way. The Saxon did likewise.

Dera repressed a groan. Such maneuverings could last all night. Alfred was strong, but not quick, and he tended to plod rather than bound. The Saxon's lean body appeared both agile and fast.

She held up her hand. "Alfred, cease." He stopped, and she faced her enemy. "You . . . whoever you are. Give me that circlet, and my man here will allow you to pass swiftly from the castle without . . ." She paused to offer a dangerous smile. "Without disturbing the placement of your bones."

Those blue eyes twinkled. "A kind offer, my lady." His gaze shifted to Alfred, then back to Dera. "But one I must refuse."

Dera frowned. The Saxon, however handsome and however well-spoken, clearly didn't value his physical well-being. "You can't refuse. I shall have my man thump you, and you shall be left for the guards, while I depart with the prize."

His brow rose into a teasing arch. It annoyed her. "Indeed?" He eyed Alfred. "Is your servant so strong?"

"He is." Dera looked to Alfred for affirmation. Alfred nodded. The massive cords in his neck bulged when he moved his head. Proof enough.

"So it seems. But I am an agile man." To prove his point, the Saxon leapt easily onto the edge of the crypt and stood balanced with casual grace.

Dera huffed to indicate she wasn't impressed. With hands skilled by hours of practice, she whipped her bow from her shoulder and set an arrow to the string. Just as fast, the Saxon jumped down from the crypt edge.

She pointed the arrow at his heart. "You are outmatched."

He held her gaze with a power so vast that she couldn't look away. She saw him move, but she couldn't react. His broad shoulders flexed with mesmerizing strength. She caught a glimpse of shining steel as he swung his weapon a hairbreadth from her throat.

Dera stumbled back, stunned beyond words. He fingered his weapon, and that infuriating smile returned. Dera's indignation overcame her shock. "An ax? You fight with an ax? What kind of primitive, barbaric fool fights with such a cumbersome weapon?"

"Cumbersome only in the hands of the unskilled." He placed the ax over his back, where it had been hidden. Dera eyed the sword at his belt. He patted the hilt. "For display only." His smile deepened, creating dimples in his well-crafted cheeks. "I like the jewels."

Dera liked them, too, but securing his sword might be more difficult than she had first suspected. "I cannot believe you fight with an ax."

"A throwback to my ancestry, perhaps. I carry the blood of both Viking and Saxon."

"A loathsome mixture."

"But quick."

She couldn't argue with that assessment, so she ignored his comment. She heard movement in the gatehouse as the watchtower guards returned from their dinner. She had timed her invasion perfectly, and this troublesome ruffian had interrupted her plans.

"I have no patience for this foolishness, Saxon. I came for the circlet. I will not leave without it."

He fingered the golden band, looking thoughtful. "Has it such value?"

He didn't know its real purpose. Good. Dera resisted the impulse to rub her hands together. "It has value of a sentimental nature only. It belonged to my . . . grandsire, and was stolen by the lord of this castle."

"Baron DuPre?"

Dera bit her lip. "Yes."

His brows rose. "Baron DuPre is not the lord of this castle."

Dera cringed. He'd caught her in a lie. "It is mine by rights."

He looked askance. "What rights?"

She ground her teeth together. "The right of the Welsh! Give it here!"

He laughed. "I don't think so. Not until I know why you desire it with such . . . passion." He fingered the circlet again, deliberately baiting her. "Yet, perhaps, a deal might be reached between us. You are a trader, I think."

She was a thief, but trader was a more respectable title. "I am."

"As I am." Ha! He was a thief, too, but let him think she believed his claim.

"Go on."

"I might be persuaded to surrender this 'sentimental' heirloom of yours." His sharp gaze met hers. "For a price."

"Name it."

"Agree first."

"Certainly not! What do you want?"

"Allow me to name whatever treasure in this room I desire, and the circlet is yours."

Several guards passed overhead. Dera heard their armor-clad feet on the stone, and her tension soared. She wanted nothing in the room but the circlet. "All the treasure in the room is yours."

"Even the gem in your pack?"

How did he know about that? Dera puffed a breath, then fished around in her pack for the gem. She found it, then held it up to the torch light. A fine green beryl—her favorite stone. She clenched her fingers tightly around it, reluctant to abandon such a prized object.

His lips curved in that infuriating smile. Dera smacked the gem on the pile of treasure. He took it and placed it in a felt bag tied to his belt. "Thank you."

She nodded and held out her hand for the circlet.

"Not so fast, my lady. This gem, though appealing, is not the treasure I seek."

Her eyes narrowed. "You requested it."

"It was a gift."

She clenched her teeth. Until this wretched moment, she had considered the Saxons dull of wit and plain. A shame this man proved himself an exception. "What do you want?"

"Then you agree to my offer?"

More guards filed into the gatehouse on the level above. "Yes. Agreed. Take what you want, and give me my circlet."

He smiled like a cat with a mouse, and Dera endured a

grim sense of doom. "Very well, then." He moved around the crypt to her side. "I choose you."

"*What?*"

"I trade the circlet for yourself, lady."

She was too angry for coherent thought. Too angry even to shoot him. "I am not a possession!"

"You are Welsh. *Wealas* in the Saxon tongue means 'slave.' I traded for you in a fair deal. You are mine."

Dera shifted toward Alfred, but her gaze remained fixed on the Saxon. "Alfred. Break his bones."

Alfred stepped dutifully toward the Saxon, his fist readied for a fine and utterly satisfying *thump*.

The Saxon didn't flee as she expected. Instead, he eyed her like a chastened child. "Are you certain of this course, lady?"

She was too angry to respond. A loud clatter of castle guards prevented her from response, anyway. Dera froze. This evil, golden-haired Saxon fiend would be the death of her.

"What say you, lady? Our friends above have heard your giant, or perhaps your own indignant yelp. They will soon discover our presence in this vault. Can he hold off the entire armed guard?"

"He can hold off ten, at most."

"But there will be twenty. At least."

Dera groaned. "You will pay for this, Saxon."

"We will discuss the arrangements between us later. After we've escaped this fortress." He didn't wait for an answer. He knew she couldn't refuse.

She decided to give one, anyway, so that he would understand she allowed only his assistance, not his ownership. "Very well. You have permission to assist us in our exit."

He chuckled as he drew his sword. Dera contemplated saving her last arrow for him.

"I thought your sword was only for show."

"An ax, my lady, is less useful in close quarters."

"You used it against me!"

He passed by her and aimed for the door. "That . . . was for show." He dared wink.

She growled, then followed him. "Alfred, come along."

The Saxon looked back at Alfred. "Doesn't he have a weapon?"

"He doesn't need one."

"Ah."

Dera's heart drummed as the castle guards proceeded down the staircase and along the corridor. "What do we do?"

The Saxon shrugged. "If we wait for them to discover us, we'll be trapped here."

"If we try to leave now, they'll see us."

"Eventually, but we should be able to reach the portcullis before we're surrounded."

"What good will that do?"

"I assume your servant can handle a portcullis?"

"Of course."

"Then we fight, and assuming we win, we cross the bridge and depart. They won't pursue us at night."

"There must be an easier way."

"If you can think of one, I'd be pleased to hear it."

They both looked back at Alfred. Alfred shook his head. They nodded and faced the door again.

Dera closed her eyes tightly and steeled her courage. Then she peered up at the Saxon. He seemed unafraid. He glanced down at her. This time, his smile was kind.

"I am Dera, daughter of Penn of Llangollen." She paused. "By what name are you called?"

"Beowulf."

Chapter Two

The events of Wulf's day had proceeded even better than he'd planned. He'd followed the Welsh girl and her giant from the Welsh borders through the villages of Shropshire and across Staffordshire, knowing she possessed a portion of his map.

She was a sneaky little person, but he had guessed her destination, and reached Tutbury Castle before her. He had only to learn what object she would choose to continue on his own quest.

Now, he needed only to defeat the castle guard of twenty mail-clad men and continue on his way. Simple.

Dera readied her bow beside him. He heard her soft, swift breaths as she prepared to fight. A brave woman, though small of stature. He had admired her as he trailed her from Wales. Nothing daunted her, perhaps because of the massive guard always at her side.

She had taken longer to surrender than he'd imagined. He

hadn't planned on a battle. But what needs be . . . "Are you ready?"

She nodded. It occurred to him that she was too afraid to speak, and his heart warmed with unwilling sympathy.

"Follow me." Wulf started forward, then glanced back at Alfred. "Quietly."

Dera nodded. "No thumping, Alfred."

Alfred issued a brief grunt, which presumably indicated an affirmative.

Wulf moved silently from the vault into the corridor. Dera followed close behind. "All clear."

They crept slowly forward. Her stealth impressed him, but Alfred's heavy footfall was easy to detect. Two guards passed the junction of two corridors, and Wulf pressed back against the wall. The guards didn't notice them, so he motioned Dera forward again.

"We just might make it."

"There! Ruffians!" Two fully armored knights charged around the corner, and Wulf sighed.

"Or perhaps we won't."

Dera uttered a small peep of fear, but her arrow was already set to the bow. Wulf shoved his sword into its scabbard, seized his war-ax, and bounded toward the guards.

They weren't expecting an attack, and both stumbled backward. Wulf swung his ax sidelong, knocking both men down. "If you'll excuse me, my good men . . ."

Wulf smiled, then waved Dera forward. She gaped at him in utter astonishment. She mouthed the words "excuse me," then shook her head in disbelief.

The guards lay stunned on the floor, but more thundered down the spiral rock stairway. If they reached the portcullis . . .

"I suggest we run."

She ran like a woodland deer beside him. Alfred lumbered along behind, keeping pace despite his bulk. They reached the heavy wooden door that separated the interior keep from the causeway and gatehouse. It was barred, naturally. Wulf positioned his ax, then remembered his new servant. "Alfred . . ."

Alfred stepped forward and bashed the door with one fist; it crunched outward. He stepped back, and Wulf nodded. "Very good."

The castle door led to a short causeway, then to the gatehouse where the guards would now be massed in waiting. "Fewer ahead than behind." He wasn't certain this was true, but one could always hope.

Stagnant odors from the dark moat rose in the misty night like a wall against them. They ran forward toward the torchlight in the gatehouse. Guards shouted from behind, and Wulf glanced back over his shoulder as the men poured from the castle.

Ahead, the gatehouse guards waited before the portcullis, their long halberds readied for defense. Wulf leapt forward, his ax singing through the damp air as he charged. The gatehouse guards advanced, forming a line to stop him. He angled right, then jerked left. He swung his ax again sidelong, knocking three men at once into the moat. He enjoyed the subsequent splash and loud cursing.

Another group clamored from the rampart above, faces flushed from too much ale. They had been celebrating, enjoying a festive mood. Such days didn't come often for men of their profession. Sympathy tinged Wulf's heart when he recalled his own past. They meant to kill him—it was their duty as castle guards. To free himself and continue on his quest, he would have to do the same to them.

Wulf lowered his weapon as if surrendering. They advanced, then swung, but he ducked, dove forward, and tripped the first man with the hilt of his ax. He liked battle this way—charged with power, leaving no man scathed. A few wet, perhaps. Wulf started to rise, and found himself looking up as a halberd rose, perfectly aimed and poised to slice him through.

Alfred stepped up, thumped the guard on the head, and the halberd clattered to the stone causeway. Wulf looked between Alfred and the stunned guard. "Well done."

Dera ran up and pointed behind them as the castle guards charged across the causeway. "They're coming! We'll never make it."

"Think defeat, and know defeat. Follow me, lady."

Wulf took her hand and they ran together, just as the portcullis creaked above them. On the rampart above, a guard worked feverishly to lower the gate. "Curses!"

Dera's arrow flew before he saw her set it to the string. It pierced the gatekeeper's hand and he lurched backward with a howl of pain.

"A good aim, my lady."

She looked smug. "I know."

They darted into the gatehouse just as the second portcullis lowered. Dera issued a squeal of dismay. "Alfred! The gate!"

Alfred took his place at the portcullis, caught it as it lowered—this time with both hands—and held it as Wulf and Dera raced beneath. He shoved it up, went beneath himself, then yanked it down with pure, brute force.

Wulf stared at Alfred, ignoring the sudden rain of ill-aimed arrows from the rampart. "A strong man."

Dera nodded as if the compliment were directed at her. "Thank you."

Dera started across the drawbridge, but Wulf hesitated. He unfastened his jeweled sword, then tossed it through the portcullis bars to the guards beyond.

A faint smile touched his lips as the guards scrambled to retrieve the valuable weapon. Wulf turned to see Alfred watching him, a look of quiet wonder on the large, impassive face.

They hurried across the short drawbridge where Dera waited. She hopped from foot to foot with impatience. She held out her hand. "Give me my circlet."

Wulf pointed back at the portcullis as the guards desperately struggled to raise it again. Apparently, Alfred's efforts had jammed the mechanism. "Perhaps we can discuss our agreement later."

"There was no agreement!"

A stubborn woman. Wulf took her arm and pulled her from the bridge. "Later, woman. Where are your horses?" The faint light from the gatehouse illuminated the stubborn set of her jaw. "Of course, I could—with the circlet in my possession—take my own horse and make my way alone. . . ."

Her eyes narrowed to slits and her full, soft lips pressed into a fierce line. "My horses are farther along, tethered by a small stream just east of here."

"Close by my own. Good."

Dera glanced back at the castle, then at Wulf. "You wield an ax, the bloodiest weapon I know, the weapon of your violent heritage. Yet through all the battle, you killed no one." She paused. "You harmed no one."

"Three men are well-soaked in foul water."

"It was a greater effort to leave them unharmed, yet still escape."

"I saw no man fall to your arrows, lady."

She looked at her feet as if ashamed of weakness. "I suppose because I've had Alfred with me, I've never actually killed anyone."

Wulf met her gaze and saw a proud innocence he had long since forgotten. "I have."

The Saxon started away, but Dera hesitated before following him. "Are you truly named Beowulf?"

He turned back, smiling again. The haunted expression she had seen on his face was gone, yet its brief flare had pierced her heart. "My sire was fond of legend. But those of my close acquaintance shorten that name to Wulf."

Dera followed him through the dark wood, Alfred stomp-

ing along behind. They retrieved his horse, then found hers.
Alfred's stout bay mare waited with the same blank expression as its master. Dera's lithe chestnut had entwined itself
in the bushes, no doubt a product of its quest for better foliage, and it stood trapped by the rope.

Wulf untangled the horse from the shrubs, then led it to
Dera. "Yours, I presume."

Despite the fact that he held her circlet and had claimed
her as a possession, Wulf was a likable man. Perhaps he had
been teasing her when he made his deal. His nature seemed
good-humored. She had seen him laugh in the midst of battle,
when the three guards fell headlong into the moat.

Nothing seemed to trouble him, except the mention of killing. She wondered why. He was obviously well-skilled with
his ax, though he wielded it in a peculiar fashion. He wasn't
a serf or any kind of peasant. By his stature, good manners,
and clear speech, she guessed he had been a knight.

A knight turned thief. Her curiosity about him gave way
to the pursuit of her quest. "My circlet."

Wulf patted his pack. "It is safe. Come, my lady, mount
your horse . . ." He paused, eyes twinkling in the darkness.
"Or perhaps I should better say *my horse*."

Her jaw set itself hard as she seized her horse's reins. "My
horse was not part of our bargain."

"Ah, but since you were, all things in your possession are
now mine."

He was not likable. Not in the least. Dera averted her eyes
in an attempt to ignore him. "Alfred! Assist!" She positioned herself at her horse's side and waved a fierce command. Alfred marched to her side and started to lift her onto
the horse's back.

Wulf stepped between them. "Alfred, from now onward,
will answer my commands, dear lady. Not yours."

"What?" She made a fist and prepared to strike him. "Alfred belongs to me. Alfred! Place me on my horse at once!"

He moved to do so, but Wulf gripped his arm. Alfred

304

hesitated, uncertain as to who controlled him now. "You surrendered yourself to me in exchange for the circlet. In doing so, you surrendered your giant to me also."

"You never *gave* me the circlet, you fiend!"

"I will hold it as assurance that you uphold your word."

She twitched with fury. He seemed to enjoy her posture. As soon as he fell asleep, she would tie him hands and feet like a hog, gag him, then dance circles around his prostrate body. "As you wish, my lord Saxon. I shall walk at your side in humble obedience."

He wasn't fooled. Perhaps he recognized the combative gleam in her eyes. "Nay, lady. You shall ride your horse lest you slow my escape. With the circlet in my possession, I see no need to restrain you."

She gazed upward through the black shadows of the trees into the starless sky, embarrassed. "Alfred always helps me to mount."

"Because you have chosen a horse too tall for a woman of your small size."

She braced in offense, but he moved closer to her. Without warning, he picked her up himself. Attack was imminent. She couldn't stop herself. Dera seized a portion of his long, shaggy hair and gripped it tight. To her fury, he laughed.

"I am not to be trifled with, you pirate! I am on a quest, and—"

"Yes, I know." He spoke with such confidence that she stopped and stared at him. He couldn't know. "You seek the mysterious artifact known as the Twelfth Night."

She wanted to deny his guess, but she gaped instead. "How did you—?" She clamped her lips shut, but he just grinned.

"It seems, my little servant, that you and I share a common goal."

Her mouth drifted open again. "You're after my artifact, too? Why?"

"For the same reason you seek it, of course. Because of

the rumor of great wealth. A wealth that never runs dry.''

''You heard that, too?'' Dera's face puckered as she considered what this might mean. ''My father gave me such a message—he said a man spoke to him in the night, in secret, telling *me* to undertake this quest. I cannot think how you intercepted it.''

''A voice in the night spoke to me, and in the morning, I found a portion of a map.''

''What portion?'' Dera's irritation eased as she considered her new fortune. The map she possessed was torn—and she needed the missing part to gauge the details of her journey. ''How did you know I had the rest?'' She cringed, realizing that perhaps he hadn't known, but Wulf didn't seemed surprised by her announcement.

''That, too, was revealed to me.''

''I do not believe your claim, of course. It is clear that the map was meant for me, and somehow you managed to tear off a section.'' She paused. ''Let me see it.''

''I don't think so.''

They stared at each other. Dera couldn't trust him, and he wouldn't trust her. For good reason. Her face puckered as she considered their common dilemma.

''You know as well as I do that we are a danger to each other. While I am obviously more deserving, you appear to be cunning in the extreme. I do not trust you.''

Wulf smiled as if this were a charming image. ''Nor do I trust you, my lady thief.'' He paused, blue eyes alive with amusement. ''*Dera* is an interesting name—in the Welsh tongue, it means 'fiend.' Appropriate, I should say.''

Dera felt proud. ''Indeed, and you would be wise to take care around me.''

''I will.'' He paused. ''Yet our common dilemma remains. At some point, I will require sleep—and I would sleep unencumbered by fear that you'll steal my map. Although waking to find your little fingers prying about might be interesting.''

She ignored his reference. ''There is only one solution.''

He nodded, understanding. For an instant, his quick read of her thoughts seemed a surprise, yet it felt normal, and her doubt eased. "I agree, lady, if your memory is as adept as your thieving fingers."

"It is, of course." Most of the time. She had mistaken the fourteenth stone in the castle for the twelfth, but Wulf needn't know that.

Wulf opened the felt bag at his belt and withdrew a small, torn parchment. Dera retrieved her own pack and found her map. They nodded at once, stood back to back, and each committed their portion to memory.

Then they stood face to face, gazes locked, and they tore their portions to shreds. Together, they tossed the bits into the swift stream.

Dera endured a sense of finality and doom, but she kept her chin high. "If one of us dies, the other is lost."

"A good reason to keep both of us alive."

"True."

He glanced at her sidelong. "Did you think I would kill you?"

"You said you have done it before."

His expression changed. "I killed a man once. And for it, I lost . . ." His voice trailed off.

Her heart moved with unwilling pity. "What did you lose?"

"Suffice to say the life my family leads today would be much altered had I chosen another course."

"You were not always a lowly ruffian?"

"No."

"You were, I suspect, a knight of some sort. It is in your manner."

He nodded. "I was the Captain of Lord Cleavedon's guard."

Dera's curiosity peaked, but he set her abruptly on her horse's back, then turned away. "Of Brinklow Castle?"

"The same."

"It is a position of high honor."

"It was."

Dera watched as Wulf mounted his horse. "This man you killed. Who was he?"

He didn't answer at once. Then he sighed, the breath torn from his chest. "Lord Cleavedon."

Chapter Three

Dera asked no further questions. Perhaps his answer had shocked her beyond the desire to know. Wulf rode ahead, with Dera and Alfred following. They traveled in silence, each with their own thoughts. Wulf knew what occupied Dera's mind—schemes to seize control of their group.

But Alfred remained a mystery. His expression appeared blank, but Wulf knew the giant was thinking something. Something that left a vague uneasiness in Wulf's heart.

They rode for an hour in darkness, then made camp east of Tutbury's domain. They weren't followed—Wulf knew the surrounding land too well for that.

"Tonight, we sleep beneath the stars, my lady thief. But as our journey progresses, we may find inns of better comfort."

Dera unfurled her bedroll and arranged her cape as a blanket. "I am accustomed to sleeping this way."

She lay flat on her back, but her gaze shifted often to him. Wulf positioned his bedroll next to hers, and she tensed.

"You need not fear, lady. I treat my possessions with great care."

Her lips curled upward in disgust, and he watched as she resisted an impulse to battle. Her fists clenched, but she kept them at her sides. "I am not your possession."

She couldn't resist arguing that point. He reached to touch her cheek, and she smacked his hand away. "I might be persuaded to take you as a mistress instead."

She rolled over on her side facing him, then propped herself up on one elbow. "If you should again consider such a vile arrangement, I shall command Alfred to pick you up and break you like a bread loaf!"

"Even at the expense of my knowledge?"

"Yes."

"Is your chastity so important?"

She rolled onto her back again, her small hands folded on her chest. She hesitated before answering him, as if her chastity had less value than he imagined. A promising thought. "I will not be an amusement to wile away any man's hours."

"I never suggested—"

She glared over at him. "You did."

"If you see it so."

She lay silent for a while, but her eyes didn't close. She looked thoughtful. Wulf waited. "What preys on your thoughts, lady?"

"Why did you kill your lord?"

"That, I keep to myself."

"Why weren't you executed for the deed?"

Wulf turned his gaze back to the dark sky. "The king had reason to keep me alive."

"Because your act was deemed just?" Dera sounded hopeful.

"Because the king considered me his assassin."

He heard a sharp gasp, and Dera went tense. "Assassin? They paid you?"

"They offered. I declined."

310

She paused as if reluctant to learn more about her new
"master."

"If that is so, how did you lose your knighthood?"

"Lose it?" Wulf sighed. "I gave it away."

"You mentioned your family. Have you a wife?"

He glanced at her. Her expression remained intent. He
allowed himself a knowing smile at her expense. "I have no
wife. My mother and sisters were sent from within castle
walls to the squalor of a crofter's hut. The fortune I had
gained was lost with my knighthood."

"So you turned to theft?"

"Trade, my lady."

"In what way was your invasion of Tutbury Castle
'trade'?"

"I consider it such."

She studied his face in silence, then arched one fine brow.
"Is that why you left your sword to the guards?"

He nodded.

"You mean to give the Twelfth Night's treasure to your
family, don't you?" He detected guilt and possible remorse
in her voice, but he doubted it would move her to relinquish
her claim.

"I do." She didn't respond. "And you, lady. For what
purpose do you seek such a mysterious artifact?"

Dera sighed. "It is necessary. That is all I will say."

"Come, I have told you my tale. What of your own?"

"And a tale might be all that it is. You are wily. I can see
that. But however just your claim may be, mine is better."

"In what way?" As he had thought—a stubborn woman.

"That is none of your concern."

"A change of subject, then."

"Good idea. What do you wish to discuss?"

"Where do we go next?"

Dera sat up and looked at him again. "How did you get
this far?" She didn't let him answer. "You followed me,
didn't you?"

"I did."

"I never noticed you."

"Of course not. My stealth is unmatched."

"Except by your conceit."

Wulf smiled. "The only thing that equals my conceit is your own."

She huffed, but she didn't argue. "How did you know about my quest?"

"The message I received told me the path to my treasure—"

She interrupted with another huff. "Your treasure, indeed!"

"The path to *my* treasure was held in an angel's hands."

She eyed him doubtfully. "And this led you to me?"

"My angel has black hair and green eyes."

"As do many Welsh women."

"And she travels with a red-bearded giant at her side. Is that trait also common to Welsh females?"

"No. It isn't. I am the only one." She paused. "The message my father received said nothing of you. He was told the path I should follow—'from out the dark wood, across the green fields where you shall find the sun which will guide you north into the hold of the Night.' There was more about this Twelfth Night, and how it would bestow upon me the only treasure worth seeking."

"It is obvious that I am the sun."

Dera uttered a short laugh. "What madness leads you to believe this?"

"I am golden-haired and of a cheerful disposition." She interrupted with a contrived cough. He continued, unabated by her scorn. "You left Wales, found me—'the sun'—and I will guide you north." He paused. "North, is it? To Scotland?"

"Not quite so far north." She paused. "I shall tell you no more of that now."

"Wise."

"I have retrieved the first key—the circlet."

"Ah! So it is a key. I guessed as much."

"You guessed nothing of the kind! You were simply following me for clues. I should not be surprised to find you eavesdropped on my conversations with Alfred."

"You have conversations, do you?"

"Well, no. Alfred isn't much for talk." A tiny smile curved her lips as she peered over at Wulf. "For that reason only, I am not completely regretful at your presence."

"And the fact that I'm handsome, young, and strong carries no weight with you?"

She groaned. "Your days as a ruffian have done little to diminish the typical vanity of a knight, I see."

"My days as a ruffian have taught me that a woman cares more for a man's skill in her bed than for his title."

"About that, I wouldn't know."

He enjoyed teasing her. In the days he had followed her trail, he had wondered at her disposition. She seemed bossy, and she was, but there was a fragility beneath her determination that appealed to him. He liked the way she issued fierce commands to her hulking servant, then eased behind him in a crowd. Yet when threatened, Dera always took the fore.

He had learned that she wore her green gown only when in towns, and that she dressed like an archer otherwise. He noticed that she had an affection for beryl stones, and that she only stole from noblemen. She had resisted the temptation of an egg-sized beryl brooch worn by an elderly widow.

He noticed that before she left town, she had given every child treats and shared what food she had purchased with the village beggars.

Men from every village watched her, but she never noticed their attention. One poor fool deliberately tripped in front of her, and Dera just stepped over him, ordered Alfred to set the fool aside, and marched on.

She walked with purpose on small, stomping feet, wearing

well-worn laced thongs or supple shoes. She always seemed to know where she was going, and she never looked back.

Wulf wandered aimlessly and could never quite look away from where he'd been.

"Tell me of yourself. You are not quite a lady, but neither are you completely a scoundrel."

"I am flattered by your assessment of my character."

"What drove you into thievery? You seem adept at the craft."

"I am. And no, I am not a lady. My mother was noble-born, and lived at Caernafon Castle. She was ruined by a lowly bard—my father—which resulted in my birth."

"Were you raised at court?"

"For a while. My mother died when I was nine years old, and her family arranged my placement in a village far from Caernafon."

"Why? Surely they didn't blame you for your mother's indiscretion?"

"Perhaps I wasn't so very well-behaved."

Wulf smiled. He could imagine her as a child, small and quick, bright and curious. "I cannot imagine that."

"At first, I thought anything would be better than living unwanted in the castle. I soon learned there is always a worse fate. I was placed with a dairy maid, who left me to do her most unpleasant tasks. My mentor was large and fat, and struck me with a butter mallet if I disobeyed." A small expression of pride formed on her face. "I saw fit to apprentice myself elsewhere."

"Dare I ask with whom?"

"I met an old thief named Penn—he was stealing fresh butter from my mentor—and I decided I liked his craft. He took me in as apprentice and taught me all the arts he knew."

"It seems an odd choice."

"To you, perhaps. Penn was the only person to treat me with kindness, to appreciate my nature. His only son was a scoundrel who died young, and he wanted an heir to carry on his heritage."

"Heritage? Of thievery?"

"Yes. I am a member in good standing of several thieves' guilds already."

"An honor."

"You, being a noble yourself, wouldn't understand, but there are some who might say a knight is little more than . . ." She stopped, but Wulf turned his gaze upward to the dark sky.

"Little more than an assassin? Aye, there are some who say so."

"I wasn't thinking of that." A nervous silence followed. Dera cleared her throat. "I am sorry."

"There is no need. You were right."

They didn't speak for a while, but Wulf drew no closer to sleep. He liked her company. He liked her quick anger and veiled smile. "How did you come by a servant like Alfred?"

"My father fetched him for me."

"Ah. Then the old thief has some fortune, anyway."

Dera's brow puckered. "No. No, he doesn't. I have wondered how he came to secure Alfred. But my father is a clever man. Alfred has proven most useful in my endeavors."

"I wondered if you might be lovers."

She cocked her brow in a doubtful posture. "Alfred is my servant."

"Alfred is *my* servant, lady. But being a maiden's servant doesn't preclude warming her lovely body at night." And she did have a lovely body. Wulf had seen enough to know that. Her small, lithe form encased in snug leggings; her round, firm bottom barely concealed by her boy's tunic . . . And her legs—it was worth following the woman just to gaze at her shapely calves and trim ankles.

She watched him suspiciously. "I find you peculiar in the extreme, and your nature reprehensibly lascivious."

He chose to ignore her comment. "I soon realized my error. No man allows his mistress to order him about as you do Alfred. When you become my lover, it shall be otherwise."

She cast him a dark look. "Saxon, you talk too much."

"I do, at that." Without warning, he leaned toward her and kissed her. He fully expected her to strike him, but she seemed too surprised to move. Her lips were soft and warm against his. He flicked his tongue to taste her, but he probed no further. He drew her closer into his arms and felt her wild, rapid pulse, the sign of her arousal.

He ran his fingers through her hair, slowly moving his mouth back and forth against her tender lips. A soft moan escaped from deep in her throat, a moan of both pleasure and despair.

Dera jerked away from him. "Alfred!" Her voice came as a tiny peep. Wulf glanced toward Alfred, who answered her whispered cry for help with a rumbling snore.

Wulf smiled, then laid his finger on her moist lips. "There is no need."

He might become fond of her, and that was a danger. She was quick to passion, yet vulnerable and sweet, qualities she tried desperately to hide. "It seems I traded well this time. You are indeed a treasure."

"I am not a possession. This agreement between us isn't lasting."

"That remains to be seen. Already you have surrendered to my kiss."

"I am still armed." She spoke through clenched teeth. He loved the sound. Wulf folded his hands on his chest, comfortable.

"With your bow, yes. Of course, since you belong to me, the bow . . ."

Morning brought new resolve. The Saxon Beowulf didn't seem an entirely loathsome man, but Dera had no intention of spending her days as his servant. *Where the will lacks nothing, a way opens.* Penn had told her that when he took her in as his daughter, and she had never forgotten.

Wulf had the circlet. His cleverness was something she had to consider, and so plan carefully. Don't act in haste. He was an able swordsman, thanks to his knightly heritage. A swordsman skilled enough to defeat Lord Cleavedon, whose skill was renowned even in Wales.

So having Wulf in her party as she followed the quest northward wasn't a bad arrangement. If only he were in *her* service!

Dera drummed her fingers on her chest and stared at the first light of dawn. Alfred lay between her and the tethered horses, snoring. He was, of course, the answer—when the time was right. Wulf didn't snore, another element in his favor.

She peered over at him. He had positioned his bedroll too close to her own, a presumptuous act she would correct at the next opportunity. When she secured him into her service, it would be otherwise. Yes. He would sleep at her feet. That image pleased her and she smiled.

The slight growth of his new beard contrasted with the perfection of his fine Saxon bone structure. This image of masculinity, combined with his tenderness, caused an odd stir in her loins. Dera forced her gaze from his sleeping face.

He must be in her service, not the other way around. But how? Such things must be handled delicately, especially with a man so well-skilled with a war ax. She had retrieved the first key, the circlet, on her own, but the next trial would be harder. Alfred was useful, but having a former knight at her disposal would ensure her success.

More satisfying still would be issuing orders he had to obey. She would have him assist her onto her horse. Make her breakfast. Bow before speaking and call her "Lady Dera."

A small chuckle rose in her throat at the thought.

"Scheming, my lady?"

His voice startled her, and she popped up from her bedding. Wulf lay on his side, propped up on one elbow. Her insides tingled in a peculiar fashion at the sight of him. He looked drowsy, his blond hair hanging over one eye in a sensual posture. His lips curved, and she remembered with vivid clarity his kiss.

"Not at all." Her voice came small and nervous—not the reaction she wished to show. "You startled me."

"In the midst of thoughts that produced the most devious expression I have ever seen. I almost fear to continue this day."

She couldn't resist a smile, but she refused to allay his concern. "Indeed?"

Wulf sat up. His chest was bare despite the cold, broad and well-formed with muscle. He pulled his tunic on slowly, then fastened a belt around his waist. Dera stared, then realized he would notice her attention, so she fixed her gaze on the nearest shrub.

Alfred was still sleeping. She needed him to break the tension between herself and her captor. "Alfred! Morning has come. Wake at once!"

Alfred rose in one motion, showing no signs of grogginess, and awaited her instructions.

Dera felt better. Alfred's immediate obedience salvaged her shaken pride. "Prepare a light meal, then ready the horses, Alfred."

Alfred started off, but Wulf shook his head. "Hold, Alfred."

To Dera's annoyance, Alfred obeyed Wulf's order, too.

"My lady servant forgets herself, Alfred. Since yesterday's events, you and she are both in my service, and it is mine to give direction."

Dera twitched. "What are your commands then, oh Lord of Fiends?"

Wulf rubbed his chin thoughtfully. "Alfred, prepare a

breakfast for our group, and ready the horses."

Dera managed no more than a low growl, but Wulf turned his innocent gaze to her, his smile veiled. "Where to today, my lady?"

"I thought you were the master." Her voice came tightly through constricted, angry passages.

"I am. But you hold knowledge of our onward path."

"So I do." Dera squirmed free of her bedding and stood up, adjusted her tunic, and faced him. "For this reason, you will relinquish your position and dominance over me, and present yourself as my servant. Then we shall proceed onward."

Alfred looked back and forth between them, revealing no emotion, but with interest as to who would command him next. Dera cast him a meaningful glance to assure him that those orders would come from her, but Wulf laughed.

"A good try, my lady thief, but I think you have as much to gain from our onward quest as I. I see no reason to alter the situation between us."

"What have I to gain as your servant?"

Wulf touched her chin, but he drew his hand away before she could strike him. "Ah, but you don't expect to be my servant, do you? By the time we reach our goal, you feel sure the battle will have turned your way."

She couldn't argue with that. "You are an infuriating man."

"I am."

Dera seized her gray cape and pinned it at her neck. "Very well. I shall bide my time for now."

"A reassuring declaration. And in answer to my question . . . ?"

"We go northeast. We must find the second key at Conisbrough Castle." She paused. "Of course, I am concealing from you the details and exact directions, which I memorized."

319

"Perhaps if you gave me an idea of what your map contained, I could better detect our destination."

"There is no chance of that."

"This much I know without seeing your portion: Our maps were two halves of a whole. Without the other, neither of us can complete the quest."

"Only one of us can hold the treasure. It will be me."

"That remains to be seen, but let us debate this matter later. Today, we begin the journey to Conisbrough." He paused and eyed her doubtfully. "Are you certain of this key's location?"

"No. Yes. Why?"

He smiled at her wavering certainty. "Conisbrough seems an odd choice. But I will trust you in this."

"You would be wise to do so." Dera looked up at the morning sky. The clouds were growing thicker, and the air was damp and cold. "Winter approaches. We will not reach our destination before the Yule. Why couldn't it be a Midsummer's Day treasure?"

"The way is cold, but we should find pleasant shelter along the way. I am well known at the inns between Warwickshire and York. When we reach Conisbrough, we will take rest at an inn called the Bull and Pheasant—a fine establishment. The proprietor is an old friend. He will give us quarters to take away the chill, and ease our hunger."

"That sounds promising." Dera sighed. "Twelve days! Let them pass swiftly. . . ."

Chapter Four

Conisbrough
December 29, 1335
Fourth Day of Yule

The Bull and Pheasant was easy to spot, a large many-winged building with a newly painted sign. It appeared both inviting and warm, festive for the fourth day of Yule. Several horses were tied near the front entrance, with a stable set back from the inn.

Smoke billowed from the center chimney, and all the windows burned with light. Dera dismounted, passed her reins to Alfred, and rubbed her bare hands together. "Alfred, see to our horses."

Wulf issued a *tsk* noise and shook his head. "The servile demeanor hasn't been easy for you to adopt, has it, lady thief? Alfred is *my* servant, therefore he must attend *my* instructions."

Dera stood face to face with Wulf. Unfortunately, he was

a tall man, and she had to crank her head up to glare into his eyes. "What other errand would you have him do?"

"You mustn't strain yourself with such tasks as delivering orders yourself, my dear." He leaned slightly toward her as he spoke, and Dera remembered his kiss. "I might require your skills later."

"My skills? What for?"

"Foot washing, perhaps?" He backed away, leaving her speechless with fury. "Alfred, find stabling for the horses."

Dera mustered a growl, but no words came.

Alfred took their horses and led them to the stable without comment. If possible, he had spoken less in Wulf's company than before, but he always seemed to be watching.

When she and Wulf argued, Alfred was watching. When they fought over who got the largest portion of the dinner stew, he watched. When Dera nabbed a round of cheese from a fat dairymaid's cart, then pretended to have nothing—Alfred watched.

Sometimes, she felt he knew too much.

Wulf went to the common room and waited for Dera. She marched past him, determined to deny whatever he commanded.

The warm scent of roasted meat met her nostrils, and her stomach churned with hunger. The noisy din of the common room's patrons rose like song to her ears. Everywhere, there were pockets to be picked, small bags that held treasure. First, she would have to study her targets to be sure they had cash to spare.

Alfred entered the common room and took position behind Dera. Several of the patrons took note of him and whispered amongst themselves. A ruddy-faced man presented himself to Wulf like a long-lost uncle.

"Sir Beowulf, it is! I am honored, sir, that you've chosen to visit us again."

Dera glanced at Wulf. It seemed his fall from grace wasn't

widely known in England. "Crighton, could I pass northward without sampling your fine wares? Nay . . ."

The innkeeper winked at Dera. "It seems you've brought wares of your own this time. My serving wenches will be disappointed."

Dera sputtered with fury. "I am not—"

Wulf clamped his hand on her shoulder, pinning her back. "A room for myself and my two servants, Crighton."

"We could put the big fellow out with the stableboys, but I'm guessing you'd best keep your handmaiden at your side." He winked again, and Dera contemplated striking him. "Any number of randy fellows who might pester her otherwise."

Dera made a fist. "They'd best not try, or they'll have Alfred to deal with!"

Wulf cast a dark glance toward the gathering room. "The woman is mine alone." Both Dera and the innkeeper looked at Wulf in surprise. He appeared surprised himself. "A room, Crighton."

"I have elegant quarters for yourself, and one for your manservant, in the south wing."

"Thank you. That will do well."

Crighton dusted his hands on his apron. "I can have provisions sent up to you there, or you can dine in the common room, as you prefer. A fine stuffed pigling, we're offering tonight"

Wulf turned to Dera. "What say you to stuffed pigling, my lady servant?"

She was cold, hungry, and keen to steal, but she disliked easy acquiescence. "It is adequate. But I will not pour your ale this time. It is beneath me."

"Agreed." He agreed too easily, because that task fell to noblewomen as well. Dera eyed him with intense suspicion, but he looked even more innocent than usual. Her suspicions doubled.

Dera glanced back toward the common room, filled with

unsuspecting targets. "Let us take our meal there. The room appears well-filled with guests."

Now Wulf gave way to suspicion. "Why do you care if it's filled?" Dera answered with a smile, and Wulf's eyes narrowed to slits. "You forget—I have seen you in action before. I know your tricks."

She ignored him and turned to the innkeeper. "I require a basin of hot water delivered to my quarters at once."

Wulf offered an apologetic smile. "My handmaiden enjoys washing my feet."

"What?" Before she could say more, he seized her arm and directed her toward the stairs.

Their room was long and low, with a fine bolstered bed against the far wall. Dera coveted the soft bed with its red canopy at once, but Wulf placed his pack at its foot and seated himself, leaving her the truckle bed. She glared.

"The chivalry of knights has been vastly overstated."

"Ah, but you forget, my lady. I am no longer noble." His blue eyes darkened. "But you are welcome to share my bed if it pleases you."

"It doesn't." Dera set her own gear near the farthest wall, beside a wooden stool. He intended to tease her, to affect her senses. That his tactics worked infuriated her.

Wulf rose and looked out the window, his gaze intent. He drew the heavy curtains closed as if . . . as if concealing himself from prying eyes.

"I've noticed that you hide our camps well, as if you fear pursuit, and now you take the position of watch. Why do you feel the need to guard our door?"

He appeared overly casual. "A custom of mine."

"Or do you know of some danger?"

Wulf left the window and stood before her. He touched her cheek, and his thumb brushed over her lips. "You have a way, my lady, of looking always ahead. I, on the other hand, often look back over my shoulder."

She nodded vigorously. "You think too much of times gone by."

"Perhaps. Yet that trait can be helpful if one is being followed."

"Are we being followed?"

"Yes."

Dera's pulse bounced with excitement and a trace of apprehension. "By whom?"

"An old friend."

"Must you be so evasive? What old friend, and why is he following you?"

"My path has not been carved without creating enemies along the way."

"And you'd best beware lest you create another in me!"

Wulf touched her cheek, so gently that fire sped along her veins. Dera gulped. "Your words imply that you are not yet my enemy."

Her gaze drifted to the side. "You test my patience, but I have no wish to injure you in a severe manner."

"What a comfort!"

"You would make an amusing and pert servant, Sir Beowulf. Sooner or later, I will have you as such."

His bright eyes sparkled. "And when I am in your control, dear lady? What then? Will you demand that I pleasure you all through the night, make love to you with such passion that you forget your name, tease you until each breath is a gasp of ecstasy?"

Dera's mouth slid open, and stayed open. She couldn't answer, though her first reaction was "yes." She shook herself and shuddered, then backed away from him. Wulf chuckled.

"You are an arrogant man. I have no interest in such . . . fleshly pursuits." Curses! Her voice quavered, betraying his effect on her senses.

"Indeed? A shame. Such demands might see the situation between us easily reversed."

Dera lifted her chin and forced herself to look him straight in the eye. "I require privacy to bathe and alter my attire."

"Is that an order?" She knew what he meant. If she ordered, he would refuse. She ground her teeth together.

"It is . . . a request."

Wulf grinned, then went to the door. "Granted. I will await you in the gathering room." His gaze whisked to her body. "Wear garb befitting a woman this night. It would please me. That, too, is an order."

He left before she could hurtle her pack at his head, or remind him that she carried but one change of clothes. Dera flung her pack to the truckle bed, then paced back and forth until a serving boy brought her hot water.

She washed herself carefully, combed out her long hair, and left it loose around her shoulders. She dressed in a cream-colored undergown and her favorite green tunic. Tonight, she wanted to be womanly, to be pretty. As she went downstairs to the gathering room, she told herself that her sudden interest in her appearance had nothing to do with Wulf.

They met outside the gathering room. Dera pretended not to notice Wulf's obvious appreciation of her new attire, nor the way he clearly marveled at her loose hair. His gaze lingered over her breasts, and a surge of embarrassment rose inside her. If he could see the swift rise and fall of her breast, if he knew . . .

"You are lovely, my lady thief."

Dera restrained a smile. "Thank you." She couldn't let him know how much his praise pleased her. She suspected he intended to seduce her tonight. The thought frightened her, because it was possible that with a few tender words and a gentle touch, she would refuse him nothing.

Wulf placed his hand on her back and eased her into the gathering room. "Shall we dine?"

She glanced up at him and noticed his dimples. She

snapped her gaze back to the crowd. "I am quite hungry. Thank you."

"You have thanked me twice tonight." He leaned closer to her, speaking low. "Perhaps you would prefer to dine in our room, after all?"

"I would not." She refused to look at him, but she knew his blue eyes twinkled. Could a man read a woman's feelings, even if she offered vehement denial? His long fingers clasped over her shoulder in a protective manner. He could.

Dera's nervous gaze fixed on a fat, boisterous merchant, who wore an extravagant scarlet tunic. His shoes bore particularly foolish, long, curled toes, complete with bells, and he jingled a felt bag of gold as if bragging of wealth. His loud voice dominated the room, which had the effect of diminishing the sounds of those near him.

Alfred entered the common room, followed by a gust of swirling, snowy wind. Someone in the gathering room cursed him, but Alfred shoved the door against the cold and took his place behind Wulf.

Wulf glanced at him, frowning. "Alfred, a man your size must have to eat." He sounded perturbed at the thought. "I suppose you must take dinner with us." He rubbed his chin thoughtfully. "Guard the horses tonight, Alfred. The stables here are often assailed by thieves."

The innkeeper overheard Wulf's words, and paused, brow puckered as he started to speak. Wulf sent him a stern look, and the innkeeper nodded, then moved on. Dera eyed him suspiciously, but then she knew. Wulf wanted them to be alone tonight.

There was no question why. She drew a quick, nervous breath, then forced her attention back to the gathering room. A thin boy of perhaps ten years stood by the fire. He moved from table to table, posing a question, then moving on. He carried a small burlap sack which he offered to the patrons. Some patrons dropped a coin into his bony hand, but others waved him on with harsh words.

The merchant laughed when the boy approached. "What are you selling, boy?"

The boy straightened with pride and drew a small wooden figure from his bag. "These animal figures, sir! I carved them myself. For a farthing only, you can have one for your children."

The merchant took the toy and examined it. Dera read his expression. He saw something of value in the figurine. Something the boy didn't recognize. "What's this you've put in for the eyes?"

The boy shrugged. "Only two blue rocks, sir."

Dera knew what the merchant saw. Beryl chips. Of small value, but easily presented as aquamarine. The merchant stuffed the figure into his bag, then turned away from the boy. The boy gulped, then tapped the merchant's shoulder.

"A farthing, if you please, sir." The boy's voice quavered, and Dera held herself tense.

"Get hence, young rapscallion, or I'll summon the innkeeper to remove you for a pickpocket!"

The boy bowed his head and aimed for the door. Dera caught his arm, and he looked up at her with teary, defeated eyes. "What is your name, small person?"

"I am called Nicholas, miss."

"Very well then, Nicholas. Perhaps I can help you, and persuade that dreadful merchant to pay you your due."

The boy shook his head. "I only wanted to make toys, but each one takes time—to be good enough for the children."

"A noble endeavor." Dera eyed the merchant. "We'll see what I can do."

Dera started toward the merchant, but Wulf caught her and pulled her back. "What are you planning, woman?"

"That is my concern."

"I will not have you hanged for thievery—not while you hold the map's secret in your lovely head."

"I have no intention of getting caught."

Wulf groaned. "That is not what I want to hear. I forbid— What are you going to do?"

She eased out of his grasp. "I am Welsh."

"That's no answer!"

Dera turned to Alfred. "Alfred, there is a harp near the fireplace, unused." She waited for him to catch the direction of her request. He smiled and nodded, but took no action. She cast a quick glance at the merchant, then back to Alfred, who appeared blank. "The harp, Alfred! Use it!"

Wulf watched with ripe suspicion as Alfred shoved his way through the crowd, seized the harp, and began to play. Dera waited until the patrons took note of Alfred's music, then eased herself up to the widest table.

Alfred's skills were unexpected, but always useful. He played like an angel. Not with airiness, true, but with a mystical sensuality she had never heard from any other harpist.

She knew exactly what to do, because she and Alfred had used this tactic many times before. Her body swayed in rhythm, until more and more patrons noticed her. Until they responded with fascination.

When she had their full attention, she danced. She danced as only the Welsh can dance, with magic and sensuality, and a witch's skill at mesmerizing those who watched. She danced on the table. She danced on the benches, her long gown twirling around her ankles.

Wulf watched her, too, and his eyes appeared dark, burning with desire. Across the room, as she moved, she knew he wanted her, and she knew she wanted him, too.

The music filled the room, and it filled her soul. From across the room, her gaze locked with Wulf's, and she felt his passion. The music carried her, but her knees felt weak as she danced. *I want you.* She heard his voice in her head— or was it her own?

The firelight glinted on his golden hair as he stood watching her. She swayed in sensual rhythm, her hips moving with a primal grace. A grace that invited him, and no other, into her secret passion.

As she danced around the crowded room, she had never been more aware of him, of the boots he wore and how they hugged his strong calves, of how his black tunic gripped his broad shoulders, how his hair touched just the collar . . .

Dera gulped and almost missed her twirl. She was forgetting her purpose, a cold, logical purpose that didn't involve a Saxon pirate. Yet all she saw was Wulf.

A man entered the gathering room and stood behind Wulf. He resembled Wulf as closely as a brother, tall and blond, with a regal bearing in his stance. She half-expected Wulf to turn and greet the man as he had the innkeeper, as a long-lost friend, but Wulf's attention remained fixed on Dera.

The man looked from Wulf to Dera, and a faint smile touched his lips. Dera danced toward them, her hands moving like leaves on a morning breeze. As she drew nearer, she realized that though the man indeed resembled Wulf, he lacked the quick, teasing expression.

The look the man cast Wulf's way wasn't friendly, and dark foreboding rose in Dera's heart. She missed her step, and nearly tripped, but the audience didn't notice. The man did, perhaps, because he turned and left. *We are being followed.*

Whatever his purpose, the man didn't appear immediately threatening. If she drew attention to him now, he might act against Wulf openly. She maneuvered herself back into the room's center, nearer to the merchant. His scarlet tunic bore signs of sweat—a disgusting image. Dera swayed, and moved closer to him. She twirled behind his bench. He gasped, and twisted to see her.

She twirled back, smiling as she gazed seductively into his eyes, reached her hand into his pack, and removed a felt bag filled with gold.

She stuffed it in her tunic, then escalated her twirling until she spun so fast that her hair covered her face, her arms

330

outstretched like wings. She heard cheers, loud shouts of approval. She clasped her hands to her breast, and stopped all motion.

The patrons howled, they shouted for more, but Alfred set aside the harp and proceeded to his dinner. Dera went to the boy, who stood beside Wulf. "That was a pretty dance, lady."

Dera smiled. Wulf just stared, his mouth agape. It was a satisfying expression. He appeared flushed. Dera took the boy's hand, then pressed the bag of gold into his palm. "The merchant has paid you now."

The boy's eyes widened. "But lady, he will say I stole from him."

"He might, but no one will believe him."

"Why not?" Wulf and the boy spoke at once, but Wulf sounded more suspicious. Dera cast a reproachful glance his way.

"Because I placed in his other bag an item belonging to his neighbor. And into his neighbor's bag, a pouch belonging to the man across the table. It will be long ere this night is resolved."

Wulf gaped at her in amazement, and even Alfred looked up from his stew, his large face thoughtful.

Wulf shook his head, then seated himself beside Alfred. "There's likely to be a riot tonight, Alfred. I hope your thumping fist is ready."

The boy peeked in at the money and his eyes glowed with happiness. "Why, this will see my mother and sister for a year, at least! And with what your husband gave me . . ." He drew an object from his pocket. The firelight glinted on a green stone, and Dera's breath caught in astonishment.

A beryl. The beryl Wulf had connived from her when they first met.

The boy let out a whoop, covered his mouth to silence himself, then darted from the common room reveling in his good fortune.

Dera stared at the door as the boy left. She looked over at Wulf who stuffed a sliver of roast pigling into his mouth, then took a draught of ale.

Alfred watched the door, too. His gaze shifted to Wulf, and a faint trace of a smile appeared on his lips before he resumed his stew.

Chapter Five

"There was a man watching you tonight."

Dera stood by the shuttered window in their guest room, watching as Wulf prepared his bedding to exact specifications. He eyed her doubtfully. "My lady, 'twas you the men watched, not me." He smiled. "And for good reason."

She restrained her pride. "Only one. He came in while I danced and stood behind you. He seemed to know you." Wulf's brow furrowed. He hadn't noticed the man. Her pride soared—because he had seen only her. "He was a tall man, like yourself, and light-haired."

Wulf's expression told her all she needed to know, and Dera nodded.

"I thought as much. He is the one following us."

Wulf went to the door and barred it, then stood fidgeting for a moment. He fingered his sword, then found his ax and positioned it near the bed. Dera watched with misgivings. "He seemed less formidable than yourself—do you think he will assail you tonight?"

"No." Wulf set the ax aside. "That is not his purpose."

"Then what is?"

"Vengeance."

Dera's eyes widened. "Was he one of Lord Cleavedon's men?"

"No." Wulf went to the window and edged aside the curtain. Dera peeked out, too, but she saw nothing but the lanterns outside the inn.

"So who is he?"

Wulf drew the curtain closed again, then faced her. Sadness shadowed his eyes and her heart moved in sympathy. "He was my first lieutenant."

"He served you?

Wulf turned away before she could issue further comment. He went to the bed and seated himself, gazing upward at nothing. "Aye."

"Sir Beowulf, yours is a complicated tale." Dera hesitated, then sat down beside him. "Why is he following you? From the look on his face, I doubt his intentions are good."

"No, not good."

Dera resisted a flare of impatience in favor of compassion. "In what way?" She touched his arm. "Does he mean to kill you?"

"Worse, my dear. He means to destroy me."

"Why?"

Wulf shrugged. "Because I destroyed him."

Dera exhaled a small growl. "You will explain."

"The route from the past to the present follows one road." She resisted the impulse to strike him, but it wasn't easy. "Lord Cleavedon wielded great power, but he wanted more. After a time, it seemed to me that he became infected with a madness. With his allies, he believed he had found a way to supplant the king and take the throne himself."

"An ambitious plan. What stopped him?"

"I did."

"You killed him to save the king?"

"That wasn't my reason, but King Edward appreciated my act. I have no great affection for our king, but Lord Cleavedon's methods were ruthless."

"What methods did he use?"

"He took King Edward's four-year-old niece and held a knife at her throat."

Dera's eyes puddled with tears. "You killed him to save a child?"

"Yes."

"Your act was noble. I take it your former lieutenant thinks otherwise."

"Ramm is a man of high ambition and pride. He was furious when I left Brinklow Castle. Often, I felt he vied with me for Cleavedon's approval. Perhaps he thought to gain Cleavedon's inheritance himself—had Cleavedon lived."

"Who did supplant Cleavedon?"

A long silence followed. "I did."

Dera turned herself on the bed, crossed her legs beneath her body, and studied Wulf as if he were a peculiar insect. "Does this mean *you* are now Lord of Brinklow Castle?"

"It does, but as I told you, I surrendered my claim."

Dera rolled her eyes. "You have a castle, you're beloved of the king, and still you feel the need to steal my artifact?" Her voice grew louder, tenser. In response, Wulf grinned.

"I will answer to no one," she continued. "I will make my own fate, and when I give the Twelfth Knight treasure to my family, no one will suffer because of my act."

Dera turned her attention to her clasped hands. "I want to give my father the life he deserves—not scraping his way from meal to meal, but with fine things, a soft bed, food, perhaps a new tunic and a black cape. He has always wanted a black cape."

"For better stealth in thievery, no doubt."

"Perhaps." When Dera realized that Wulf hadn't meant

this as a compliment, she frowned. "You do not understand my father."

"That old Welshman is not your father, just a wily thief who took you in. He probably recognized your cleverness."

"Of course! Penn knew at once that I was capable of much . . . well . . ."

"Mischief?"

"Skill!" Dera looked into Wulf's eyes. He appeared doubtful. "I matter to him. I had never mattered to anyone before, not my mother, not the ladies at court. To no one. I was a nuisance. But Penn loves me."

Wulf's expression softened. "That I can believe. I am certain you are dear to him. But surely there is a better life for you than stealing." He hesitated. "Although after tonight's performance, I will say that I approve of your methods."

"I noticed that."

His brow lifted, and his blue eyes flashed. "I wondered . . . I mean, I imagined . . ." As he spoke, his voice lowered, and he moved closer to her. Before she realized his intention, he touched her cheek. "I thought perhaps your dance was meant for me."

She wanted to deny him. She intended to, but the words wouldn't come. Instead, she found herself touching his face, too. "I think, perhaps, it was."

This time, she kissed him. She didn't mean to, but it happened without her consideration. Her lips played against his, a soft, hesitant exploration. Wulf held himself still, neither deepening the kiss nor drawing away. His reaction inspired her to further study. Dera ran her hand over his shoulder, down his arm. He felt tense. Stiff.

An intoxicating response, though she wasn't sure why it inspired her so. She tried parting her lips. He drew in a sharp breath, then parted his, too. She tasted his lower lip with the tip of her tongue. He moaned. She clasped both his shoulders in her grip to hold him fast. She squirmed to face him so that she might deepen their kiss.

Her hair fell loose around her face, shrouding them both in its dark veil. Dera's breath came swift and shallow, almost like gasps. She wanted more of him, she wanted to be part of him—part of his sorrow, his courage, his kindness, and his joy.

Her lips brushed over his, and she kissed the spot where his cheeks dimpled when he smiled. She kissed the side of his face, just in front of his ear, because she had noticed it was a strong, flat portion—admirably formed. She kissed his temple because it seemed somehow vulnerable.

She kissed his forehead because it made him seem young.

Wulf caught her waist in his hands, steadying her. "You are a sweet lover, little thief."

A lover. Dera drew back and looked at him. His face was flushed with desire; his blue eyes burned. She felt the same. "That is what I want to be."

His breath exhaled in a shuddering sigh of relief. "Good, good. I thought perhaps you'd lost your mind."

Before she could assess the meaning of his comment, Wulf eased her into his arms, then lowered her gently back on his bed. It was large, low, and comfortable. A bed fit for a knight.

And his lady. But not his servant.

Wulf pressed fervent kisses along her neck, at the corners of her lips. His attention focused lower as he eased her tunic off her shoulders with quick, sure fingers. "How lovely you are, Dera! How sweet, how beautiful!"

His words had resonance, passion. They lulled her from her discordant thought. "Do you know how much I want you? I've wanted you since I first saw you." He paused to kiss the skin beneath her collarbone. "You were stealing a loaf of bread." She felt his tongue on her flesh, and her nerves tingled like a summer storm raging. "You looked so hungry, my angel, but you didn't eat. Do you remember?"

"No."

He moved to kiss her mouth again, then pressed his cheek

against hers. "You gave it to some children instead."

This clarified nothing for Dera, since she had often done this, but she didn't care. At least, Wulf admired her more noble qualities. She hoped he didn't recall her lesser deeds.

"Then you stole a nobleman's cart, and got it stuck in mud. Even your giant couldn't get it out." He kissed the corner of her mouth again, then her neck. "The noble almost caught you, my dear. Did you know that?"

"He never did!"

Wulf drew back to look down into her face. His eyes glittered. "Only because I told him his horse freed itself of its own devices and wandered off."

"An unlikely story. He wouldn't have believed you."

"No, but to defy Sir Beowulf of Castle Brinklow? Never."

Dera caught his hair in her fists and drew him down to her. "Saxon, you talk too much."

"I do, at that . . ."

She didn't let him finish as she pressed her mouth firmly against his. He braced his strong arms on either side of her and kissed her with wanton abandon. He moved to lie above her, until she felt the weight of his body—almost touching, but not quite.

Desire flamed inside her. It would be bliss to lie in his arms, to revel in his passion—to be his love. Dera closed her eyes, and she remembered the dreams of her youth. A sweet fantasy of a kind, handsome knight who would love her, who would bring magic into her lonely world, who would share with her his endless passion.

Imagination's delicate wings carried her, and Wulf cast her tunic to the floor. He seemed to be fumbling with her undergown, but he still kissed her. He slipped his hands beneath the gown and grazed his fingers up her leg to her hip.

His touch felt intimate and sweet, a worshipful adoration.

In one swoop, Wulf pulled the gown over her head and tossed it aside.

Dera lay stunned, staring up at him through wide eyes. Naked. Completely and utterly naked. She gulped, but he didn't notice. He sat back to view her. He dampened his lips as if savoring a feast. She was too shocked to move.

"You are a perfect sight, little servant."

Servant. He considered her a servant. The wings of fantasy crashed, and Dera remembered who she was, who he was. She yanked the coverlet up to her breasts and started to sit up. "You are well-skilled, I see. No doubt many a tavern wench has found herself as swiftly unclothed." She refused to show embarrassment—simply disdain.

Dera moved away from him to the far side of the bed, then seized her discarded undergown. Wulf didn't try to stop her. He didn't argue or cajole or beg. He did something much, much worse. He smiled.

Dera glared, but that smile deepened until his cursed dimples appeared. He looked innocent, but his eyes twinkled far too brightly for innocence. She couldn't look away.

He held out his hand for her. She chomped her lip, winced, then placed her hand in his. He drew her back. He paused to look into her eyes, and she felt as if he absorbed her soul into his.

So slowly that she ached with need, he bent to kiss her. Not a demanding kiss, but so tender that she had to believe she mattered to him. They lay down together as if there were no other choice between them. He tangled his fingers in her hair and rolled her under him.

"I won't hurt you, Dera. Let me please you."

A sweet promise, and one he meant, she had no doubt. The window rattled beneath the wind's force, and Dera shivered. Wulf smiled as if her every act was dear to him. As if she were dear to him. He pulled a thick blanket over her, then sat up.

Dera watched, spellbound, as he removed his black tunic. His gaze locked with hers, as if he savored her reaction to his masculinity. She had seen him bare-chested before and thought the sight admirable, but now, lying in his bed, about to become his lover, her whole body trembled. Nervousness overtook her, combined with a desire that seemed stronger than any lust for gold.

She knew how a man and woman became one, because among her many childhood crimes was a tendency to spy on unsuspecting couples. She knew men were intent on touching the secret parts of a woman's body. Wulf had already revealed similar inclinations.

He began unfastening his black leggings. His male organ pressed against the cloth, straining . . . for her. Wulf hesitated, then reached for her hand. He held her clenched fist against his mouth and kissed the backs of her fingers.

"Do you fear me, little thief? There is no need."

Dera glanced at his face, then back at his groin. His male organ was larger than she had realized—full and cylindrical. He pried her tense fingers open, then pressed her palm against his length. It felt warm, even through the cloth. Dera's curiosity overcame her fear, and she moved her hand over him, exploring his size and shape. Wulf's sharp breath told her the action pleased him.

She liked her power. No servant had such power, she felt sure of it. She tried squeezing her fingers around him and he shuddered. He pulled off his leggings, and his erection strained upward to his navel. Dera beamed with pleasure. "You are far more interesting than other men."

Wulf's eyes widened, and his jaw slackened. "You have done this before?"

She shrugged. "Not exactly." She paused, reluctant to reveal her intense interest in such matters of the flesh. "When I was young, I . . . happened upon a couple performing this . . . function."

He grinned. "You were spying."

She frowned, but her lips twitched upward into a smile. "Only a bit."

"And what did you see, little Dera?"

"Oh, the most interesting things! Such grappling they did! Cries of passion, moans . . ."

His brow rose. "So you 'happened upon' the entire love-making?"

She decided there was no need to deny the obvious. "Yes. And after that, I happened upon several more such encounters." She hesitated as guilt from her past resurfaced. Even now, the remorse she mustered wasn't heartfelt. "On the last occasion, I was apprehended. It was this that inspired my removal from the keep."

He chuckled and shook his head, but his blue eyes darkened with interest. "Did your exploration stop there?"

"For a time, my study of thievery took its place. But when I turned sixteen, the matter returned to me."

He gulped, then cleared his throat. "In what way?"

She gazed upward at the ceiling, recalling the innocent passion of her youth. "In the form of a stableboy who tried to sell my father a horse. A lame horse, I might add."

"Go on." For reasons she didn't understand, Wulf's voice took on a husky tone.

"He was most interested in conversing with me without my father's presence."

"I'm sure he was." Dera noted a small frown on Wulf's brow, which he replaced with a look of detachment.

"I knew what he wanted, naturally." She paused, allowing his erotic anticipation to grow. "So I accompanied him to the stables. Actually, our stable was a small hut where Penn kept chickens, but no matter."

"I trust it was comfortable."

"The floor was covered with new hay."

"Good." He seized a short breath. "What happened?"

Dera sighed. "Not what I anticipated. To be honest, I had worked myself into a frenzy of expectation." Wulf interrupted her with a small moan. "I undressed myself before him—as I had seen the ladies do at the castle." Again, a

341

moan, this time harsher. "But at that point, my would-be lover acted in a most peculiar manner."

"He fell on the floor, facedown?"

Dera eyed him doubtfully. "No. Why would he do that?"

"I don't know. I might."

"He did not. He tore off his own garb, which was not at all what the knights had done." She glanced down at Wulf's concealed male organ. "His bits were . . . not quite as I expected. Slender. Then he lurched at me, seized my left breast, and pinched. I struck him, of course, and left him stunned." Dera sighed. "My desire was left disappointed, and I decided such matters were far less interesting than they appeared."

Wulf looked down, but Dera suspected he was hiding laughter. "What did you expect?"

"Tender caresses, a kiss that would inspire my blood to greater passion."

Wulf cupped her face in his hand. "You wasted your temptation on a boy your own age, my dear. You need a man instead."

"You are no older than myself."

"Ah, but I am a man." He bent close to her, his lips bare inches from hers. "Had you done the same to me at sixteen, my reaction might well have been worse than your stable-boy's."

"I cannot imagine you pinching." She paused. "You look like the man in my fantasies."

"Do I?"

"Yes."

"Have you many fantasies?"

Dera closed her eyes. "So many! There is an ache inside me, and it plagues me with such a fever at times, but there is no answer to it."

Wulf touched her lips, and she felt his breath. "There is an answer, Dera." He paused, his voice husky. "Tell me these fantasies of yours."

"I am having one now." She opened her eyes and saw

all her dreams in Wulf's face. Such a beautiful face! Eyes darkened with desire, lips tender from kissing . . . "There is a man—a knight." The title disturbed him because he had denied his heritage, but it still belonged to him. Dera placed her hand on his face, feeling the stubble of his blond beard. "He is a beautiful man, and strong, like you. His eyes tease me with what they see, his lips tease with kisses."

He smiled, and she knew he wanted more. "He resists me because he is noble." He was resisting her. She wasn't sure how, because he was naked, but she felt it, beneath the surface.

"How do you lower this man's guard?" Wulf's eyes twinkled with delight, with play. Dera sat up, and he sat up, too. She straddled his powerful legs and seated herself on his lap, facing him. His full length rose between them, and she squirmed closer.

"Like this."

Wulf closed his eyes and his head tipped back. "This would do well to reduce a man's guard, aye."

She bent to kiss his throat. "I thought it might." She tasted the faint saltiness of his skin, then reached between them to grip his length in her hand. She caressed him from the base to the blunt tip, then back, over and over until his hips moved with her skill. "It is just as I imagined." She sounded breathless, and her pulse raced. "Better, I think."

He nodded, but he didn't answer. It pleased her to think he couldn't.

Wulf looked at her, fire in the depths of his blue eyes. He caught her hand and held it tight. "My guard is lowered, angel. But yours . . ."

Chapter Six

He had known many women, pleasured many with his skill. But nothing, no one, had prepared him for the erotic innocence of his new Welsh servant. Dera's curiosity fueled his desire, and her reaction drove him beyond control. Her swift, eager breaths fanned him like wind on fire.

She sat on his lap, her woman's mound pressed against his engorged manhood. Her damp curls teased his heated flesh, and he felt the demand of her wild pulse. She needed of him the one thing a man could not refuse—satisfaction. The culmination of erotic fantasy.

Wulf slid his hands slowly up her sides to her round, full breasts. She seemed tense when he touched her there, but pleased when he didn't pinch. What fool would dampen a woman's desire that way? Even as a boy, he would have known better. An image of himself and Dera enjoying the first flush of desire flooded his mind. Had they found each other then, she would have had no time for thievery. He might have been a simple farmer, with no ambition toward knighthood.

Wulf circled his finger around the small, pink tips of her breasts. He watched her face as she waited, eager for his progress. With infinite care and tenderness, he grazed the delicate peaks with his thumb, back and forth, then in circles until her eyes closed and her breath came as gasps. The small peaks hardened like rosebuds against his touch, and he bent to sample their fullness.

She caught her breath when his tongue flicked to taste her, then moaned when he took one rosy tip in his mouth. Dera responded like no woman he had ever known, with complete trust and eagerness to feel whatever her body could experience. He had sensed this quality from the first moment he saw her, but she surpassed his most fevered dreams.

As he teased her with his tongue, he slipped his hand between her open thighs, over the soft, damp curls, to the heart of her desire. With the pad of his thumb, he found the tiny bud that would drive her to mindlessness, but she didn't seem surprised. With a flash of erotic understanding, he knew she had found this spot before.

She loved everything he did. Her slender hips moved with primal rhythm against his hand; her flesh seemed to tingle against his touch. She clasped his shoulders hard as she balanced herself above him, and he watched her face as the passion seized control of her.

She kissed him wildly, with such primitive female demand that he couldn't think of resisting.

"Wulf . . ." He loved the sound of her voice this way, breathless and sweet, confused by the power of her need.

"Yes, angel."

"There is more, and I want it."

He laughed at her demand. No, this woman would never accept a role of servitude for long. Odd that so many queens lived passive to their heritage, and Dera, an ignobly born Welsh girl, had every instinct of a ruler.

He knew what she wanted. The deep, passionate thrusts of a man's desire, the satisfaction of pure union. He wanted it, too. Desire warred with compassion. Her need was quick and easily reached. He could restrain himself and seek release outside her body. It seemed a sensible decision, given the state of his desire.

"As you wish, my lady thief."

Wulf cupped her bottom in his hands and lifted her above his erection. He lowered her slowly over his rounded tip, and her eyes opened wide as he entered her.

"Oh!" She seemed surprised. He wondered why. A woman with such fierce desire couldn't deny herself this for long. Surely she had sought greater pleasure after the stable-boy failed her fiery needs.

A determined expression formed on her small face, and she sank herself over him. He met her inner barrier with a thrill of shock. Her determined expression wavered, then solidified, and she took him inside herself.

His surprise faded before bliss. She was hot and tight inside, damp with desire, and feverish with need. She moved before he had the chance, up and down in a rhythm that mirrored her dance at dinner. He braced his arms behind himself and let her follow her own course.

She did so with abandon, her head tipped back, her beautiful throat cloaked by her long, raven hair. The firelight caught each strand as she moved and twisted over him. Her fingers clenched into his muscle, but he stared at her face with wonder as a second wave of ecstasy swept through her lithe body.

His own drove deep inside her, pounding his release as his passion spilled into her. She recognized his bliss, and her own doubled. Their pulses mingled, then stilled. Wulf stared, stunned, into her green eyes. She smiled, with such satisfaction on her little face that he laughed. He flopped back on the bed, filled with happiness.

"The deal I made for you, my little servant, was the best trade I've ever made."

A tense silence followed his comment. She detached herself from his body, then glared down at him. "After this between us, you still call me your servant?" The tone in her voice indicated that her bliss passed as quickly as it rose.

He turned to look at her and offered the smile that had won her over earlier. Her lips pressed into a thin, downward curve. "You are a fiendish man."

Not the reaction he'd hoped for. "I gave you your fantasy, my little thief. You reveled in it. You were made for it."

He saw both hurt and resignation in her eyes as she turned her head away. "I have become your whore. It is not surprising that I should do so, given your skill and your smile, and such." She sounded wistful, but not a broken-hearted maiden. Her expression altered from forlorn to determined. A dangerous mood he now recognized first-hand. Her slender back straightened as she looked back to him. "This . . . revelry doesn't alter the situation between us. You call me your servant. You have the knowledge I need to complete my quest."

She lay down beside him, looking sure of herself and satisfied. "The situation between us will turn, Sir Beowulf." She adjusted the blanket over her body. He noted that though she hadn't accepted her role as his servant, she gave no thought to leaving their bed. She peered over at him from beneath long, black lashes, from drowsy eyes. "When that time comes, my friend knight, I may praise the deal I made for *you*."

Despite her anger and disappointment, Dera slept well past sunrise. She told herself the heavy snowfall accounted for her late rising, but discovering herself wrapped comfortably in Wulf's arms proved a sore trial to explain.

He beamed with happiness and male pride when she woke snuggled against him. Every passionate caress they had shared the night before glimmered in his eyes. Dera flushed hot and pink, then stuffed herself into her tangled undergown. She fixed her tunic over it, then tied her soft boots as he watched.

"You appear well rested this morning, my dear thief."

Dera pinned her attention on the thongs of her boots, and not on Wulf, but she saw him from the corner of her eye. He lay on his back, arms folded behind his head. His skin looked golden in the white morning light, but the fire had burned low and Dera saw her own breath in the chill air.

"Aren't you cold, or do Saxons feel nothing of ill weather?"

"I am heated from our evening in bliss."

He intended to remind her of her indiscretion at every opportunity, that much was certain. "There are small bumps on your skin such as a goose's plucked flesh reveals." She meant to insult him, but his smile deepened into dimples.

"You notice every detail of my body. I should have heeded that right away. It would have made our journey northward more enjoyable." Dera cast him a dark and forbidding look, but he seemed unaffected by her cold manner. "Perhaps we should stay at the Bull and Pheasant another night?"

One quick glance at his bare, muscular, and completely unbumpy chest told her she would easily weaken to his request. She wanted him now in those secret depths of her body he had discovered. She felt hot and congested inside, damp and aching. An infuriating state, and one she should have foreseen. The reveling did nothing to diminish her desire. Instead, it seemed to lend fuel to the unwelcome fire.

There was only one solution. Reverse the situation between them so that she became master, and Wulf her servant. A perfect balance. A small smile formed on her lips. "I see

348

no reason to delay our onward journey. We must secure the second key for the final stage of my quest.''

''*My* quest.'' He enjoyed annoying her. Dera tried not to watch as he issued an exaggerated sigh, then dressed himself too slowly. He fiddled with his shaggy hair, then eyed her doubtfully. ''What did you do to me, woman? My hair is tangled in knots.'' His lips formed a kissing expression and he made a smacking noise. ''Love knots.''

Dera grimaced. Strange that they should be so intimate, yet their adversarial relationship remain the same as before. She wanted to best him, more now than when he first claimed her. A plan formed already.

''We should be on our way.'' Her eagerness to best him overtook her desire for treasure, and she aimed for the door with undisguised glee.

Wulf caught her arm and drew her back. She tried to remain detached and uninterested in his purpose, but he waited until she peeked up at him. He was so tall and so beautiful. He touched her, and the passion she had imagined came to fiery life. The wanton young woman she had been, in search of passion, disappointed by its lack, then finally disinterested—this woman had met her equal in Wulf.

An equal who considered her a servant. She tried to muster defiance, but he smiled, and her resolve was lost. He didn't speak, he just looked at her, seeing far more than she would have allowed.

Very gently, he kissed her forehead. ''You and I, we will seek this place again.''

''This inn?'' Curses! Her voice came too small and wistful.

''Each other.''

A fierce energy sped along her veins. She didn't respond, but her determination returned as if fueled by lightning. ''I suppose we will.'' *We'll return here, all right. But when we do, you will be mine.*

Wulf eyed her suspiciously as she went to the door and opened it for him. "Shall we go?"

He nodded. "The journey before us is still long."

"And it will have many unexpected twists."

How pleasing! He radiated suspicion, but he certainly knew better than to question her. Dera followed him down the long, low hall and into the front room. The innkeeper awaited them, with a cloth over one arm. He looked less jolly in the morning, but the chamberlain stood beside him, cheerful and ready for the day.

"We've prepared a basket for your journey, Sir Beowulf. A jug of elder wine, and of ale, too." The innkeeper handed a large basket to Dera, and Wulf made no effort to intercept it, as a chivalrous man would. The innkeeper cast a quick, knowing glance Dera's way, then winked at Wulf. "I trust you slept well?"

Wulf smiled, with no pretense of innocence, though Dera shifted her weight and gazed around the room at nothing. "Perfectly. You have another guest, I think. A tall man, blond."

The innkeeper's brow furrowed. "No, sir, I don't recall anyone but yourself fitting that description."

The chamberlain stepped forward as if entering a confessional. "There was a man here last night. Inquired about rooms, but didn't take one. Said he had to move on."

Wulf didn't appear surprised by this, but Dera felt uncomfortable. A man was following them—a man who hated Wulf, and perhaps suspected the nature of their quest. She doubted he had "moved on." More likely, he was lying in wait for them to pass, before then continuing his pursuit.

She followed Wulf from the inn. Both were surprised to find Alfred waiting with their horses readied. He looked slowly from Wulf to Dera, and Dera endured excruciating embarrassment. He knew what they had done. She wasn't sure how he knew, but he did. The innkeeper's jocularity hadn't truly rattled her, but Alfred did, even though he said nothing.

Wulf took his reins and mounted. "Well done, Alfred." Dera noticed that he didn't meet Alfred's too-knowing eyes, either. Ha! He was embarrassed, too. Odd that a man as unassuming and silent as Alfred could muster Wulf's guilt.

Dera stood by her chestnut's shoulder. "Good morning, Alfred." She tried to sound casual and innocent, but her voice pierced the air and radiated guilt. She cleared her throat and noticed that Wulf chuckled. "If you please . . ."

Alfred positioned his hands as a stirrup and she mounted. Wulf's horse was considerably taller and more impressive than her own, though hers was the best Welsh mount she could steal at the time. When she took Wulf captive, she would take his horse, too. Then he could ride the smaller animal, and she would look down at him.

They rode through Conisbrough to within sight of the Castle. Wulf dismounted and studied the fortress, his brow furrowed as if in confusion. Conisbrough Castle was an impressive structure, with six massive buttresses and a white, circular keep. Dera shaded her eyes against the sun. "I wonder if it's well heated by fires?"

Wulf turned to face her. "Woman, you have led me astray."

"Not yet!" She cringed and forced an awkward smile. "I mean, I have led you according to my map."

His lips curved to one side. "I will let your slip pass for the moment. It is necessary that you reveal to me the location of the third key."

"How do you know there's a third key?"

"A hunch. York?" He sounded hopeful.

"No. Not York." There seemed no harm in alerting him, since he needed her knowledge to secure the artifact. "Pickering."

Wulf groaned. "I guessed as much."

"You guessed York." Her eyes narrowed. "What ails you about Pickering Castle?"

"Never mind that now." Wulf plucked a willow branch and knelt while Dera watched with interest. He proceeded to draw a map of their journey, marking the castles along the ancient Roman roads. She noticed that he also added small mountains and occasional rivers for effect. After he completed his drawing, he sat back and studied it. "As I suspected, Conisbrough Castle cannot be our current destination."

"Why not?"

"For one thing, it was built too late to harbor an ancient key. For another . . ."

"Why are we wasting time with your peculiar, although exact, drawings? We've found the castle already."

"It's the wrong castle. Look." Wulf broke off another thin branch from a bare willow, straightened it, and laid it between Tutbury Castle, York, and Pickering. Following the straight line to its natural conclusion, their journey would end at Scarborough Castle. "As you can see, Tutbury and Pickering are connected by a straight line with the ancient fortress in York. Conisbrough, however, is off that line."

"What of it?"

"It is an ancient treasure, this Twelfth Night. Its keys won't be found in a new structure."

"Does this mean we should seek the second key in York?" Dera frowned. "But I am certain my map indicated a castle southwest of York."

"It did." Wulf tapped a spot on his map. "Here."

Before she could examine his map, Wulf scratched it out, then mounted his horse.

"Where are we going?"

"It adds to our journey, but I'm afraid we must ride northwest. Not to Conisbrough, but to the Castle of Pontefract."

"I hope you're right."

352

"If you doubt me, we can search in Conisbrough Castle, but you will find no key there."

Dera considered this. She trusted Wulf's judgment, if nothing else. "Very well. I will take your word in this. But it will take longer to reach Pickering."

A dark look crossed Wulf's face. "About that, I cannot be sorry."

"Why?"

"There is no place I would less rather go."

"What does trouble you about Pickering Castle?"

"After the king's victory over the Scots at Halidor Hill two years ago, he gave the charge of Pickering to a knight he deemed worthy."

"Not to Ramm?"

"No." Wulf sighed as if hell beckoned. "To me."

Dera's brow knit in confusion. "You have ties to many grand castles, it seems. I do not understand you."

"It was not my wish to become steward of Pickering, although I was obliged to visit occasionally."

"Why not?"

"For one thing, though I did my duty as an Englishman, I did not favor our tactics against Scotland."

"Your kind is ever ruthless against my Celts."

He didn't argue, but his discouraged expression didn't waver. "Nonetheless, it would not be my choice to go there now."

"Tell them you're visiting, casually. We'll nab the second key and be off."

"That sounds good . . ." He spoke as if it sounded of disaster.

"Wulf—it's your castle, more or less. What's bothering you?"

"When I abandoned my title, I left the stewardship of Pickering to one I considered deserving."

"Who?"

"Ramm."

Dera bowed her head and issued a defeated moan. "Ramm. Your enemy. Well, *that* doesn't sound promising."

"No. It doesn't."

"What shall we do?"

Wulf shrugged. "There is a saying, my dear. 'Cross that bridge when you come to it.'" With that, he sighed, and urged his horse onward.

Chapter Seven

Pontefract Castle
West Riding, Yorkshire

Dera made thievery seem easy. They entered Pontefract castle disguised as servants, with Alfred lumbering behind. Dera had used a vile mud concoction to darken Wulf's hair, lest anyone recognize him as Sir Beowulf. Wulf suspected she'd used a grimier mixture than necessary in revenge.

She hadn't forgiven him for denying her freedom. He could have let her go, treated her as his equal. But he needed the Twelfth Night more than she did, whatever she believed, and though he desired her, he couldn't trust her once the artifact was in hand.

He had every intention of sharing its fortune with her. Once he had secured his mother and sisters in France, he and Dera might take up together in trade. He had nothing to offer a woman now, but they might become partners. Lovers.

Since they left Conisbrough, she had pretended nothing

had happened between them. Wulf half-believed it was that she was embarrassed in front of Alfred. More likely, she was using her wiles to gain power over Wulf himself.

But one night in her arms wasn't enough. Dera gave love like a goddess, with an earthy appreciation of coupling he'd never encountered before. Once he secured the Twelfth Night, he would keep Dera in high honor as his mistress, or perhaps his wife, and she would treat him as her lord, whether she wanted to or not.

If he gave her any freedom, she would use it against him. At first, he needed her to complete his quest. But he enjoyed her company. He delighted in her sensuality. He loved talking to her, and watching her scheme. It came as a surprise, but he couldn't deny it.

He wanted her in his life. But on his terms. Not hers.

He had maintained his position as leader by superior knowledge. Though he hadn't visited Pontefract Castle before, its structure closely resembled that of York Castle, which he knew well. Finding the crypt seemed the only challenge to another easy victory.

They reached a long, narrow arcade which inconveniently split in three directions, each with finely arched ceilings. Alfred's great size was bound to attract attention sooner or later, and attracting attention was the last thing Wulf wanted to do.

Dera stopped beneath the center of the arcade, her hands on her hips. No matter how she tried, the woman couldn't look servile. "Which way do we go?"

Wulf crossed his arms over his chest. "What do you mean, 'which way?' I trusted you to memorize your portion of the map!"

"I memorized it perfectly!" Her lips twisted to one side. "Almost. I remembered this archway and the four corridors."

"Yes . . . ?"

Her eyes shifted to the side with guilt. "I do not recall exactly which one leads to the crypt."

Wulf started to respond, but a small man carrying full armor clattered down the hall toward them, accompanied by an even smaller valet, who carried several weapons, all of which appeared to be on the verge of scattering from his grasp. Wulf lowered his head to disguise his face, and Dera pretended to dust the sconces.

Alfred stood looking out of place, like a beacon of wrongdoing.

The small man stopped and scrutinized Alfred. "Big fellow, you are. I could use a man your size to bear my armor."

Wulf rolled his eyes, but Alfred nodded. The giant took orders from anyone. Wulf cleared his throat. "Begging your pardon, sir, but Hetchfield here can't be spared."

The armorer turned his pointed attention to Wulf. "Who are you?"

Dera spun her cloth to the armor and dusted a shoulder plate. "This here's Piddlesqueak, sir."

Piddlesqueak. Wulf turned his coldest glare her way, but she offered a pert smile and went on. "Piddlesqueak is supposed to carry out the hogs, but he's a mite too small, so he has to get Hetchfield here to help him."

The armorer puffed his chest, causing the breastplate to clank against the grieves he held. "Hogs do not take precedence over the head armorer's request, wench."

A mistress, definitely a mistress. He couldn't tolerate a wife who would call him Piddlesqueak at the earliest opportunity.

Wulf bowed his head, forcing his clenched jaw to relax enough for speech. "Miss Roundbottom speaks truly, sir." He caught her sharp look and repressed a smile. "Hogs got loose, and Lord Percy has asked me to remove them." Fortunately, he knew the current Lord of Pontefract Castle, a man of quick and renowned temper. Hogs would not please Lord Percy, so Dera's explanation was adequate.

The armourer hesitated. "Very well, but have him back—Hetchfield, did you say? Have him back by mealtime."

"Yes, sir."

The armorer clattered onward, then disappeared into the castle's center courtyard. Wulf turned to Dera, ready with a long series of objections concerning her servile behavior, but she waved her hand dismissively. "Which way do we go?" She paused, green eyes glittering. "Piddlesqueak."

He decided to ignore her teasing manner, though her attitude had a certain appeal, despite her defiance. "Since your memory of your map appears faulty, I suppose we'll have to try each hall."

Alfred looked between them, uttered a short grunt, then headed up the northern passageway. Wulf and Dera looked at each other, shrugged in unison, and followed him. They reached the end of the hall, which branched both left and right. Dera clapped her hands in excitement.

"I remember now! Left!"

She sped off left, then darted left again around a sharp corner. Before Wulf and Alfred caught up with her, she darted back, a sheepish expression on her small face. "Sorry, it was right around the turn."

Wulf shook his head, then followed. The torches burned low in the corridor, and dust covered the stone in a thick layer, indicating a long-unused passageway. Dera found a narrow staircase going down, but Wulf hesitated before going in after her.

She stuck her head out the entrance, looking impatient. "Well? It's down here, I'm sure of it. Alfred! Proceed in here!"

Alfred didn't hesitate, though he had more to fear from the small space than Wulf. He scrunched his massive shoulders and somehow squeezed past Dera. Dera stomped her foot. Demanding woman. "Hurry up!"

Wulf seized a short torch from the sconce, then took a tentative step into the passage. As he feared, it was small and dark, with a damp, moldy odor. He disliked small, damp spaces, partly because of their inclination toward harboring snakes and rats, but he refused to admit his squeamishness to Dera.

She took off ahead, but he disliked her superior bravery, and he caught up with her. "I am leader." She huffed as he passed her, but she didn't argue, though he felt sure she muttered, *not for long, Saxon.*

Better to pretend he hadn't heard than to demand an explanation now.

The passage slid downward, with stairs so worn they were barely recognizable, and ended in a small, circular room that Wulf guessed to be beneath the armory. His dim torch cast an eerie, greenish-orange glow on the rock walls.

He looked around, but saw no crypt, only a hinged trapdoor embedded in the rock floor. "A pit prison, I would say." He shuddered in disgust. "Interesting that these keys should be placed in a castle's worst dungeon."

Dera straightened. "One of us has to go in there. Since Alfred and I are mere servants, and can't possibly be trusted, and since you are, or were, once a knight of vastly heroic proportions and deeds . . ."

"Say no more. I'll go." He felt sure she had guessed his dislike of small, putrid spaces, but he restrained himself from saying so. "Alfred, the trapdoor."

Alfred seized the iron ring in one hand, grunted, then hoisted it upward. Yes, noxious, damp fumes rose from the depths, but an old rope-strung ladder descended inward.

From what he could see from the torch light, a long, narrow tube, two-men deep, led into another dungeon, probably cramped, putrid, and generally unpleasant. A dungeon prison he would wish on no man.

Wulf handed Alfred the torch, inhaled a great sigh of misery, then lowered himself into the pit. "Alfred, pass me that torch!"

Alfred did so, and Wulf descended the rope ladder. Once

359

he set foot on the uneven floor, he examined his surroundings. Other than the pit entrance, the dungeon was barely a man high, and Wulf had to move hunched beneath the jagged stone ceiling. Worse still, a shallow layer of slimy water covered the floor, making it both slippery and foul. When he moved, his boots made sloshing noises.

He spotted a small rock crypt in the corner. Wulf pulled a crowbar from his pack and pried it open. He held up the torch to examine its contents. "A triangular shape this time! Interesting." He picked up the key, and found that it was also made of gold. "I wonder what shape the third key takes?" Interesting, but unimportant.

Dera might have insight on the shape's meaning. He turned back to the ladder and found it missing. His jaw firmed, his lips pressed into a thin, straight line. "Madam, you will restore this ladder at once, or bid your precious quest farewell forever!"

He maneuvered himself from the cramped hole to stand beneath the opening. Dera peeked down at him. His dimming torchlight illuminated the most infuriating, pert expression he'd ever seen. Her long hair dangled down around her face, as if it knowingly joined her efforts to tantalize him.

"Dera . . ."

"You seem to be stuck. In a disgusting, cold, dank, and rather foul pit. I am under the impression that you dislike such places."

He could muster no more than a growl.

"A shame for you."

Wulf hopped and tried to catch the cavern's rim. It was a futile gesture, as the rim was over a man-length above his head. He moved back, forgetting the cavern's ceiling was much lower, and bumped his head on a low-hanging rock. He cursed violently, and Dera issued a lively *tsk* from above.

"Take care, Sir Beowulf, lest you knock yourself senseless, and we be forced to abandon you here."

"Not without the key, lady. You want it as much as I

do.'' He wanted to add that she wanted the passion between them just as much, but he decided that angering her now wouldn't be wise.

''I do. There's no denying what we both want.'' She spoke with an added intimation, indicating that she was also considering their passion. To his irritation, he found himself becoming aroused despite the situation.

''Woman, get me out of here!''

''Toss up the key, and Alfred will lower the ladder.''

''Alfred! You are in my service . . .''

''Not anymore!'' She was delighted with her antics. Wulf twitched with anger. ''Alfred has resumed his rightful station as my guard and servant.'' She hummed a bit, musing, then peeked back down at Wulf. ''It seems, however, that I shall need two servants. One, Alfred, to assist me with matters of strength, and one . . . Yes, one to do such things as pour mead into my goblet, prepare my bath water on a nightly basis, brush my hair with soft brushes, sing pleasant melodies while I go to sleep . . .''

''Never.'' He would gladly brush her hair, and with delight prepare—and share—her bath. He might even sing to her, but not when ordered to do so. ''Lady, it was a good effort, but unsuccessful.''

''It would be a shame to have you rot down there, what with the rats and all. The floor appears rather damp. Lying down for your naps might be treacherous and possibly smelly. I would think it a place such as a leech might favor.'' She looked back over her shoulder—a contrived gesture. ''Alfred! Squash that bug at once! It appears to have tongs. No, those are teeth . . . How loathsome! It's slipping into a hole that leads into poor Sir Beowulf's new solar chamber.''

''You are a devilish little fiend, woman. You can't expect me to surrender this way.''

''I expect no more of you than you expected of me. I expect you to yield to the inevitable, call me Lady Dera, your mistress—in the sense of my power and position over you—

and acknowledge yourself as my faithful servant henceforward."

Her little foot tapped impatiently. "Well? I'm waiting."
She said "waiting" in a sing-song voice, in time with her
taps.

"You won't get the last key without me."

"And you won't get out of this filthy, stenchful, leech-
infested pit without *me*."

She had him. For the time being.

"The key, Saxon." She paused. "Both of them."

"One only."

Her tapping stopped. "Very well. Toss it up."

He flung the triangular key out of the pit, furious that he
couldn't trust her not to leave if he didn't hold the first key.
*A woman should be more faithful, tender to her lover. He
should be able to trust her.*

"What did you say?"

Wulf realized with horror that he'd muttered his thoughts
aloud. "Nothing. The ladder, wench."

A short laugh followed. "Wench? Wench is not the title
I requested."

She poked her head into the hole, one brow raised. It was
possible that he loved her. "As I meant to say . . . Lady Dera,
Queen of Thieves, and Creator of Vast Ruckus."

She beamed in her triumph. "Alfred, lower the ropes."

Chapter Eight

"Piddlesqueak! I require assistance mounting!"

Dera's newfound power pleased her even more than she'd fantasized. Wulf glared. His fair face appeared permanently etched with displeasure. His blue eyes cooled to the shade of winter ice. His lips curled in perpetual grumpiness.

He walked to her, then stopped, his proud head angled to one side. "Madam, I have tolerated your vengeful antics up to this point, but I will not be called foolish names by a woman . . ." He moved closer to her as he spoke. Dera forced herself to maintain her position, but it wasn't easy.

". . . by a woman who has shared my bed, kissed my lips and other portions of my body, cried out her pleasure while lying in my arms, then surrendered to rapturous lovemaking and ecstatic bliss."

A tiny squeak erupted from Dera's parted lips, and her face flushed scarlet. She didn't dare look to see Alfred's reaction, but since he was standing directly behind her, it seemed certain he had heard.

"Henceforward . . ." Oh, no! Her voice quavered. "You will be more . . . restrained in your outbursts."

He pointed his finger at her. "So long as you refrain from calling me the abominable name Piddlesqueak, I might temper references to your passionate embrace."

"I shall call you Wulf from now on."

"That's a sound plan." He still looked sullen. "You requested help mounting."

Good. A change of subject was welcome at this point. "I did. Proceed."

He seized her without grace or care, then aimed her at her restive chestnut. The manner in which he held her indicated disrespect. He might as well have flung her over his shoulder.

"Not that one."

He stopped. "What do you mean? This is your horse."

She twisted in his arms to meet him eye to eye, not easy in this position. "They are *all* my horses." She cranked her head around to deliver a pointed look toward Wulf's fine gray steed. "I will ride the gray."

The muscles in his arms tightened around her. He hated this subservient position, having to obey her commands. But no more than she had disliked obeying his.

"Allow me to warn you, Lady Dera, that my horse—"

"My horse now. You are in my service, as concluded in our most recent deal. Therefore, all things in your possession must be considered mine. You were saying . . ."

"The horse that until recently was mine . . ." He couldn't quite bring himself to say it. Most satisfying. "He has only been ridden by one master, myself, and only I can handle him."

"Ridiculous. I am well skilled with horses. Place me on his back at once."

Those blue eyes narrowed to slits, and an evil smile formed on his lips. He hoisted her upward without preamble, and she bumped into his saddle. The horse started, and Dera rolled backward. She scrambled to steady herself, but instead plunked down on the other side.

She opened her mouth to insult him, but no air came. He fell to his knees beside her, white-faced and . . . terrified. Dera stared up at him, unable to speak because the wind had been knocked from her chest, and stunned because he cared.

"Dera—are you hurt? Can you speak?"

Her lips parted for speech, but no words came. She motioned him closer with her finger, and he bent down to her. When his face came within inches of hers, she seized his hair, pulled him close, and kissed his mouth. "No . . . But I can kiss."

He exhaled a breath of relief, then rested his forehead against hers. "That you can, my lady, that you can."

The little demon could ride. No denying that. Dera handled his powerful gray as easily as he did. Wulf rode behind her on her nervous chestnut. As much as he hated to admit it, her horse was harder to control than his. It started at squirrels, falling leaves, and imaginary wolves, and always seemed to be on the lookout for trouble. No wonder she had wanted to switch mounts.

More annoying still, it jigged constantly to keep up with his long-legged gray, which after time caused his backside considerable stress.

Alfred's fat bay mare plodded peacefully along behind them, in no hurry to catch up, but neither did she fall far behind the leaders. Wulf noticed that Alfred barely touched his reins, often riding with them hanging loose by her withers. He allowed the mare to seize bunches of leaves from bushes, though Wulf had trained his own horse into perfect obedience, thanks to an early start when it was a prized foal.

A shame he hadn't gotten control of Dera when she was young. He might have guided her into obedience, into respectful silence. Yes. If he'd known of her existence, he might have persuaded King Edward to betroth them—the

English liked connections with the Welsh, after all—and she would have been schooled as a proper female.

Wulf pinned his gaze on her back, contemplating the surest method to regain his control. It was only a matter of time, of course. But how to do it . . . Alfred was no help. The man would obey a serf if the serf had the presence of mind to issue orders. Whether or not Alfred bore Dera any true loyalty, Wulf wasn't sure.

As well as he knew her, he had no real idea of Alfred's nature. At first, he'd had no interest in Alfred, because Dera fascinated him, because she was beautiful and intriguing, and he desired her. Alfred rarely spoke, which made him seem dull, yet Wulf had seen him talk to the animals, so the giant wasn't mute.

Nor was he simple. Despite his cumbersome size, a keen intelligence sparkled in Alfred's dark eyes. Another troublesome factor was Alfred's ancestry. At first, Wulf had assumed he was a Scot and attributed his silence to a preference for the Gaelic tongue. But when he spoke to the horses, Wulf detected no Scottish burr.

Dera knew little more about her giant, though she'd probably never asked. He hadn't been in her service long, and seemed to be more or less a gift from her thief father, Penn. If Penn knew more about his daughter's servant, he'd kept it to himself.

Wulf wasn't sure why it mattered, or if it mattered, but perhaps out of boredom, he slowed the prancing chestnut to walk beside Alfred. Alfred looked pleasant, but offered no comment. "That's quite a mare, Alfred . . ."

Dera halted at once and looked back at them. With annoying confidence, she poised her hand on the gray's powerful rump. "I will not have my servants conspiring against me. You"—She snapped her fingers at him as if she'd forgotten his name—"You ride up here with me, and leave Alfred be. He does not need you confusing his duties."

"Fiend."

She smiled, then waited as he urged the chestnut forward. He must have urged too hard, because it bounced into a canter and bounded up to the gray. It was as well that he was an expert in the saddle, for the chestnut's random, jarring gait would have dislodged a lesser rider.

Dera studied the chestnut and shook her head. "Irritating when he does that, isn't it? Yet you handle him with passing skill." She gazed thoughtfully up at the sky toward the feathery clouds. The winter sun shone on her beautiful face with a golden light. Wulf found himself wishing for snow. "You will school that horse until he ceases his annoying behavior. The role of stable boy suits you admirably."

Demonic. Wulf contorted his lips into an innocent smile. "I would be more than honored to use my years of knighthood in training your skittish little horse, my lady." He urged the horse forward, in front of Dera. "In fact, while practicing my skills in Castle Brinklow's Feat of Arms, I learned several tricks."

"Tricks?"

"Aye. A horse that can unexpectedly lurch forward, to the side, or perhaps roll over on command is useful in battle."

"You will not teach my horse those tricks."

He chuckled to himself. So, she didn't expect to stay in command of him long—she expected to have her old horse returned to her. What else did she expect? That they go their separate ways, she back to Wales, he on his uncertain journey nowhere?

As he mused, Dera overtook the lead, then rode on ahead. He had to regain control of her at once. There was only one way: seduction. Yes, he would obey all her commands, brush her hair, lave her skin with fragrant warm water, perhaps lick the droplets. . . . They would stop in York to replenish supplies. It would only take one night. . . .

Chapter Nine

Once they had settled themselves in York, Wulf went to the servants' quarters instead of attending her room. Dera lay in her bed fighting tears; she had looked forward to this night with such overpowering anticipation. She had even allowed herself to consider a marriage between them. On her terms, of course. Not his. Wulf was too dangerous when left to his own devices.

She had ordered him to pour her wine and to serve her partridge-and-pear squeak in tiny portions. Perhaps she had been a trifle bossy, but it was as he deserved after all the tedious tasks he'd made her perform. She hadn't quite summoned the courage to order him to her room, though the thought of hair brushing tempted her. It was too brazen, and despite her desire, she couldn't issue the command.

He had looked handsome on purpose. He had deliberately dressed himself like a young nobleman, despite their need to maintain secrecy in this city. He wore a pale blue cote-hardie, with gray hose that revealed the strength of his well-formed legs.

Several times, he had caught her peeking at him, and each time, he had smiled that knowing smile that sent her nerves tingling. He had clearly bathed, because his golden hair shone and had a slight curl from moisture at the nape of his neck, which was extremely appealing.

Yet now, she lay alone.

No wonder ladies cried such tears over men!

A shadow passed by her door and her breath caught. The shadow passed by, and footsteps faded down the hall. She started to roll over, but the light beneath the door went dark, as if someone had doused a torch. The door opened a crack, then more. What if Wulf's enemy had come for her?

She fumbled in the darkness for her bow. He wouldn't succeed without a fight.

"There is no need."

Wulf.

Dera dropped the bow. "You frightened me. I thought you might be one of Ramm's men."

Wulf closed the door, then barred it, and Dera's heart bounced to a wild pace. He fumbled with her low-burning fireplace, and it glowed to brighter life. "Why should Ramm seize you? I am the target of his vengeance."

"I thought he might have mistaken our rooms." No, she thought Ramm might believe Wulf cared for her and use her against him. Obviously, Wulf hadn't considered that possibility—because it had no foundation.

He crossed the room and stood by her bed. "You called. I am here."

"I never called."

"There is the matter of . . ." He paused, looking upward as he mused. "Hair brushing."

"Hair brushing?"

He moved closer, then sat beside her on her bed. "And bathing . . . And singing . . ."

"I have bathed already."

"Then I will save that service until tomorrow, when your body will be flushed with its passion."

"Oh!"

He seized a soft brush from her bedstand, and proceeded to stroke her long hair. Dera responded like a kitten to his attention, closing her eyes, and feeling . . . cared for.

"The inn has set a Yule log on the fire. We have only four days left to accomplish our task."

"My task." Her voice was almost too small to be heard, but his lips twitched in irritation.

"Four days, Dera, can see many changes."

"You seek to gain power over me through—*this!*" He frowned, but he didn't offer an immediate denial. Dera snatched the brush from his hand and flung it aside. "That's why you came to me tonight, you devil. You probably mean to steal my key. Well, you won't find it!"

"I already did." He reached up his tunic sleeve and withdrew the triangular key. His smirk was almost unbearable.

Dera reached into her tunic and held up the circlet key. "I've noticed you keep it with you at all times. In the inner hem of your tunic."

His eyes snapped open, and his smirk faded to astonishment. "It seems we are well matched." He paused. "When did you nab it?"

Her mouth curled to one side. "No doubt at the same time you nabbed mine."

"As I brushed your hair?"

"Yes."

A silence followed. Without words or agreement, they exchanged keys, then sat side by side facing the fire.

"You are still my servant, Saxon."

"For now."

"I wouldn't expect you to agree, of course."

"Wise." He glanced over at her. "I didn't expect agreement from you, either."

"Good."

Another silence.

After a time, a tentative smile formed on his sensual lips. "Since I am—temporarily—still in your service, have you any commands of me tonight?"

Her stomach fluttered. The look in his eyes was unmistakable. "I might, given time, think of ways you might please me."

"Perhaps you would like me to wash your small feet."

"Later."

He nodded. "Set your slippers by the fire to warm your little toes come morning?"

"That might be good."

He tugged her new slippers off her feet and tossed them toward the fire. Dera gasped, ready to strike him, but the slippers landed neatly by the hearth. "You have considerable luck."

"I have considerable aim."

"It is pleasing to have a man of your skills in my service."

"Is it?"

"Yes. Your nature is domineering and bossy, qualities which should be tempered by servitude."

He turned to face her. "*My* nature is bossy? Woman, you could teach the king, the queen, and all the rampaging popes new tricks!"

"Frustrating, isn't it, to be faced with one slightly more capable than yourself?"

He seized her shoulders and held her facing him. "You trifle with me, Lady Dera. It might seem unwise."

"You won't hurt me. Not even to regain your power over me. You won't even go back on your word to me. Your knightly heritage forbids it."

"I am no longer knightly."

She smiled, but said nothing.

371

He drew her closer, but he didn't kiss her. "Command me."

Dera gulped, but her pulse turned warm and swift.

"Does it trouble you, Dera? Do you fear to summon me, to demand that I do your bidding?"

"Not fear . . ." She averted her eyes from his. "It seems unwomanly."

"Why consider that now?"

She frowned. "I don't know."

"Because you want fantasy from me. You want to believe yourself a lady, and me your faithful suitor. Dear lady, we are thieves, nothing more."

"You're not a thief."

"I am a thief with scruples, but a thief nonetheless. "Dera, I can't give you the life you want. I can give you fleeting delight and more passion than you've ever dreamed, but I can't promise you a lifetime I do not have to give."

Dera didn't look away, though she knew her disappointment showed too clearly. He was right. They both needed the Twelfth Night, but it wouldn't change the essence of their lives. Because neither wanted its riches for themselves.

Dera touched Wulf's face, and her heart ached. "Then I command you to please me, and to let me please you."

She slipped her fingers into his soft hair, and he responded in kind. Their kiss met as an equal demand. Dera eased his tunic off his shoulders, baring his golden skin to the firelight. She kissed his shoulder, sampling his taste with small darts of her tongue.

He tossed his tunic aside, then freed himself from his hose. His male length stood poised from his body, gold like his skin, engorged with need. Dera pulled off her chemise and held out her arms to him. Perhaps satisfaction was meant to be fleeting, to touch but not hold. Perhaps love was never more than a dream.

Dera lay back on her bed, waiting, but Wulf didn't proceed as she expected. He knelt beside her. "My lady, your expectations are limited by your experience, which though fanciful, offers little new.''

''What are you talking about?''

''Would you have me lie atop you, and thrust deep inside you?''

''Yes!''

He ran his finger from her chin, down her neck, to the swell of her breasts. ''Nothing more?''

''You have permission to touch me also.''

''With my fingers?''

''Do so.'' It might prove irritating to tell him each step. ''Use your imagination.''

''Imagination, lady, is a dangerous thing, but you are warned.''

Dera endured a flutter of apprehension. He positioned himself between her legs and she awaited his entrance. Instead, he ran his hands along her side, then cupped her hips. ''You have approved my fingers. What do you say of my tongue?''

''That it talks too much.''

''It does, at that.''

He bent low, until she felt his breath on her inner thighs. Dera started to sit up, but he reached to press her back down. ''I'm using my imagination. Hold still.''

''It is mine to give orders, and yours to obey. I defeated you fair and square, in a battle of wits, in which I proved superior. I do not understand why you have such a difficult time accepting—''

His tongue flicked across her most secret spot, and her words caught in her throat. ''Oh, my! Behave!''

He didn't. Instead, he teased, and circled, and tormented the tiny spot until she could think of no objections, of nothing but the pleasure he gave. Her breath came as gasps, then moans. He sucked and nibbled, and she screamed in fierce, passionate delight.

Desire twisted and spiraled beyond her control, and she lay powerless to resist its force. She gripped his shoulders, her toes curled tight. Wild surges of rapture flooded through her, seizing her and lifting her like an oncoming storm. Dera gripped his hair and pulled him up.

He obliged with a man's raging need, and she realized that his teasing had sent him into a similar state. He held himself above her, looking down, then thrust inside her until he touched her deepest core. They moved without thought, demanding and giving.

He gripped her ankles, then set her legs around his neck. The posture afforded deeper pleasure, and she braced herself against the headboard to receive his thrusts. In his control, without thought of her, she reached her fiery pinnacle, then watched his face as he reached his own inside her.

They made love with abandon, over and over, until they collapsed against each other, exhausted. Dera lay in Wulf's arms, contented. Whatever he had said, he had given her all she wanted, and there was nothing more to ask.

"Take them both!"

The door burst open, shattered with the force of several men. Dera screamed and Wulf leapt from the bed for his ax. The guards wore Ramm's insignia, and two aimed crossbows at Dera's heart.

Wulf gripped his ax, but he couldn't act before they could shoot. "The first man who touches her dies," he hissed.

"Then you would surely be dead by now, Sir Beowulf." Ramm entered behind his guards. Behind him, Alfred stood, waiting obediently like a servant. Ramm's servant.

Dera gasped, and Wulf looked between his captors. "Alfred . . ." He had no idea what order carried weight with the giant, but Dera appeared too frightened to issue commands. Wulf hesitated, then shrugged. "Thump them!"

Alfred didn't respond, and Ramm grinned. "Your giant takes orders from me now, Wulf."

Dera issued a fierce hiss. "Alfred! You traitorous fiend!"

Wulf shrugged again. "Why stop now?" He faced Ramm,

fighting to retain his composure. "What do you want?"

"Only what is my due." Ramm's sharp gaze shifted to Dera. Her hands shook as she fumbled for her gown. "What fascination does this pretty wench hold for you, Wulf?"

"The fascination of any beautiful woman."

Ramm shook his head. "It's more than that, I think. You followed her from Wales, in secret. If you merely desired the woman, you would have taken her and been done with it. She is obviously apt to your hand."

Wulf didn't look at Dera, but he felt her pain. She had no reason either to believe she meant more to him. "I was wary of her guardian."

Ramm glanced at Alfred. "My guardian now, Wulf."

Wulf frowned. Alfred's betrayal stung far deeper than he would have expected. "Let the woman go, and I will not resist you."

Ramm laughed. "What kind of fool do you think me? I know you, Wulf. I know what you seek."

It wasn't possible. Unless Alfred had spoken at last. Wulf kept his expression blank. "Indeed?"

"This woman holds something you value—knowledge, perhaps. Of what? Tell me what you seek, and what power it holds."

Wulf laughed. "I seek nothing but a night's bliss."

"I am not fooled by your pretense, Wulf. You are on the king's mission, and I will hear of it."

"My allegiance to Edward has never been strong, Ramm."

"Not strong? In your effort to gain his favor, you killed your own father."

Wulf heard Dera's sharp gasp. "Your father?"

The past always returned to haunt him. He would never be free.

"Lord Cleavedon was my father."

Chapter Ten

Pickering Castle
North Riding, Yorkshire

"Your father? Why didn't you tell me?"

Dera sat shackled on a stone bench beside Wulf in the vile oubliette into which Ramm had thrown them. They were in Pickering Castle, in total darkness. She couldn't see Wulf, but she felt his presence.

"It isn't a point of honor for me."

"So you really are Lord Cleavedon's son?"

"His bastard son, yes."

"Why didn't he marry your mother?"

"He was married to another at the time of my birth, but the woman remained barren, though he doubtless had many bastard children. Of those, I am the eldest."

"Did your mother love him?"

"Who can say? He was a handsome man, well loved by women."

"Like yourself." Wulf didn't respond, but Dera knew she'd guessed well. "You said you have sisters."

"My mother fled Brinklow Castle with Cleavedon's steward, then married him—much to Cleavedon's fury. The steward fathered my sisters, but Cleavedon insisted I be raised at the castle. For this reason, my mother and her husband were allowed to stay also."

"How uncomfortable for all of them!"

"Aye, since Cleavedon never relinquished his passion for my mother."

A long silence followed.

Dera twitched with irritation. She had a duty to follow, and Penn needed her. "If you hadn't insinuated yourself into my quest, we wouldn't be caught in this dungeon now."

She felt certain Wulf glared in response, but she couldn't see him. "If you hadn't tempted me to your room, we wouldn't have been caught."

"Tempted you, indeed! You have been a severe trial to me from our first meeting."

"And you, my lady, have been a distraction to me."

"I might say likewise. If not for your interference, I would have avoided taverns entirely."

"Unless you had a fancy for thievery."

"Which I would have done swiftly and without trouble if not for you!"

They both fell silent, furious. After a moment, Dera's fury eased and tears puddled in her eyes. "We'll never find the artifact by Twelfth Night now." She dried her tears with the back of her hand, but more came. "Penn trusted me. He believed I could do it."

Wulf patted her knee. "You could do it. We still have time."

"How? We've lost Alfred." She paused. "I cannot believe he betrayed us this way."

Wulf took her hand, then faced her. "Us. That is what we've been missing, Dera. We've both fought working together—truly together—because we're both cursedly independent fools.''

Dera squeezed her fingers around his. "Or maybe we're afraid we'll grow accustomed to each other, and then . . ." Her voice faltered, but Wulf touched her cheek.

"And then lose each other. Dera, I don't want to lose you, either." She heard the new resolve in his voice. "We'll get out of here somehow. Then we'll continue our journey, find that artifact, and share it."

Her throat constricted with new tears, with hope. "Yes."

"We still have our keys. The third is in this castle somewhere—probably near."

"In a dungeon."

Together, they looked down at the bench beneath them, then at each other. They stood up at once. Wulf shifted his weight from foot to foot, then cleared his throat. "It's a crypt."

"So it is. Can you open it?"

Wulf fumbled with the crypt, and Dera helped. They pried it open. Wulf held it while she extracted the key. Wulf lowered the top, and they sat down again. "What shape is this one?"

Dera felt it. "It has many points . . . five. It's a star!" The star slipped out of her fingers. "Wulf! Why did you take the star?"

"I didn't."

Someone grunted just behind them. Dera gripped Wulf's hand in sudden terror. They weren't alone in the dungeon.

Someone moved toward them. Dera screamed, and Wulf jumped to his feet, then banged his head on the oubliette's low ceiling.

"Who is there? Who are you?" Dera's voice shook. She moved in Wulf's direction and bumped into him. He eased her behind him.

The stranger shoved the back wall of the tiny dungeon, and it gave way. Only one person could do that.

"Alfred!" Dera nearly collapsed with relief, and Wulf breathed a long sigh.

Wulf slapped Alfred's shoulder. "Well done, Alfred! Now, how do we get out of here?"

Alfred retrieved a dim torch from the hall outside the dungeon, then started off without a word. Dera eyed Wulf, who shrugged. She saw suspicion in his eyes. "What is he doing?"

"I don't know—but there's more to Alfred than we've realized, my dear."

"What do you mean?"

"The tables have turned, though he says nothing."

"In what way?"

"We're following *him*."

They met outside Pickering Castle. Alfred had mustered all three horses, though Dera had no idea how he managed to evade Ramm's substantial guard. It was early morning, and a light snow covered the ground. Dera saw her breath mingling with Wulf's.

He knelt in the snow and motioned for her to join him. "Now is the time, my lady."

"For what?"

He smiled. "For trust."

She took a breath, then knelt beside him. She had trusted no one in her life except Penn. She had been often betrayed. But today, love mattered more than fear. He passed her a willow branch, and she drew her portion of the map in the snow.

Wulf took the branch silently, then added his own drawing to hers. They looked at each other. The tears in her eyes were mirrored by tears in his.

Dera looked up. To her wonder, she saw the mist of tears in Alfred's dark eyes, too.

Wulf studied their map. "Our journey leads to Scarborough Castle, if my guess is correct."

Dera peered at the drawing. "That is the direction my memory indicates also."

"We will reach Scarborough Castle tomorrow. By evening tomorrow, everyone in the castle should be occupied with Twelfth Night festivities. We won't be noticed."

Wulf pointed to a section of their map. "The crypt we seek appears to be in the old portion of the keep, which is the side closest to our position here. We need only enter through the west gate portcullis, turn right, and there should be a small staircase leading down." He nodded to Dera.

Dera added little scratch marks to his perfect drawing. "On the level below, here, we should find another pit."

They drew simultaneous breaths, knowing the end of their quest was near, then rose. "We'll have to ride tonight before Ramm realizes we've escaped. With good speed, we should reach Scarborough Castle by Twelfth Night."

Dera passed by Alfred to join Wulf. "Perhaps we can disguise ourselves as mummers! Alfred, you'll have to fetch us costumes." Her excitement grew as they mounted their horses.

January 5, 1336
Scarborough Castle

Twelfth Night festivities had always been Dera's favorite time of year. Mummers dressed up as oxen, a King and Queen of the Bean were chosen, and the people danced, both nobles and peasants, laughing and singing. As a child, she had dreamed she was lady of the castle, and that she and her beloved husband would stage these festivities.

They entered the castle disguised as mummers, intending to slip away unseen when they passed the west hail. The decorations and music thrilled Dera, but Wulf didn't seem as excited. She guessed he had known many such occasions, or perhaps celebration lost its thrill after his father's death.

Wulf wore an ox mask complete with a ring in its nose.

Dera giggled each time she looked at him, though the guise of ox that Alfred also wore suited him better. She was dressed as a winter sprite with a sheer white veil covering her hair and face.

Wulf was obviously trying to ignore his ridiculous garb, so Dera seized each opportunity to lean close and offer small *moo*s.

"You are abominable, woman. Here, find that passageway before we're forced into dancing around the wassail tree."

"We have time for a little dancing."

"No. We don't."

Dera skipped beside him. "You will certainly be chosen as best beast, and you'll get a cake placed on one of your fine little horns, which you'll have to shake off. What fun! I'm sure you'll be spectacular."

Wulf uttered a muted groan. "Over there—the western passage." He stopped, allowing the other mummers to pass by. "Curses!" Armored guards stood by each passageway.

Dera forgot her glee. "Now what? We'll never get by them!"

Several guests complimented Alfred's costume, and he nodded gallantly to each. Dera pinched his arm. "Alfred! Pay attention. We can't get by the guards. You'll have to thump them when no one's looking."

Alfred didn't appear perturbed by the delay. He seemed more interested in dancing. Wulf eyed him doubtfully, then shook his head. "After the supper, the guests will go to the outer court to toast the oldest tree of the hall, and then, at midnight, the mummers will perform the play of the three magi. All light will be doused, and that will give us a few moments to make our exit."

It seemed a good plan, and beyond that, Dera was hungry. Wulf, however, appeared pained and reluctant to join in the Festivities. She prodded his ribs with her elbow. "I look forward to your dancing, Sir Beowulf."

His frown tightened. "I do not dance."

Stobie Piel

"Even in your grander days at Brinklow Castle?"

He didn't answer at once. "Those days are gone."

She touched his arm. "You did dance, didn't you? You were happy there." She wasn't sure he considered her a friend, maybe just a lover, but Wulf kept too much to himself. "Did you care for your father once?"

"Once." His sorrow was easy to read, and Dera's heart ached in sympathy. "Cleavedon was a good father when I was a young boy. I was favored because I resembled him and took on many of his skills. Yes, my father favored such festivities as this tonight. Twelfth Night was his favorite."

Dera's eyes misted with tears. "Can you not claim those moments for what they were, and not let the ending overwhelm their meaning?"

He looked at her, pain etched in his fine brow. "It is too late for that."

Dera took his hand in hers, and they entered the Great Hall. As lively music began, Wulf issued another miserable groan. Dera stopped to look around. "What is wrong now? It's lovely. See all the banners—and all the food! Cakes everywhere!" She noted that Alfred was already sampling a collection of nuts and pastries.

"Are you blind, woman? Look. Ramm is seated with the castle lord."

"Oh, dear." He was right. Ramm sat on the high dais with the other noblemen, and he was definitely looking for someone. "It's a good thing we're disguised."

"Keep your veil lowered, and have an eye on Alfred. I doubt he'd be fool enough to draw attention . . ."

"Don't count on it." Dera pointed—Alfred had taken up a raucous dance around a tree in the center of the hall. Other mummers joined in, and Wulf clasped his hand to his forehead, bumping his mask.

"Curses!"

"You'd better do something."

"Such as . . . ?"

"Dance over there and speak to him!"

Apparently Wulf could think of no better solution, but Dera heard the echo of another groan as he maneuvered himself toward Alfred. Wulf refused to dance at first, but Alfred seemed to be deliberately provoking him. As Wulf drew near Alfred, Alfred twisted away, with a peculiar hip action. Dera giggled.

Wulf's reluctance to dance shifted. He began to mimic Alfred, perhaps part of his plan to get close enough for an order. Wulf danced well, and Dera found herself imagining him as lord of a fine castle, herself as his lady.

Each time he danced near to Alfred, Alfred danced in the other direction, leading Wulf on a chase that amused the celebrants greatly. Dera clapped her hands, forgetting her real purpose at the castle. She felt sure Wulf was enjoying himself, despite his many groans.

Wulf leapt toward Alfred, but Alfred twisted away, and Wulf sprawled on the floor. The audience roared with laughter, and Dera laughed, too. Ramm stepped down from the dais, his attention fixed on Wulf. Dera held her breath, desperately considering a way to warn Wulf.

Ramm watched the two vigorous dancers, and Dera's teeth sank into her lip. Alfred danced the most peculiar steps she'd ever seen, moving his hips side to side—much belying his cumbersome shape. Wulf threw up his hands and gave up, still laughing.

From across the room, Dera caught Ramm's veiled smile as he returned to the dais with his host. Perhaps he couldn't imagine Sir Beowulf as a dancing ox. For now, Wulf was safe.

The King and Queen of the Bean chose Alfred as the best beast and stuck the cake on his horns. Dera heard Wulf's laughter as Alfred tried to shake it off.

When the dance ended, Wulf returned to her side, though Alfred remained surrounded by admirers. "If that didn't do us in, nothing will." Wulf sounded happy despite his dire predictions, and Dera took his hand.

She wanted to tell him she loved him, but she couldn't alter the casual ease between them and the words wouldn't form. "I enjoyed your performance, Sir Beowulf."

He lifted his mask enough to see her, and he smiled. "As much as I enjoyed yours in Tutbury? If so, this night might end better than I hoped."

Why did intimacy of the body come so much easier than intimacy of the heart? "Do you think Ramm noticed you?"

"I doubt it." A frown twitched on his lips. "He has never seen me dance as an ox before."

"It's time we fetched Alfred. Do you think we can get him away from that crowd?"

"He'll come. I think he's more interested in this treasure than we've realized."

"What do you mean?"

"Has it occurred to you, little thief, that there might be a better thief than either of us?"

Dera's mouth slid open. "Alfred? You think he's after the Twelfth Night, too?"

"It's possible. He has shown no particular loyalty to us. He wasn't long in your father's service, either."

"No, that's true. Penn had no idea where Alfred came from."

"Yet he freed us from Pickering Castle. That wasn't easy, and it was done all by his own cleverness. Why?"

"I see. Because he wants the treasure for himself."

"No doubt."

Dera couldn't restrain a surge of admiration. "Then it was well done to attach himself to both of us for this journey."

"Aye."

Dera sighed heavily. "Together, we can wrest it from him."

"Aye."

The prospect didn't please her, though she should have

384

welcomed the challenge. "All I have done, all the good I thought to do . . . Everything I wanted was based on factors outside myself. Yet now . . ."

Wulf looked back to her. "And now?"

"Now I wonder . . . would all the treasure in the world ease this ache in my heart?"

Wulf lowered his mask over his face. "I have asked myself the same question."

They waited until the hour of midnight. The candles and torches were doused one by one, and Wulf nodded to Dera. The final play of the magi would soon begin. As the Great Hall grew dark, Alfred joined them.

Wulf looked between them. "The hour is short. If we are to gain this Twelfth Night, now is the time."

Alfred revealed nothing of his mind's inner workings, but Dera's suspicions intensified, and she cast him quick looks. He was intelligent, and he had always watched them closely—because he intended to best them in this final hour. That much seemed certain now.

He rarely spoke, but she had heard him muttering to the animals, and sometimes to village children. So he kept quiet for a reason—to conceal his true purpose and intelligence from Dera and Wulf.

They made their way from the hall to where the guard stood by the western passage. Alfred veiled his short torch until it gave almost no light. Wulf doused the wall torch, and Dera heard a solid *thump*, followed by the collapse of the stunned knight's body.

They hurried down the dark passageway, then stopped near its end. Dera felt along the wall for an entrance. "It should be here."

Someone tripped and stumbled next to her, followed by Wulf's sharp curse. "It is."

Dera chuckled, then picked her way carefully after him. They went down a long, winding staircase until her head spun with dizziness. When they reached the bottom, she stopped, and Wulf took her hand. "Truly, we are in the bowels of the earth, lady thief."

"There's a comforting thought."

Alfred edged past them and marched onward.

Dera squeezed her fingers around Wulf's. "How does he know where to go?"

"I'm not certain, but the time of our leadership has passed."

Though she couldn't see, Dera heard Alfred's firm footsteps ahead—a sound strangely comforting in the dark. He stopped, and she heard another *thump*. Stone ground against stone as an unseen wall slid open.

They entered another passageway, so narrow that Dera could feel walls on either side of her. As they progressed, the walls became eerily smooth, though before this point, even the floor had been rough and uneven.

"Where are we?"

Alfred stopped short, and Wulf bumped into him. Dera bumped into Wulf, then gripped his hand again. "Is this the end?"

Alfred unveiled his small torch and held it up to a door. He pointed to strange symbols engraved on the door's smooth, black surface. Dera edged around Wulf to examine them.

"A circle, a triangle, and a star! Our keys!"

Wulf ran his finger over the carvings. "So it seems. Shall we try them?"

Dera withdrew her circlet and pressed it into the round spot. It embedded instantly, with a small clank. Alfred nodded to Wulf, and Wulf fit the pyramid key into its slot. It clicked, and seemed to become one with the door.

Alfred held up the star and it glowed with light. In the darkness, the glow seemed a beacon. Dera stared in awe. "It truly is magical."

As she spoke, the door slid soundlessly inward. Alfred

stood back, allowing them to enter first. Wulf stepped in, and Dera followed close behind. She caught only a glimpse of the interior before the door closed behind them—blocking all light.

"Alfred! Your torch!"

Alfred didn't answer. Wulf moved toward the door. "Alfred?"

Again, no answer. Dera kept her hand on his shoulder, afraid to lose herself in the darkness. "Do you suppose he's locked us in here?"

"I can't think why."

Something filled this invisible room, something powerful. Dera trembled. Wulf drew her close against him, and suddenly she knew she mattered. He had no idea what threatened them, but he intended to protect her against anything.

"What treasure do you seek?" A strange voice spoke, one Dera had never heard before, yet it seemed familiar.

Her trembling increased, but Dera fought panic. "Who are you?"

"What treasure do you seek? Take care with your answer, for in many, there is only one."

Wulf squeezed Dera's shoulder in a comforting gesture. "We seek the Twelfth Night."

Low laughter warmed the dark space. "You have found him."

"*Him?*"

A torch blazed to life, and both Dera and Wulf winced at the brightness. When they looked up, Alfred stood before them.

But not Alfred.

The man before them was garbed as a knight. His golden plate armor glistened, and he held a full helm in the crook of his strong arm. The torchlight shone on his red hair and beard, and his eyes glittered like stars.

The symbol on his breastplate was that of a circle and a pyramid linked by a star.

Dera stared at him in astonishment. "Alfred . . . You are the Twelfth . . ." She paused and looked up at Wulf. She saw a mirror of her shock on his face.

"The Twelfth . . . *Knight*."

Alfred nodded, looking pleased with himself. "You have sought me—I am here."

Wulf smiled. "I would say you led us here. For what purpose?"

"You seek treasure. You have found it. Here, in this forgotten hold, you will find all you desire."

Dera gazed up at Wulf, her lost heart sure at last. "I have already found my treasure, Alfred. It was here all along." Her eyes filled with tears, and the words she feared came easily. "I love you, Wulf. The treasure is yours. I will find another way to help my father."

Wulf cupped her face in his hands, and to her wonder, she saw tears in his blue eyes—tears like her own. "Dera, there is no need. For your love, I would give you the world. A treasure is nothing compared to the love I feel for you."

They stared at each other, shocked that in one thing, finally, they were truly a team. Wulf kissed her mouth, and she hugged him tight. "Then I have all that I need, forever."

Dera dried her eyes, then turned back to Alfred. "What are you? Why did you come to me?"

"I am the last of the Twelve Knights of Yule. An age ago, we were great magicians of this isle—England, Scotland, and Wales. Aye, we were *kings*, but not kings such as now rule England. No, we were kings of such power that none could withstand us. An age ago, there was none prouder than we, none with a magic stronger."

"An age ago?" A chill sped down Dera's spine. "Why did you come to me?"

"In life, we Twelve had all magic could bestow, yet we went to our graves, each lacking the great hope of life. One lacked truth, one lacked generosity, one lacked joy, another

388

forgiveness, another understanding. Despite our glory, we died without life's fullness.''

Wulf's brow furrowed. ''I think I understand.''

Alfred smiled. ''I think you both understand. In time, we all understand. For those of great power as we were then, it wasn't enough to understand. We wanted to share with those who followed. And so, each of the Knights took upon himself a task—to find that which he in life scorned, and bestow it on one who deserved it most. On the night of Yule respective to our title, we would give that gift to another.''

Dera watched his ageless face in wonder. ''Alfred . . . What did you scorn?''

He looked between them before answering, then bowed his great head. ''I scorned love.''

''Oh!'' Tears flooded Dera's eyes. ''But what changed you?''

''We kings sought power beyond Britain, beyond all shores we knew. No conquest was great enough, no land wide enough. We traveled south into lands where Rome held sway. And there, we learned that there is only one treasure, and one magic that holds sway over all. And that is love.''

Tears dripped to Dera's cheeks. ''Love.''

''Fear blocks it, and tries to hide it. Lust and ambition try to shove it aside. But when it rises stronger than all else, when it forsakes all else, there is nothing beyond its power.''

''But why us? Why did you become my guard?''

''I have watched you, Dera. In a form other than you see me now. Your mother abandoned you, the nobles sought to humiliate you, they left you with a woman who beat you. Yet when one aged thief, starving and thin, came to rob you, you fed him, and you praised him, and you loved him.''

''How did you know?''

''Each year, my brethren and I seek out new souls to watch. The gift I bestow is not meant for one, but for two who become one.''

Wulf didn't appear as happy as Dera felt. He lowered his

389

gaze to his feet. "But why choose me? Surely Dera deserves a better man, one without his father's blood on his hands."

"A child lives because of you, and a broken man is given another chance in a new form. You released your father from madness, Wulf. Death is not the end of a soul's journey, and always there is hope beyond of a new beginning, and a new wisdom."

Wulf didn't appear convinced. "But I have done nothing to deserve this treasure."

"Haven't you? A young man, proud and willful, assailed you, threatened you, and demanded your inheritance."

"Ramm?"

"You could have banished him, or had him killed. Instead, you gave to him the stewardship of Pickering Castle. You don't give to improve yourself in another's eyes—you proved that by giving the beryl to the boy at the inn in secret, rather than in front of Dera. Ramm hated you, yet you gave him the power and title he desires."

Wulf sighed. "He has always resented me, yet I can't help feeling fond of him. He reminds me of someone."

Alfred smiled. "Yourself?"

"I suppose so. Neither of us had a real father, and we both sought honor as knights. And we were both betrayed by Lord Cleavedon's madness."

Alfred lay his broad hand on Wulf's shoulder. "Because you are both Lord Cleavedon's sons."

Wulf's eyes widened in shock, though Dera wasn't surprised by Alfred's revelation. Dera clasped Wulf's hand. "I thought you looked alike! He recognized you as an ox, Wulf. And he didn't capture you."

"Dera is right, Wulf. There is good in Ramm. Good begets good. All living things have magic within them. All living things, from the highest king to the lowest peasant, have power. When that power is wielded with kindness, with love, then that magic becomes eternal."

Wulf smiled, but tears glittered in his eyes. "Thank you."

He kissed Dera's forehead. "For myself, and my future wife, you have changed two lifetimes."

Alfred took Wulf's hand and Dera's, then placed them together. "I walk the earth now because it gives me the greatest joy to see love prevail."

Dera gazed up at Wulf. "Do you truly wish to marry me?"

A teasing expression formed on Wulf's face. "Will you obey me in all things?"

"Only if you'll obey me!"

He laughed. "Then, yes, my lady, I will take you as my wife. This night. Perhaps my brother will attend."

Dera smiled. "He will."

"After that, you and I will travel to Brinklow Castle, where you will live as a queen. I loved my father. By leading as he once led in better years, I will honor his memory."

"That is all I ever wanted." Ramm spoke behind them, startling both Wulf and Dera. Alfred, however, didn't seem surprised. Ramm's blue eyes were filled with tears, but Wulf gaped, astonished.

"You knew?" He glanced toward Alfred, and Ramm smiled.

"I knew my brother was running, and I couldn't stop him. This man—or whatever he is—said he could lead you home. It was close, though. A miserable old thief seemed to hold sway with him already."

Dera's breath caught. "An old thief? Penn?"

Alfred nodded. "Your father came to plead with me for you, Dera. He said he couldn't give you life's treasures. He was terrified you'd steal your way to a hanging."

"I never would!"

Wulf chuckled. "The old man knows you well."

Dera's lips formed a tight pout. "I only wanted the treasure for him."

Alfred patted her shoulder. "That is why I accepted."

Wulf kissed Dera's forehead. "Would the old fellow enjoy guarding my castle treasure, do you think?"

"Would you allow him to finger it, and sift the jewels through his fingers?"

Wulf sighed and rolled his eyes heavenward. "Aye, though I may end up a poor lord."

Dera beamed. "He won't steal, if he can keep an eye on the gold and gems, and such."

Wulf eyed Ramm. "Perhaps my lieutenant can keep an eye on my new head thief. Will you return to Brinklow with us, Ramm?"

Ramm bowed before Wulf. "I will."

Dera turned to Alfred. "Will you come with us, Alfred?"

"My dear lass, my duties for this Yule already wane, and with this last night, I retire for another year."

As he spoke, the glow of Alfred's armor expanded around him until it enveloped all in the room. Dera stepped toward him, reaching to touch him, but her hand met only air. "Thank you, Alfred."

The glow spread until the human shape within was lost and became part of the aura. Wulf took Dera's hand as the glow filled the room, then vanished to nothing.

They stood in silence for a moment, awed by the Twelfth Knight's magic. Ramm slapped Wulf's shoulder. "I should have known your salvation rested with a beautiful woman! I'll go now, and arrange your wedding."

Ramm left Wulf and Dera alone in the dark room, but in the wake of Alfred's departure, the dungeon air was as warm and fresh as if the sun itself had come down to cleanse it.

Wulf bent to kiss her mouth. "He said, that first day, that you were my angel, and you would lead me to my treasure. That treasure is my love, Dera, and it is yours forever."

Dera returned his kiss, knowing all she longed for had come true. "All my life, I have longed to matter to someone, to be loved. I thought it would be the greatest happiness. But now I know better. The greatest happiness is loving another—loving you.''

Wulf held out his hand, smiling. ''Tonight, we marry. The first and last toast we drink will be to the Twelfth Knight of Christmas.''

Dera placed her hand in his. ''The Twelfth Knight of Christmas, who brought my true love to me.''

Christmas means more than just puppy love.

"SHAKESPEARE AND THE THREE KINGS"
Victoria Alexander

Requiring a trainer for his three inherited dogs, Oliver Stanhope meets D. K. Lawrence, and is in for the Christmas surprise—and love—of his life.

"ATHENA'S CHRISTMAS TAIL" Nina Coombs

Mercy wants her marriage to be a match of the heart—and with the help of her very determined dog, Athena, she finds just the right magic of the holiday season.

"AWAY IN A SHELTER" Annie Kimberlin

A dedicated volunteer, Camille Campbell still doesn't want to be stuck in an animal shelter on Christmas Eve—especially with a handsome helper whose touch leaves her starry-eyed.

"MR. WRIGHT'S CHRISTMAS ANGEL"
Miriam Raftery

When Joy's daughter asks Santa for a father, she knows she's in trouble—until a trip to Alaska takes them on a journey into the arms of Nicholas Wright and his amazing dog.

___52235-7 $5.99 US/$6.99 CAN

TIMESWEPT

Christmas Carol FLORA SPEER

Bestselling Author of *A Love Beyond Time*

Bah! Humbug! That is what Carol Simmons says to the holidays, mistletoe, and the ghost in her room. But the mysterious specter has come to save the heartless spinster from a loveless life. Soon Carol is traveling through the ages to three different London Yuletides—and into the arms of a trio of dashing suitors. From Christmas past to Christmas future, the passionate caresses of the one man meant for her teach Carol that the season is about a lot more than Christmas presents.

_51986-0 $4.99 US/$5.99 CAN

Molly In The Middle

STOBIE PIEL

"An exciting new voice!" —*Romantic Times*

Sheep, sheep, sheep. Ach! The bumbling boobs are everywhere, and as far as Molly is concerned, the stupid beasts are better off mutton. But Molly is a sheepdog, a Scottish Border collie, and unless she finds some other means of livelihood for her lovely mistress, Miren, she'll be doomed to chase after the frustrating flock forever. That's why she is tickled pink when handsome Nathan MacCallum comes into Miren's life. Sure, Nathan seems to have issues of his own to resolve—although why people are so concerned about righting family wrongs is beyond Molly—but she knows from his scent he'll be a good catch. And she knows from Miren's pink cheeks and distracted gaze that his hot kisses are something special. Now she'll simply have to herd the spirited Scottish lass and brooding American together, and show the silly humans that true love—and a faithful house pet—are all they'll ever need.

__52193-8   **$5.99 US/$6.99 CAN**

APOLLO'S FAULT

TIMESWEPT

MIRIAM RAFTERY

Taylor James's wrinkled Shar-Pei, Apollo, is always getting into trouble. But the young beauty never expects her mischievous puppy to lead her on the romantic adventure of a lifetime—from a dusty old Victorian attic to the strong arms of Nathaniel Stuart and his turn-of-the-century charm. One minute Taylor and Apollo are in modern-day San Francisco, and the next thing Taylor knows, a shift in the earth's crust, a wrinkle in time, and the lovely historian finds herself facing the terror of California's most infamous earthquake—and a love so monumental it threatens to shake the foundations of her world.

_52084-2 $4.99 US/$6.99 CAN

Dorchester Publishing Co., Inc.
P.O. Box 6640
Wayne, PA 19087-8640

Please add $1.75 for shipping and handling for the first book and $.50 for each book thereafter. NY, NYC, and PA residents, please add appropriate sales tax. No cash, stamps, or C.O.D.s. All orders shipped within 6 weeks via postal service book rate. Canadian orders require $2.00 extra postage and must be paid in U.S. dollars through a U.S. banking facility.

Name _____

Address _____

City _____ State _____ Zip _____

I have enclosed $_____in payment for the checked book(s).
Payment <u>must</u> accompany all orders.☐ Please send a free catalog.

Heart's Magic

Flora Speer

Bestselling author of *ROSE RED*

In the year 1122, Mirielle senses change is coming to Wroxley Castle. Then, from out of the fog, two strangers ride into Lincolnshire. Mirielle believes the first man to be honest. But the second, Giles, is hiding something–even as he stirs her heart and awakens her deepest desires. And as Mirielle seeks the truth about her mysterious guest, she uncovers the castle's secrets and learns she must stop a treachery which threatens all she holds dear. Only then can she be in the arms of her only love, the man who has awakened her own heart's magic.

___52204-7 $5.99 US/$6.99 CAN